We hope you enjoy this b
renew it by the due d

You can renew
by using c

Oth

GOOD REASONS TO DIE

Morgan Audic

GOOD REASONS TO DIE

Translated from the French by
Sam Taylor

MOUNTAIN LEOPARD PRESS
WELBECK · LONDON & SYDNEY

Originally published in French as DE BONNES RAISONS DE MOURIR
in 2019 by
Éditions Albin Michel, Paris

First published in the English language in 2022 by
Mountain Leopard Press
an imprint of
Welbeck Publishing Group
London and Sydney

www.mountainleopard.press

9 8 7 6 5 4 3 2 1

Designed and typeset in Albertina by Libanus Press Ltd
Printed and bound in Great Britain by
CPI Group (UK) Ltd, Croydon, CR0 4YY

This book is supported by the Institut Français (Royaume-Uni)
as part of the Burgess programme

INSTITUT
FRANÇAIS
ROYAUME-UNI

FSC
www.fsc.org

MIX
Paper from
responsible sources
FSC® C171272

To my mother, my father, my brother

THE CITY OF SILENCE

1

"This must be the worst place to die," said Officer Galina Novak.

To the north, towards the Belarusian border, black clouds were swelling on the horizon, unleashing cold rain onto the forests of Polesia. Novak took a cigarette pack from her pocket and tapped it nervously on her knee.

"You think it's murder?"

Surprised by the question, Captain Joseph Melnyk turned his gaze momentarily from the road. With her blonde hair neatly scraped back into a ponytail, her childlike face, and her brand-new, American-style uniform, the young recruit – fresh from the police academy – seemed out of place in Melnyk's shabby old Lada.

"Do you think someone killed this guy?" she insisted.

Melnyk shrugged. "I bet you anything it's just a tourist who had a heart attack or some old drunk who fell off a balcony. It'll be done and dusted in a couple of hours. There's no point imagining the worst."

Unconvinced, Novak settled back in her seat and put a cigarette between her pinched lips. She muttered: "All the same... What a horrible place to end your life."

There was a tense silence, broken only by the squeak of the windscreen wipers. Novak was terrified: you didn't have to be a detective to work that one out. She was about to get lugged with her first real corpse. Not one of those bodies from the morgue in Kyiv that new recruits were shown during their training. A real one, with a real family. Not only that, but the body was in Pripyat, a ghost town since it was abandoned in 1986 when the nuclear reactor in Chernobyl exploded. It was enough to make anyone want to smoke their way through a whole pack of those cheap, disgusting Belomorkanal cigarettes.

Thickets of pine and birch flashed past the roadside, alternating with vast grassy stretches that had once been fertile fields. Melnyk had to slow down at a junction for a herd of wild Przewalski horses blocking the road, nibbling at the short grass on both sides of the cracked tarmac. In the late 1990s about thirty of those horses had been captured on the Askania-Nova nature reserve in southern Ukraine and brought here. The authorities had hoped to kill two birds with one stone: allowing this endangered species to prosper far away from human beings, and preventing the vegetation around Chernobyl from becoming too wild. The ecologists said it was a bad idea to further endanger an endangered species by putting it in a place like this, but Melnyk liked seeing the horses frolicking in what once were farmers' fields. It gave him the impression that, thirty years after the nuclear disaster, life was returning to this evacuated zone.

The Lada passed a large Orthodox crucifix and Novak's dosimeter started crackling furiously. Its screen showed levels of radiation that you might get after a year in Moscow or Kyiv. A triangular red and yellow sign, planted near the cross, warned them that they were entering a highly contaminated area. A radioactive furnace saturated with caesium, strontium and plutonium.

"Turn that damn thing off," Melnyk instructed her.

He hated the sinister crackles the dosimeters made. His own had been tucked away for years inside the Lada's glove compartment. It was bad enough working in a place infested with radiation without a machine forever reminding you of the fact. He knew the worst spots by heart anyway, the places that had to be avoided. Other than that, he had no choice but to walk on contaminated earth and to breathe air where radioactive particles sometimes floated.

Novak grudgingly dropped her device into the inside pocket of her parka. He wondered what kind of fuck-up she'd made at the academy to find herself catapulted into Chernobyl for her first assignment. No twenty-something dreams of being sent to a police station surrounded by thirty kilometres of irradiated fields and ruins. You dream of working in Kyiv or on the shore of the Black Sea, in the sun. Seven years before, he himself could never have imagined he would one day end up working in the zone. . . not until his boss summoned him to his office and gave him a choice: resign or be transferred to Chernobyl.

Seven years. . . He looked at himself for a moment in the rear-view mirror. Heavy build, dense bushy hair, pale blue eyes, thick blond beard with a scattering of grey hairs. . . Working in the zone had transformed him into a woodsman.

"Do you have any advice about the. . . the radiation?" Novak said anxiously.

He noticed that she had still not lit her cigarette. She was just chewing on the filter.

"Is there a way to protect ourselves from the radioactivity?" she demanded.

Melnyk frowned as if thinking deeply about this, then said in a serious voice: "A few years ago, when I got here, I asked the same question. They told me: 'If you're planning on having kids, you should wrap your balls in aluminium foil.'"

Novak stared wide-eyed at her superior.

"Aluminium foil? Does that really work?"

"Does it work? Ask the other guys at the station. They all do it."

"You don't?"

"I already had three kids. That stuff's for young men."

Melnyk kept a straight face. The old hands always played the same joke on new recruits, who invariably cleaned out the local supermarkets' stocks of aluminium foil to protect their testicles. Obviously it wasn't quite as funny in this case.

A few kilometres further on, the dilapidated towers of Pripyat appeared above the treetops. Melnyk saw a minibus at the far end of Lenin Street. Big stickers on the doors boasted the merits of a tour operator specialising in visits to the zone. He parked the Lada at the side

of the road and cursed inwardly as he got out of the vehicle. The drizzle
had turned to a fine rain that slipped behind coat collars and froze necks.
But at least the raindrops glued the radioactive dust to the ground,
making it briefly less dangerous.

A dozen tourists scrambled out of the minibus. They all wore yellow
bracelets confirming that they had bought the mandatory insurance
before entering the contaminated zone. God only knew which company
insured people against that kind of risk.

The official guide – a tall figure in a camouflage jacket – stepped
forward from the group and called out in Ukrainian to the captain.

"*Ekh!* We've been waiting here for an hour!" he whined.

"Heavy traffic," Melnyk replied deadpan. "Are you the one who
called? Where's the corpse?"

"We should go there by car. The body's–"

Before he could finish his sentence, one of the tourists walked up to
Melnyk and addressed him in broken Russian: "When we leave? We not
want stay!"

Melnyk glared at him before telling him coldly and slowly: "You'll
leave when I say you can."

"Here dangerous, not stay, leave quick we want!"

The guy had an American accent and his Russian was not good: two
reasons to send him packing.

"You wanted a special experience, right? The thrill of danger? Well,
here you go – enjoy! You'll have a great story to tell your oncologist."

"What is last word?"

"A cancer doctor," Melnyk said.

The man's face turned a shade of green. The other tourists looked
anxiously at the guide, who jabbered a few words in English and then
asked Melnyk: "Can they at least wait in the minibus?"

"Sure. As soon as they've shown my colleague their identity papers."

The guide relayed this information to the tourists, who immediately
held out British, American, Latvian and Lithuanian passports. Melnyk
leaned close to Novak and whispered in Ukrainian: "Take their names
and their witness statements. I'm going to see the body. Whatever you

do, keep the vultures waiting for as long as you can. They came here to get an adrenaline rush, so I think we should give them their money's worth!"

Then he signalled to the guide to follow him to the Lada. As they walked past the minibus, Melnyk noticed for the first time the slogan in enormous letters on the vehicle's sides: "The trip that'll make all your friends jealous."

"Cretins," he mumbled into his beard.

Thirty thousand tourists had come to visit the irradiated zone the previous year. All you needed to get in was to be eighteen years or older, to not be pregnant, and to deal with one of the numerous travel agencies in Kyiv specialising in Chernobyl Tours. There, for a few hundred dollars, you could get all the necessary permits stamped by the Ukrainian authorities.

The latest fad was to have your stag party in Cheronobyl. Skydiving and strippers were so *passé*! For several months now, Melnyk had seen contingents of drunken morons arriving and bellowing their way through the abandoned streets of Pripyat. He was almost nostalgic for the era of Russian tourists. They had become increasingly rare since Russia had annexed Crimea, triggering the civil war that dogged the Donbas region in eastern Ukraine.

"So where's the damn corpse?" he said as he got into the Lada.

"You don't seem too bothered that a man is dead," the guide said reproachfully.

"The only thing that 'bothers' me at the moment is finding the body before the wild dogs start gobbling it down."

A joyless smile flickered across the guide's face.

"Don't worry. Given where it is, I don't think anything like that is going to happen to it."

"Why? Is it in a building?"

"Not *in* a building, *on* a building."

The guide pointed to a tall apartment block at the end of Kurchatova Street. The top of the building was decorated with the emblem of the Soviet Socialist Republic of Ukraine: a hammer and sickle surrounded by ears of wheat and crowned with a red star. On the second-highest floor of the apartment block, a corpse was hanging between two windows, arms outstretched.

Melnyk felt his stomach heave.

"*Blyad!*" he swore, shaken.

He started the car and drove up the street, slaloming between the saplings that had grown up through the tarmac. His mind was racing, going through all the steps he would have to take: call the station for reinforcements, call the prosecutor, warn the morgue that a potentially radioactive body was going to arrive... In front of the apartment block, he raised his eyes to the corpse and was again stunned by the morbid spectacle above him. Metal cables were wrapped around the dead man's wrists, tensed diagonally towards the inside of the building. From a distance they'd been invisible because they were the same greyish colour as the building's façade.

For an instant he had the impression that he saw one of the victim's legs move. Was it the wind or just his imagination? Or maybe...

"Have you been up there to check he's actually dead?"

"Huh?" The guide shrugged, arms wide and turned his palms upward. "Isn't it pretty obvious that he's dead?"

"For you, maybe. Not for me."

Melnyk looked up at the body again. The slight swaying movement he thought he had detected had stopped. Probably it was just the wind, but the idea that this guy might still be alive had chilled him. He thought about the rickety staircase leading up to where the body was, about the radioactive dust on the concrete floors, about the apartment building that had partially collapsed the previous winter on the corner of the street. He hesitated, then at last resolved to go and take a closer look.

"I'm going up. Wait here."

"Don't worry, I'm not going anywhere," the guide said.

Melnyk strode to the front door of the old Soviet apartment block. The first floor had been a public library. The books had long ago disappeared. Occasionally you would find a few pages of Russian poetry caught in the branches of trees lining the road.

Once inside, he had no difficulty finding his way. The building was almost identical to the one where he lived in Kyiv with his wife. In the days of the U.S.S.R., the whole country had been littered with these cheap concrete eyesores, from Berlin to Vladivostok. The buildings were so similar that he could have navigated his way around this one with his eyes shut.

When he reached the fifth floor, he took a break. He was out of breath. Not enough exercise, too many cigarettes. While he got his breath back, he listened to the sounds of the abandoned building. The whistling of the wind through the broken windows, the shutters creaking and banging... Suddenly he noticed a regular clicking noise.

The claws of a dog on the bare concrete.

He took out his pistol and held it against his thigh. The dogs in Pripyat had long ago lost all respect for humans. The ones that had survived the cull after the evacuation of the city had formed packs that slept in the empty buildings and went out only to hunt. Some of them, with their thin bodies and long muzzles, looked more like wolves than dogs.

He went on up the stairs. On the seventh floor, the air was thick with the stink of wild animals. He heard a muffled growl and realised that the beast's lair must be somewhere close by. He thought briefly about firing a shot through a window, hoping that the noise would scare the dog and encourage it to run down to the ground floor. But then it occurred to him that he had no way of knowing whether the person who had crucified the man on the outside of the building had left. His weapon raised in front of him, his whole body tensed, Melnyk went on up.

On the penultimate floor, he walked to the apartment where the body was hanging. Outside the smashed front door he froze, alert for the faintest noise: the crunch of broken glass under a shoe, a sigh, the rustle of clothing, anything that might betray a hostile presence. He waited a good minute before deciding to go inside. The entrance hall was empty; he made for the living room. There he was greeted by a sight so surprising that his index finger slipped from the trigger of his pistol.

The room was full of animals. Fifteen, twenty, maybe even thirty of them. Foxes, wolves, lynxes, wild boars. A strange herd, their backs turned to him. It took a while before he realised that all of them were stuffed. Motionless, he waited for his heart to stop speeding, then walked through the living room and leaned out of the window to examine the hanging man. His naked body bore the marks of burns, cuts, bruises. Worse: his eyelids and his lips were sewn shut. Melnyk reached out to the greyish neck, but could detect no pulse. It must have been the wind that made the corpse move.

A pile of clothes lay in one corner of the room. In the pocket of a pair of trousers, Melnyk found a Russian passport in the name of Leonid Vektorovich Sokolov. The photograph matched the victim: the guy had a red birthmark at the edge of his scalp that enabled Melnyk to identify him despite the stitches on his eyes and lips.

There was also a wallet inside the trouser pocket. Opening it, Melnyk found a large quantity of rubles and hryvnia: a small fortune, four or five months' salary for a Chernobyl police officer. The idea of taking the money for himself crossed his mind. God knows he needed it, if only for his son, Nikolai, who was fighting in Donbas without a bulletproof vest. But he put the money back where he had found it. He had lived his life as honestly as possible; he wasn't about to start stealing from corpses at his age. He took out his mobile and called the police station.

One of his colleagues answered: "What's the corpse like?"

"It's a fucking mess. We've got a murder case on our hands. I'll need reinforcements. Equipment too. The guy's hanging on the side of an apartment block."

"Is it a local?"

"No, he's Russian. His name is Leonid Vektorovich Sokolov. Find out everything you can about him and call me back when you know more."

He walked down to the ground floor. On the seventh floor, the growling had stopped. In the dust that covered the floor of the building's lobby, paw prints had criss-crossed the neat traces left by his boots.

Outside, the guide was standing exactly where Melnyk had left him.

"Have you seen this guy before?"

He handed the guide the dead man's passport. The guide examined it closely, but the man's face meant nothing to him.

"Think: maybe you saw him yesterday or the day before during one of your visits. He might have been part of another group."

"I've never seen him before," the guide said.

During the short drive to the central square, Melnyk thought about how much hate you would have to feel to destroy someone like that and to exhibit his body. When they got close to the minibus, he dropped the guide off and took Novak aside.

"It's a one-fifteen," he murmured.

In the Ukrainian penal code, Article 115 refers to premeditated murder. He had not wanted to utter aloud the word 'murder' because the tourists were spooked enough already.

Novak's pupils dilated.

"Cause of death?"

"Hard to say until we've got him down."

"Down?"

"He's hanging by metal wires on the front of an apartment block."

Novak said nothing for a moment before frantically reeling off the criminal procedure code: "We can't leave the crime scene without surveillance... we have to... to create a secure perimeter around the body..."

"Calm down, officer," Melnyk said. "We're in the middle of nowhere. Who do you think is going to intrude on the world's most radioactive crime scene?"

"But it's procedure..."

"In Kyiv maybe. Not here. Did you get anything out of the tourists?"

Novak took out her notebook and read out her notes in a shaky voice: "They all reserved their excursion yesterday in Kyiv, after a visit to the National Chernobyl Museum. The minibus picked them up at seven this morning outside McDonald's in Maidan. Their drive lasted a little over two hours and they passed the Dytayatki checkpoint around 10 o'clock and did the usual visit: first the city of Chernobyl, the monument to the liquidators, then the abandoned villages, the reactor, and after that they came here, to Pripyat. They had been here ten minutes before one of them, a Frenchman named... Gallois... noticed the body. You think one of the tourists killed the guy?"

Melnyk dismissed this idea: "No. Just hanging the body must have taken hours."

His mobile rang. It was his colleague at the police station.

"What can you tell me?"

"I didn't find much, but I did discover something freaky about his family." His colleague's voice wavered between excitement and nervousness. "His mother was called Olga Sokolov. She was murdered nearby. It was really bad: multiple stab wounds, mutilations. . . a horror show. They found her body along with another woman's body in a house in the village of Zalissya."

Zalissya was only a stone's throw from Chernobyl, yet Melnyk had heard nothing about this story.

"Doesn't ring any bells. When did it happen?"

"That's the crazy thing. It was in 1986. April 26th."

Melnyk felt his guts twist.

"Are you sure about the date?"

"Certain," his colleague said.

Melnyk hung up, staring into space. April 26, 1986. . . All Ukrainians, young or old, knew that date. It was the day that the nuclear reactor exploded.

THE LANGUAGE OF NIGHTINGALES

2

Metallic creaks, wheezing breaths.

He woke in darkness: green and blue lights flashed across his vision every time he blinked. The air was heavy, thick with the bitter stink of unwashed bodies, antiseptic and alcohol.

Where am I?

His eyes adjusted to the dim light in the room and he made out a row of beds against the opposite wall. They were occupied by shapeless, moaning beings that slowly moved their limbs the way half-crushed beetles wave their legs before dying.

Get out of here!

He tried to stand, but his wrists and ankles could not be raised from the mattress. Horrified, he realised that they were strapped to the bedframe. He pulled with all his strength, trying to free himself, but the effort made his head spin so that he thought he would faint. Disorientated, his body bathed in cold, greasy sweat, he tried to remember how he had got here.

Dry mouth, aching head, throat scorched with the aftertaste of alcohol: apparently he had drunk too much. Each time his heartbeat suddenly accelerated, he felt as if the bells of St Basil's were pealing inside his head. Stabbing pains in his ribs, the tang of metal oozing from his split lips, a burning sensation in the knuckles of his fingers: he hadn't just been drinking, he had been fighting too. Fragments of the previous night came back to him. Zenit St Petersburg had been playing against

Spartak Moscow. In a bar, he had yelled at the Zenit supporters that they were goat-fuckers, or something like that. Or had it been the other way round? Maybe he had insulted the sacrosanct Spartak team, may God forgive him! In any case, the result hadn't been long coming. When he left the bar, three men had jumped him. Skinhead ultras with a black-white-gold crest sewn onto their khaki bomber jackets: the flag of imperial Russia. The kind of morons who usually attacked Chechens or Dagestanis or basically anyone with darker skin than their own.

With his mixed features, he was the perfect prey. The ultras must have thought they'd found an easy target. Big mistake. Elbows to their eye sockets, roundhouse kicks to their ribs, knees in their balls, head-butts: he had given them the full works. In a rush of drunken pride, he thought to himself that his attackers must be feeling a lot worse than he was right now.

The sound of footsteps in the corridor.

A door creaked open, then the fluorescent ceiling lights came on, clinking sharply, blinding him. He closed his eyes against the dazzle while a man's voice speaking Siberian-accented Russian exploded in his ears like a firecracker at the back of a cave: "Which of you is Alexander Rybalko?"

The light. . . the fluorescent lights were burning into his brain. He leaned to the side and squinted. A young guy in glasses wearing a white coat.

"Alexander Rybalko?" the man repeated.

Another explosion inside his hangover-racked brain. He groaned and the doctor walked towards him.

"Are you Alexander Rybalko? Do you understand what I'm saying? Do you speak Russian?"

"Not. . . so loud," he said. His tongue was heavy, clumsy. The sound of his own voice made the bones inside his head vibrate. Even thinking was painful.

"Where. . . am I?"

"In hospital. Are you American? European?"

"I'm Russian, *mudak*."

The young doctor looked shocked. Rybalko wondered if it was surprise at the idea that someone of mixed blood could speak Russian, or simply the fact of being insulted in his native language.

"Why... I... here?"

The doctor's face quickly resumed its expression of arrogance and weary resignation.

"The police picked you up near the station last night," he said stiffly. "You were lying in the street, totally drunk."

Rybalko raised his head a few centimetres to look around. The other beds were occupied by pathetic, wild-eyed alcoholics, hairy guys with dirty fingernails, red cheeks and purple noses: human beasts. He hoped – without really believing it – that he did not look as they did.

He seemed to be the only one strapped to his bed.

"Why... tied up?"

"Because of your attitude when you were being undressed. You tried to bite one of the nurses."

A new memory came to him: he was in the corridor, being dragged by three men struggling to subdue his almost two-metre-tall, eighty-eight kilo frame as clumsily he tried to shake them off. He felt a pain in his arm, the cold floor pressing against his face: they'd put him in a shoulder lock to calm him down. He'd shouted: "I don't have time for this shit! I don't have time!" They undressed him down to his underwear. He spent a long time yelling. Then he fell asleep.

The doctor began undoing one of the leather straps.

"Before letting you leave, I'm going to examine you to make sure everything's alright. O.K., Mr Rybalko?"

He did not like being spoken to as though he were some kind of backward child, but he nodded all the same.

"Please sit on the edge of the bed."

He obeyed, taking his time. His muscles ached and his movements were awkward. The doctor asked him question after question and he answered them with monosyllables. Do you often drink that much? No. Do you drink regularly? No. Do you remember last night? No. Or the one before? No. Does your head ache? Yes. On a scale of one to ten, how would you rate your pain? Eleven. Does your stomach ache? Yes. What triggered your excessive drinking?

Rybalko stared at the doctor.

"I killed someone."

The doctor froze.

"Someone? How? Who?"

He paused before replying, with a mocking smile: "Some quack. He was asking too many questions."

The young doctor blushed and angrily strapped the cuff of a blood-pressure monitor around Rybalko's arm.

"You shouldn't joke about things like that. Last month, a guy in the same state as you fell asleep on a railway track. The driver didn't have time to brake. That could have been you. We have a group therapy class for alcoholics that meets twice a week. Tuesdays and Thursdays. I would advise you to sign up."

"I'm not an alcoholic," Rybalko said.

Ignoring this, the doctor gave him the usual long-winded speech about the harmful effects of alcohol, like a preacher trying to convert a heathen. Thankfully the rest of the examination took place in relative silence. Finally the young doctor told him he was free to leave. As the doctor left the room, Rybalko closed his eyes and sank into a restless sleep for twenty or thirty minutes before being shaken awake by a female nurse. She had brought him the crumpled clothes he had been wearing for the previous several days. He tried to stand up to get dressed, but felt so dizzy that he had to sit down again.

"I can find you a wheelchair if you need one," the nurse said kindly.

I'm not a fucking invalid, he thought, his pride stung.

But all he said was: "I'm O.K." Each word was so painful to articulate, and getting angry only made his headache worse.

With difficulty, he somehow put on his trousers, while the other drunks watched with amusement. After that, he put on his socks, his still-wet shoes, his T-shirt, his sweater with its stale beer stench, and his parka with its torn sleeves. The nurse gave him some pills, which he swallowed with a glass of water so cold that it made his teeth hurt.

She left the room then and he limped after her through the tiled corridors, breathing in the smell of iodine. At each junction, she waited a few seconds for him to catch up. He had the impression that she was walking along the edge of a swimming pool while he was at the bottom in a diving suit, trudging through the water.

It was humiliating.

"Are you sure you don't want a wheelchair?" she said.

He mumbled an inaudible insult. Another ten metres at least and they reached the lobby. The nurse left him at a counter, where a bored-looking woman gave him back his coat and a black plastic bin-liner containing his belongings. The bin-liner was tied shut, but his fingers were too clumsy to undo the knot. In the end he angrily tore the plastic open, spilling its contents onto the countertop: a wallet, car keys, metro tickets, and in the middle of it all. . .

An MP-443 pistol.

The woman stared open-mouthed at the weapon.

Rybalko knew what was going through her head: dark skin, gun on the counter. Just as she looked about to scream, he said: "It's my service pistol."

The receptionist gave him the same incredulous look that the doctor had given him earlier. Rybalko searched through the mess of his belongings on the counter, found his police card, and showed it to her.

"Do you see that? Moscow police."

The woman inspected the card with the scepticism of a supermarket cashier examining a 5,000-ruble note. While this was happening, Rybalko stuck his pistol into his belt and lowered his T-shirt over it. The receptionist decided at last that the police card was genuine and handed him a stack of documents including his bill, various forms, and – slipped between the pages – a brochure advertising group therapy for alcoholics. He shoved all this paperwork into the pocket of his parka and unblinkingly paid the bill for his hospitalisation.

Before leaving, he went to the men's room to splash some cold water over his face. In the mirror above the sink, he almost did not recognise himself. His cheeks were covered with a three-day beard, his coffee-coloured skin had turned an earthlike tone, and his pale blue eyes were bloodshot. The doctor's words echoed in his head: "Last month, a guy in the same state as you fell asleep on a railway track. The driver didn't have time to brake. That could have been you."

It could have been him. . . Asleep on the train tracks, killed by the morning's first suburban train before he even woke. . . Maybe that would have been better for everyone, he thought, pulling up his jacket collar.

He dried his face, walked out through reception and left the hospital. Outside, the air was crisp, the sun weak. An aspirin-coloured taxi was waiting, double-parked. He climbed in, showed the driver his police card, and was about to ask to be taken home when he spotted the police car on the other side of the street. He instantly recognised the man inside: cropped black hair, hooked nose, physique of a bodybuilder running to fat, looking as though he was about to burst out of his leather jacket. He, too, had rings under his eyes and his cheeks were darkened by a nascent beard.

Vasily Chekhov, his partner.

3

Chekhov's Lada Priora was parked in a spot reserved for ambulances. Inside the vehicle, the air was pleasantly warm. He buckled his seatbelt and Chekhov set off, heading towards the clogged arteries of central Moscow. Despite the early hour, the city seemed to spew out automobiles – on pavements, in car parks, on two-lane, four-lane and six-lane roads, making their progress slow and halting.

"I've spent forty-eight hours looking for you. Where were you?"

His partner's deep voice boomed like a bass drum in his head.

"Not so loud," he said.

"Where were you?"

"Everywhere and nowhere. . . What day is it?"

"What day? Fucking hell! It's Wednesday."

Wednesday? Already? Rybalko rubbed his temples.

"You've been missing since Friday. What the hell have you been doing all that time?"

"*Zapoï*" Rybalko said.

The Russian language had helpfully developed a single word to describe the fact of having got drunk for several days in a row, to the point where you couldn't remember a thing. Rybalko figured he may as well use it.

"Seriously? A *zapoï*?"

Chekhov could not believe his ears.

"We've spent days searching for you, and you've just been getting pissed? Fucking hell! A *zapoï*," he repeated incredulously, slamming the car's horn because someone had cut in front of him. "And you didn't think maybe you should have warned me? Or called the office on Monday morning to tell them you were sick or whatever crap you thought they might have swallowed? Why didn't you contact anyone?"

"I didn't feel like talking."

"You didn't feel like. . . Jesus fucking Christ, what is wrong with you?"

"Calm down, Tolia," Rybalko said, using his partner's nickname to mollify him. "Nobody died."

"Oh yeah, Alex? You sure about that?"

Chekhov's hand dived into the inside pocket of his jacket, fingers grazing the butt of his service pistol, and pulled out a spiral notebook. He tossed it into Rybalko's lap. On the first page there was a list of names and addresses that he recognised: his own apartment, his ex-wife's, a few bars, his gym, the homes of his closest friends. Each one had been furiously crossed out. There were also a few notes scrawled underneath: drunk and disorderly, assault and battery, insulting a police officer, nocturnal disturbance, death threats, damage to public property. . .

"Given the number of crimes you committed while you were out of your head, I actually wouldn't be surprised to find a corpse floating in the Moskva with your name carved into its forehead. You'd have ended up in one of those *avtozaks* if I hadn't found you first."

Chekhov pointed at some sinister prison vans that were heading towards Maiakovskaia square, where an anti-corruption protest march was taking place.

"Pankowski's on the look-out. He's ready to sign an arrest warrant for you."

Rybalko shrugged, indifferent. He had no respect for Anatoli Pankowski, their chief. He was a bureaucrat devoid of courage or charisma. Exactly the kind of policeman who would sacrifice his men if his career were at risk.

"If they start jailing every officer in Moscow who drinks too much, they're going to need a shitload of new prisons," he said with a yawn.

"This isn't a joke! Even your mate Kachin started freaking out when you vanished."

"Kita?"

"Yeah, Kita. He turned up at my place on Sunday evening. You can imagine how thrilled I was to have a drug-dealer ringing my doorbell. He was desperate to see you."

"Why?"

"No idea. Maybe you can ask him yourself. But it must be important: he gave me a nice wad of cash to find you."

Rybalko forced a smile. "And I thought you'd gone looking for me because you were worried about my health. . ."

"I must have called you a dozen times before he came to my place," Chekhov said.

"If you ever disappear, I won't wait until someone pays me before I go looking for you."

"Don't start on me, Alex. I'm not the one who screwed up here. What got into you anyway? Was it because of Marina?"

Rybalko's jaw tensed at this mention of his ex-wife.

"Did you talk to her?"

"Nobody knew where you were, so I went to see her. She told me she was getting remarried soon. Is that what triggered this?"

"I don't want to talk about it."

With perfect timing, Chekhov's mobile rang just then and he had to answer it. End of round one; the interrogation would begin again later. Rybalko watched the streets of Moscow speed past his window until he began to doze. When he woke, they had come to a stop outside his apartment block, a large, bourgeois building dating from before the First World War.

"Come on, let's go!" Chekhov said, shaking him gently.

Rybalko stretched and yawned, then got out of the car. They went into the lobby and climbed the stairs to his apartment. While he was searching his pockets for his keys, Chekhov stared wide-eyed at the five doorbells next to his front door.

"You live in a *kommunalka?*"

Rybalko nodded. Since his divorce, he had been renting a room in a communal apartment, a sort of temporal anomaly left over from the painful beginnings of the U.S.S.R., when the Soviets had attempted to provide better housing for the proletariat by confiscating rich people's apartments and dividing them into as many parts as there were rooms. There were five tenants and so there were five of everything in the communal areas. Five bars of soap in the bathroom (well, four actually, because he had forgotten to buy one), five gas cookers in the kitchen, five dish towels next to the sink, five washing machines, and – of course – five electric meters to measure the consumption of five penniless Muscovites.

"Go take a shower," Chekhov said. "I'm going to call Pankowski." As Rybalko walked up the hallway to the bathroom, his partner called out: "And while you're getting clean, try to work out what Kachin might want from you."

Since nobody was willing to pay for the maintenance of the apartment's communal areas, the bathroom was in a pitiful state. Rust-coloured water dripped from the sink tap, the bottom of the bathtub was covered in dark stains, and the yellow and green wall tiles had fallen off in places, exposing the concrete beneath. To prevent any other tiles coming loose, someone had taped a plastic sheet over the dividing wall next to the bath, the dampest spot in the apartment.

He stood motionless for a long time under the jet of lukewarm water, then began to rub himself half-heartedly with a large bar of soap that belonged to one of the tenants – it must have been a woman, because it smelled of vanilla and apricot. The bottom of the tub was slippery and Rybalko was still feeling dizzy. Incapable of keeping his balance in such a hostile environment, he leaned his head against the wall tiles to stop himself falling while he soaped his left foot, then his right.

His head was a little clearer by the time he emerged from the shower, but he still did not understand why Kachin had wanted to see him. Was it something he had done that weekend? He glanced at his clothes. The dark blue jeans were stiff with the fluids they'd absorbed: alcohol, sweat, and blood. As he focused on the brownish stains, a memory came to him, like a bubble bursting as it reaches the surface of a glass of champagne.

Soldiers coming back from the front, with their comrades in body bags. Prisoners thrown in the back of a truck, spitting blood onto their shirts. Men tied to chairs, being pistol-whipped. The image of a tank guarding the crossroads of an ash-coloured city filled his head. That was far away, in a country where people knelt down to pray. No, not in another country, in his country: in the Caucasian mountains, in Chechnya, years before. A country that was concrete-grey, army-green, blood-red.

He held his head in both hands. It was impossible to take stock of his recent memories with all this crap cluttering the shelves of his mind. He needed other objects to focus on. He searched in his pockets and took out the belongings that they had given back to him at the hospital. Try to remember what you may have done in the last few days, he said to himself as he examined them.

Suspect: Alexander Rybalko, born 1978 in the Union of Soviet Socialist Republics, a country that died in 1991. Citizen of the Russian Federation. Eighteen years in the police. Divorced from his wife, Marina, for almost two years. Non-smoker, since their daughter's birth. . .

First mistake.

He stared with a mixture of surprise and disappointment at the pack of cigarettes in his hand. Immediately he felt the old need, powerful and imperious. He lit one and cracked open the bathroom window to let the smoke out, cursing himself for his lapse after years of holding firm.

When he had finished the cigarette, he continued his self-investigation. The bunch of keys with a matryoshka hanging from the end of a small chain were his car keys. At the base of the Russian doll, "Tassia" had been written in a child's neat handwriting. This was his daughter, Anastassia, who had given it to him years before. The painting was faded and peeling off in places, even though he took care to varnish it now and then.

He lingered a little longer on his wallet. It was stuffed full of cash withdrawn from his bank account a few days earlier: money that he had put aside for emergencies. Stuck between two business cards, he found some bar receipts. One of them was from the football supporters' bar where he had done battle with the skinheads. Deep down, he knew he had not gone into that bar by chance; he had gone because he wanted to find some guys stupid and drunk enough to fight him, as a way of venting all the anger and frustration that had been building up in him for days. The skins had been the perfect candidates. He had beaten the shit out of them, but he did remember that they had still been breathing when someone had pulled him off them. Half-collapsed against a wall, blood pouring from between their smashed teeth. . . but alive.

He moved on to the next piece of evidence. An empty bottle that he recognised. To his shame, it was a 100ml bottle of Boyarychnik, a concoction made from hawthorn plants that was normally used as a bath oil. But in Russia, everyone knew that hawthorn oil was the drunkard's fallback option: even when the shops and bars were closed, you could find it in vending machines right there on the street. It had three big advantages: it contained up to 90% alcohol, it was easy to find because it was not subject to the same restrictions as hard spirits, and it was ridiculously cheap. On top of all that, it was less disgusting than cologne and less dangerous than antifreeze. Then again, dozens of people had died the year before in a housing estate in Siberia after drinking bottles of adulterated Boyarychnik. A local manufacturer of bath oil had exchanged the ethanol with methanol, a deadly poison.

What a wonderful world we live in, he thought as he tossed the hawthorn bottle into the bin near the sink.

The last item in the wallet was a scrap of paper that looked like a credit card receipt, so thin it was almost transparent. It was a ticket for an *elektrichka*, a suburban train. He had bought it in Lyubertsy, the city where he used to live with his wife before their divorce. Marina still rented their old two-bedroom flat, only now she shared it with her new boyfriend. It was when he had gone to see her there that everything had spun out of control. Needing courage, he had started to drink. In the end, he had staggered to the apartment building, had climbed the stairs, but just as he was about to knock, he had chickened out. Beyond the door, he had heard the laughter of Tassia and Marina. And the voice of the other man. He knew in that moment he did not have the strength to talk to them. So he had fled into the night. And woken up a few days later in the drunk tank of a hospital.

He came out of the bathroom with a towel wrapped around his waist. He could smell coffee coming from the kitchen, but Chekhov, mobile to his ear, was having a row with Pankowski. Rybalko headed to his bedroom, nothing more than a bed, a wardrobe, a chair, and a coffee table on which stood some cans of Jigoulevskoie beer and a photograph album opened to a page with pictures taken ten years earlier. Souvenirs of happier times with Tassia and Marina.

From the wardrobe where he kept the few clothes that he had unpacked, he took a woollen jumper. He put it on over one of his old counterfeit T-shirts, the one with a portrait of Kurt Cobain and the name of the band Nirvana misspelled. Most of his clothes were in a box somewhere on the outskirts of Moscow. He had no space to keep it all here. Besides, if he moved out completely, that would be tantamount to admitting that it was all over between him and Marina.

His headache flared up again. He reached into the wardrobe and picked up a plastic box with a green cross on it. It was full to the brim with medicine. An old Soviet habit, dating from an era when you could never be sure when the shelves in the shops might be empty.

"Pankowski wants you to report to the office immediately," a gravelly voice announced.

Chekhov was standing in the doorway.

"What did you tell him?"

"I said you were sick. That way, we can pay a visit to Kachin. He wants to see you as soon as possible."

Rybalko swallowed two pills, watched anxiously by his partner.

"Alex, what happened to make you go off the rails like that? I know you're no angel, but skipping work to go on a five-day bender is something else."

"Forget it, Tolia," Rybalko said. "Just take me to Kachin."

4

Nikita Kachin ran a business in the southern suburbs, an abattoir and butcher's shop that made the best sausages in the area. Rumour had it that he used it to get rid of the corpses of people who got in his way. Rybalko hoped it was rumour. He often left their meetings with a few pounds of freshly ground meat.

The man behind the counter in the butcher's shop led them into a backroom and then into the abattoir itself. Kachin was working alongside his employees. Thin and stooped like a steel blade ready to spring up, he was methodically cutting up meat with precise, almost surgical motions. Even if most of the money he made came from his illegal activities, Kachin enjoyed the time he spent in his abattoir. He found it relaxing, however weird that seemed to most people.

As if noticing a change in the air, Kachin turned when they were still about six metres away from him.

"Alex!" he said when he saw Rybalko.

He stabbed his knife into the piece of meat he had been cutting and took off his gloves.

"I've been searching for you for days. Good thing your friend's a detective!"

A metal tooth glinted at the back of his smile as he gave Chekhov a friendly pat on the shoulder. He whispered into his ear: "Go to the till. They've got your money. And take a nice roast for Sunday."

Chekhov glanced hesitantly at his partner.

"Shall I wait for you outside?"

"Don't wait," Rybalko said. "Kito and I haven't seen each other for a long time. This might take a while. I'll get a taxi."

Chekhov nodded and disappeared without another word. Kachin took off his apron and hung it on a stainless-steel hook.

"It'll be quieter up there," he said, making for a metal staircase.

Kachin led Rybalko to his office from which he could keep an eye on his employees. The room was spacious, without any kind of decoration. No photographs, no souvenirs, no paintings. The white walls were lined with identical metal filing cabinets. An old fridge hummed in a corner.

When Kachin closed the door behind him, Rybalko noticed that the edge of the handle was a dirty brown colour, as if touched by blood-covered hands. There were stains of the same colour on the carpet. The memory of this mafioso hitting a man flashed up in his mind. The guy had been some Chechen civilian who refused to say where his money was hidden. Rybalko lit a cigarette and took a long drag on it to blot out the memory. Below, through the window, he saw a pig's carcass being sliced with a boning knife.

"Beer?" Kachin said.

Rybalko grimaced. The idea of drinking alcohol turned his stomach, as did the smell of blood and viscera that permeated the office through a half-open fanlight.

"I'm not thirsty. Why did you pay Chekhov to find me?"

"He's not cheap, your friend, but he gets the job done. Where were you?"

"Get to the point, Kita. I don't have any time to lose."

Kachin sighed.

"Always in a rush. Alright, let's get down to it. I need a discreet police officer who speaks the language of nightingales. So I thought of you."

The "language of nightingales" was what Ukrainians called their language, due to its musicality. Contrary to popular belief, Ukrainian and Russian were two very different languages, no closer than Spanish and French.

"Do you know Vektor Sokolov?" Kachin asked in Ukrainian.

"The name rings a bell."

"He was the energy minister, back in the days of Boris the Sponge."

Boris Yeltsin had been the first president of the Russian Federation, after the end of the U.S.S.R. He was also the only world leader capable of governing with three grammes of alcohol in his bloodstream.

"Hang on. This Sokolov – he's not the PetroRus guy?" Rybalko said.

Kachin nodded. "That's him."

During the period of rampant privatisation of state organisations in the mid-1990s, Sokolov had used his position at the Ministry of Energy to acquire part of Siberia's vast oil resources. It was at this time that he founded PetroRus, one of the most substantial oil companies in the country.

"His family recently suffered a bereavement," Kachin said. "An unpleasant affair. Vektor's son was killed in Ukraine."

"Many people die in Ukraine, especially now."

"But this was a murder. In a city you know well."

"Kyiv?"

"No. Pripyat."

Rybalko thought this must be a sick joke. "*Pripyat?* That's impossible. Nobody's lived there for thirty years. It's sealed off by the police and the army."

"Not altogether. It has been welcoming tourist groups for the past few years."

"Tourists? Why?"

"So people can view the last vestiges of the communist world apparently. It's like an open-air museum."

"What bullshit!"

"Tell me about it! But to get back to our story, Vektor Sokolov suspects the Ukrainian authorities of wanting to bury the official investigation. He asked me to find someone competent to look into his son's death."

"Hang on. . . Are you suggesting I go to Pripyat? You really think I would agree to go back to that shitty place?"

"I know, I know. I haven't forgotten what you told me when we were in Chechnya. Your parents' death, your exile. . . You had a hard time there, I know. But Vektor Sokolov is ready to pay serious money for–"

"I'm not interested. But tell me, how do you know Sokolov?"

"We have some mutual friends. It is well known that I have some influence over the Ukrainians in Moscow."

In spite of his illegal activities, Kachin was regarded as a benefactor by the Ukrainian diaspora. He funded a number of charities, the Ukrainian cultural centre and the Ukrainian library in Moscow. It was to Kachin that members of the community would go when they had a problem whose solution demanded discretion and minimum scruples.

"I know you swore never to return to Ukraine, Alex, but I'm offering you a great deal. This guy is ready to pay a fortune. And I'm not exaggerating, we're talking about a *lot* of money. Enough to pay for your daughter's surgery."

Rybalko froze. "That would cost millions of rubles," he said.

"I told you: this guy will do anything to find his son's murderer."

Kachin opened a drawer, took out a business card, put it on the table and – with his faintly bloodstained fingers – pushed it towards the policeman.

"Call him. At least find out how much he's offering for the job."

Rybalko stared at the glossy card for a long moment. Part of him wanted nothing to do with it. Another part whispered that he should agree, for Tassia.

"What do you get out of it?"

"Sokolov's going to invest in Crimea. If you find his son's killer, he'll take me on as a business partner. Goodbye, grey Moscow. Hello, sunny beaches! I'll take care of security for his businesses there."

"To stop racketeers like you extorting money from them?"

The mafioso's thin face lit up as he roared with laughter.

"You understand everything, Alex! So. . . will you talk to him?"

Rybalko stood up and pocketed the business card.

"I'll let you know."

5

Rybalko took a taxi to Lyubertsy, to the south-east of Moscow. In the 1990s, the city had been the Russian Chicago. Gangs, racketeers, hitmen. . . after the fall of the communist regime, the city's streets had given birth to a generation of young bodybuilding delinquents, conceived from the mix of widespread poverty, the new temptations offered by capitalism, and the dissolution of the Soviet moral order. Young tearaways wearing improbable clothes – check trousers, baseball caps, leather jackets and skinny ties – would lead raids into the heart of Moscow. These days the city was calmer and the rundown tower blocks were inhabited by couples benefiting from the "Young Families" housing programme.

He found his car, still on the pavement where he had abandoned it. It was a charcoal-grey Volga M24 from the 1970s, with a chrome grill like a straight moustache between the two headlight eyes. Empty half-litre vodka bottles littered the carpeted floor, along with the remains of a *chebureki* in its greasepaper packaging. The car smelled of deep-fried dough and ground beef.

He collected it all and threw it in a bin. At the end of the street he could see the balcony of the apartment he had once shared with Marina. Had their love simply been worn away by time? Was it his job? Marina had endured his absences for years as he immersed himself, body and soul, in his life as a policeman. And then, one day, it had all crumbled. She no longer wanted to wait, fearfully, for a telephone call to tell her that he had been shot in the course of an operation. She no longer wanted to share her life with a ghost. She wanted someone who would be there for her.

Maybe she had at least understood that she could not mend him.

Women love to believe they can change men. Improve them. He was a perfect example of the broken male. The deaths of his parents, the trauma of being expelled from Chernobyl, the war in Chechnya. . . he had so many wounds that needed to heal. She thought that creating a stable home life would be enough to soothe his angst. But he needed the conflict with evil to keep moving forward. He needed to explore the dark veins of Moscow to remove the cancerous cells; he needed to lock up killers and rapists to scour away some of the perversion that he had seen in Chechnya, and which was also corrupting the capital.

For him, the violence had not come to an end when the war ended. The battlefield had just moved. All those men who had learned to kill, some of whom had developed a taste for it, had been spilled into society. One day, in one of the city's northern suburbs, he'd arrested an old comrade from his regiment. At the front, he was nicknamed Popovich – a reference to the clown Oleg Popov – because he was always joking around. Rybalko had found two decomposed bodies in Popovich's apartment. The corpses of prostitutes. When the policeman had asked his former comrade why he had killed them, he had said that nobody had asked him that in Chechnya. That he had killed all the time there and it had been normal.

So how could Rybalko quit the police when there were so many madmen living in the same city as Anastassia?

Tassia. Maybe it was because of her that they had separated? Maria was a violinist at the Tchaikovsky Conservatory, Russia's most prestigious music school. When she had discovered that her daughter was practically deaf, it had broken her heart. Rybalko felt sure that his ex-wife blamed him for that – because his genes had been damaged by radiation. In any case, it had been around the time that Tassia's hearing problems had first been diagnosed that his relationship with Marina had hit the skids. For him, this was no coincidence; it was a confession. Marina never came out and said it, but he was sure of it all the same: for her, it was his fault that Tassia was not "normal".

Sitting in the M24, he spent the journey thinking about Kachin's offer, while staring out at the usual sights of the street: skinny-armed junkies parading past like walking skeletons in search of their next fix, the armada of single mothers pushing their prams towards a dingy park, the babushkas in their coloured headscarves slowly carrying bags of anaemic vegetables back from the market.

Depressing as hell.

Was this what he wanted for Tassia? A mediocre life, in a mediocre neighbourhood, with a mediocre job and a husband who was either absent or dead? He started his car and drove towards his daughter's school. He got there just before the lunch break. As soon as the bell rang, kids ran screeching into the playground. A moment later, the teacher opened the gate for the waiting parents and he went in search of Tassia.

The children whirled around him happily, a hurricane of laughter, blonde braids and blue eyes. After a while, he spotted his daughter's figure in the middle of the playground. She was wearing a bright pink puffa jacket, as if to ward off the greyness of the school's walls and the steel-coloured sky above. From behind, you hardly noticed the unsightly hearing aids attached to her ears. Two ugly brown plastic devices that she had to wear to escape her world of silence.

Suddenly she turned around and her face lit up. *Papa! Papa!* She leapt into his arms.

"What are you doing here?" she said.

"We're going out for lunch. To McDonald's."

"We're going to MacDonald's?" she shouted, hopping in excitement.

"It's a sort of surprise birthday, just the two of us," he said.

His daughter stared at him wide-eyed.

"Will there be a present, like for a real birthday?"

"Yes. We can go to GUM to pick something out."

He held her little hand in his. She had traces of red and blue paint on her fingernails. That morning, an artist had come to their class. She told him this while he drove to a car park not far from Manezhnaya Square, near the Kremlin. There was a McDonald's there that he had never visited before. He wanted a place with no memories other than the ones they would create that day.

As they queued up to order, he remembered the first time he had eaten a Big Mac. It was in 1990, on Pushkinskaya Square. The U.S.S.R. was still standing, but the Iron Curtain which separated it from the rest of the world was already full of holes. The first fast-food restaurant in Russia had just opened. The biggest in the world. He had gone there with his aunt, for his birthday. It was pure luxury: the meal cost six rubles, at a time when the average monthly wage in Russia was less than 200 rubles.

Tassia ordered a kids' meal, with a toy for girls. She wolfed down her food, while he ate slowly: every moment spent with her was precious, even the sad, banal ones, as when he wiped the corner of his mouth with a napkin or watched his daughter laughing in the Play Place.

When their meal was almost over, he suggested they go to Gorky Park to do some rollerblading.

"The park? But it's time to go back to school!"

"Not this afternoon. We're going to have fun, just the two of us."

"Great!" she shouted before swallowing her last mouthful of vanilla ice cream.

On the way, she told him about her life. Friends, clothes, Christmas presents. She said she wanted to be a painter. The last time, she had wanted to be a surfer. When he was her age, Rybalko remembered, all the boys had wanted to be cosmonauts and the girls gymnasts, like Nadia Com neci. All her stories were wonderful, he thought. So why hadn't he listened to them before? He had always been too busy. Too many things to do. Now it was too late, he realised that he had missed out on the most important moments of his life.

The imminence of death forces you to redefine your priorities.

*

A week ago, in a hospital room that smells of surgical spirit. He is sitting on the table where the doctor has just examined him. The two men know each other well. The old man has been his doctor since his first visit to the militia's medical centre in the late 1990s. Now Rybalko asks this man the most important question he has ever asked anyone:

"Is it operable?"

The doctor hangs the photographs on the light box fixed to the wall. A cold light floods the black and white contours showing a cross-section of his brain. The doctor points to a dark mass in the middle of the image. The beast's lair.

"The tumour is here," he says.

"Can you remove it?"

The doctor turns off the light box.

"At this stage, it's impossible to operate. I'm sorry."

*

They arrived in Gorky Park and rented rollerblades. While he tied her laces, he explained to Tassia that during the Soviet era, the park had been one of the few places where people could really relax, even if the loud-speakers broadcast speeches by communist leaders all day long. Tassia asked if he used to walk her here in her pram when she was a baby. He told her that the park had been too dangerous back then. After the demise of the U.S.S.R., it had fallen for a while into the hands of junkies and gangsters. Tassia looked baffled: for children of her generation, Gorky Park belonged to the young women of Moscow Beach who sunbathed topless there in the summer, to the ping-pong players and to teenagers smoking their first cigarettes, to nannies pushing prams.

They saw other children. Tassia nervously touched her hearing aids. Whenever she went out, she always tried to hide them under a hat or her hair. And more and more often, when she could not hide them, she would simply take them out. She just wanted to look normal.

A series of black-and-white photographs flash up on the light box. Liver, lungs, stomach. . . the doctor points to large dark masses on each of these X-rays. The cancer is everywhere inside him.

"Some cancers spread very quickly," the doctor says. "Yours is extremely aggressive and it's metastasised into most of your major organs."

His throat is dry and tight. He feels like he can't breathe. Three months earlier, he'd had a check-up and the doctor had found nothing worrying in any of the tests. He can't be sick, it's impossible. Let alone dying.

Tonelessly he asks: "I was in Pripyat when the Chernobyl nuclear reactor exploded. I was eight at the time. Could that have. . ."

He leaves the sentence unfinished. Frowning, the doctor nods.

"That could explain why it's spread so quickly. A lot of people affected by that disaster have had cancers. Your immune system was undoubtedly weakened by your exposure to radiation."

They walked past the place where, every winter, there was a skating rink. Unfortunately, it wouldn't open again until mid-November. A shame. He would have liked to go ice skating with Tassia. On rollerblades she was a bit clumsy, but on ice his daughter was as light and graceful as a fairy with wings. She got that from her mother. He was a terrible skater.

The doctor's voice sounds distant, as if he's speaking from the depths of a cave. But Rybalko isn't really listening anymore. Memories of the explosion, suppressed for years, are surging into his mind.

Six in the morning in Pripyat. The apartment is quiet. The alarm clock rings. It's Saturday; he hasn't slept well. His mother makes him breakfast. She keeps looking nervously out of the window. For him, it's just another day.

But time stutters.

*

It's Saturday and he's going to school. What's going on? His mother makes several attempts to tie his laces. At school, the older kids mutter rumours. Around nine in the morning, some unsmiling women come into the classroom. He and all his classmates are given strange pills that they have to swallow with a glass of water. He does not know this yet, but the pills are iodine, which is supposed to protect them from the effects of radiation. After that, everyone is sent home. On the way back he is scared. People are driving weirdly. Grown-ups whisper to one another. Little boys look as serious as old men. Something bad is happening, they can tell, but nobody knows what it is.

Then evening comes, and they enter hell. His father has not returned from the reactor. His mother has stopped talking. She waits beside the telephone. He waits too. Finally, exhausted, he falls asleep at around one in the morning. When his mother wakes him, her eyes are red and her face is puffy from sleeplessness. It's Sunday, April 27. The city is going to be evacuated. He asks where his father is. His mother says that he is fighting the dragon.

As they wandered around the park, the sound of traffic faded to silence. There were lots of other families on the paths, babies in prams. He bought some birdseed from a vending machine. Tassia threw it to the animals and birds in the park. She saw a little squirrel with a red and white tail and spent a long time trying to coax it towards her.

*

The dragon in the Russian forest.

Back when he was a little boy of four or five, his mother used to tell him that his father put out fires started by the dragon imprisoned inside the reactor. She said that Russian scientists had captured it and made it submit to their will. That they were using its fiery breath to heat houses and produce the electricity that lit streetlamps and powered the television in their living room. She said the beast was sleeping peacefully, but that his father was there to put out the fire if the dragon ever woke up and began breathing fire. It wasn't much of a lie, of course. But he was only a kid. What could he possibly understand about atoms, nuclear fusion, radioactivity?

Nothing.

*

Autumn melancholy. In Moscow, the season began on September 1 and unfolded like a dream. Soon the trees would blaze with red and orange leaves. Even now, he could see patches of yellow among the green. Tassia picked up some fallen leaves and threw them towards the sky.

*

His mother gathers a few belongings. The authorities have told them to take only the bare necessities because the evacuation is temporary. So she hesitates. Which dresses, which coats, which shoes should she pack? Should she take the samovar, a gift from her mother-in-law, in case there is looting? He asks her what toys he should take. His teddy bear? No, not the bear. Anyway, he's a big boy now. He doesn't need that anymore. His mother tells him this as she holds him by the shoulders. She is usually so gentle, but today her hands squeeze him hard. It scares him. They get on a bus with their suitcases. Their bus is joined by another bus, and soon they are part of a long line of buses. Young as he is, he understands that the entire population of Pripyat is leaving on those orange buses. A city on wheels, almost 50,000 people who do not yet know that they will never return to live there, that their city of the atom — so young, so proud, the exemplar of triumphant communism — is already dead.

*

There was a big wheel in Gorky Park. Tassia was a little bit scared, but she agreed to go on it, as long as he was with her. When their pod reached the summit of the circle, she pressed herself tight against him. He thought about another big wheel, the one in Pripyat, which he had dreamed about for a long time when he was a kid. The fairground was supposed to open on May 1, but the city had been evacuated before that could happen, and he was never able to go there with his father as he had been promised. A tear welled up in the corner of his eye, without him noticing.

"Are you crying?"

"No, it's the wind. I got some dust in my eye."

*

After the evacuation, they move in with his paternal grandfather, Vadik, an old colonel who went to war against the Nazis. A real communist, solid as a piece of artillery. Not the kind of man to be scared of his own shadow. One night, a Party representative comes to the house. After the man leaves, Vadik slumps into his chair and starts to sob. Alexander is shocked: he has never seen his grandfather cry before. That's when he understands: his father will not be coming back. The dragon defeated him.

His father is buried in Moscow, at the Mitinskoe Cemetery, along with his fellow firemen, who suffered massive doses of radiation during the early hours of the disaster. He is wrapped in a plastic sheet then placed in a wooden coffin, and that coffin is placed inside a zinc box. Then the zinc box is buried five metres under concrete, like nuclear waste. His father's face is engraved on the dark grey tombstone, frozen in perpetual youth.

His mother goes to the funeral. When she returns, they visit the local hospital. X-rays, scans, blood tests. They are monitored with devices that make crackling noises. The needles dance on the screens of dosimeters. The number of microroentgens goes up to 100, 200, 500. They do not know what that means. All they know is: the higher the numbers, the more serious it is. The doctors make them take baths every ninety minutes and swallow vitamin pills. This is all the great U.S.S.R. can do to save its heroic proletariat. But he is just a kid and he thinks everything will be alright.

And, until now, it has been.

Later that afternoon they went to GUM, the former "State Department Store", now transformed into a luxury shopping centre. In a jeweller's they chose a necklace for Tassia's birthday. He wanted to give her something that would outlive him. He had the gift wrapped and told her she would not receive it until the day of her birthday. Tassia pouted: she did not want to wait three months.

The doctor is writing a prescription.

That's when he asks him the worst question of all:

"How long do I have?"

The doctor looks up from his papers and stares at him for a long time, as if trying to read from the lines on his forehead the precise number of seconds remaining to him.

"A few months. Three, four. . . maybe six. But not much more than that."

A scream turns silent in his throat. The Chernobyl dragon has caught him at last, the monster that destroyed his childhood and killed everyone he loved. His father, burned by an invisible fire. His mother, taken by leukemia. The night when Reactor 4 spewed flames and shards of graphite, she had tried to reach the power plant to find out what was happening to her husband. She had been stopped at a checkpoint, but the harm had been done. She had suffered a massive dose of radiation.

He remembers her poor bald head, because of the treatment. He remembers her gold locks falling. She used to have such pretty hair, his mother. She was so proud of it.

His phone rang. It was Marina.

"Alexander? I just got a call from the school. Anastassia isn't in her class. They said a man came to fetch her. Was it you?"

"Yes, it was me. . . I forgot to call you. Sorry, I–"

She interrupts, furious: "What is wrong with you? I was worried sick. . . I almost called the police! Why the hell would you do that?"

The moment had come. He should tell her now. Or maybe not. Announcing his imminent death on the telephone did not strike him as a great idea. He decided to postpone that ordeal a little longer.

"I'll explain later."

"You're so inconsiderate. . . Bring her home right now!"

He hung up. Tassia was on the swings. She was laughing. He caught a few more sweet memories of her, then told her it was time to leave.

*

The consultation is over. The doctor stands to accompany him outside.

He asks one last question: "If you were me, what would you do with the time you had left?"

The doctor doesn't think long. He has a standard answer for this kind of situation.

"I would put my affairs in order and spend time with my family."

*

When he left the doctor's office, that had been his plan. He was going to tell Marina about his cancer. Then, outside the door of her apartment, he hesitated. He felt so miserable that he decided to walk away and satisfy every whim that popped into his head. Drugs. Women. Gratuitous violence. Speed. Alcohol. He maxed out on everything, one last time.

"Are you coming to my birthday party this year?" Tassia said as they entered Lyubertsy.

"I'll try to make it."

But would he even be alive in three months? They parked outside Marina's apartment building. His ex-wife was waiting at the front door, arms crossed, face like thunder. She hugged Tassia and told her to go up to their apartment. Once the little girl had gone inside, she vented her fury.

"Are you out of your mind? Can you imagine how scared I was?"

He knew all he had to do to calm her down was utter two little words: "I'm dying". But he couldn't.

"I wanted to spend some time with my daughter. . ."

"Spend some time with your daughter? Oh my God, what a joke! You had nine years to spend time with her. But you always had something better to do. You spent more time with your dealers and killers than with her. . . or with me."

She fell silent. She was on the verge of tears.

"I'm warning you, Alex, the next time this happens I'm pressing charges. You can't just pick up Tassia whenever you feel like it."

"There won't be a next time."

She frowned.

"I know you and your promises. Alex, listen to me."

"It's the truth, Marina. I . . . I . . ."

"You what?"

He suddenly had a vision. Anastassia at 20. She's at university. Studying medicine. Sitting in the front row of the lecture hall, she pushes her hair behind her ears. She's forgotten the unpleasant sensation of having those ugly brown hearing aids in her ears. It's noon. Early autumn. She touches the gold necklace that they chose together at GUM. Maybe she remembers their walk in Gorky Park.

In his vision, he did not want her to remember her mother in tears in the small kitchen of their apartment.

"Go on, Alex, what's your excuse this time?"

He took a deep breath.

"I'm leaving."

They weren't the two words he had meant to say, but they were the right ones.

"Leaving?" Marina said, surprised. "Are you taking time off work? Moving house?"

"No, it's a special mission. I'm going to be a long way from Moscow for a while, so I wanted to see Tassia, just in case. . . in case anything happens to me."

Marina observed him in silence for a moment. He knew that look. She was trying to work out if he was lying or telling the truth.

"So where've you been these last few days?"

"On a stakeout."

"In a bar?" Marina said sarcastically. "I've seen you off your head often enough before to know when you've been drinking."

"One of my colleagues had a retirement party last night."

She didn't believe a word of it. And she was right.

"What you do at night is none of my business anymore. But I'm telling you again, you can't just pick up Tassia whenever you like. The judge gave me custody. You have to follow the orders."

He nodded, then took the box containing the necklace from his pocket.

"I don't know how long I'll be gone. Could you give this to her, if I'm not there?"

Martina squinted suspiciously at the package, as if it might be a parcel bomb.

"That's exactly what I was saying," she said, reluctantly taking it from him. "With you, work always comes first."

"Marina..."

"Not one word. I've heard too many of your excuses. I'll tell your daughter that you have to arrest bad guys. Just like I did all the other times. At least try to call on the right day this time. And to be sober."

She turned around and walked into the lobby. He felt a faint pang as he watched her disappear. It was maybe the last time he would see her and he had not managed to make peace with her.

6

The call he made to Vektor Sokolov was brief and concise. Rybalko introduced himself, explained that Kachin had given him his business card, and the former minister immediately invited him to his villa. It was on the Rublyovka, the most prestigious road in Moscow. His colleagues in the station called it Zabor-City, the city of fences, since all the houses were surrounded by high, protective fences or walls. The first had appeared in the 1930s, under Stalin, to shelter all the dachas of the Nomenklatura from prying eyes, the Party elite. Since then, the 100-million-ruble villas of rich oligarchs had supplanted those of the communist leaders, and the walls and fences had shot up like mushrooms after rain. The neighbourhood was the sanctuary of the city's most powerful people: politicians, captains of industry, mafiosi, all of them imprisoned in this incestuous little island of wealth, protected by video-surveillance cameras and walls as impenetrable as those of the Kremlin.

There was a security guard in a little hut at the entrance to the neighbourhood – a former policeman who stared contemptuously at Rybalko. After the barrier, the only people with dark skin he saw in that place were nannies from the Philippines and labourers from Caucasia who wore themselves out building the foundations of new villas. These men were hired for less than 100 rubles an hour on Three Station Square in the centre of Moscow, among the hundreds of workers from the former Soviet socialist republics that comprised the old U.S.S.R. – Tajikistan, Uzbekistan, Turkmenistan, Kyrgyzstan – all of them there trying to make a new life in the Russian capital.

Sokolov's high metal gate was topped with three large cameras. Two bodyguards came to meet Rybalko and he had to hand over his service pistol. Behind the gate stretched a wide paved driveway and a garden as long as a golf course. After following a path marked out by slates, he arrived at a patio door that led into a very large and pretentiously decorated living room. Paintings by contemporary artists, no doubt extremely expensive, lined the walls; crystal chandeliers hung from the ceiling. On one wall, a flatscreen TV the size of a snooker table overlooked an assemblage of leather chairs.

A young blonde woman walked across the room just then, airy and ethereal in a haute-couture dress that looked as if it had been designed by Mondrian. Ten-centimetre Louboutin heels, Cartier jewellery, Hermès handbag. . . Sokolov was evidently something of a Francophile. The girl flashed him a charming smile, then put on a long sable coat handed to her by a maid who had appeared out of nowhere. Without a word, this blonde angel left the room and walked out to the driveway where a Bentley limousine, complete with chauffeur, was purring.

"Your boss' daughter doesn't look too upset by her brother's death," Rybalko said to the bodyguards.

The two bodybuilders exchanged a look of amusement.

"That's Mr Sokolov's wife, not his daughter," one of them said.

"Ah, a love match – how sweet!" Rybalko said with a smile.

Footsteps echoed from the marble staircase and soon afterwards Vektor Sokolov appeared in front of him. A fit-looking fiftysomething, the ex-minister wore a fitted suit jacket and his heavy, unremarkable face was enhanced by his bright blonde hair. In place of natural charisma, he wore a Rolex Cosmograph Daytona on his left wrist, gold rings on his sausage fingers, and diamond cufflinks.

"Ah! Alexander Rybalko!" he said. "I'm delighted to meet you at last!"

They shared a solid handshake.

"My condolences for your son," Rybalko said.

A shadow passed over Sokolov's eyes.

"Thank you. You're a father too, so you can imagine what I'm going through."

"Yes, I. . . I can imagine," he said.

"Let's go to the smoking room. We'll be more comfortable there."

Sokolov dismissed the bodyguards and led Rybalko to the smoking room. Two leather club chairs, a coffee table with a humidor, a small cabinet containing spirits and sparkling waters. . . it was quite cosy compared to the living room. One of the walls, painted peacock blue, was covered with hunting trophies. Stags, wolves, bears.

A copy of *Kommersant* lay on the coffee table, along with a magazine opened to an article on how to choose diamonds.

Sokolov poured himself a glass of Cognac and offered one to Rybalko, who shook his head and asked for a glass of water. The ex-minister opened a bottle of foreign mineral water and poured it into a glass, explaining that it was from Norway and was probably the purest water in the world. He talked briefly about his plans for an electric factory there, then swallowed a mouthful of his ridiculously expensive cognac before saying in a more serious voice: "It's been more than a month since my son was killed and I still don't have any idea what exactly happened. Since Leonid died in Ukraine, I cannot use my contacts to direct the investigation."

"How far have the local police got?"

"What investigation?" Sokolov said bitterly. "It's a joke. From the Russian embassy, I discovered that those scumbags have not even ordered an autopsy, supposedly because the body had absorbed too much radiation."

Suppressed rage swelled the veins in his neck and hardened his features.

"They just want to punish Russia by punishing me, those bastards. Because I used to be a minister. But they won't get away with it. If they think I'm just going to let them do this, they've got another thing coming!"

Sokolov's jaw muscles tensed, the corner of one eyelid twitched, and his chest rose and fell too fast. And yet, just as his hatred seemed on the point of exploding in a volley of insults, he composed himself: his face became stoical again and his voice resumed its cold, professional tone.

Rybalko watched all this, surprised and somewhat disturbed.

"When I realised that I couldn't trust the Ukrainian police to discover the truth, I began to look for a detective who would agree to investigate near Chernobyl. A few people turned me down, then I contacted some old friends who put me in touch with Nikita. When he told me you were from Pripyat, I knew you would be the perfect candidate."

On the cabinet containing all the bottles, there was also a silver platter that was presumably used for serving patisseries prepared by Sokolov's French chef. Today, however, it contained two dossiers.

"This," he said, picking up the first stack of documents, "contains the information I have so far gathered to help with your investigation. There's not much, unfortunately: it's mostly bank statements, the list of calls my son made on his mobile, and of course a few photographs that I was able to procure. It was my contact in the zone who took them."

Rybalko leafed through the dossier, then stopped at an I.D. photo of Leonid. With his heavy face and false smile, he looked a lot like his father, except for one detail: where Vektor Sokolov's eyes were blue, his son's were ink-black. In the other photographs, taken after his death, the dark gaze had vanished behind eyelids sewn shut with clear fishing line.

"If you already have someone there, why send me?"

"It is a person who has no experience in criminal investigation. I want a professional. And I want him to be from here," Sokolov said, articulating every syllable. "I want to know exactly who I'm dealing with. I want to talk to him face to face."

He picked up the second stack of documents. This time, he did not hand it to Rybalko, just leafed through it himself.

"I was able to procure a copy of your dossier, Alexander. I saw a few things in there, tiny details, but put them all together and they tell a story: delayed promotions, holidays in autumn, at the worst time of year, official reprimands. . . I conclude from this that you are not in your bosses' good books. I suppose you're more the independent, rebellious type?"

Rybalko smiled. "Just like you're the egocentric, careerist type who's used to being obeyed by everyone you meet."

Sokolov nodded slowly.

"Nikita Kachin warned me that you might be quite. . . direct. That suits me fine. For this job, I need someone who doesn't waste time beating around the bush."

"Doesn't waste time," Rybalko repeated, frowning.

Flustered, he looked through the photographs to cover up his emotion.

"Apparently Pripyat has loads of visitors now. Tourists and thrill-seekers, some of them. Others are people who used to live there and want to see the city of their youth again. Or their children, wanting to trace their roots. . . Which category did your son belong to?"

Sokolov thought about this for a few seconds before responding.

"I think he went there because of our family's connections to Pripyat."

His expression became grave.

"I was in Pripyat too. I was the first secretary of the *Gorkom*."

The head of the city committee. And yet Sokolov's face meant nothing to Rybalko. No doubt he had been too young to recognise an obscure politician from the 1980s.

"So Leonid wanted to see the city where he was born. . ."

"I don't think that was really it. . . I think he was there to carry out an investigation. My wife. . ."

Sokolov seemed suddenly very old and tired. His face pale, he slumped down in one of the leather chairs.

"My first wife, Olga. . . Leonid's mother. . . she was killed on the day the reactor exploded."

Rybalko was intrigued.

"You think your son went there to investigate her murder?"

"I suppose so, even if it makes no sense. I was an influential man in Pripyat at the time of the catastrophe. If I hadn't been able to find Olga's murderer, with all the authority and influence I had at that time, how could he possibly manage it thirty years later?"

"Your son never told you about his intention to return to the Chernobyl region?"

"No. He told me he was in Dubai, so this whole disaster came out of the blue."

"So this is your second family tragedy, and both of them were connected to Pripyat. . ."

With sharp little wrist movements, Sokolov swirled the cognac around his glass. He stared at the oily spiral left in the spirit's wake.

"I know what you're thinking. My wife's murder, Leonid's death. . . It can't be coincidental. They must be linked in some way."

"Did you have enemies in Pripyat?"

Sokolov laughed softly.

"What politician doesn't have enemies? When I was at Gorkom, everyone in the hierarchy below me wanted to take my place. As for my superiors, they were afraid I'd replace them."

"Had you received any warnings or threats before your son's death?"

"No."

"Do you have enemies here in Moscow who might have planned his murder?"

Sokolov leaned forward and said: "Alexander, nobody gets to where I am without making a lot of enemies. If, on your way home, you stopped to visit every person I offended during my career, you wouldn't get to Moscow before Christmas. And that's only my political enemies. If you add my business enemies to the list. . . well, you wouldn't even get out of Rublyovka!"

"And who might have wanted your wife dead?"

Sokolov gazed gloomily at his hunting trophies on the wall.

"I have no idea. The militia did everything they could to find Olga's killer, but the killing happened at the worst possible moment. The security services were all stretched to breaking point. They had to evacuate the civilians, monitor the danger zones, turn over the contaminated earth, bury all the heavily exposed buildings. . ."

Sokolov's words stirred Rybalko's memories of the evacuation. He saw himself at the back of a bus, sitting next to his mother. The kids around him were excited because they thought they were going on a camping trip. But he could feel no happiness about that: his father had not returned from the reactor.

He lit a cigarette and listened distractedly to the former minister.

". . . to carry out investigations. . . insufficient human resources. . . everyone was so busy dealing with the consequences of the explosion. . . I wish I never had to think about those years again. . . But it would be crazy to believe there's no connection between Olga's death and Leonid's. . . The autopsy's supposed to take place in Donetsk. . ."

Rybalko was torn from his thoughts. "Donetsk is hundreds of kilometres east of Chernobyl in the Donbas region. What is your son's body doing there?"

Sokolov took a deep breath before answering.

"The Ukrainian authorities did not want to give it to me, supposedly because of the risk of contamination if we brought it into Russia. A few days ago, I managed to bribe enough people to have the body sent in a refrigerated truck to Donetsk."

"Why not use a plane?"

"Maybe I wasn't clear. The authorities did not agree to return my son's remains. I paid people to let his body 'escape' from the morgue."

"I see. But how do you expect to get it out of the country without the correct paperwork?"

"I have contacts in the Republic of Donetsk. They'll take care of it."

Rybalko had heard about this. The Republic of Donetsk was the name that the separatists had given to the territory they had set up in the Donbas around the city of Donetsk.

"I arranged for Leonid's body in a coffin to cross the border. He came in one of those trucks that bring back the bodies of Russian soldiers from the front."

"I thought there were no Russians involved in the Ukrainian conflict," Rybalko said sarcastically.

Sokolov sneered. Russia was regularly accused of offering the separatists military support, but had always proclaimed its innocence where the Donbas was concerned.

"No-one can prevent our brave citizens from going off to fight the Kyiv fascists, can they? Anyway, to return to the subject in hand, we found a coroner who agreed to carry out the autopsy at the morgue in Donetsk. He's waiting for you."

Rybalko crossed his arms, frowning. "I get it, you want me to cross through a war-torn country so I can try to find a killer in a nuclear wasteland? Am I missing anything?"

Sokolov's smile did not falter.

"I'm well aware of the dangers of this mission. That's why I'm willing to pay you fifty million rubles to carry it out."

Rybalko was stunned. Fifty million rubles! He could not make that much as a policeman in two or three lifetimes. With that kind of cash, Tassia could have her operation and go to whatever university she wanted. She would never have to worry about money. . .

"How would the money be paid?" he said.

"Into a numbered bank account in Switzerland, upon completion of your mission."

His mouth was suddenly very dry. He picked up his glass and swallowed some Norwegian mineral water.

"What if. . . what if I die during the investigation?"

"I understand your concern. This is a risky mission. If anything were to happen to you, I guarantee that a quarter of the promised sum would be paid to your widow, or to the person of your choice."

That was a weight off Rybalko's mind.

"In return," Sokolov went on, "I expect total discretion from you. Nobody must know that I sent you to Ukraine. My name must never be mentioned and you are not to talk to anyone about our arrangement. That will be one of the clauses in the contract that we'll sign." He finished his Cognac, then added: "One last thing: you will only receive the money on one condition, which will not appear in the contract."

"What condition?"

"When you find my son's murderer, I want him to *die*." Sokolov stared at him, as if trying to read his reaction, then asked: "Would that pose a moral problem for you? If you need time to think about my offer, I can give you a day."

A day of reflection. It was a luxury Rybalko could not allow himself.

"No need," he said, getting to his feet. "I'll find the killer. And I'll kill him."

7

When Captain Melnyk arrived at the police station in Chernobyl, he found on top of his desk a cardboard box sealed with brown sticky tape. On it in capital letters in black felt-tip pen: "FOR CAPTAIN MELNYK. ATTENTION: FRAGILE."

The box was light as a feather, and when he shook it to work out what was inside it made a quiet, fluffy sort of sound. It was covered in stamps, but there was no postmark, and no addresses on the parcel – neither the sender's nor the police station's.

He called reception.

"There's a package in my office. Who left it here?"

"It was me," the receptionist said. "Is there a problem?"

"There's no sender's address on it and I wasn't expecting a delivery. Did the postman make you sign something when he brought it in?"

"Nah, I just found it in the letter box."

"Did you wear gloves when you picked it up?"

"Um, no. . . Why would I have done that?"

"Never mind," Melnyk said before hanging up.

He examined the parcel as if it were a suspect who refused to talk. He grabbed a pair of latex gloves from one of the drawers in his desk, put them on, then picked up a flick-knife. He slid the blade along the sticky tape that covered the box's opening and slowly lifted the flaps. Inside were small pieces of white plastic that seemed to invite him to plunge his hand into their velvety softness. His fingers touched an object buried beneath. It was light and silky to the touch. Melnyk parted the sea of polystyrene and something round and electric blue emerged. A little more digging and soon a bird's head appeared. It was a stuffed swallow, frozen in such a realistic pose that he found it somewhat disturbing.

Despite the coolness of his office, Melnyk felt beads of sweat roll down his forehead. The last time he had seen a stuffed animal had been in that apartment in Pripyat, with Leonid Sokolov's corpse hanging outside the window. He observed the bird from every angle, then checked there was nothing else inside the box. After making sure that he had missed nothing under the packing materials, he turned his attention to the stamps. They were all from the communist era, and they were so old that they'd had to be sellotaped to the box because the glue on their backs had dried up. The stamps had been issued to celebrate the 90th anniversary of the first modern Olympics. A quick search informed Melnyk that the first Olympiad had taken place in 1886.

So those stamps had been published the same year that Olga Sokolov, Leonid's mother, had been murdered. The killer must have sent him this parcel. Was it a warning? An act of provocation? The announcement of another murder?

From the metal cabinet where he kept his automatic rifle, Melnyk took a bottle of vodka and poured himself a glass. The alcohol burned his throat, then a gentle warmth spread through his chest, slowly untying the knots in his stomach.

Everything had gone wrong from the start of this investigation. The autopsy had been cancelled because, according to the coroner's office, Leonid's body was too radioactive. They had had to make do with a quick external examination, which had provided them with practically no clues whatsoever. Since that first setback, things had just got worse for the captain and his team. There had been no witnesses to the murder. The samples from the crime scene had turned up nothing other than a few size 14 shoe prints and some splatters of blood belonging to the victim.

Not only that, but the murdered man had left the fewest possible traces of his time in the region. They had found out that he had flown from Moscow to Kyiv one week before his death. Three days later he had passed through the Dytiatky checkpoint with a group of tourists. He had paid in cash for a guided visit with two days in the zone and one night in Chernobyl. After that, he had booked four nights at the only hotel in Slavutych, which he had left on a fine morning wearing a backpack and hiking boots. Then he had vanished, until being discovered hanging from a tower block in Pripyat.

Melnyk was sure that Sokolov's killing was connected to his mother's death thirty years earlier, but he had not yet been able to find any evidence to back up his belief. He poured himself another glass of vodka and went through the records of the 1986 double homicide again.

While the sealed evidence had long since disappeared – either lost through negligence or simply abandoned in the radioactive Pripyat police station – some of the pleadings were still available, kept inside a slender cardboard folder. That in itself was almost a miracle: for budgetary reasons, the digitalisation of Soviet-era documents had been endlessly postponed, leaving most of the pre-1991 dossiers mouldering in storage rooms, nibbled by rats and ruined by damp.

He carefully took the yellowed pages from the folder and spread them out on his desk. He put on his glasses and read through the militia's typed notes on the 1986 discovery of the bodies of Olga Sokolov and Larissa Leonski, the second victim.

Larissa's corpse had been found upstairs in her dacha, in the conjugal bed. She was wearing only underwear – western styles not readily available in the U.S.S.R. The only way to get hold of such items was through the black market or by way of diplomats posted in capitalist countries. Piotr Leonski, her husband, was on duty at the nuclear reactor the night of the murder. He claimed to know nothing about the underwear. Was he lying, out of fear of being accused of smuggling? He also denied that his wife might have had a lover who joined her that night in their dacha. On this point, the coroner's examination appeared to contradict him: the evidence suggested that Larissa had engaged in sexual intercourse shortly before her death.

As for Olga, she was fully dressed. Her body was found on the ground floor, close to the open front door. She had a torch in her pocket.

Melnyk imagined Olga in her own dacha nearby, a few hours before her murder. She was sleeping. The heat in her bedroom was stifling, so the windows were open. She was deeply asleep: she was a teacher and at her school everyone had been busy preparing for the May 1 holiday. She was exhausted. In the middle of the night something woke her. Maybe the reactor explosion, at 1:23 a.m. Or maybe a woman screaming? She sat up, turned on her bedside light, then looked at her alarm clock. She glanced outside. The Leonskis' dacha, the only one inhabited that night, was about forty-five metres away. Olga decided to go there to check that Larissa was O.K. She took her torch and walked quickly over the dry grass. She was a brave woman: the investigation dossier stated that she had been a nurse on the front in Afghanistan before moving with her husband to Pripyat.

The night was pitch black. Tree branches shook in the wind. Their creaking and moaning accompanied Olga on her walk. Outside the Leonskis' front door, did she hesitate? Was her hand trembling when she opened it?

She went in. The living room was empty. Its usual disorder seemed strangely disturbing now. The clothes thrown on the sofa. The bottle that left wine circles on the coffee table. The candles, their wax oozing onto the pale wood of a shelf. Did she guess that Larissa was at home with a man who was not her husband?

She smelled a familiar fragrance in the air. Upstairs, in the bathroom, the militia's investigators would find a bottle of Red Moscow smashed on the floor. The spilled perfume overpowered Olga's olfactory nerves as she climbed the stairs. Suddenly, in the hallway, she stopped. Something wasn't right here. Another smell was mingled with the Red Moscow. The stench of death.

What did she do then? We can presume that Olga kept going. The militia found her fingerprints on the bedroom door. Melnyk imagined the shock she must have felt when she saw her friend's body lying in a pool of her own blood. The preliminary report made several mentions of the quantity of blood spread around the room: on the walls, on the furniture, and particularly on the bed. The investigators recorded twenty-four stab wounds on Larissa's body. The mattress beneath her was soaked through with blood. It was also lacerated in places. Melnyk imagined the killer sitting astride the victim, stabbing her torso, her neck, her face, with such fury that sometimes his blows missed the mark and the blade sank instead through the sheets, burying itself in the mattress. Larissa also had defensive wounds on her forearms: four clear, deep wounds. The murder weapon was found in the undergrowth outside: it was a kitchen knife belonging to the Leonskis.

Olga was stabbed only once, a fatal blow to the heart. Why only once, when Larissa had been killed with such savagery? The investigators had a theory for that: the first murder was a crime of passion, the second motivated purely by the desire to cover up the first. The murderer had killed Larissa in a moment of madness; Olga had seen him; she had tried to run away, but he had caught her before she could escape the dacha . . . and he had executed her.

Melnyk read and reread the documents, but nothing in the dossier made any reference to a swallow. And to make things worse, the crime scene photographs had disappeared. There was, however, one detail that seemed to connect Olga's murder with her son's: Leonid's eyelids were sewn shut. Both Olga's and Larissa's eyes had been gouged out.

Did the killer feel too ashamed to meet his victims' gaze? The investigator who had written the preliminary report saw in those mutilations the influence of an old Russian legend – that the murderer's image was imprinted on the eyes of his victims. Melnyk did not dismiss this explanation: in the superstitious lands of Polesia, such a legend was likely to be widely known.

As he stared at the illegible signature at the foot of the document, Melnyk had an idea. The investigators who had worked on the 1986 double homicide had long retired, but it was possible that one of them might still live in the region. Maybe he would know why the killer was obsessed by stuffed animals?

Well, it was worth a try. Melnyk found the name of the man in charge of the investigation – a Arseni Agopian. An internet search revealed that the man now ran a fishing shop in Strakholissya, a village on the edge of the exclusion zone.

He dialled the shop's number.

"Arseni's Lure. What can I do for you?"

The voice sounded too young to belong to a retired policeman.

"This is Captain Melnyk at the police station in Chernobyl. Are you Arseni Agopian?"

The young man confirmed his intuition: "No, I'm Ruslan. Arseni is my father. Are you a former colleague of his?"

"No. I'd like to speak to him about a case he investigated when he was in the militia. Could you pass him to me?"

"Sorry, he doesn't work here in the afternoons."

"Is he at home?"

"Yes and no. He's on his boat. It's his home from home!"

"Is it possible to contact him?"

"He doesn't have a mobile phone. It's not really his thing, electronics and all that."

"And when will he be back?"

"Oh, an hour or two at most. Can I give him a message?"

It was Friday and Melnyk had to return to Kyiv that evening. Strakholissya wasn't too far out of his way. He looked at his watch. Almost five o'clock.

"I'm going to drive to your shop. If you happen to see your father before I get there, please ask him to wait for me."

8

The Nuclear Riviera – that was the village's nickname.

When the authorities had marked out the perimeter of the evacuation zone after the explosion, Strakholissya had narrowly escaped destruction. The barbed-wire fences laid out by the military cut through countryside 150 metres from its outskirts, to the great relief of the village's inhabitants. Strakholissya accordingly became a "clean" place, even though nobody was permitted to pick mushrooms, apples or raspberries in the fields and woods beyond the fence because of the risks of radiation.

Melnyk got a strange feeling as he drove through the village. It was quite close to some of the ghost villages inside the zone, but Strakholissya had nothing in common with them. Its long streets were well-kept, its dachas' gardens were planted with sweet-smelling flower-beds, the kitchen gardens bursting with vegetables. And most of the people he passed looked happy. He saw busy construction sites almost everywhere, with men labouring to build ultra-modern dachas. With the human genius for transforming shit into gold, property developers had bought ridiculously cheap plots of land overlooking what was known as the "Kyiv Sea" – an artificial lake one hundred and ten kilo-metres long formed by the Vyshhorod hydroelectric dam – so that they could build luxurious second homes for the wealthy inhabitants of the Ukrainian capital. Since the lake stretched all the way to Pripyat, it might have seemed impossible that anyone would want to live next to it. But in fact, dozens and dozens of them had paid through the nose to move to the Nuclear Riviera.

Melnyk parked his Lada Riva outside Arseni Agopian's fishing shop. It was next to a pontoon where a number of canoes and motorboats were moored. There were some large yachts further off, along the lake's grassy banks. Inside the shop, he found a wide selection of fishing rods, baits, hooks, lures, spinners and corks. By the entrance was a board with notices of prices for boat rentals and guided fishing trips. The prices were offered in hryvnias, rubles and dollars. For several years now, enthusiasts from all over the world had been coming to the Kyiv Sea to try to catch enormous fish that were not to be found anywhere else. Since the local fauna had been spared the damage of overfishing for the past 30 years by the perils of radiation, the fish in the Kyiv Sea had been able to reproduce freely and had been given the time to grow to unusual sizes. Photographs pinned to the wall above the noticeboard showed happy tourists brandishing catfish so long and heavy that they had to be held in both arms, as big as bags of flour. Each picture showed an old man smiling proudly, as if he were the one who had caught the fish. Melnyk was sure that this was Arseni Agopian.

The son was behind the counter, fixing a reel onto a fishing rod. He was a handsome young man, at least one hundred kilos, with bluish interlaced tattoos all over his forearms. His olive-green T-shirt proclaimed that the Loch Ness Monster lived in the Kyiv Sea.

Melnyk got out his card. "Captain Melnyk. I called you an hour ago."

"Yeah, the policeman from Chernobyl," Arseni's son said.

"Is your father back?"

"Yeah, he's working in his shed. It's the first building to the left."

Melnyk soon found himself outside a building he would probably have called a hangar rather than a shed. Inside, it smelled of damp rope and sawdust. A sailing boat in dry dock occupied part of the space.

"You the policeman from the zone?"

Melnyk jumped. He had not seen the old man standing near a carpenter's bench. With his skin tanned and wrinkled by the sun, his dark brown clothes and his leather hat, the man was almost perfectly camouflaged in the shed's dark corner. "Commander Agopian?"

"Just call me Arseni," the man said, putting the tool he was holding onto the workbench.

He walked steadily across towards the captain.

"You don't have a partner? In my day, militia members went everywhere in pairs."

"One who could read and another who could write," Melnyk said, remembering the joke that did the rounds back in the Soviet era.

Agopian laughed politely and shook his hand.

"My son told me your name, but I forgot it."

"Joseph Melnyk."

"Melnyk," Arseni repeated. "I've heard about you. Some colleagues of yours go fishing around here sometimes. And you know what happens when two cops go fishing together: they tell each other cop stories. But tell me what brings you here, captain."

"An old case. A double homicide that you investigated in 1986."

"Olga and Larissa," Arseni muttered. "Why are you interested in that case?"

"I think it's connected to a murder I'm working on now."

"The guy they found in Pripyat?"

"Exactly. He was Olga Sokolov's son."

Arseni's face tensed.

"Are you thinking that his death is linked to his mother's?"

"That's what I think, and that's why I came to see you."

Agopian stared out at the surface of the lake as it glimmered in the setting sun.

"Can we talk about this on the boat? I was about to go out. This may be one of the last warm days of the year."

"I'm expected in Kyiv for dinner."

"Let's make it quick then."

There were lots of people enjoying the mild weather on the river-bank. Melnyk realised that Agopian wanted to have this conversation away from prying ears.

"We can go out for a short trip. But I have to be back on land in less than an hour."

"Not a problem."

Agopian led him to the pontoon and untied his boat, a large motor-boat with huge Japanese engines that must have cost a fortune.

"Nice boat. I don't know many former militia members who could afford something like this."

Agopian smiled.

"I did some good business in the late Nineties, when they started selling off public land. I bought the land where they built those dachas over there."

He pointed to a line of buildings with gardens backing onto the artificial lake.

"It was going for peanuts at the time. I kept one plot of land to build myself a house, and sold the rest for a small fortune."

Arseni turned the steering wheel and the boat curved around a group of teenagers in wetsuits trying to master stand-up paddleboarding on surfboards.

"And the fishing shop?"

"That's just a retired man's hobby. It hardly makes a profit, but my son gets a job out of it and it gives me something to do. Do you have children?"

"Two sons and a daughter," Melnyk said.

"Do they live around here?"

"The two older ones are in Kyiv and my youngest just went to the eastern front."

"Regular army?"

"No, volunteer brigade."

Agopian nodded gravely. "I've heard that the boys at the front don't have all the equipment they need."

"It's true. We try to help him out, but he still can't afford a bullet-proof vest."

"A dirty war," Agopian said. He pushed down on the accelerator and the boat sped away from the beaches and their palatial dachas.

"If you made so much cash, how come you haven't gone somewhere else?"

"Somewhere else? Like where?"

"The coast. Crimea, for example."

"Ah! My wife would love that. She's got a sister over there. But I spent my whole life in this place. It's my home. What would I do on the Black Sea? I'm a freshwater fisherman," he said with a grin.

"Most of the people in this region only stay here because they're too poor to move away."

"Not the ones who live in Strakholissya."

The boat engines were so loud that conversation became impossible. Rather than yelling to make himself heard, Melnyk decided to wait until they had reached their destination, an island in the middle of the lake. Agopian handed him a fishing rod.

"Do you fish?"

Melnyk took the rod and cast out with a supple flick of his wrist.

"Sometimes. Not usually this close to the zone though. I prefer my fish without radiation."

Everyone knew there was radioactive sediment at the bottom of the Kyiv Sea and that the fish there were contaminated beyond safe levels.

Agopian smiled ironically. "In that case, I hope you don't buy fish at the markets in Kyiv. The fishermen here don't stick a label on their catch when they sell it to the fishmongers in the capital. You know that?"

He took a rod too and, casting out, began talking about the investigation thirty years before.

"It started when Olga's husband, Vektor Sokolov, summoned me to the Gorkom. He was overwhelmed by the evacuation. The phone lines weren't working and he was worried because he hadn't heard from his wife. She was spending the weekend at their dacha, a few kilometres from Pripyat."

"In Zalissya."

"He was supposed to join her there, but when the reactor exploded he was stuck in the city, dealing with the crisis. He asked us to go to the dacha and evacuate her. Of course we had other fish to fry, but he was a senior Party member. So we did what he asked."

Agopian's line twitched. He reeled it in and landed a small fish, shiny as a silver spoon.

"One-nil, captain."

"It's quality that counts, not quantity," Melnyk said, unperturbed. "So what happened when you got to Sokolov's dacha?"

Agopian unhooked his bloodied catch and threw it into a tray filled with water.

"We found the front door to the dacha open and nobody inside. The car was parked outside. We went to the neighbours' houses to make sure that Olga was not there. The door to the Leonskis' dacha was open too and there was a bloody footprint on the doorstep. Big feet – size 14 at least. We went inside and found Olga's body on the ground floor, and Larissa's upstairs in the bedroom. But I assume you know all of this already."

"Why do you think the killer didn't try to hide the bodies?"

"You think like a modern detective. Back then it was the U.S.S.R. People didn't watch true-crime shows or police dramas as they do now. Besides, we had only the footprints to go on. There was no D.N.A. testing in those days. Most of the murders I investigated either had their victims' bodies dumped in woodland or they were left where they died. Olga and Larissa's killer could have been interrupted, of course."

"By who? According to your report, the other dachas were unoccupied and some distance away in the forest."

"You misunderstand me. I'm not saying the killer was interrupted by someone. I mean by something."

"The reactor explosion?"

"Precisely."

That makes sense, thought Melnyk. After the accident, the fire from Reactor 4 could be seen for huge distances away. If the murderer had seen the sky turn bright red, he might have decided to get as far from the reactor as he could rather than waste time disposing of his victims' bodies.

He felt a tug on his line. He reeled in only to find strings of algae caught on his hook. He threw them back into the water just as Agopian caught another fish. The old man told him a few fishing stories before Melnyk could bring him back to the investigation.

"Your report suggested that Larissa had company that night," he said.

"That's correct. A bottle of nice wine, fancy lingerie. . . Larissa had apparently planned to spend the night with a man who was not her husband."

"Did you ever find out who it was?"

"No, we never did, and to be honest, we didn't look into it so closely. We were focused on Piotr Leonski."

"The husband? I thought he was working at the reactor that night?"

"He deserted his post immediately after the explosion. He was stopped at a roadblock and brought to the police station in Pripyat. Once we had discovered that his wife had been killed, we interrogated him. He said he had nothing to do with it, of course, that he was making for Kyiv to be safe from the radiation. But certain evidence suggested he might have killed Larissa."

"The size 14 shoe on the doorstep?"

"It matched a pair of his boots that we found in the dacha. He claimed the killer must have put them on to frame him."

"I saw that in the dossier, but there were no crime scene photographs."

"Can't say I'm surprised. A lot of things went missing during the evacuation."

The old policeman's seeming indifference was starting to irritate Melnyk. He decided to bring up another detail that had been bothering him.

"I read in the coroner's report that Larissa had had sexual intercourse just before she was killed, but they found no trace of semen. Didn't you find that strange?"

"Why? Should I have done?"

"In the 1980s it was almost impossible for a woman to buy condoms. Abortion was the main method of birth control."

"Perhaps her lover had some. Or her killer used an object to simulate penetration."

"That's not the only thing that worries me. The investigation began on April 26 and the final entry in the dossier is dated the 30th. Between that and the missing evidence, the whole thing feels a bit rushed."

Agopian glared at him.

"Have you come here to accuse me of not having done my job properly, captain?"

Melnyk could hear the anger in his voice, so he decided to calm things down: "I'm not looking to blame you. It was a difficult period."

"You're telling me! It was worse than the war. We had to manage the evacuation of thousands of people, prevent looting, set up roadblocks, patrol the abandoned villages. . . It was madness. We hardly slept. But I did my job, captain. If I didn't catch the killer, it's because I wasn't given enough time."

"You weren't allowed to finish your investigation?"

"No, I was taken off the case."

"Who took over it?"

"The K.G.B."

"The K.G.B.? Why would the secret services take over a militia case?"

"I wasn't given an explanation and I didn't ask any questions. But if you want my opinion, the K.G.B. wanted to check there wasn't something else hidden beneath that double homicide."

"Such as what?"

"The sabotage of Reactor 4."

Melnyk stared at him, shocked, then turned towards the Chernobyl arch, just visible in the distance above the treetops.

"Olga was married to the Gorkom chief in Pripyat," Agopian said. "Larissa's husband was an engineer at the power station. It looked a little suspicious."

"But how could two women on their own have sabotaged a nuclear reactor?"

"By giving information to foreign powers."

"Are you talking about the Americans? That's ridiculous!"

"Oh yeah, because the Americans have never plotted to destabilise another country, have they?" Agopian said mockingly. "Ever heard of Pamir?"

"It's the name of a mountain range in central Asia."

"It was also the codename for a highly confidential operation that would have given the U.S.S.R. the advantage over the United States in the arms race if it had been seen through to completion. In the Seventies, Soviet researchers started work on a mobile nuclear power station."

A mobile nuclear power station? Melnyk could not believe his ears. How could anyone have seriously considered such a thing?

"The Americans could use their satellites to target our nuclear silos very precisely. The idea behind Pamir was to provide enough energy to power the launch platforms for mobile atomic missiles, fitted to the backs of trucks. That way, the American attacks would be unable to neutralise Soviet weapons. Chernobyl blew up thirty days after the first mobile nuclear reactor was completed. So, as I said, it was suspicious. Larissa had access to the power station and Olga had access to sensitive information through her husband. And they both died on the night of the explosion. Quite a coincidence, don't you think?"

"But if they were giving secret defence data to the Americans, why would they kill them?"

"Don't be naïve. You think they were planning to take the women to Washington? Much easier simply to get rid of any witnesses."

Melnyk was bewildered. On the one hand, he thought that if the K.G.B. had found any proof of sabotage they would immediately have accused the Americans. On the other hand, it was possible that the Soviet authorities had decided to bury the case. To denounce the US would have meant admitting the weak safety protocols of Russian power stations and the incompetence of the K.G.B. And that's without even talking about the military consequences: sabotage would have constituted an act of war and the U.S.S.R. would have had to reply in kind – by launching nuclear warheads.

"Do you remember the name of the K.G.B. officer who took over the investigation?"

"From thirty years ago? How do you expect me to remember that?"

"It's not every day you investigate a double homicide."

"As I said, it was total madness after the explosion. When they took me off the case, I simply moved onto the next thing."

"You never tried to find out what really happened? You weren't tempted to keep investigating?"

"Why would I have done that?"

"Some detectives are obsessed by their unsolved cases."

"Oh really? Well, I'm not one of them. I quit the job more than ten years ago and it was the best thing I ever did. I don't have to lug a briefcase around. I don't dream about terrible killings. I don't wake up in a cold sweat in the middle of the night. I sleep like a baby now. And I don't rake over the past. I hadn't thought about that double homicide for years. And if you hadn't come here, I might never have thought about it again until the day I died."

He caught another fish. This time, he took a knife and quickly, neatly sliced open its body before emptying its guts into the lake. The birds circling above them dived down and fought, squawking, over the viscera. Arseni Agopian repeated the operation with the other two fish he had caught.

"Looks like it's not your day, captain," he said, glancing at the empty bucket next to him.

Melnyk still had caught nothing, apart from the algae.

"I concede defeat," he said, reeling in his line.

He leaned the fishing rod against the cockpit.

Agopian said, "We could try another spot."

"No thanks. It's time I was going home. So what do you think happened to the K.G.B. dossier?"

"I have no idea. It's probably in the archives, somewhere in Moscow."

He started the engines and the set off back towards land. When they reached the pontoon, Melnyk asked him: "So who do you think killed Larissa Leonski – her lover or her husband?"

Arseni looked him straight in the eye.

"Half of the murders I investigated during my career involved alcohol and chronic domestic violence. The other half were crimes motivated by very simple urges, mostly greed. Larissa was a very beautiful woman and rumour had it that she had several lovers. My opinion is that her husband found out she had cheated on him. He waited for her lover to leave then went into the dacha and killed her. He thought there was no-one else around, but Olga Sokolov heard her screams. And he had to kill her, too, to shut her up."

Simple sexual jealousy. . . It made sense. Among other things, it explained the number of stab wounds in Larissa's body. You would have to be full of anger or hate or both to do that.

"One last question: was there a bird at the crime scene?"

"A bird? There were no birds here after the reactor exploded."

"I was thinking more of a stuffed bird. A swallow, to be precise."

Agopian stared thoughtfully at a group of cormorants drying their wings in the sun.

"It's strange how certain details can come back to you. I couldn't tell you the colour of Larissa's hair or whether the bottle in the living room was red wine or Soviet champagne. And yet you're right – I do remember that damn stuffed bird."

He picked up the bucket and emptied the gutted fish into an icebox.

"As I said, there weren't any birds left round here after the explosion. They fell from the sky or they flew into walls, as if they were trying to commit suicide. It was because of all the radioactive crap in the air. When we went to the Leonskis' dacha, a whole flock of them fell onto the roof of our car. I still remember the noise: *tam-tam-tam-tam*. As if someone was machine-gunning rubber bullets at us. There was even one bird that smashed into the windscreen. It made a big bloodstain that spread over the glass when I used the wipers."

His voice was shaky. He was more affected than he wanted to admit.

"In Larissa's bedroom, there was a chest of drawers with a stuffed bird on top of it. It's one of the few things I remember clearly from that night. I went into the room, I saw the corpse, all that blood, and then I noticed the bird. It seemed to be observing me. It looked so. . . so alive. I felt as if I ought to walk on tiptoes so it wouldn't fly away."

"Was it a swallow?"

Arseni nodded.

"That's right. A blue swallow. With blood all over its feathers."

9

Melnyk left and drove to Kyiv, his mind turning over his new discoveries. When he reached his apartment, he heard voices raised in the living room. By the time he took off his parka and hung it on the coat rack, his wife had appeared in the entrance hall.

"Your future daughter-in-law is here. We've been waiting for an hour!"

He had almost forgotten. Nikolai was coming for dinner with them that evening. It was the first time he had brought his new girlfriend. What was her name again?

"Nadia?" he guessed.

"No. Oksana."

"The last one was called Nadia."

"Maybe. But he's going to marry this one."

Melnyk had been surprised when his son had announced he was getting married. His wife, on the other hand, had reacted with joy. At last some good news! Since Nikolai had dropped out of university to fight on the eastern front, she had not had much to celebrate.

"But where were you?" she hissed. "You were supposed to be here at seven!"

She seemed torn between two contradictory desires: to yell at him and to be as quiet as possible so that her future daughter-in-law would not hear.

"I had to stop in Strakholissya for a case I'm working on."

He leaned down to kiss her. She recoiled slightly.

"First take a shower, Joseph."

He sighed. This was the ritual whenever he came home. Tatiana had an excessive fear of radiation. She refused to touch him until he had spent at least ten minutes in the shower.

She looked down at his combat boots.

"You didn't leave your boots outside?"

Oh yes, he was always supposed to leave his shoes on the landing. She was afraid he might bring radioactive particles into the apartment on his soles.

"I'll take them out now."

"You can throw the doormat out too. I'll put it in the bin. It's worn out anyway. And don't hang your jacket with the others."

They had had plenty of fights already over her quarantine rules, and he was in no mood to have another one. He lived alone in Chernobyl for most of the year, in a State-owned apartment, so he had no desire now to be quarrelling in the moments they had together.

She opened the cupboard in the entrance hall, took out a heavy-duty bin liner, and handed it to him.

"Join us in the living room when you're ready," she said. "I put your clean clothes in the bathroom."

"Darling, she might see me! Just for once, couldn't we—"

"Absolutely not. All it takes is one time and we'd be contaminated."

End of discussion. She turned on her heel and went back into the living room. He stood on the doormat for a moment, uncertain. Then, quickly, shamefacedly, he undressed in the entrance hall, put all his clothes in the bin liner, and walked on tiptoe to the bathroom.

Tatiana had always been terrified of anything related to radiation. When he had started working in the zone, they came close to divorce over the issue. She had not wanted to touch him anymore. Had not even wanted him to come home. The development of the homecoming ritual had been the only way of rescuing their marriage. He had hoped it would be temporary. But seven years later, the ritual was still going strong. That evening, like all the other evenings, he had ended up obeying, but he hated the idea that someone – in this case his potential future daughter-in-law – might find out that he was forced by his wife to strip naked before he could come into his own apartment.

After his shower he joined his wife in the living room. She was showing family photographs to Oksana, who smiled as she looked at them, obviously enjoying the sight of her boyfriend in a romper suit in those old photographs. Melnyk liked her straightaway. She was much more discreet than the flashy girls Nikolai generally went out with. No piercings, no tattoos, no hair dye. She was medium height with a generous figure, and she wore tortoiseshell glasses that gave her a serious look.

"Pleased to meet you, Mr Melnyk."

"Call me Joseph," he said, shaking her hand. "Isn't Nikolai here?"

"His train was delayed. He should be here soon."

"The Melnyks are not known for their punctuality," Tatiana said, winking at her future daughter-in-law.

It was clear that the two women got along. Melnyk sat on the sofa and nibbled his wife's still-warm savoury appetisers.

"We were talking about Oksana's position at the university," she told him.

Oksana was an historian. She and Nikolai had met during the 2014 revolution. After the old president, Viktor Yanukovych, had fled, thousands of paper documents had been found in the government buildings, shredded into confetti. Dozens of Ukrainians had volunteered to reconstruct those "archives of corruption". As a historian, Oksana had been given the task of supervising the volunteers. Nikolai had been part of her group. According to him, he had fallen in love with her at first sight.

"Oksana is writing about fashion during the communist era," Tatiana said. "I showed her the dresses I used to wear when I was young. She took pictures of them for her thesis, would you believe?"

Oksana explained that her thesis began in 1959 with the Dior fashion show in Moscow, because before that the U.S.S.R. had banned such parades and persecuted anyone who wore "fashionable" clothing. Then Oksana and Tatiana started talking about 1970s fashions, and Melnyk withdrew a little, smiling now and then to give the impression that he was listening. Oksana must have sensed this, because she began asking him questions about his work. In particular, she wanted to know if her future father-in-law was a member of the militia or the police. It was true that the government had recently decided to replace the word "militia" with the word "police", a more modern word. And this was no mere cosmetic change: former militia men like Melnyk had had to go through a readmission procedure intended to check their proficiency and probity. He was about to explain this to Oksana when the doorbell rang.

His mother welcomed Nikolai so effusively, you would have thought she had not seen him for ten years. After hugging him tightly, she looked with distress at his uniform, which hung off him. He must have lost six kilos in weight, Melnyk guessed.

"How long are you staying?"

"Just for the weekend, mum. My unit goes back to the Donbas at the end of the week."

"Only two days?" she asked sadly, realising she would hardly have time to fatten him up.

She finally let him go and Melnyk found himself face to face with his son, separated by a distance of several metres and the wall of reserve that had always existed between them.

"Hi, dad."

"Hi, son."

No hug. No handshake. It was late, so they went straight to the dining-room table. Tatiana had spent a long time preparing dinner: beef Stroganov followed by *Kievskiy tort*, a Ukrainian cake that was a delicious slab of butter cream, meringue and cashew nuts. This epic confection had to be planned three days in advance. A true Soviet meal. The meringue alone took 36 hours to prepare. So Melnyk was not allowed to tell his wife that there was too much cognac in one of the layers of butter cream or not enough cocoa powder in the other.

During the meal they spent a long time talking about the wedding, as if there was no war happening: a way of exorcising their fears. Nikolai announced that it would be a small wedding, to his mother's dismay. They also agreed a date for the two families to meet. They had to move quickly: Nikolai insisted that the wedding day should be fixed as soon as possible. After that, they talked about the dress, the feast, the band.

At the end of the meal the women went to the kitchen and the men to the balcony for a cigarette. Melnyk chose that moment to ask the question that had been nagging at him for some time: "How come you decided so quickly to marry her?"

Nikolai shrugged.

"You and mum were married at my age."

"You know what I mean. You've known each other for only a few months. Your mother and I had been going out for two years."

"I can tell she's the one. I'm ready."

Melnyk let his gaze dwell on his son. How much he'd grown in a few weeks of war. No, he hadn't grown – he had matured. He was still quite boyish and awkward, but there was something in his eyes which made it obvious that he had left adolescence behind for good. He was an adult now.

Suddenly Nikolai asked: "Have you ever shot anyone, dad?"

Surprised, Melnyk turned the question on his son: "Have you fired at an enemy?"

Nikolai nervously chewed the inside of his cheek before answering: "Yes. But I don't know if I..."

He took a drag on his cigarette and left the sentence unfinished, floating in the air amid the wreaths of bluish smoke.

"You don't know if you killed him?" Melnyk said.

The young man rubbed his left temple, blocking his father's gaze for a moment.

"We were guarding the checkpoint as usual. It was late evening. And then, out of nowhere, we heard gunfire coming from a building at the other side of the street. Bursts of machine-gun fire. We hid behind some concrete blocks, waiting for it to stop, then returned fire. We shot at the windows until there was total silence. It was an old government building that had been shut for a long time. Nobody was supposed to be living there anymore."

He stared at the tower block opposite as if the gunfire had come from there.

"We waited fifteen minutes then we decided to send in a patrol. I volunteered. We moved slowly because we were afraid that it might be a trap. That there might be a sniper somewhere. It happens. The separatists pretend to retreat, then they fire at us as soon as we show our faces. But that didn't happen this time."

Melnyk exhaled a large cloud of smoke. The smell of tobacco seemed as bitter as gunpowder to him.

"Inside the building, everyone was dead. Two men and a woman. They'd been hiding in a room full of frescoes. You know, those old communist murals with loads of people parading past. There was blood everywhere. On the flags, the uniforms, the aprons. As if the people in the paintings had come out of the walls to massacre them. But they were still smiling. It gave me the creeps."

Melnyk thought about all the Soviet murals he had seen over the course of his life. So many cosmonauts, children, old people, marching towards progress with their suspiciously happy faces. The contrast with the spectacle of bullet-shredded bodies must have been startling.

"The people on the floor were my age. They were Ukrainian, like us. And one of them had a train ticket for Kyiv."

Nikolai paused and used his foot to brush away a cigarette stub that had somehow escaped his mother's vigilance.

"I thought about how he too must have a family in Kyiv. Maybe I had passed him in the street. Maybe we had even gone to the same school, or lived in the same neighbourhood, without ever meeting. Maybe we had drunk a beer in the same bar. Loved the same girl."

He smiled bitterly.

"The worst thing is that I don't even know if I killed him. I fired in his direction. We all fired in his direction. I don't know if I should feel guilty. Would he have felt guilty, if he'd killed me?"

He reached into his pocket and took out a plastic bag containing a few objects: a watch, a wallet, a locket, a wedding ring. . .

"He had a few personal belongings on him. I took it all. I don't know why. The others shared out the money, the guns, the more valuable equipment. I just asked for this stuff. I think. . . I'd like to give it back to his family. I'm not going to talk to them, just put it in their letter box with a note explaining how their son died. I don't know why I want to do that. I suppose I'd want someone to do it for me, . . ."

Nikolai fell silent. Both men knew that there would be no-one from the ministry who would call the family if he were killed. They would have to rely on his comrades to do the dirty work. Nikolai was not in the regular army, so officially his battalion did not exist. They were not trained soldiers, just some young people who'd taken up arms to defend their country.

"You could just quit. Why don't you stop fighting?" Melnyk said.

His son gave him a penetrating look, a smile playing at the edges of his lips, as if he'd been expecting this question since the start of their conversation, since his arrival in the apartment, since the day he had decided to join the war in the Donbas.

"Why don't you quit the police?"

"You know very well that your mother and I need my salary to get by."

"You could find another job."

75

"We're in the middle of an economic crisis. Who would hire an ex-policeman of my age?"

"Is that the only reason? Don't you believe in what you're doing?"

"Yes, but. . ."

He did not know what to say, which pawn to advance. If he acknowledged that he loved his job, that he considered it important, that would be tantamount to admitting that his son's choice to defend his country was similarly important. Claiming otherwise would be lying, and Nikolai knew it.

"When I was a kid," Nikolai went on, "when the others made fun of me, I would tell them you were a militiaman, and that used to scare them. I thought it was because you went after bad guys and you had a gun. When I was older, I realised everyone was afraid of the police because they could arrest you or fine you, even beat you, even though you'd done nothing wrong. After that, I didn't tell my friends what you did."

"I was never one of that kind."

"I know. You think you have to be part of the system to change it. That you have to do something instead of just protesting. Well, I want to do something too. I gave it a lot of thought. I can't just sit around complaining that things are bad in Ukraine. I want to change this country. I was at Maidan. I took part in the revolution and the elections. Now my country is under attack, now they want to divide us, I have to do something. I can't just hope that others will do it for me. Other sons and other daughters. I have to take my share of the risk."

Nikolai did indeed appear to have thought it through.

"So if I asked you to go back to your normal life, you'd refuse?" Melnyk said.

"Yes."

"Did Oksana ask you that?"

"She believes in what I'm doing. But yes, of course, she tried to convince me to stay."

"And your mother?"

Nikolai looked more embarrassed.

"Don't bring mum into this."

"If you die at the front, it will kill her. Literally. You've always been her little Niko. You're her youngest. Her last son. And your brother and sister don't have kids of their own yet. . ."

"Oksana and I are planning to have a baby."

Nikolai dropped this sentence like a plane drops a bomb.

"When?"

"Soon. We've already started trying."

He should have been happy, but Melnyk stared sadly at his son. A quick wedding, a child. . . he had the impression that Nikolai was rushing everything because he was afraid of dying before he had a chance to live a normal life.

The women returned to the living room. Melnyk and his son left the balcony. It was time for their goodbyes. Tatiana warmly embraced Oksana and Nikolai. Melnyk hugged his future daughter-in-law, then gave the usual distant, macho nod to his son, the two of them incapable of holding each other even though they both feared this separation might be their last.

The young couple left and the apartment grew gloomy and silent once again. Melnyk sat in his old chair while his wife washed the dishes. He thought about their discussion. And then he thought about Vadim Moutko.

Moutko had been a third-rate petty criminal whom Melnyk had arrested for theft on several occasions. One day, during his arrest, Moutko had grabbed a knife and tried to stab him. The policeman still had a scar on his side where the blade had slid along his ribs. He had managed to get hold of his gun and to shoot his attacker. A single bullet. He had aimed for Moutko's arm but penetrated his lung instead. Moutko had died a few hours later in hospital. Nevertheless, though he had been a piece of shit who beat his wife, had raped several teenage girls, and abandoned his children to the welfare state, Melnyk still sometimes dreamed of him and could not help feeling guilty about killing him. And that's what he should have told Nikolai: that the ghosts of those young people in the room with the murals would always haunt him, whether or not he returned the dead man's belongings to his heartbroken parents.

"They're going to have a baby," Tatiana announced from the kitchen.

"Oh, really?" he said, feigning ignorance.

"Oksana says she stopped taking the pill a few weeks ago. She's sure it'll happen soon."

"What about her thesis? It could be complicated with a child and Nikolai at the front."

"We'll help her!"

"You're over the moon, aren't you?"

"Of course! He'll be my first grandson."

"Oh, you already know it'll be a boy?"

"I saw him in a dream."

"Ah well, in that case. . . I had no idea you had scientific proof."

"Don't make fun of me, Joseph. I had a vision in my dreams that we would have two sons and a daughter. And that's what happened."

"Well, let me know when you see the lottery numbers."

"Idiot!" she shouted.

Later, when he went to bed, he thought about his talk with Arseni Agopian. If the K.G.B. really had taken over the case, as the ex-militiaman claimed, there had to be a dossier somewhere. The Ukrainian section of the K.G.B. had been dissolved not long after the fall of the U.S.S.R. and the country's independence. He had no idea what could have happened to the documents compiled by the old Soviet secret services.

Then suddenly it hit him. Oksana! She was a historian. He should ask her. He turned to look at the alarm clock: 11:30pm. Too late to call now. She and Nikolai were no doubt catching up on lost time. His gaze lingered on the chest of drawers opposite the bed. There was a jewellery tree on top of it. Necklaces and rings hung from its branches. Tatiana was brushing her teeth in the bathroom. When she came out, he asked her: "What did you do with your grandmother's ring?"

She lay next to him, but not too close.

"It's at the jeweller's. The diamond was coming loose."

It was a slender gold ring with a tiny stone, not much more than a speck.

"You're the worst liar I know," Melnyk said.

She leaned on her elbow and sat up to face him. He stared her out.

"I sold it," she said eventually.

"Sold it? Why?"

"Because our son is fighting a war in his T-shirt, Joseph. I couldn't go on living if I found out he'd been killed by a bullet to his chest."

She turned onto her side. He looked at her back. He knew every contour, every freckle.

"Was it enough?"

She sighed. "Do you know how much a bulletproof vest costs?"

He had no idea. But she was not expecting an answer.

"A lot more than the price of an old ring," she grumbled.

"We could borrow some money."

"From whom? We're already overdrawn at the bank."

"Your mother, the children. . ."

"They're finding it as hard as we are to make ends meet."

She gave another heavy sigh. "If you hadn't been transferred to Chernobyl you might be the head of a department by now, instead of stagnating there."

"Darling, we've been through this before. . . Do you think I like having to strip off before I am allowed into my own home? Seeing the fear in your eyes every Friday when I get back from work? You think I like you refusing to touch me unless I've scrubbed my skin until it bleeds?"

He felt tired. How many times had they had this argument?

"It's entirely your fault. If you could have put your principles aside for once, we wouldn't be here!"

Seven years earlier, he had testified against his boss in a corruption case. The chief had had a racket going with some of the capital's gambling dens: they paid him money for his "protection". Since Melnyk had been the only person who had dared to testify, the investigation had fallen through and he was the one who had been punished: exiled to Chernobyl.

"If you'd kept your job in Kyiv, we'd be together all week long and your son wouldn't have joined the army to defend all those values that you profess!"

"It's my fault he enrolled?"

She turned to face him, her eyes red with tears.

"If you'd been there during the Maidan protests. . . if you'd asked him not to enrol in his stupid unit. . . if you hadn't been so far away when we needed you here. . ." She stopped her litany of reproaches. "I know. It is unfair. But it's hard enough already knowing that you work in the zone. And now Nikolai is at the front. I'm terrified of losing you both."

Melnyk moved closer and held her tight. He understood her feelings. There was nothing she could do to protect herself against the death of her loved ones. She couldn't put Nikolai's boots outside the door, put his clothes in a bin liner, and make him take a shower to exorcise her fear of one day receiving a phone call announcing that her son was dead.

"Nothing will happen to him," he said soothingly.

"How do you know?"

"The same way you know he's going to have a son."

She did not reply. He held her for a long time, until her breathing grew slower and more regular. She was sleeping at last. He took much longer to fall asleep, his eyes riveted to the changing red numbers of his digital alarm clock. He thought of what his wife had said about his principles, and the money he had found in Leonid Sokolov's wallet. Enough to buy his son a bulletproof vest, if only he had been able to transgress his moral code for once.

Long after midnight he slipped into a restless sleep. At the same moment, somewhere in Russia, a Russian police officer he did not know was packing his rucksack to go and die in Ukraine.

CIVIL WAR

10

Saturday morning. A flight from Moscow to Rostov.

Rybalko stared at the infinite steppes below, punctuated here and there by reed-lined marshes. The new grass, tall and dense, that grew on the sunny slopes of ravines. . . the dull smell of black earth. . . the wind scattering the fragrance of violets and tulips. . . Snatches of Sholokhov's *And Quiet Flows the Don* ran through his mind. As a teenager, he had devoured that novel by the Russian Nobel Prize winner. Strange to think that his youth belonged to another era, another century, another country, when it all seemed so close in his memories. The landscapes were still the same, the men almost identical, but the U.S.S.R. of his childhood had fragmented. It had become Russia, Ukraine, Belarus, and so many other countries.

The steppes gave way to the straight lines of fields, as boring and rational as a computer's circuit board. Soon, Rostov-on-Don appeared at the horizon.

A slight jolt on landing. Everyone filed out of the plane.

Inside the airport, he walked straight past the baggage claim carousels. He had not brought much with him. He was planning to buy clothes here and to get rid of them before he went back to Russia. . . if he ever did. He had no desire to bring back clothes that might be contaminated.

He did not have to wait long to meet his contact outside the main entrance. The man hired by Vektor Sokolov to drive him to Donetsk was there on time. A man in his fifties, his face and forearms tanned and tattooed, his name was Joseph, although everyone called him Ossip.

His car was an ancient Lada Niva, its pale beige paintwork flecked with rust. The seats and the boot were packed with cardboard boxes and the roof was loaded with petrol cans covered by a khaki tarpaulin. The vehicle was carrying far more than the recommended weight and its suspension whined disturbingly when Rybalko sat in the front seat.

During the trip to the border post, Ossip told his passenger that he crossed the border several times a week to sell products in Ukraine that could be bought cheaply in Russia, such as fuel – which explained the occasional whiff of petrol that escaped from the tarp covering the Lada's roof. There were forty-five gallons of unleaded up there, a fact that was not enough to dissuade the old smuggler from chain-smoking cigarettes. On the way back he mostly took Ukrainian vodka, he said, because it was less than half the price of the stuff you could buy in Russia. But, Ossip swore on all the orthodox saints, he never smuggled arms. He had no desire to have a relative's death on his conscience: here, everyone – him included – had family in Russia and in Ukraine.

They reached the border post around noon. It was an open-air hangar with several lines of vehicles passing through. The lines from Russia were fairly short, while those from Ukraine seemed to stretch all the way back to Kyiv. There were also some pedestrians crossing the border with shopping baskets or prams transformed into makeshift trolleys so they could visit shops in Russia and fill up on all the things that were unavailable in Ukraine. Ossip told him that at the height of the crisis, up to 4,000 Ukrainians crossed the border every day.

Rybalko noticed a flag he did not recognise hanging from a tall radio antenna. It featured three horizontal stripes – black, blue and red – with a crest at its centre showing a two-headed eagle and a shield embossed with the image of an archangel.

"It's the flag of the Republic of Donetsk," Ossip told him. "The rebels took over the border post, so they're the customs officers now. They want to join Russia again, just as Crimea did."

Rybalko remembered how heavily-armed, well-organised men in

combat fatigues had suddenly appeared in Crimea just after the Maidan Revolution, driving the weak Ukrainian forces out of their shabby barracks. Separatists, according to Moscow; Russian soldiers, according to Kyiv. Once they had taken over the region, the separatists organised a referendum proposing Crimea's reattachment to Russia. Unsurprisingly they won the election. Not long after that, the whole of eastern Ukraine was in uproar. In the Donbas, and especially in Donetsk and Luhansk, part of the population refused to recognise the new revolutionary government. The pro-Russian groups attacked official buildings and declared the region independent. And then it was war.

"Are you in favour of the Donbas becoming part of Russia again?" he asked his driver.

The old smuggler considered the question for a moment, as if he had never thought about this before. "I'm in favour of the war ending," he said. "That's all."

"But if the war ends, so does your business."

"Not really." Ossip grinned. "There's always something to smuggle round here."

Rybalko didn't know what to think of all this. When he was a child, the borderlines here had been imaginary. There was Ukraine to the left, Russia to the right, but hardly any evidence of a border between them. After the fall of the U.S.S.R., those lines had become visible, like a nightmare turning real. People had fallen asleep Soviets and woken up Ukrainians or Russians. But they shared the same language, the same culture. Most of the region's inhabitants spoke either Russian or Surzhyk, a dialect blending Russian and Ukrainian that had been woven together over decades.

Once past the border, they drove through many kilometres of steppes dotted with the black and grey masses of anthracite mines, dormitory towns and metalworking factories. From time to time, a dark pyramid would loom in the distance, a slag heap made up of residues from coal extraction. Other than that, the Donbas was exhaustingly flat, leaving no space for surprise or imagination. In the industrial zones, they passed factories silent as churches, rusted hangars smeared with coal dust, abandoned miners' cottages. The region was ravaged by unemployment. And that was the primary reason behind the war. In the days of communism, the miners and workers of the Donbas had been the heroes of State propaganda. The motherland gave them medals, comfortable apartments, and spa holidays in sunny Crimea. What did they have now? Nothing but a nostalgia for the old world. To get by, some people dug illegal mines. The precious coal was everywhere – so much so that gravediggers would often bring some back in the boot of their hearse after a day's work. But those were temporary measures. The truth was that the Donbas had been rotting in its Soviet juices for thirty years. Kyiv was far away and seemed powerless to solve the region's problems. All Moscow had had to do was breathe on the embers and the coal country had burst into flames.

All the same, not everyone in the Donbas agreed with the separatists. While in some towns pro-Russian graffiti (*Stavai Donbass* – "rise up, Donbas") covered the walls, in others it was the yellow and blue flag of Ukraine that fluttered in the wind.

"The war here is brother against brother, or at best cousin against cousin," Ossip said. "And even if you shoot at a Russian, there's a good chance you'll hit a distant relative. What a shitty war! There's something. . . ah, what's the word?. . . my daughter's a psychologist, you know, she told me the story of this Greek bloke, a long time ago, who slept with his mother and killed his father. Do you know what I'm talking about?"

"Oedipus," Rybalko said.

"That must be it. Anyway, I've thought about it and for me, this war is connected to the story of Oedipus. The troops from Kyiv want to kill their Russian father; the pro-Russian rebels are fighting to rejoin their Soviet motherland. And for that, members of the same family cheerfully kill each other!"

He pointed to a black pyramid near a mine shaft, with a red star at the top.

"My wife was from here before she moved to Rostov. She said that when she was a kid they used to have fireworks on the first of May and she would stand on top of a slag heap to watch them. These days, the kids go up there to watch Grad missiles falling on the next town. What kind of future are those kids going to have?"

Rybalko knew what it meant to belong to a sacrificed generation. He had been twenty in the late 1990s when the U.S.S.R. collapsed. A cataclysm that only those who had lived through it could understand. The shattered illusions, the unemployment, the country's fall from global superpower to secondary power, the cities invaded by criminals and capitalists, the daily shootings, the four-figure inflation, the disappearance of all reference points, the drugs. . . Growing up in the post-communist world had been an endless series of humiliations and sacrifices.

They drove for what seemed an eternity. Every fifteen minutes Ossip would take out his mobile and check Twitter or VKontakte, the Russian version of Facebook. That way, he could check troop movements and changes of nationality at the roadblocks controlling strategic crossroads in real time. Sometimes they would hear gunshots in the distance. Ossip was careful not to get too close to the front, where death seemed to be biding its time.

Of course, they were not completely free of danger. A shell could be fired the wrong way. Or a group of bandits could kidnap them or beat them to death. Rybalko felt relaxed, however. He experienced the journey across the Donbas with a feeling of almost total detachment, as if the sagging seats of the Lada were a sofa and the windscreen a television screen. He had the strange impression that nothing could hurt him. That his appointment with death had already been arranged and that the Grim Reaper would not seek him out before that date.

At last, Donetsk appeared on the dark horizon. Its outskirts had the disturbing peacefulness of all cities next to battlefields. The outlying housing estates, closer to the fighting, were full of tall tower blocks that looked like grazed knees. Part of the metal cladding with which they were covered had been smashed by explosions, leaving behind a layer of grey cement with gaps where the reddish bricks showed through. On the streets below you would sometimes see the still-smoking carcass of a car destroyed by a shell. Blown-up sandbags were spilled everywhere and shards of glass sparkled on the roads: was it the heat from the bombs that had vitrified the sand? In the city centre, the stigmata of war were less evident. The windows of buildings had brown sticky tape crosses over them to reduce the vibrations from the shellfire. Those windows overlooked deserted streets, the tarmac pockmarked by shrapnel.

They reached the Kalinina hospital around five that afternoon. Ossip dropped his passenger outside an adjoining building decorated with Greek-style columns, as if it were a temple to some antique god. The people who went inside held handkerchiefs to their noses; the ones who came out were pale as ghosts. And every time the door opened, the street was filled with the fierce, disturbing stink of rotting flesh. Yes, this was definitely the morgue. It was time to find out what Leonid Sokolov's body had to tell him.

11

The lobby reeked of gunpowder and dried blood. Corpses in combat fatigues were piled on the floor like firewood. A little further off, in a corridor that led to the examining rooms, he could see the bodies of old people and children lying on bloodstained stretchers, wrapped up in horribly ordinary bedsheets decorated with daisies or bluebirds.

A coroner entered the lobby from one of the doors on the side. He was a tired-looking man, perhaps in his thirties, in a white apron splattered with reddish-brown stains. Rybalko intercepted him before he could disappear towards the examining rooms.

"I have an appointment with Dr Tcherep. Do you know where I could find him?"

The coroner looked him up and down.

"Are you the one who's come for the radioactive body?"

"That's me. Where can I find Tcherep?"

"Tcherep is dead," the coroner said without the slightest hint of emotion.

"Dead? When?"

"This morning. A shell hit the building."

His voice was as clinical as a scalpel. Seemingly Dr Tcherep had not been his closest friend.

"Who is replacing him for the autopsy?"

"Nobody. Tcherep was only a few months from retirement and he had throat cancer. He didn't care if he had to cut open an irradiated corpse. But no-one else here is going voluntarily to put his hands inside something like that."

"We paid a lot of money for that autopsy," Rybalko said.

"Talk to Tcherep's widow about it. She's the one who got the money."

Rybalko could hear someone sobbing in the background. An assistant was asking a mother to identify her son's body. It was trapped under two other corpses. They had to push aside the feet of the body above his to see the face of the boy.

"Could you bring in someone else? From Luhansk, for example?"

The coroner was annoyed. "Listen, I covered up for Tcherep's schemes when he was alive, but I'm not going to do his dirty work for him now. I have twenty bodies to autopsy and my team is one man down. And we weren't exactly overstaffed before. It's your problem – deal with it yourself. All I can do is put your friend back in his lead box and wait for someone to pick him up. And the sooner he's out of my morgue, the better."

Rybalko looked at the bodies piled up in the lobby while he thought this over. It would take days to find another coroner or to transport the corpse to another morgue. For now, he would have to forget about the autopsy report. But he could still carry out an external examination of the body, so at least he wouldn't have completely wasted his time by coming all this way.

"Can I at least take a look at the body?"

"I don't think so. The radiation levels are—"

Rybalko took a wad of 5,000-ruble banknotes from his pocket.

"I'm sure we can come to an arrangement," he said, counting out ten notes. "You must need money for electricity, equipment, repairs. . .

And I do need to see the body. I don't have any time to lose, do you understand?"

He held out the bait to the coroner, who hesitated for an instant before surrendering.

They walked up the windowless corridor that led to the examining rooms. It was lit only by bare bulbs whose yellowish light bounced off the walls. Passing close to one of the stretchers, Rybalko felt a dead man's fingers brush against him and he shivered.

The coroner opened a door. The room they entered was like a slaughterhouse in a third-world country. Bodies everywhere. Stiff, swollen, grotesque. Bodies so thin you could see their ribs. Bodies with limbs missing. Bodies where the head was nothing more than a mass of pulped flesh and a few tufts of hair. Bodies of miners with blackened faces. Naked bodies, bodies in combat gear, bodies in tracksuits. Lying on rusty stretchers, or on dissection tables. Piled up four or five deep on the blue-tiled floor or on clear plastic sheeting. Many of them had their eyes closed, but occasionally Rybalko would find himself being stared at by the unseeing eyes of the dead. Only the day before, these people were making plans. Rybalko had suddenly the chilling thought that he would soon be one of them.

"Yesterday's bombardments," the coroner explained.

"Is... is Tcherep in here?"

The coroner pointed to the windows. His index finger was stained with dried blood. Rybalko looked out through the glass at a courtyard where some refrigerated trucks were parked. On one of them, someone had painted "200" in black paint. Rybalko understood: those trucks were being used to store the bodies of Russian soldiers. When he had been in Chechnya, Grüz 200 had been the codename used by the army to designate the corpses of soldiers brought back from the front. On another truck there was an advertising slogan in French: "*Produits frais, pour bien vous servir*".

"We had to put Tcherep in there," the coroner said. "With the power cuts here, we couldn't use our cold rooms anymore."

He sighed.

88

"At the worst point of the war, we were getting twenty or thirty bodies a day. We had to find a way to keep them cool before we examined them. We were so overrun that we had to bring colleagues in from Sloviansk to help. And even then we couldn't perform all the autopsies. There were so many bodies that we had to store them in an ice cream warehouse. When that was bombed, we began burying the corpses without examining them. And burying them without coffins, because there were so many dead that the city ran out of coffins. We put the unidentified bodies in a communal grave, without death certificates. Every time there was a ceasefire, we'd dig them up to autopsy them. There are so many people in this region whose relatives have died and who don't even know. We're doing our best to identify the bodies. So maybe now you understand why your radioactive Russian is not my top priority."

He went over to a door with large orange and yellow triangular sign taped to it. Two messages, one in Russian and one in Ukrainian, warned whoever entered against the risk of radioactive contamination.

"The corpse is highly radioactive, so don't stay near it for more than ten minutes. And don't touch anything in there."

He opened the door. In the middle of the small room was an examining table surrounded by clear plastic sheets that hung from the ceiling. Through those transparent strips, Rybalko could see the mutilated body of Leonid Sokolov.

"When we took it out of the coffin, the dosimeters went crazy," the coroner said. "And before you ask, no, we don't have any anti-radiation equipment."

Rybalko took out three 5,000-ruble notes. "I'd like to be alone for a moment."

The coroner looked at him, intrigued. "What are you planning to do?"

"Just a brief examination."

"Didn't you hear what I just said? The body is radioactive. Ra-di-o-ac-tive."

Rybalko added another two notes. The coroner took them.

"Well, it's your life. Throw it away if you want to. Tcherep put a decontamination shower in the room next door. You should get washed before you leave. And throw away your clothes. I'll tell one of the assistants to find you something else to wear."

The coroner left the room and Rybalko was alone with the corpse. He passed through the thin transparent curtain that marked out the safety zone around it. Inside, the floor and the ceiling had been taped with plastic film, presumably to prevent any splatter of organic matter contaminating the morgue.

The stench of the decomposed body made him retch. He turned on an old operating lamp to illuminate Leonid Sokolov's remains. The raw white light flooded the wounds that striped his body.

He smoked a cigarette to give himself time to get used to the smell and the presence of the cold, pale, lifeless body. Although the corpse bore the traces of many cuts, burns and bruises, its face and hands were relatively unscathed. Of course, the eyelids and lips had been sewn shut, but the murderer had used transparent thread and performed the task with precision. The stitching on Sokolov's stomach was something else altogether: ugly and chaotic, the thread thick and dark. The aim of those mutilations had not been to disfigure the victim. Clearly, the killer had wanted him to be identified – with the aid of his fingerprints and his face.

Why was he so determined that we should recognise you? Rybalko wondered, examining the reddish birth mark at the top of the dead man's forehead.

On a stainless steel table on rollers close by, there was an old cassette recorder and a Polaroid camera. There were also some second-hand surgical tools. Saw, scalpels, angled scissors, all of it mismatched and worn. The instruments were intended to be thrown away after the autopsy, so there was no point using new equipment.

He picked up the camera and took photographs of the corpse, starting with the face and moving down to the feet. He looked away when he snapped pictures of the genital area, so the photograph was badly framed. This was not a question of modesty: Rybalko had seen plenty of other penises at the gym or when he had done physical training with the men from the police station. It was simply disgust: the killer had castrated his victim, and the sight of the pinkish flesh where the testicles should be revolted him.

He tried to sort through the information provided by Leonid Sokolov's body to work out what had happened during his final days. First, his hands: some of the nails were broken, but that did not seem to be the result of torture. Rather, Rybalko had the impression that the young man had been scratching at something. There was a black residue under the nails that were still intact. Earth, perhaps? The laboratory analysis would tell him more, if the samples were usable. He had no idea how radiation might alter soil. In any case, the killer had not bothered cutting or cleaning the nails. Either he wasn't afraid that they would find his D.N.A. or he did not care.

Other than the marks left by the cables that had hung the body outside the apartment block, the dead man's wrists also bore circular traces that suggested he had been tied up while still alive. There were also traces of abrasion on the torso and abdomen, as if the skin had been subjected to intense, prolonged rubbing. Adding these facts together, Rybalko created the mental image of a man stretched out on his back, held in place by straps. By tying him up like that, the murderer would have ensured that the victim was at his mercy while he tortured him.

The more he examined the body, the greater the contempt and disgust he felt for whoever had done this. Killing someone was one thing, but destroying a man in this way was profoundly inhuman. He memorised all the details he now observed and put the photographs in his pocket. There wasn't much else to be done in the absence of a qualified coroner. Unless. . .

No.

He pushed the idea away. He was not going to cut the stitches to see what horrors lay behind the long, winding scar on his stomach, like a giant hairy caterpillar. And as for the eyes. . .

No. He definitely was not going to do that.

And yet. . . he had to. He lit another cigarette while he took his time weighing up the pros and cons. The radiation was not a concern. He was already dead anyway: why worry about something that might give him cancer ten years from now when he only had six months to live? There were morgue employees in the autopsy room next door, but that was not a problem; none of them were going to want to come into a room containing a highly contaminated corpse. The real problem was knowing whether there was a risk of destroying any clues if he removed the stitches.

In an instant he made his decision. With a trembling hand, he picked up one of the scalpels.

The head first, or the abdomen?

It was undoubtedly the stitches on the face that most repelled him, but there was a good chance that opening up his stomach would reveal far more sickening things. The body was more than a month dead, and even if it had been kept cold all that time there was a risk the intestines would be little more than putrefying slop.

So he opted for the face.

Nausea rose inside him when he put his hand on Leonid Sokolov's right eye. The skin was cold to the touch and slightly sticky. He pulled apart the lower and upper eyelids, then made little incisions to remove the stitches. Leonid's eye appeared. His iris was a perfect blue. Rybalko was overcome with a feeling of unease. Something wasn't right here, he could feel it in his guts. With the tip of his index finger, he forced himself to touch the eyeball. It was cold, hard and slippery. Its consistency was strange, however. It did not have the elasticity he was expecting. He tried rolling the eyeball and, to his surprise, encountered no resistance. It rolled around until the blue iris disappeared. Horrified, Rybalko recoiled. Vektor Sokolov had blue eyes, he remembered. But his son's had been black.

So Leonid Sokolov's eyes had been gouged out and replaced with glass eyes.

Controlling his disgust, Rybalko inserted his scalpel between the eyeball and the socket. The heavy, smooth, sticky glass eye popped out, revealing a metal object lodged in the mass of tissue around the severed optic nerve. He pulled it out with a pair of surgical pliers and discovered that it was a coin.

"A kopek," he muttered.

A loud clicking noise behind him. His stomach contracted, his heart hammered. He turned in a flash and found himself facing the plastic curtain. There was nobody there. He took a few seconds to understand that the noise had been made by the old cassette recorder on the table next to him.

"Stupid machine," he groaned.

The recorder was voice-activated. Presumably his conversation with the coroner had taken place too far away to trigger the machine into life.

He turned it off, then concentrated on the other eye. After ejecting the glass eyeball, he discovered another kopek. This time, the coin was stuck to the back of the eye socket and he had to lever his finger into the slimy orifice to get it out. After cleaning the coins, he noticed that they were quite old. One was dated 1986, the other 1957.

He put the coins aside and cut the stitches sealing the victim's lips. Inside the mouth he found the severed testicles. The killer had stuffed a piece of cloth at the base of the throat to prevent them slipping into the oesophagus. Grimacing with disgust, Rybalko took out the man's balls and then the cloth so he could examine it. White, with a floral pattern, it was very worn; he guessed it was extremely old. He took a picture of it before putting it back inside the corpse's mouth.

Now he had to search through Leonid Sokolov's guts. He hesitated for a long time as he stared at the long scar with the coarse stitching that reminded him of a baseball. He had pins and needles in his fingers. Was it the stress, or his cancer, or the effects of the radiation? He opened and closed his right hand several times to rid himself of the numbness. When at last he put his palm on Leonid Sokolov's abdomen to support his weight as he cut through the stitches, he had the strange sensation of kneading a pillow. He pressed down more firmly and the stomach sank down in a very unnatural way.

What horror would he discover next?

He had no choice but to find out. The operation was tedious and time-consuming: the scar was long and the thread thick. Once he'd cut open all the stitches, he grabbed both sides of the gaping wound, held his breath and pulled the flesh apart. The stomach yawned open, revealing Leonid Sokolov's intestines, the thin layer of yellow fat, the pink muscles, and a dark mass that horrified him.

In place of the stomach and viscera, there was now only a sort of stuffing made from straw and horsehair. And in the centre, a ball of feathers. He pulled it out and, shocked and incredulous, saw that it was a bird – a falcon. He placed it carefully on the dead man's white chest.

12

The sun was high in the sky when he emerged, pale-faced, from the morgue. He walked to the nearest bar, ordered a vodka and drank it in silence. He noticed a small bloodstain on his glass then looked at his fingernails. He'd scrubbed them so hard in the decontamination shower that he had made himself bleed. He asked for another vodka and drank it straight down to calm himself before calling Vektor Sokolov.

"Alexander? Is the autopsy over already?" the former minister asked with surprise.

"No, it... it was cancelled. The coroner was killed by a bomb."

Sokolov was silent for a moment, then said in a firm voice: "I'll call my contacts in Donetsk. I'll find a replacement in less than a week."

"What do you want me to do in the meantime?"

"Wait."

Rybalko immediately dismissed this suggestion. "There's no point. I made a brief examination of the body. It wouldn't do any good for me to stay here for the full autopsy. Just send me the report when it's ready."

"You saw my son's body? How... what was it like?"

"The coroner can give you a better explanation than I could."

"I want to know," Sokolov said in a voice that brooked no argument.

Images flashed through his head, framed like the Polaroid pictures he had taken of Leonid's body.

"That's not a good idea. Your son's body showed traces of torture and it had been severely mutilated."

"What. . . what kind of mutilations?"

"Really, I think the coroner should be the one to–"

"I want to know!" Sokolov yelled. "What did that bastard do to my son?"

The former minister's breathing was heavy and menacing. Rybalko gave in: if he wanted the truth, that was his right.

"His eyes had been gouged out and he had been castrated. The testicles were put inside his mouth and he had glass eyeballs in the sockets."

Silence at the other end of the line. Sokolov's breathing swelled again, became husky, bestial, almost a growl. Then there was an explosion of noises: smashed wood, breaking glass, curses. A surge of rage that sounded as though it was destroying everything in the enormous living room. It went on for a long time before finally quieting.

At last Sokolov spoke in a horrifyingly neutral tone: "What was the cause of death?"

"I couldn't tell. There was no obvious trace of a fatal blow, no signs of strangulation, no bullet holes. . ."

Sokolov cut in angrily: "What the hell am I paying you for if you can't even tell me what killed my son?"

The silence between them now was venomous, like a snake poised to strike.

"I'm not a coroner."

"I know that! I know you're not a fucking coroner, because the fucking coroner who was supposed to do this fucking autopsy died in this fucking shitty war!" There followed a litany of insults in Russian and Ukrainian before Sokolov calmed down again and spoke in that disturbingly cold voice: "Excuse me. You understand, it's just too much, all this. You're a father. Imagine if someone did that to your daughter. . . What else can you tell me? What are your preliminary conclusions?"

"For now, I only have theories," Rybalko began cautiously. "This is a killer who stays in the shadows but makes no attempt to hide his crime. Who exhibits it, even, almost like a sort of. . . a sort of artwork. Before asking why he killed your son and not someone else, the most important question we must ask ourselves is: why display it the way he did?"

"And do you have an answer?"

"As I told you, it's too early to draw any definitive conclusions. I'll have to see the crime scene with my own eyes and find some other clues. But based on what I observed, I think the killer is using symbolism. The irises of the glass eyes were pale blue, like yours. And behind them were two coins. One kopek from 1957 and another from 1986. Does that suggest anything to you?"

Sokolov stammered: "Fifty-seven? I. . . my wife. . . that was the year Olga was born. . . And 1986. . ."

"The year she was killed," Rybalko said.

He quickly absorbed this new information. The coins indicated that Leonid Sokolov's death was connected to his mother's. He wondered if the cloth in the victim's throat had a special meaning too.

"What was your wife wearing the night she was killed?"

"A dress."

"What colour?"

"White, I think."

Rybalko took out the Polaroid pictures he had taken during the examination and spread them out across the bar.

"There was a piece of fabric jammed into your son's throat. I thought it was just to prevent his. . . Anyway, the fabric was white with flower patterns."

"Yes, I. . . I remember, she was wearing a flowered dress that day. . . Do you think. . . do you think. . ."

Sokolov's firm voice started to tremble, as if it had been broken. Rybalko thought about Marina and his daughter. How would he have reacted, in Sokolov's place?

He spoke the sentence that the other man could not articulate: "I think it's highly probable that your son's killer and the person who killed your wife in 1986 are one and the same person."

Another silence, but this one was different to those that had come before. Like the silence in a forest just before a mighty tree falls.

"My God," Sokolov mumbled finally. "How is it possible, after all these years... how... and why this terrible display?"

Rybalko said slowly: "The killer is sending you a message, through your son's body."

"But why now, more than thirty years after... my wife's death?"

"I don't have an answer to that question. All I can do is make suppositions about the meaning of that message. Inside your son's abdomen, I found a bird. A falcon, to be more precise."

He left Sokolov time to digest the killer's macabre sense of irony: *sokol*, in Russian, meant "falcon".

"If Leonid really was investigating his mother's death, this might be a warning addressed to you. Something like: 'stay out of this or you will die too'."

Sokolov blew his top. "Who does this madman think he is? He thinks he can threaten me? Kill my son and get away with it? I'm not scared of him!"

Easy to say, thought Rybalko, when you're hundreds of kilometres from danger, surrounded by bodyguards. No, it was he himself – Rybalko – who was threatened. He was the one who risked ending up like Leonid Sokolov, his eyes gouged out and his balls in his mouth.

"Get on with the rest of your investigation," Sokolov said. "I'll organise a new autopsy as soon as I can."

He hung up. Rybalko put his mobile back in his pocket and ordered a third glass of vodka. After swallowing it, he looked at his hands: they were not trembling now.

13

Melnyk emerged from sleep to a familiar ringing sound. He fumbled for the button on his alarm clock, then realised he had not set the alarm the night before. The muffled melody was coming from the kitchen. His mobile. . . he had left it there. Too far, too early. He closed his eyes again, hoping that whoever was calling would give up. But after stopping for a moment, the ringing started again. Beside him, his wife grumbled. He decided to get up and answer his phone.

"Melnyk," he said in a dry-mouthed voice.

"Captain? I hope I'm not waking you?"

Novak. Unlike him, she had to stay at the station all weekend. He opened the fridge and took the plate containing the remains of the *Kievskiy tort*.

"What's up?" he said, cutting himself a slice.

"The guard at Duga just called."

"Let me guess. Someone broke in."

"Yes," Novak said.

Melnyk was unsurprised: Duga was a former military base containing a gigantic anti-missile radar dating from the Cold War. It was one of the favourite spots for the "extreme tourists" who liked illegally to enter the zone to visit the Soviet ruins.

"Did he arrest the guy?"

"No, but he found the place where he'd been camping."

Melnyk started the coffee machine. He might as well make

himself breakfast: there was no chance he would get back to sleep.

"So? What are you expecting me to do about it? I'm in Kyiv for the weekend."

"I know, but I think there's a connection with Leonid Sokolov's murder."

Tatiana came into the kitchen.

"Who's calling at this hour? Is everything O.K.?"

"Yes, darling, it's. . ." He didn't want her to know it was a work call, in case it caused another row. The first thing that came to his mind was the name of one of his cousins. "It's Nikodim."

He took refuge on the balcony. Novak asked who he was talking to.

"My wife. The phone woke her up."

"Sorry."

"What makes you think the visitor to Duga might have a connection to Leonid Sokolov's death?"

"Apparently he left a stuffed bird behind."

Melnyk felt his pulse accelerate.

"A bird? What kind of bird? A swallow?"

"The guard didn't say. Do you want me to go take a look?"

He looked at the kitchen clock. Two hours to drive to Chernobyl, at least two hours there to clear things up, and then the drive back. . . If he decided to go to the zone, he couldn't hope to be home again until mid-afternoon or early evening.

"Captain?"

"Wait for me at the station. I'll be there in two hours."

He hung up, lost in thought. He had been planning to visit Oksana that morning to ask if she knew where the Ukrainian K.G.B. archives might be. He would have to put that back to another time. And find an excuse for his wife. If he told her he was going back to the zone during his time off, she would not be happy.

At the table in the living room, he sipped his coffee and watched the morning news.

"The bombardments in the Donetsk region have started again," Tatiana said. "Thank God Nikolai is in Kyiv."

The reporter was saying that there had already been more than 10,000 deaths since the start of the conflict, and that more than one and a half million people had been displaced by the fighting. He ended by wondering when Ukrainians would be able to return to normal life. Normal life. . . Some days, Melnyk wondered if Ukraine was really made for normality. The revolutionary wars at the start of the twentieth century, the great famine caused by Stalin, the massacres carried out by the Germans, the Chernobyl explosion, the civil war in the Donbas, the economic crisis, the mass unemployment. . . what constituted normal life for a Ukrainian?

"Nikodim has a problem with his car. I told him I'd go and give him a hand," he told Tatiana.

He hated lying, but it was better for everyone if she believed he was in the suburbs of Kyiv helping to fix his cousin's old Zhiguli.

"Remind him that he hasn't given you back the tools you lent him last summer," she said without taking her eyes from the screen.

"I'll try to remember. Don't wait for me at lunch. It might take a while."

"Alright."

He was surprised she didn't argue about that. In fact, he felt almost disappointed. They had not seen each other for two weeks because he had been on duty in the zone. She ought to have been upset that he wasn't spending the day with her. And yet she showed no signs of emotion at all as she flicked between Russian and Ukrainian channels in search of information about the situation in the Donbas.

"Shall I bring something back for dinner?"

"With all those leftovers in the fridge? No, thank you. Anyway, we need to save money."

Guilt rushed through him again. The bulletproof vest. . . He absolutely had to get hold of one for his son before Nikolai returned to the front. But where could he find the money?

Later. Right now he needed to join Novak. This case could be his ticket out of the zone. If he could quickly catch this monster, he'd certainly get a promotion, maybe even a bonus. Yes, that was it. He could catch two fish with one worm: arrest Leonid Sokolov's killer and provide his son with the protection he needed.

He gobbled down the rest of his *Kievskiy tort* and left.

The traffic in Kyiv was not bad for the time of day. Despite being in a rush, he drove within the speed limit. Petrol was scarily expensive these days, and he could not count on the State to pay his travel expenses when he was working on the case during his time off.

He picked up Novak at the police station, and took a patrol car to Duga. The base wasn't far from Chernobyl. After they left the city, they took a back road built out of slabs of reinforced concrete. It ran through a forest of pine. Novak was surprised by how perfectly aligned the trees were.

"It's a man-made forest," Melnyk explained. "It was planted when the radar was being built, to hide the military base."

At the end of the road, the massive outline of the radar tower blotted the horizon. It was composed of two immense rectangular structures. The smaller one, for high frequencies, was ninety metres tall. The other, which spied on low frequencies, was closer to one hundred and fifty metres. From a distance, the two metal walls looked like gigantic scaffolding erected to paint a coat of bright blue over the grey sky.

"What did it do, that thing?"

"It's what they call an 'over-the-horizon' radar. Theoretically it was capable of detecting a nuclear rocket launch in the United States."

Access to the base was blocked by a wide green gate embossed with a huge silver star. Beside it, a white brick house served as a checkpoint. A man came out. He was wearing military trousers and a combat jacket. His mouth dropped open when Novak got out of the car. You did not see many women in the Chernobyl region. Particularly not in police uniform.

"So you had a visitor, eh, chief?" Melnyk said.

"Yes."

"Were you able to identify the intruder?"

"No. I didn't see him."

"But he left a stuffed bird behind?"

"Yes. He left a few things."

"Things?"

"A sleeping bag, some tins of food. . ."

"So he was camping here for several days?"

"Yes."

"And you noticed nothing?"

The guard shrugged. "It's a big place."

"How do you know he was here for several days?"

"He made himself at home. See for yourself."

Not exactly chatty, Melnyk thought. At Duga there was no need for anyone talkative to guard the installations. The radar was not yet on all the tourist routes. Whole days might pass before anyone turned up at the gate. Most days, the guard's only company was a pack of half-wild dogs that came to beg for food.

The man went through a small door beside the big green gate. Melnyk signalled to Novak to follow them. The young woman hesitated. She had taken out her Geiger counter almost as soon as she stepped out of the car. Melnyk wondered how long she would last here before resigning. One week? Two? At the station, the others were already betting on this. Most of them thought she wouldn't last the year. They had discovered that she commuted from Kyiv every day rather than rent an apartment in Slavutych or use official accommodation in Chernobyl. This was always a bad sign: it was only a matter of time before she cracked.

The Geiger counter crackled faintly as she passed through the door.

"See? It's no more radioactive here than it is at the station," Melnyk said.

This remark did not have the effect he had been hoping for: Novik grew even more tense. But she put the device away and the three of them walked in silence towards the radar.

Melnyk tried to relax her by telling her what he knew about the place: "In the U.S.S.R. days, the Duga site was top secret. The people who worked here needed somewhere to live, so the Soviets built a town next to it. It was altogether independent: there was a stadium, shops, a theatre, even a hockey rink. More than fifteen hundred people lived here. Scientists, soldiers, technicians, their families... Yet the town was not any map or any census. It didn't even have a name of its own. Like all the U.S.S.R.'s secret cities, it was designated by a postcode based on the name of the nearest city. So this was Chernobyl-2."

Novak pulled a face. "Sounds like a lot of fuss over nothing. I mean, you can see the radar kilometres away. People must have asked questions about this enormous thing in the middle of the forest."

"You're forgetting that, at the time, asking the wrong questions could get you in a lot of trouble. The K.G.B. had eyes and ears everywhere, so nobody divulged the secret. On the official maps it was a summer camp for Soviet pioneers."

"Oh, the 'Soviet scouts'? My father was one of those. You too, I imagine."

"No, I didn't have the opportunity."

"I thought everyone was a member, in the U.S.S.R. days. Except..."

Novak stopped speaking. Too late. He knew what she'd been about to say.

"Apart from idiots, thugs, and the children of enemies of the people?"

The young woman stared at her feet.

"Sorry. I didn't mean to be unkind."

They walked for a few minutes in silence before reaching the base of the radar. The last time Melnyk had been to Duga, it had been to pick up the corpse of a tourist who had fallen to his death after trying to climb one of the two gigantic antennae. The ascent became more dangerous every year. The ladders were growing twisted through lack of maintenance and the rungs were slippery from corrosion. Other accidents seemed inevitable as long as the radar remained standing, so there were frequent discussions about dynamiting it. But to demolish a structure the size of ten football stadiums, a structure that weighed more than 14,000 metric tons, was inherently risky in a zone affected by the Chernobyl disaster. The collapse could create a microearthquake, sending radioactive particles into the air. In Kyiv, its destruction was not a subject of discussion.

The guard led them to a large, austere-looking building.

"This is the command centre of the radar," he said as they entered.

Inside, everything was in darkness. Holding out their torches, they crossed through rooms full of empty metal filing cabinets. The floor was covered with a gritty dust and various circuit boards, cables and punch cards for ancient computers. There was too much metal here, Melnyk thought, for this mess to be the work of looters. More likely the military had destroyed everything, for fear that their precious technology might be stolen. At the time of the reactor explosion, Duga had been home to one of the most cutting-edge computer systems in the world.

They came out into a room that was a reproduction in miniature of the radar's control room. Coloured signs showed the various American missiles with which the radar's operators might be confronted. A door lay on the floor, on a bed of bricks. On top of it was an old foam mat and a sleeping bag.

"Looks like your visitor left in a hurry," Melnyk said.

"There are dogs and wolves prowling round here sometimes," the guard said. "The smell probably drew them."

An open tin stood on a shelf. Melnyk put on a pair of gloves and picked it up. The food inside had gone mouldy. It must have been open for several days. Which meant that whoever had been here could be practically anywhere else in the zone by now.

"And the bird?" Melnyk said. "Where's that?"

"In the old cafeteria."

Cosmonauts, space stations, satellites: the walls of the old officers' canteen were decorated with colourful murals depicting the U.S.S.R.'s glorious future in outer space. In the middle of the room strewn with dead computers and scraps of metal, they found a small stuffed bird perched on a stool. It wasn't a swallow: it had grey and green feathers.

Novak took a picture with her mobile phone.

"Any idea what species it is?" she said.

"None at all," Melnyk said.

Behind them, the guard's voice murmured: "I bet it's some kind of green woodpecker."

They turned. The man was smiling, clearly pleased by the looks of surprise on their faces.

"You know about birds?"

"No. But I know about radars."

Melnyk understood. Back when it was still active, the Duga radar emitted a radioelectric signal that disturbed radio links. Rapid and regular, the signal had quickly been given a whole host of nicknames, such as the Caviar Machine-Gun and the Russian Green Woodpecker.

He explained this to Novak.

"But why leave this bird here?" she wondered aloud.

"Maybe it's a sort of artwork," their guide suggested. "The bloke did a drawing in another room."

"Show us," Melnyk said.

The guard took them to what had once been a propaganda room. On one of the walls was an old black-and-white photomontage showing American soldiers terrorising unarmed civilians and a man in a cowboy hat with a large gold signet ring on his right ring finger. Opposite this, someone had recently spray-painted a horrified face frozen in a silent scream. One of those disturbing Edvard Munch-type faces. At the foot of the mural were a few used aerosol cans and cardboard stencils. Melnyk noticed that the artist had signed his work.

Artyom.

"*Blyad*," he cursed, then told Novak: "Take some pictures and let's get out of here. I know where to find our man."

14

The last time he had come across Artyom – or Yegor, to call him by his real first name – the artist had been an awkward, insolent sixteen-year-old. Artyom's adventures in the zone had been his way of escaping his humdrum everyday existence: the boring classes, the empty weekends, the holidays spent working at his parents' farm. He must have been caught in the zone four or five times, but Melnyk suspected he had gone there far more often.

"You really think he could have killed Leonid Sokolov?" Novak asked once they were back in their vehicle.

"No, I don't think so. He was a difficult kid, but not a killer."

Melnyk glanced in the rear-view mirror at the green woodpecker on the backseat. Artyom had been a crazy teenager back then, spending nights at the police station while he waited for his father to come and pay the fine he had incurred for entering the zone. When he wasn't in trouble with the law, he spent most of this time smoking, playing ultraviolent video games, hanging around at the youth centre or at the football pitch near his school. But Artyom could have changed since their last encounter. Had he moved on to more dangerous hobbies?

Melnyk decided to go to the kid's father's house to find out more. The man had a farm in Bazar, a small village to the west of the zone. Technically, Bazar was inside the perimeter marking the area of fallout from Chernobyl, but there were no guard posts or barbed-wire fences nearby. In 1986, the authorities had told the inhabitants to lock themselves in their houses. There had been talk of evacuation, but nothing had happened for years. It was as if they had been forgotten about. And then, one fine day in 1993, the 2,600 inhabitants had been ordered to leave their village. Most of them had found new homes elsewhere, but a few hundred had refused to budge despite the urgent demands of the police and military.

"There are loads of young people here," Novak said, surprised, when they reached the centre of the village.

Nine or ten blank-faced adolescents were lounging miserably outside the youth centre; they stared at the passing police vehicle as if it were the highlight of their day.

"There's a secondary school in Bazar," Melnyk said. "It's the only one in the region."

Unlike most of the villages on the edge of the zone, Bazar's population numbers had been on the rise over the past few years. To attract new inhabitants, the mayor was practically giving away old houses in the centre of the village. In exchange, all the newcomers had to do was renovate the house they were given, and pay 150 hryvnias per year – about twenty or thirty times less than the rent on the cheapest house anywhere else in Ukraine. Result: Bazar had gone from 2,030 inhabitants in 2005 to more than 5,000 in 2010.

"Why's it called Bazar?"

"In the Middle Ages, during the era of Mongol rule, this place had the biggest slave market in the region."

"Nice," Novak said.

The village's main street was full of bumps and potholes. They passed the park, with its obligatory statue in memory of the victims of the Great Patriotic War. By the roadside, in among the buildings with broken windows and overgrown gardens, they saw one or two renovated houses. There were far more of them than there had been the last time he had been here. He had heard that, since the war in the Donbas had started, a new kind of colonist had come to live in Bazar: pro-Ukrainian families chased out by the separatists, hoping to build a new life here, far from the conflict.

The further they moved away from the centre, the more man's grip on the wild loosened. As elsewhere in the zone, nature was slowly, insidiously devouring everything. Old fences collapsed. Virginia creeper wound its way through dilapidated apartment blocks. A fox slept on a park bench. It was hard to tell if this land belonged to people or to wildlife.

Novak's eyes widened at the sight of fields planted with cereals and vegetables.

"There's agriculture here? Isn't the soil contaminated?"

"Apparently there are some places where it's not so bad. Radioactive pollution isn't uniform. You can have dozens of kilometres of fertile land, then suddenly there's a small, highly radioactive zone."

Artyom's father's farm was a five-minute drive from the centre of Bazar. He had bought two old Soviet-era agricultural buildings for a tiny sum and renovated them to raise sheep here. He also cultivated eighty or ninety acres of land around the village. When he saw the police vehicle entering his property, the farmer at once guessed the reason for their visit. He left the lamb he was examining to one of his labourers and came over to greet them, but first he knocked off some straw that had stuck to his quilted jacket; there was something oddly stiff about the movement of his arm as he did this, and Melnyk remembered that the man had suffered a serious shoulder injury several years before. Back then, Artyom's father had owned a farm in the Donetsk region. When the conflict in the Donbas began, he had provided food to the loyalist forces, and the pro-Russian forces had punished him with a savage beating. It was to avoid further reprisals that he had moved to Bazar.

"Captain Melnyk. . . It's been a long time. And, to be perfectly honest, I was hoping never to see you again. Has Yegor been in the zone again?"

"That's right. We found some of his graffiti near the radar."

"That junk yard. . . Why would he go there? Oh well, I assume I'll have to report to Ivankiv's courthouse and pay a fine again?"

"I'm afraid it might be more serious than that, this time."

"What? You mean. . . prison?"

"Maybe. First, I have to talk to your son, so we have a clearer idea of what we're dealing with. Is he at the farm?"

The farmer looked stunned. He passed one of hands through his greying hair.

"Yes, yes. . . He comes back from Kyiv on weekends. . . He's at university there."

"What's he studying?"

"Art. He's in a private school."

Melnyk was not surprised. Artyom had already been a graffiti artist three years ago when he had gone into the zone on a regular basis.

"It costs a fortune and there are no job prospects," his father said grimly. "But, well, I thought surely he'll end up finding a real job."

They left the sheep pen and walked towards the house. It was built on the edge of a large field.

"That's all going to be winter wheat," the farmer said with a sweep of his arms to indicate the extent of his land. "All organic. No pesticides."

"Organic food from Chernobyl?" Novak said, looking horrified. "And people buy that?"

"Of course. It's better and safer than most of the stuff you can find in the Kyiv markets. We export it abroad too."

A big wolfhound was sleeping peacefully outside the house's front door. The old floorboards in the entrance hall smelled of rotten wood, and the doors leading to other rooms were warped in their frames. The building had been left empty for years before the farmer and his family moved there.

"Yegor must be in his bedroom," his father said, heading to the staircase.

"Which one is it?"

"End of the corridor. First floor."

"Stay here. We'll go and get him ourselves."

"But. . ."

Without giving the father time to protest, Melnyk climbed the stairs, closely followed by Novak. Just before they reached the door, she opened her coat and put her hand on the butt of her pistol. She had already donned her bulletproof vest after getting out of the car. Melnyk was wearing his too. This was the first time he had worn it since his days at the crime squad in Kyiv.

He took out his pistol and opened the door onto the usual chaos of a teenager's bedroom: clothes on the floor, a guitar with shredded strings, an upturned schoolbag vomiting out folders, posters of popular bands, an unmade bed. The air was thick with the stale smell of sweat and ketchup punctuated by notes of cannabis.

Artyom had not heard them come in. He was sitting in front of a video game on his computer, giving orders through a built-in microphone on his headphones. He had to stop the opposing team getting in and to blow up a bomb before time ran out.

Melnyk raised his voice: "Artyom!"

Startled, the boy turned around. Seeing the police officers, he went so pale that Melnyk was worried he was about to faint.

"Captain. . . Captain Melnyk. . . I. . . what are you doing here?"

His eyes flickered between the officers in his room and the bong on his chest of drawers.

"Turn that off and follow us. We'll talk downstairs."

Artyom hurriedly obeyed. The chubby boy that the captain had arrested in the zone so many times had become a tall, skinny nineteen-year-old whose torn T-shirt and jeans looked way too big for him. His cheeks had narrowed too, but he still had the fresh-faced look of a well-fed kid. As they sat around the living-room table, Melnyk was finding it difficult to imagine that this was the face of a ruthless killer.

"Did you call them?" Artyom hissed at his father.

"I swear I didn't."

"So how did they know then? I only come here on weekends. How else would they know that I smoke?"

"That's not why we're here," Melnyk said. "We know that you went in the zone."

The boy attacked his father again: "Yeah, well, you shouldn't have let them in. Now I'm in the shit because of you. You won't be laughing if they send me to prison, will you?"

"Show some respect to your father, kid," Melnyk said sternly. "And I repeat: we're not here because of your grass. We want to know what you were doing in Duga."

Artyom threw himself back against his chair and crossed his arms.

"I haven't been in the zone."

"Stop lying. We found your sleeping bag and saw your graffiti inside one of the buildings near the radar."

"So? I've done loads of graffiti over the last few years."

"The painting was recent."

"Can you prove it?"

"I can find plenty of proof in your bedroom if I want to. Possession of cannabis is worth three years in prison, if I recall correctly."

"But you said–"

"Yeah, I said that's not why we're here. But if you keep acting like an idiot, we'll seize it all and take you down to the station."

Artyom scowled.

"That's illegal. You didn't have a search warrant."

"Ha, you're an expert on the law now, are you? I'll remind you that you're living in your father's house and he let us in."

"Yeah, well, thanks a lot, dad. You're a real pain in the arse."

Melnyk slammed his fist down on the table.

"Don't talk like that to your father or I'll give you a slap! You should thank him instead of being an insolent little shit. How many times have the police turned up here because of you? Loads of parents would have kicked you out long before now."

Artyom held Melnyk's gaze for a long moment, before turning to look at his father.

"I'm not saying anything. I want a lawyer."

"A lawyer?" Melnyk was almost choking on his rage. He threw a few insults at the boy, threatening with him serious punishment if he wasted any more of their time, but Artyom remained silent.

"Just tell them what you were doing!" his father begged.

"I have nothing to say."

"They're willing to let you off on the drugs!"

"They had no right to enter my room. They've got nothing on me."

Melnyk was seething. He was very close to grabbing this snotty little brat by his collar when Novak's calm, composed voice stopped him in his tracks.

"Your nickname, Artyom. . . that's a reference to *Metro 2033*, right?"

The boy eyed her curiously. So did Melnyk.

"It's a dystopian novel," Novak explained to him. "It's set on the Moscow metro, twenty years after a nuclear apocalypse. The hero's name is Artyom. They made a video game based on the book a few years ago. Have you played it?"

Artyom nodded. "Yeah, it wasn't bad. Although my favourite F.P.S. is 'Stalker'."

"Your favourite what?" Melnyk asked.

"First-person shooter," the young woman translated. "One of those games with a subjective viewpoint. '*Stalker*' is a game set in the contaminated zone of Chernobyl. Have you played *Call of Duty* too? The sniper mission?" she asked the boy.

"Yeah, yeah. But what do you care?"

Having got over his surprise, the boy had reverted to his cold, disdainful attitude.

Melnyk lost his temper again. "Talk like that to the lady one more time and we'll finish this discussion at the station."

"Was it the video games that made you want to be a stalker?" Novak asked, unruffled.

Stalker was the nickname often used for those who sneaked inside the zone, to visit or to loot. It was a reference to *Roadside Picnic*, a science-fiction novel by Arkady and Boris Strugatsky. In 1979, Andre Tarkovksy made a film adaptation entitled "Stalker". The term designated secret guides who enabled people to enter a dangerous zone surrounded by police. At the heart of this zone there was supposed to be a place where all wishes would be granted.

"Young people influenced to do bad things by video games?" Artyom sneered. "Give me a break from your stupid clichés. Do you have any idea what it's like living here? Being young in this place. . . it's like rotting. There's nothing to do. No jobs, no fun, no future. . . In Donetsk, at least I had a life. And then one day, I had to leave it all behind. My girlfriend, my mates, everything. The only exciting thing here is the zone. That's why I used to hang out there when I was at school."

"But now you're in Kyiv. So why go back there?"

"I just wanted to see the zone again. It's hard to understand for anyone who doesn't know it, but it's a magical place. Once you've been there, you always want to go back. You can never see everything there. That's just how it is. There's always something else you want to see."

"Like the Russian green woodpecker," Novak said quietly.

Artyom hesitated.

"As I said, we'll let you off the drug charges if you tell us everything," Melnyk said.

The boy relaxed a little.

"O.K., it's true. I went there last week."

"When?"

"From Monday till Sunday."

"I thought you were in Kyiv, at the art school!" his father protested.

"Yeah, well, I wasn't. I shared a taxi to here, then walked to the edge of the zone. After that, I just wandered around."

"Why did you go to Duga?" Novak said.

"'Cause it's a good place to take photos."

"And paint," prompted Melnyk.

"Yeah, it's good for painting too."

"We found a stuffed bird in the building where you were squatting. Can you tell us what it is?"

Artyom smiled.

"The green woodpecker? That was a stroke of luck. See, I didn't go in the zone just to hang around. I've got a project to complete for the end of the year. Right from the start, I wanted to do something with the zone. So I took photos, painted murals. . . I wanted to show every aspect of that place. The melancholy, the sadness, the fear, the beauty, the ugliness. . ."

"The bird," Melnyk interrupted. "Tell us about the bird. How did you get it?"

"It was just luck. I'd spent quite a while looking for good places to take my photos and then I found this old shack with some stuffed animals inside."

Novak moved forward on her chair. Without thinking, Melnyk did the same.

"What sort of animals?"

"Just, like, from the forest."

"Were there other birds?"

"Yeah, yeah, loads of them. I should probably just show you the photos I took. They're on my laptop, upstairs."

"Go and get it," Melnyk said.

The boy obeyed, returning soon afterwards with the laptop under his arm.

"It takes a while to boot up," he said, tapping nervously at the mouse he'd connected to the computer.

He opened a file and the screen showed a hundred or so thumbnail pictures. The boy began scrolling through them, then clicked on one.

"That's it. It starts here."

He showed them the photographs. Stuffed animal after stuffed animal.

"They're the same as the ones we saw in Pripyat," Novak noted.

"Except they're more damaged," Melnyk replied.

Most of the animals were in a pitiful state: twisted wings, missing teeth, flayed skin. . . Was that why the killer had abandoned them?

"Where did you take these pictures?" Melnyk said.

"In this little hut not far from the train station in Yaniv."

Artyom showed them a photograph of a small building on which he had spray-painted a white dove.

"The house was next to this one."

Melnyk stared attentively at the image, then stood up.

"Come to the police station tomorrow with your father," he said. "Officer Novak will take your statement. If you've told us the truth, we'll drop the other charges. But if I see you in the zone again, I'll lock you away, you understand?"

"If you catch me," Artyom said with an insolent smile.

His father thanked the police officers and offered to give them some freshly slaughtered mutton. Melnyk refused out of principle, Novak from fear of radiation. They went back to their patrol vehicle and the captain radioed his colleagues to drive to Yaniv and look for a building with a dove painted on its façade.

"It would have been simpler to take Artyom with us to find it, don't you think?"

"And spend two hours on the road with that little turd? No thanks."

It was late afternoon when they reached the disused train station in Yaniv. It was only a stone's throw from Pripyat, next to an old road leading into the centre of the city. It was blocked by a big mound of earth where trees had grown, so nobody had driven on that road for years. The mound was presumably the remains of an embankment built in 1986 to prevent looters entering the town by car.

As soon as he got out of the car, Melnyk had a bad feeling. The smell of burning was stronger than the smell of the pines. It was coming from the charred remnants of a small house whose windows looked out on Artyom's spray-painted dove. Its roof was partly collapsed, but Melnyk went inside anyway. In what had once been the living room, amid the blackened debris covering the floor, bright white bones peeked out. Melnyk went back outside to find a dead branch and used it to sweep away the cold ashes. Animal skeletons embedded with metal wires appeared.

He threw the branch against the wall and roared his rage at the earth.

The swallow killer had covered his tracks.

15

Rybalko stretched and yawned as the outskirts of Kyiv came into view. The drive from Donetsk had lasted all night. He and Ossip had taken turns behind the wheel every three hours, but unlike the old smuggler, Rybalko had barely slept when he wasn't driving. Too much stress, too much caffeine, too many questions. At least he had had plenty of time to think through what he'd discovered during the autopsy.

First thought: obviously Sokolov's murder had been meticulously planned. The killer had not acted on an impulse. He'd set a trap for his victim and prepared the corpse to carry a message to the victim's father. That required self-control and almost inhuman determination. And stuffing the body with a bird of prey also involved certain logistical demands. Perhaps this was the most interesting angle of attack for his investigation: how did one go about getting hold of a dead falcon? Answer: either hunt it yourself or buy it from a poacher, because that species was undoubtedly protected.

It was probable that the killer had a place where he could deal with the victim without attracting unwelcome attention. Where could you torture someone without their screams alerting anyone? The answer seemed obvious: in the exclusion zone. An uninhabited place, hundreds of abandoned buildings, not a living soul within a day's walk, and hardly any police presence: it was the ideal spot for murder. He felt it: that was where the tragedy had been formed.

Nature, isolation, a dead bird... Perhaps the murderer was a hunter?

As agreed, Ossip dropped Rybalko close to the Maidan, at the café where he had a meeting arranged with the contact who was supposed to take him to Chernobyl. Their goodbyes were brief but warm. Ossip wished him good luck and a long life. Rybalko almost smiled at that.

He sat at a table and ordered a coffee, then went to the men's room to splash cold water on his face. In the mirror above the sink, his tired face looked back at him. With his waxy complexion and the rings under his eyes, he looked like one of those piled-up corpses in the Donetsk morgue. He realised that the clothes that the coroner had given him when he came out of the decontamination shower must have belonged to one of the dead men.

The café grew noisier as more and more customers came in. Young executives, ordering an espresso before going off to work. Pasty-faced students who had spent the night partying. Outside, the Maidan was quiet. Hard to imagine that, at the height of the 2014 revolution, the square had been a battlefield of sound and fury, smoke plumes, barricades, explosions and gunshots, during those weeks when the Ukrainian special forces had confronted the insurgents who wanted to be part of Europe and to end the corrupt reign of President Yanukovych.

Time passed slowly. His contact was late and, alone in the middle of the crowd that now occupied the café, Rybalko found himself missing Ossip. The smuggler talked constantly, filling each silence with a story or a question – behaviour that would have exasperated Rybalko a week earlier, but which now had the benefit of preventing him from thinking about what awaited him at the end of this trip.

Death.

Around 10 a.m., a car doubled-parked on the pavement opposite the bar. An ash-blonde woman got out. Small snub nose, bushy eyebrows, cigarette dangling from between sulky lips, she strode over, looking energetic and resolute. She reminded him of Alexandra Shevchenko, one of the founders of the Ukrainian feminist group Femen.

She entered the bar and looked around with eyes as blue as Lake Baikal. When her gaze reached Rybalko, he felt his heart start to pound.

Their eyes met for what seemed like an eternity, then she walked over to his table and stood in front of him.

"Are you Alexander?"

Sokolov must have shown her his photograph. But given that he looked like a freshly dug-up corpse, she may have not recognised him.

"Yes, but you can call me Alex."

He noticed she had a slightly pinkish scar on her throat, like a crack in her porcelain skin.

"I'm Ninel."

"Ninel what?"

"Just Ninel," she said coldly. "I'm double-parked, let's go."

He left some money under his cup and followed her outside. They walked to her vehicle, which was – yet again – a 4×4 Lada. The back window was partially covered with stickers: an orange sun against a yellow background with the words "NO NUKES!"; the logo for a charity supporting the children of a free clinic; a pink rectangle promoting the Gender Museum in Kharkiv; a green square with a black diagonal line across a picture of a wild boar, the words denouncing poaching in the forests of Belarus... Before getting into the passenger seat, Rybalko had to move a box full of posters announcing a meeting for the protection of fauna in Chernobyl.

"You were supposed to be here earlier," he told Ninel.

"I was trapped in Donetsk longer than expected because of the bombing."

She took a device from a bag and attached it to the dashboard, then fixed a small camera to it and turned the lens towards the road. Rybalko had seen such devices before: they were being used more and more often in Russia. In the event of an accident, the camera recording allowed the driver to support his version of the story. Apparently, in Ukraine as in Russia, nobody could trust other drivers or their insurance companies. And they particularly didn't trust the police.

Ninel set off into the dense morning traffic.

"So you're the one taking me into the forbidden zone," Rybalko said, to make conversation.

"Looks like it," she said without taking her eyes off the road. "If we don't hang around, we should get to Pripyat at the same time as the guide who discovered Leonid's body. That way, you can ask him your questions before we go to see the apartment building where he was hung."

Efficient, he thought. She was not wasting time: that suited him perfectly.

"How do you plan to get me into the zone?"

"I work for an N.G.O. that I founded in Chernobyl. It's called 1986. Part of our activities consists in measuring the impact of radiation on the fauna and flora there, so we have a permit to take samples."

"You're a biologist?"

"Ornithologist."

"Did you go to university in Moscow? You have a slight Russian accent."

Ninel shot him a strange look.

"I'm going to be up front about this: talking about my private life is not one of the services I'm being paid for."

He had not expected her to be so cold. Shrugging, he took the pack of cigarettes from his pocket.

"And no smoking in my car," she said.

What a bitch, he thought, putting his pack away.

"How long until we get there?"

"Just under two hours."

"That's going to feel like a long time, if we avoid personal questions."

"You can talk about yourself if you want. Are you married?"

"That's a very personal question."

"You don't have to answer it."

"I'm divorced."

"Recently?"

"About two years ago. But my wife's about to get remarried."

"What about you?"

"You think I'd investigate a case in a radioactive zone if I had a girlfriend?" he said.

Ninel gripped the steering wheel a little tighter and her eyes clouded over for an instant. He noticed she wasn't wearing a wedding ring. He guessed that she did not have anyone to share her life either.

"You're single," he said.

"I told you: I'm not going to answer questions about my private life."

"It wasn't a question."

She frowned.

"I hope you'll be that perceptive in your investigation," she said. Then, changing the subject: "You were in the Donbas. What do you think about what's happening there?"

This sounded like a trap to Rybalko. He tried to be diplomatic.

"I don't know what to say. I was born a Soviet. Russia is my country, and so is Ukraine. Choosing between the two of them would be like choosing between my father and my mother."

"Did your father beat your mother? Because Ukraine's covered in bruises right now."

Ninel nervously pushed a strand of hair back behind her ear. Anger deformed her delicate features.

"You don't seem very fond of Russia. . ."

"What? Me? I adore Russia. I adore Russians. I speak Russian, I eat Russian. I love Russian authors. Tolstoy, Gogol, Dostoyevsky. I love the Russian soul. I love its fucking endless plains, I love Moscow in the snow. I smoke Russian cigarettes, I drink Russian vodka. I use Russian gas to keep me warm, when they don't cut off our supply. I've fucked Russians."

There was a silence punctuated by a quiet crackling noise. In front of them, a truck transporting wheat was scattering grains on the road. They were escaping from the tarpaulin intended to prevent the wind blowing them away, and now and then they would patter against the windscreen like hail.

"The problem isn't Russia," Ninel said, "or even Russians. It's power. All those generals, all those politicians, all those businessmen who always want more power and more land. They're destroying everything. The east is in ruins, but look at the west: we're screwing things up too, between Ukrainians. Have you heard about the illegal amber mines?"

"Amber? That brown stone that people make jewellery with?"

"It's not a stone, it's fossilised tree resin. In the amber triangle, between Zhitomir, Rivne and Volyn, there's the second biggest reserve of amber in the world. Prices have quadrupled in recent years, so prospectors come from all over the country to illegally pillage the deposits. They've destroyed hundreds of acres of nature, digging up amber from the subsoil. First they cut down the trees, then they tear out the stumps and inject pressurised water into the earth. Amber is lighter than sand and soil, so it rises to the surface and they catch it in nets. By the time they're done, the earth is good for nothing and trees can't grow there anymore. It looks like a lunar landscape. And you know what the worst thing is?"

He said nothing, but she was not expecting a response.

"When they turn over the earth, those morons release radioactive dust from the Chernobyl disaster. They've destroyed about two hundred and fifty square kilometres of forest and put hundreds of people in danger just for some stupid jewellery! It's got so bad that the government has sent in the National Guard. It won't do any good though. One in ten people in that region makes their living from amber mining. The mafia take care of distribution, and the police and politicians are bribed to turn a blind eye."

Anger was digging a deep furrow between her eyebrows.

"I hate all those men who destroy the world for wealth and power. I hate them."

"And yet you work for Sokolov. One of the greediest men on the planet."

She glared at him fiercely.

"I would prefer not to make that sort of compromise. But my N.G.O. needs funding. The money Sokolov is giving me to help you allows me to keep it going for months. I don't have the luxury of getting paid for my scruples. Even if I hate the person that *you* are working for too."

At least he now knew where the woman's hostility was coming from. To cut short their discussion, she put a CD by the band Kino into the stereo. The voice of Viktor Tsoi singing "I want change" filled the car and Ninel kept her mouth shut for a good hour. . . until a barrier brought them to a halt about thirty kilometres from Chernobyl.

"This is the checkpoint for the city of Dytyatky. We have to get out and show them our permits."

There was a line of vehicles in front of the control post, mostly 4×4s and tourist minibuses.

Ninel parked next to a sign saying in Ukrainian and English that travellers were entering the zone affected by radioactive fallout from the Chernobyl nuclear accident.

"This'll take at least fifteen minutes. If you want to smoke, now's your chance."

She strode over to a sort of pergola sheltering a statue of the Virgin Mary, then made the sign of the cross in the orthodox way – touching her right shoulder before her left, unlike the Catholics. While she muttered an inaudible prayer, Rybalko smoked a cigarette and watched her. He had read somewhere that the statue had been erected in memory of the zone's victims. Had someone from Ninel's family been among the dead?

When her prayer was over, they queued up in front of the counter of the guard who controlled access to the zone. Sounding like an unfriendly tourist guide, Ninel briefly explained to Rybalko how the zone worked: "The exclusion zone is divided into two parts. We're about to enter the outer section, Zone 2. It extends to a perimeter of thirty kilometres around the power station. To get in, you need State authorisation. Further on, we'll go through another checkpoint to Zone 1, which contains all the most sensitive sites. It covers a radius of about ten kilometres. Theoretically, access to Zone 1 is more strictly guarded. But we have all the papers we need, so don't worry about it."

At last it was their turn to show the guard their permits. The guard, a fat man in combat fatigues, was sitting on a torn chair with yellowish foam showing through. After spending a long time examining the paperwork, he handed Ninel the passes and they got in the car to continue their journey to the power station.

There was very little change to suggest they had entered a poisoned land. The country roads they drove along were the same, except for the occasional glimpses between trees of collapsed fences, ruined houses, abandoned farms, wireless electric pylons.

A bird took off from the branches of a birch tree and flew past their windscreen.

"A woodcock," Ninel told him mechanically.

Remembering that she was an ornithologist, Rybalko took the autopsy photographs from his pocket and leafed through them until he found the one of the falcon.

"Does this kind of bird live in the region?"

She paled when she saw the picture of the blood-covered bird.

"What happened to it?" she asked, looking appalled. "Where did you find it?"

"Believe me, you really don't want to know. So?"

"It's a Eurasian hobby falcon."

"Is that a local species?"

"It's not an endemic species, if that's what you mean. You see them all over Europe and Asia. Including inside the zone."

"Is it possible to find out if this falcon was captured in the region?"

She shot another disgusted glance at the photograph.

"There's no ring. Impossible to know where it came from. I guess you'd have to autopsy it, if where it's from is really important for your investigation."

"Autopsy it? Why?"

She waved an arm vaguely at the forest around them. "You see all this? It's poisoned. The earth, the trees, the plants. It looks like nature is thriving again here because you see horses, wolves and wild boar. But the only reason there are more of them is that hunting has been banned for the past thirty years and there's hardly any traffic – so they don't get hit by cars."

He looked around. The treetops of the pines rose up to the blue sky where birds swooped and soared. A few deer were grazing in a grassy clearing. The forest, the lakes, the meandering rivers, the houses overgrown with weeds and brambles. . . It was hard to imagine this place as some toxic wasteland.

"Between 1986 and 1996," Ninel said, "studies were made on rodents to measure the impact of radiation on their organism. Twenty-two generations were examined. Between the tenth and the fifteenth generation, the number of *in utero* deaths started to rise dramatically before stabilising after the twentieth. The genome of those rodents had been badly damaged."

She stared intensely at Rybalko.

"You know what that would mean for human beings, twenty generations? Three to five centuries. And this earth will be poisoned for even longer. Thousands of years. Plutonium 239, for example, will be dangerous for about twenty-four thousand years."

The thickets of birches and pines looked suddenly sad. Twenty-four thousand years. . . by then the Great Wall of China would be as flat as a road and the Great Pyramid of Giza would be nothing more than a pile of rubble.

"O.K. So, the falcon?"

"If you autopsy it, you could find evidence that would allow you to determine whether the bird came from Chernobyl. For example, by studying swallows from the region, we realised that their feathers are greyer and that many of them are partly albino. About fifteen per cent have white markings on their heads. There are also more tumours and the number of swallows with below-average sized brains is higher here than anywhere else. And the females. . ."

She paused.

"A lot of them are sterile. During the reproductive period, about a quarter of them have no brood patch. That's an area on the bird's abdomen that loses its feathers a few days before the nesting season. It helps ensure better heat transmission during incubation." She left another silence, then added: "If a specialist carried out a serious analysis of the body, he could find those kinds of clues. Of course it would provide only part of the answer, not absolute proof."

The abandoned tower blocks of Pripyat appeared suddenly amid the trees. It was a disturbing sight: the model city where he had been born had become a disintegrating Disneyland whose only working attraction was the ghost train. And yet Pripyat had once been a wonderful place to live. The shelves in the shops had been full, the people had earned decent incomes, and everything had been new and well-maintained. As a child, Rybalko used to believe that all Soviet citizens lived in a city like that. It was only after he and his mother had moved to a seedy suburb of Kyiv that he realised Pripyat was the exception, not the rule. All Russians knew the legend of how, in the eighteenth century, the Russian minister Grigory Potemkin had ordered luxurious facades to be built from pasteboard for the villages of the Crimea to fool Catherine the Great into thinking that all was well in Russia. Pripyat, essentially, had been the same thing: a modern Potemkin village intended to mask the misery of life in the U.S.S.R., a place to be proudly displayed to foreign dignitaries visiting the region. The shopfront window of Soviet nuclear power, hiding a filthy back room.

They drove slowly up Lenin Avenue, the main street that led to the centre of the town. The road was in a poor state: there were potholes and even a few saplings growing through cracks in the tarmac. The windows of the apartment blocks had been broken years before and the wooden window frames banged in the wind. The rooms inside looked weather-beaten.

One of the buildings struck him as familiar.

"I lived there," he said, surprised.

He had not recognised his old neighbourhood, District 1, because of the trees that had grown anarchically and the skeletons of buses parked on the roadside, the Hungarian Ikaruses that had been used to evacuate the city. But there it was: the place where he had lived as a child, on the third floor of Apartment Building 28. Less than three hundred metres behind it was School 3 Sonyshko (Little Sun), where he had been as a kid. For a brief instant, he thought about asking Ninel to stop the car on the pavement so he could revisit his old home. Then he felt sick at the idea of finding the place wrecked.

If he went back there now, it could ruin his memories of happier days when his parents had been young and fit, before the power station destroyed their lives. Better just to keep moving forward.

Ninel turned her wide blue eyes to him. "I didn't know you used to live here."

"My father was a fireman. He was on duty the night of the accident."

The young woman's face seemed to relax slightly. "It's thanks to people like your father that the disaster was contained. We wouldn't be here now if they hadn't sacrificed themselves for us."

It was the truth, but how many people knew it? He thought bitterly that the world remembered dictators, Brazilian footballers, and artists who painted white squares on white backgrounds, but that nobody could name a single one of the people who had saved Europe from an unprecedented nuclear catastrophe. Who knew Oleksii Ananenko, Valeri Bezpalov or Boris Baranov? Who knew that they had volunteered to dive into the flooded steam suppression pool under Reactor 4 to activate its pumps and drain it before the water could reach the reactor's heart? Who knew that if the uranium magma and graphite had entered the pool, it would have led to an explosion of several megatons that would have made large parts of Europe uninhabitable?

Who knew any of this?

16

The sky was overcast when they got out of the car. On one of the apartment buildings surrounding the large square, the giant letters of an old propaganda message were still visible. "The party of Lenin is the strength of the people leading us to the triumph of communism." Rybalko remembered those words.

Clusters of tourists were photographing the emblematic buildings in the city centre. Ninel scanned their faces in search of the guide who had discovered Leonid Sokolov's body.

"That's him," she said, pointing to a man outside the Palace of Culture Energetik.

He was wearing a beige parka and there was a grey ushanka on his head, the fur-lined ear flaps lifted. Around him, a group of Japanese tourists were listening awestruck to his explanations, as if they were in a temple. Some of them were wearing white biohazard suits that made them look like crime-scene investigators in an American T.V. show.

Ninel turned back towards her vehicle. "I'll meet you here when you're done," she said.

When he reached the group of tourists, the guide was describing the inhabitants' lives prior to the disaster. He said that in the spring of 1986, just before the explosion, the people here had led a carefree existence. They had strolled through the streets, picnicked in the forest, sipped beers at the Café Pripyat on the riverbank. They had gone swimming, they had had sex (this made the Japanese giggle). The guide added that the average age of the population had been twenty-six and that the city had boasted fifteen primary schools to cope with the fast-rising birth rate. There had also been a theatre that put on productions of Soviet classics, a modern cinema, swimming pools. . . Two big shopping centres were planned, along with an art centre and two sport centres. The future had been bright.

But everything comes with a price, and cities built on volcanoes are vulnerable. He described the eruption of Reactor 4 as if it were an Old Testament story: the flames, almost black, leaping from the burst reactor; the metallic taste of the air; the firemen sacrificing them-selves to prevent the blaze spreading; the exodus of Pripyat's inhabitants; the city cursed forever by the power of the atom. . . Listening to this account of the city's fall, the Japanese tourists looked up in silence at the yellow pods of the big wheel, due to be inaugurated on May 1, 1986. What were they thinking as they stared at it? About the Fukushima power station, their very own Chernobyl, where three reactors went into nuclear meltdown in 2011 after a tsunami had destroyed the cooling system?

The guide's voice suddenly lost its lyrical power and switched to a businesslike tone: "You can walk around the square, but do not stray from the roads. As long as you remain on the tarmac, you will not be in any danger. If you get off the road, it's like going off-piste in a mountain region. Except that the avalanche will kill you ten years later."

The tourists nodded obediently, then divided into groups of three or four, some heading towards the big wheel, others towards the Hotel Polissya. The guide took a pack of Marlboros from his pocket and lit one, shielding the flame with his hand.

Rybalko approached him. "Do you have a minute?"

The guide looked irritated and raised his palm. "If you're not part of my group, I won't answer your questions."

"I was born here," Rybalko said. "I probably know more than you do about Pripyat."

The guide frowned. "What do you want then?"

"I heard you were there when they found Leonid Sokolov's body."

"The Russian guy? Why are you interested in that?"

"His family have hired me to investigate the circumstances of his death. I thought you could help me."

The guide exhaled a cloud of smoke. "I don't see how."

Rybalko took out a few banknotes. "Start by telling me where you were when you spotted the body."

The guide pocketed the money discreetly, then pointed to where the minibuses were parked.

"It was over there, on the corner of Lenin Avenue and Kurchatova Street. We'd just got off the minibus when one of the tourists cried out. I thought he must have hurt himself. Sometimes one of them will be so focused on taking pictures that they'll walk in a pothole and twist their ankle. But then I noticed that everyone was looking in the same direction."

He turned to one of the apartment blocks that lined Lenin Square, the one with the rusted emblem of the Soviet Socialist Republic of Ukraine on the roof.

"The Voskhod tower," Rybalko muttered. "Do the guides always park their vehicles in the same place?"

"Mostly, yes."

This was an important detail. With its sixteen floors, the Voskhod was one of the tallest buildings in the city. It was impossible to miss from the spot where the minibuses were parked. The killer must have known that, if he hung the corpse on the building's façade, it would inevitably be seen by tourists. That meant he knew the guides' habits. Maybe he was a guide himself. . .

"Were you the only group in the city at the time?"

"Yes."

"Had any others been here before you?"

"No. We were the first of the day."

"What did you do after you saw the body?"

"I called the guard at the checkpoint on the edge of the city."

"And he examined the body?"

"No, he called the police."

"What did you do while you waited for them to arrive?"

"Nothing. We waited inside the minibus."

"Nobody went to check if the guy was alive?"

"We were all terrified. One of my clients even had a panic attack, so I had better things to do than going to check on the body. That's the police's job."

"What happened when the police turned up?"

A Geiger counter started crackling loudly near the fairground. At the base of the big wheel, some old bumper cars sat motionless on a rusted circuit. The guide made a loudspeaker with his hands and yelled at a woman who was trying to sit in one of them.

"Do not get in! The seats are contaminated!" he yelled. "Bloody hell, some of them have no respect. . . What were you saying?"

"The police officers who came to examine the body – could you tell me about them?"

"They were two from Chernobyl. The first was called Melnyk. A surly guy, big beard, bushy hair, looks like a lumberjack. He seemed pretty shocked at finding the corpse here. The other one was a woman, really young, like she'd just got out of the police academy. This Melnyk guy asked me where the body was, then we went over to the apartment building. He went up to take a look and a few minutes later he came down looking really pissed off. We went back to the minibus, and he called his colleagues asking for reinforcements. After that, we went to the police station to make our statements."

Rybalko wrote all this down in his notebook.

"Did you notice anything else unusual that day?"

The guide raised his eyes to the sky, as if searching for an answer among the clouds.

"There were many unusual things, but no more unusual than usual if you know what I mean."

"Not really. Can you be more specific?"

The guide scratched the back of his head.

"Well, there are always little things moving around here, like ghosts passing. When we visit the school, for example, one week there'll be a doll on a bench, the next week there'll be a book there instead. Today, I noticed that the bumper cars had moved. Those kind of details, you don't notice unless you come here regularly."

"Someone's prowling around Pripyat?"

For Rybalko, the city was a fortress within the exclusion zone. Surrounded by a high fence topped with barbed wire, it was accessible only via a road monitored by a guarded checkpoint. The fence had been built thirty years earlier, when looters had started showing an interest in the abandoned buildings. Since the evacuees had only been able to take one small suitcase each, the apartments were full of televisions, fridges, radios, telephones and furniture that had rapidly found their way to the markets in Kyiv, exposing those who bought them to massive radiation levels.

"Not someone in particular," the guide said. "But there are sometimes stalkers."

Deep within Rybalko's brain, a memory stirred. A book he'd read when he was a kid. . .

"That word, 'stalker'. . . Is that a reference to the novel by the Strugatsky brothers?"

"That's right. Have you read it?"

"A long time ago. You think the killer could be one of those stalkers?"

The guide stared at the big wheel, as still as the hands of a broken clock.

"I'd be surprised. Those guys are generally pretty harmless. They're mostly dropouts, or students in search of a thrill, or romantic types who feel like they're experiencing something unique. Your killer's more likely to be a smuggler or a criminal on the run. Some of them come to these abandoned villages to hide. The police and the military can't check everywhere. The zone is vast and they're understaffed and under-equipped. They have a helicopter to monitor illegal tree-cutting, for example, but they only have enough fuel to get it up in the air once a month."

"But Pripyat's sealed off, isn't it? I saw a hut at the checkpoint, on the edge of town. There's a guard there, watching the road night and day, right?"

The guide grinned, as though Rybalko had just told him a good joke.

"That guy? A division of Russian tanks could pass by and he wouldn't even react!"

"So you're saying the killer could have stopped his car, leaned down on the counterweight to open the barrier, and driven into the city, and the guard wouldn't have lifted a finger?"

Again, the guide smiled. "On paper, Pripyat is supposed to be as safely guarded as the Kremlin. But in reality, it's probably more difficult to get into Disneyland without a ticket than to sneak in here. And the checkpoint isn't the only problem: the barbed-wire fence around the city is full of holes."

"Even so, once the killer got past the fence, he could still get caught by a patrol," said Rybalko.

This time, the guide laughed in his face. "A patrol? Ha, that's a good one! Would *you* go out in the pitch dark to check that no-one was hanging around a bunch of radioactive ruins? A patrol... You're kidding. The men on duty here spend their nights cooped up inside, watching T.V. or sleeping."

With the security forces short of numbers and equipment and being lazy too, the killer had the perfect conditions for preparing his macabre artwork. Unable to think of anything else, Rybalko handed the guide some more money and took his phone number in case any other questions came to mind.

"And, of course, I never talked to you," he said, shaking the guide's hand.

"Talked about what?" The guide winked at him, then wandered off to rejoin his tourists.

Rybalko went back to Ninel's car. The ornithologist had put on a white biohazard suit.

"Here," she said, giving him an outfit of his size.

"No need. It won't do me any good at the crime scene: it's already been contaminated."

"You're supposed to be an ornithologist. So put it on."

Rybalko sighed as he took the white suit, and grudgingly put it on before getting into the 4×4.

"Leonid's body was hung from the fifteenth floor of the Voskhod," she said as she drove towards the apartment building.

"I know. Vektor Sokolov showed me some photographs. Was it you who took them?"

"No, that was Sveta."

"Who?"

"She co-founded 1986 with me. You'll meet her soon. She works at our Chernobyl office."

Ninel parked the car opposite the tower block.

"I'll come to get you in forty minutes."

"You're not coming?"

"Up there? No way. I'm going out to take some samples, just in case the guards stop us at the checkpoint."

"From what I've just heard, they don't seem exactly meticulous."

"Better safe than sorry. And if a guide or a policeman finds you up there, tell them you're looking for raptor nests."

Rybalko peered up at the eyeless face of the Voskhod for a moment, then walked to the staircase.

The apartment where Leonid Sokolov's body had been hung was in an advanced state of disrepair. The blackened wallpaper was peeling off the walls and the ceiling was green with mould. Everything of any value had been stolen, including the radiators. There were pale rectangles on the walls, as if the radiators' white shadows had been etched there permanently.

The most surprising room was the living room, filled with stuffed animals: wolves, foxes, lynxes, every predator to be found in the nearby forests. The animals had been naturalised with such skill, Rybalko thought, that they looked as if they might attack him if he got too close. He walked past them and took a closer look at the wall near the window. There was a sort of rock-climbing bolt, with a snap link hanging from it. He understood that the killer had used this to hoist the corpse up the building. The concrete façade was still red in places where Leonid's lacerated back had rubbed against it. That explained the scrapes he had spotted during the autopsy.

Rybalko turned back to the thirty or so animals staring vacantly at him. The fastidiousness of the arrangement made him think of those history buffs who reconstruct battlefields using model soldiers, taking care to paint each stripe on their shoulders. He felt certain that Leonid's killer was himself an expert taxidermist. It tallied with the stitches on the corpse's eyes and lips and the incision in his abdomen. The killer was practiced in such actions, from cutting open dead animals and stuffing them.

Rybalko touched the coarse fur of a wolf's head and some greyish dust stuck to his palm. He rubbed his hands together to get rid of it, and the dust rose into the air. He watched the motes dance in a beam of sunlight and realised that the Ukrainian police had most likely not taken the stuffed animals as evidence because of the risks of radiation. They must have feared that there would be radioactive particles stuck to their fur.

Remembering the bird inside Leonid Sokolov's stomach, he scanned the room in search of a stuffed falcon. There were no birds of prey, but he did find a swallow perched on top of a dilapidated wardrobe. Surprisingly, its feathers were brightly coloured, while all the other animals' furs had dulled over the years. Not only that, but the bird was placed in a position directly in front of where Leonid's body had been hung. Clearly, the swallow had some significance in this morbid *mise en scène*. Rybalko decided to put it in a plastic bag so he could examine it later.

A glance at his watch: he had only twenty minutes before Ninel returned. He needed to get on with his inspection. He began by taking a few samples, especially from the top of the wardrobe where the swallow had been placed, then he took his own photographs of the living room. He spent a long time photographing the floor, even if he had little hope of detecting the killer's footprints. The local police had made such a mess with their muddy boots that probably all the evidence had been covered up.

He went downstairs at the agreed time. Ninel was waiting for him.

"What's that?" she asked, pointing at the plastic bag.

"A stuffed swallow. I found it at the crime scene."

"Why did you take it?"

Rybalko hesitated. Should he tell her that the falcon whose photograph he had shown her had been inside Leonid Sokolov's corpse? Should he tell her that the killer had a morbid obsession with stuffed animals? He decided to remain evasive.

"Just a hunch. I have a feeling this creature might mean something to the killer."

He put the swallow in the boot, next to Ninel's things.

"Make sure the bag is tightly sealed," she called from the driver's seat. "I don't want that horrible thing contaminating my samples."

17

As they drove into Chernobyl, they passed the monument dedicated to "those who saved the world", the hundreds of thousands of liquidators who cleaned the zone and built the concrete sarcophagus that imprisoned the radioactive particles inside Reactor 4.

"So where now?" Ninel said as they headed towards the city centre.

He hesitated. He needed to reconstruct Leonid Sokolov's schedule, talk to the people he had met, find the original crime scene. . . The visit to the apartment with the stuffed animals had made it clear to him that that was not where Leonid had been killed. There was no blood on the floor, no sign of the table or the straps that had been used to keep him motionless while he was tortured.

"I'd like to see the place where Leonid Sokolov stayed," he said at last.

"He stayed at the Hotel Slavutych. I booked you a room there. I thought it'd give you a chance to chat with the manager if you have any questions for him."

Good thinking. Once again, Ninel was helping him save precious time.

"I'll also need you to find me a taxidermist."

"Because of that swallow? I don't think it'll be very useful."

"Even so, I'd like to look into it."

At the end of Kirova Street, Ninel turned left into the heart of Chernobyl.

"I know someone at the Natural History Museum in Kyiv," she said. "They have collections of stuffed animals. I'll ask him to put me in touch with the person responsible for conserving them."

"Try to make the meeting as soon as possible. Every day that passes reduces our chances of finding Leonid Sokolov's killer and–"

"Those bastards!"

Ninel's yell made his ears ring. The ornithologist's cheeks went bright red. She was staring angrily at the wall of a building where someone had spray-painted the word PROSTITUTKA alongside a large swastika and the numbers 14 and 88.

"In broad daylight. . . in the middle of the city. . . those bastards!"

He realised that the wall belonged to Ninel's N.G.O., the 1986 charity. Before he could say a word, Ninel had yanked the handbrake on and run over to the building. He followed her and they went together through the front door. Inside, everything on the desks had been thrown onto the floor and the walls had been covered with graffitied insults. They heard sobs coming from behind a door at the far end of the room. Ninel stepped over the objects on the floor to reach it.

"Sveta? Is that you?"

The sobbing ceased.

"Ninel?"

"It's me, Sveta. You can open up."

They heard the clicking sound of a lock being unbolted, then a very frightened woman in her thirties appeared in the doorway. Her dark hair was dishevelled and her pale cheeks were mottled dark grey with mascara tearstains.

Ninel hugged her. "What happened, Sveta? Who did this?"

"Those thugs from the Pravyi Sektor. . ."

The Right Sector. . . Since the insurrection in the Donbas, Russian public radio had broadcast hours of reports on that far-right organisation. To begin with, it had just been a paramilitary group that fought against the president Viktor Yanukovych during the Maidan Revolution. Since then, however, its members had formed a political party and were seeking power. They found new recruits from among football club ultras, army veterans, young unemployed people, and they dreamed of establishing a Ukrainian "new order", purging the country of Russian influence. But that wasn't their only target: the previous year, they had turned up at the Pride march in Kyiv and beaten up a dozen participants.

"They came here in their big black jeep," Sveta went on. "I just had time to lock myself in the lab and–"

Sveta withdrew her head from Ninel's shoulder. She'd just noticed that they were not alone.

Ninel made the introductions: "This is Alexander Rybalko, the ornithologist from Kyiv I told you about. Alexander, this is Sveta, our rodent specialist. And a brave soldier, aren't you?" she said, ruffling her friend's hair.

"Ow!"

Sveta rubbed her head, at the edge of her scalp and her forehead.

"Are you hurt?"

"I banged my head when I was hiding under the table in the lab."

Ninel held her head in both hands and examined her scalp.

"It's swollen, but not bleeding. I'll put something on it to bring the swelling down."

Ninel vanished for a moment into the laboratory and came back with a medical kit. She took out a tube and, after putting on a pair of nitrile gloves, rubbed some ointment onto Sveta's head.

"Gently," her friend protested, pulling her head back.

"Keep still. It has to penetrate the skin."

"Did you see the faces of the men who attacked you?" Rybalko said.

"No, they were wearing balaclavas."

Her eyes welled with tears.

"I thought they were going to kill me," she sobbed.

"It's alright, calm down," Ninel murmured. "Remember the Maidan? When the police officers fired at us? We really did almost die that day. You're not going to let a couple of Nazi shitheads make you cry, are you? You're tougher than that."

Ninel spoke in a warm, gentle voice – a marked contrast to the cold hostility she had shown him on their drive from Kyiv, Rybalko thought.

"Why would a far-right organisation target you?" he said.

"Because they're rabidly anti-Russian and some of our financial support comes from Russia," Sveta said.

"Stop moving," Ninel told her, her eyes fixed on Sveta's forehead. "And don't tell lies. The truth is that we cause trouble for a lot of criminals in the zone. We regularly inform the media about what goes on there, and that bothers them. Someone paid those morons to come here from Kyiv to scare us. That's why."

She massaged the swelling a few seconds longer, then took off the greasy gloves.

"Who in particular is bothered by what you are doing?" Rybalko asked.

"Who isn't?" Ninel said. "Between the ones organising illegal hunting on the Belarusian border, the ones growing vegetables and selling them on the markets in Kyiv, the ones who pick mushrooms from radioactive forests. . . there's a whole black economy in the zone. And when we denounce them, we become targets."

She announced that she was going to call the police and that, in the meantime, they should take photographs of the premises so they could put them online and alert the public. Sveta immediately began taking shots with her mobile of every corner of the room.

Not wishing to appear in any of the pictures, Rybalko went into the laboratory. This room was big enough for four or five researchers. Inside its tiled walls there were microscopes, several machines whose purpose he could not even guess, an expensive brand-new computer, two fridges to keep the samples cold, and stacks of supplies. Russian or not, the financial backers of Ninel's N.G.O. were clearly not short of money.

A dead vole lay on top of a wooden plank on a lab bench. A red line ran along its stomach and the scalpel beside it was bloodstained. The attackers must have come as Sveta was in the middle of a dissection, he thought. He also noticed a bat on a polystyrene board. The animal's wings had been pinned in place. He was reminded of a medieval torture chamber. The specimen bore a label marked Museum of Texas Tech University.

"We work with researchers all over the world."

Rybalko spun around at the sound of Sveta's voice and his elbow knocked a plastic box to the floor. When it hit the ground, it opened a little and some blackish earth escaped.

"Sorry," he said, trying to stuff the humus back into the box. "I didn't hear you come in. I hope I didn't damage anything. . ."

"Don't worry. It's just deer shit. Or maybe elk shit? It's hard to tell the difference in the field."

Rybalko looked down at his shitstained palms. "Can I use your bathroom?"

"Of course."

He ran the hot water and used a large squirt of antibacterial soap. Who the hell collects faeces from the most radioactive place in the world? he wondered, as he washed his hands.

"So, what do you do with this. . . shit?"

"A French ecotoxicologist works with it. He uses the molecular biology to study the dietary regime of animals in the zone so he can gain a better understanding of the transfer of radionuclides between flora and fauna."

"A Frenchman, huh? Why don't I find that surprising?"

For Rybalko, the French seemed to spend most of their time wondering what to eat next, so it seemed only logical that their scientists would study the diets of elk – or deer – by examining their excrement. He wiped his hands with an old napkin while Sveta clumsily put away a collection of rodent skulls stored in a plastic tray taken from an old box of chocolates. She was a pretty woman, perhaps a little plump from eating too much good food. She had beautiful curly hair, as dark as Ninel's was pale. He guessed she must be in her early thirties.

"Ninel told me you're an ornithologist," she said.

"That's right."

Sveta shot him an ironic smile.

"Strange. You don't look much like an ornithologist."

"And what does an ornithologist look like, in your opinion?"

Ninel's face appeared in the doorway. "The police are here."

"That was quick!" Rybalko said.

"The station isn't far."

Two police officers came into the office. The first was a very young woman wearing the American-style uniform of the new Ukrainian police. The second looked like a lumberjack crossed with a bear, dressed in the old militia uniform. Thick, bushy hair; long blond beard. He gazed around at the room's disorder with a mix of resignation and annoyance.

"What happened here?" he said.

"We were attacked by the Right Sector. What do you plan to do about it?" Ninel demanded, hands on hips, as if challenging him to act.

"We'll begin by taking fingerprints," the young woman said, like a teacher's pet reciting the previous day's homework.

"No point," muttered the lumberjack. "Those guys wear gloves."

Ninel turned to Sveta. "Did they?"

"I think so."

The policewoman examined the graffiti on the sliding glass doors at the front of the premises.

"Eighty-eight. . . I remember those numbers before, at the Maidan, during the revolution. H is the eighth letter of the Latin alphabet."

"And two Hs is for Heil Hitler," her colleague said. "But what does the 14 mean?"

"Um. . ."

"It's a reference to a fourteen-word sentence by an American white supremacist," Rybalko told them.

The two police officers turned to look at him.

"We must secure the existence of our people and a future for white children," he recited in English, then translated the phrase for them.

"And who are you?" the lumberjack said.

Rybalko opened his mouth to speak, but Ninel answered in his place: "This is Professor Rybalko. He's come from Kyiv to give us a hand with our analyses."

"Rybalko, huh?"

The lumberjack looked him up and down.

"Captain Melnyk," he said, holding out his hand.

Shaking hands with Melnyk was like shaking hands with a grizzly; the palm of his paw was rough and calloused, and his grip was firm.

"My colleague, Officer Novak."

The young woman nodded at him.

"Go get the briefcase with the thingamajigs for taking samples and see what you can get," Melnyk told his colleague.

She nodded again and left the office. Melnyk turned back to Rybalko.

"So, tell me, professor, what's your area of expertise?"

"Falcons," he replied without missing a beat.

The policeman raised his eyebrows. Ninel turned a little pale.

"That's funny," Melnyk said, unsmiling. "I've had some problems because of a falcon recently."

"What sort of problems?"

"I found one dead on the front of a building. He was nesting in the wrong place."

"He was probably disorientated by the radiation."

"Probably."

The two men sized each other up for a moment. Then Melnyk turned to the graffiti-covered doors.

"The Right Sector. As if we didn't have enough on our plates already... I'll check the list of people who've entered the zone in recent days to find out who did that. Until they've been identified and taken into custody, however, I would advise you to close your office."

"Out of the question," Ninel said. "We're not going to let ourselves be intimidated by a bunch of stupid Nazis. This is my home."

Novak reappeared looking sheepish.

"The boot won't open."

"You don't know the protocol for when that happens?"

"I... no."

"You hit it."

"I don't want to damage a patrol car..."

"Ha, you'd be lucky! You're the one who'll get damaged. That old banger has been breaking my back for years. Come on, I'll show you how to do it..."

They went out. Ninel turned to Sveta.

"Go and ask them how long they will need to take fingerprints."

"Um, O.K.," Sveta said, looking confused. "But I don't see—"

"Just go."

Sveta obeyed. As soon as she had left the office, Rybalko felt Ninel's hard little fist pound into his shoulder.

"A specialist in falcons?" she hissed. "Are you a total idiot or what?"

She's got quite a punch for a featherweight, he thought, rubbing his shoulder.

"I had to think on my feet. I figured if he asked me about them, I could just repeat what you told me about Eurasian hobby falcons."

She glared at him. "What a brilliant idea. Now Melnyk probably has doubts about you. That's just going to make things more difficult for you."

"There's no need to get upset. Everything will be fine."

"I hope so. The charity could lose its accreditation if they find out who you really are."

He lowered his eyes. He had no idea he was endangering her N.G.O.

"I'm sorry. I should have thought more carefully."

She handed him a stack of paperwork and a bunch of keys.

"These are your permits to be shown at the checkpoints, the key for the office and the key for the charity's pick-up truck. It's parked out there. You can't miss it: it has our logo on the doors. Use it whenever you want. Sveta and I can drive our own vehicles."

"You're not coming with me to Slavutych?"

"No, I'm going to stay here and tidy up. Besides, I wouldn't be any good to you there."

She took a G.P.S. from a drawer.

"I've put a few locations in here to help you find your way around. There's the address for the hotel in Slavutych and the one for my apartment in Kyiv. Call me if you need anything. And one more thing. . ."

She picked up a large ornithology manual from a shelf.

"Read this! It'll help prevent you saying something stupid if you're asked any questions about falcons."

18

The vehicle was parked opposite the office: an off-white pick-up truck painted with the logo of a blue bird whose folded wings curved around the number 1986. Inside the vehicle, Rybalko set up the G.P.S. and drove to Slavutych.

The town was just under fifty kilometres west of Pripyat. The Soviet authorities had commissioned the construction of Slavutych just after the explosion of Reactor 4. They needed to replace the now uninhabitable Pripyat as a home for the power plant employees and their families. As crazy as it might seem, the other reactors continued working until 2000.

The air there was thick with boredom, the landscapes monotonous.

In Slavutych, he found the streets almost as empty as in Chernobyl, lined by identical tower blocks, punctuated by lifeless squares. The cemetery was filled with people who had died before the age of forty. A quarter of the town's 20,000 inhabitants were under eighteen and they were bored out of their brains. So they would take drugs, go dancing, fuck each other and drink too much. Since the power plant had shut down, the whole region had sunk even deeper into the mire of mass unemployment.

The town's only hotel was the imaginatively named Hotel Slavutych. It was recently built, and while the décor of the lobby was somewhat sterile and impersonal, at least everything looked to be clean and new. A man was doing crosswords behind the reception desk. He had the yellowish complexion of someone with liver problems and his worn jumper seemed to date from an era when listening to the Beatles could land you in prison.

"I have a reservation in the name of Rybalko."

The man wearily consulted the register.

"You said Rybalko? I have nothing in that name, sorry."

"Try with Ninel."

"Ninel what?"

"Just Ninel."

Another weary look at the register.

"Ninel. . . reservation for a week, single room. It's on the first floor. If you'd follow me. . ."

The man struggled to his feet.

"Hang on, first I'd like to ask you a few questions about one of your clients."

The man sat down again, reluctantly.

"Let me guess. You want to know about the man who died. You're a policeman, are you?"

"Private detective. I'm working for the dead man's family."

The man made a dismissive gesture. "I already told the police everything."

Rybalko took out a bundle of banknotes and lined four of them up on the counter. Greed lit up the receptionist's hitherto vacant eyes.

"And what exactly did you tell them?"

"Not much," the man said, his gaze riveted to the money. "The Russian turned up just over a month ago and booked a room."

"He was alone?"

"Well, the room was booked for one person, but there was nothing to stop him taking a girl up to his room."

"And did he?"

"Dunno. . . I did see him with a woman once, in the car park, when I came in for the morning shift."

"Could you describe her?"

"Um. . . pretty."

"Go on. Height, eye colour, that kind of thing. . ."

"She was blonde, I think."

"Can you be more specific?"

"I dunno, I saw her from a distance."

Rybalko removed one of the banknotes from the counter.

"Hey, what are you doing?"

"The information you're giving me is useless. Try being more precise if you want to be paid. Did Leonid Sokolov tell you the reason he was staying here?"

The man scratched his head.

"No. But then I didn't ask him. . . Mostly we just said hello to each other."

Rybalko reached out to remove another note.

"Hang on! One evening, he asked me how to get to Poliske. He wanted to see someone there."

"Poliske? I thought all the villages in the zone had been evacuated."

"They had. But some people have gone back to live in certain villages, like Lubyanka and Kupovate. We call them *samosely*."

"And the police do nothing?"

"Most of them are just harmless old people going back to live in their old houses. The police used to drive them out, but they just kept returning, so in the end they turned a blind eye."

"O.K., so Leonid was trying to get to Poliske. . ."

"I told him to reserve a tour with an operator, but he wanted to go there without an official guide. I explained that wasn't possible, but he wouldn't let it go, so I said he'd have to either get through the barbed wire and find his own way there or ask a stalker to guide him."

Rybalko sighed. Tourist buses, stalkers, people living in supposedly evacuated villages, smugglers, neo-Nazis. . . Clearly the population of the zone was much higher than he had imagined. A fact that complicated his investigation.

"And this person he wanted to see in Poliske, do you know their name?"

"Um. . . Kazimira. . . Kazimira something. He asked me if I knew her. Apparently she lived here, in Slavutych, before she went back to the zone. I told him her name didn't ring any bells for me, but that he'd have no trouble finding her in Poliske because there were only a handful of people living there."

"Did you tell the police about this Kazimira woman?"

"No, I just remembered it now."

"Good. Well, try to forget her name again."

Rybalko pushed the cash towards the man, who swiftly pocketed it.

"Is the room that Leonid Sokolov occupied vacant at the moment?"

"Um. . . yeah. . ."

"I'll take it, if that's not a problem."

The man reached for the key and put it on the counter. Rybalko went up to the room. He gave it a cursory search but didn't find anything that might have been left behind by Leonid Sokolov. Next, he spent a while observing the stuffed bird he had brought with him from Pripyat. It really was quite a work of art, if you can use the word art for something that consists of stripping a dead body of its skin and organs. The illusion of life was perfect: he had the impression that if he let it go, it would fly away. Alive on the outside, but dead inside. . . the bird was a bit like him, in fact. He thought about Marina and Tassia. It was lunchtime. He imagined them eating *pelmeni*, that Ukrainian ravioli dish that Marina was so good at.

God, he missed that.

He had to be content with a sandwich from a local minimarket, a *buterbrodik* with paté, then he took out the dossiers that Sokolov had given him: immersing himself in work was an excellent way of not thinking about the future. When he finally looked up from the papers, the sun had set and the sky over Slavutych was dark. In the apartment buildings he could see from his window, there were only a few lit rectangles remaining. They too would soon be plunged into darkness. In Slavutych, electricity was a precious commodity: ironic when you considered that hundreds of the city's inhabitants used to get up every day to work at a nuclear power station. The White Angel, the monumental statue erected in the centre of the Soviet housing estate, was one of the few illuminated spots in the city. Its ghostly figure rose up in the anaemic light of the streetlamps around its base. Rybalko had heard that the local authorities had cut spending on gas to fund its construction, so everyone in the city had been forced to take cold showers for a month. Did the inhabitants feel a measure of pride, looking out at the sculpture from their darkened windows?

At last he collapsed onto his bed. He was exhausted, yet sleep would not come. The bed base creaked every time he moved. Questions circled his head. Why had Leonid Sokolov been willing to break the law to go to Poliske? Who was Kazimira?

Staring up at the darkness, Rybalko spent a long time thinking of how the killer had displayed his dead victim. He visualised the body's slow rise up the side of the apartment building, then the movement of its arms, unfolded at the last moment, held outstretched by metal cables wrapped around his wrists, like the wings of a bird that might otherwise fly away. Suddenly all of this slotted together in his mind: the ascent, the abdomen gutted then stuffed, the dead falcon. . .

He turned on his bedside lamp and took out the notebook he was using for the investigation. He turned to the page where he had written that the murder's *mise en scène* featured the image of a crucifixion, crossed that word out and wrote in the margin: "Flight".

146

The killer had not intended to show a crucifixion, but a man in flight, arms outstretched like wings.

A sort of spectacular, monstrous naturalisation.

19

The next morning, after struggling awake, Rybalko examined his reflection in the bathroom mirror, particularly the nascent beard that was taking over his cheeks and neck. Before learning he had only a few months to live, he used to shave every day. It was a ritual that went back to his military service. One of the consequences of knowing he would soon be dead was that many things which used to eat up his time now seemed pointless. Washing his car? Shaving? Ironing his clothes? Who cared? Making plans? Forget it. . .

Before leaving for the zone, he stopped at a café in the Estonian quarter, the Staryi Tallinn, and ordered a hearty breakfast of pork, cheese and fresh bread. He ate in silence, listening distractedly to the conversations around him. He heard the same things he might have heard from the person next to him in a carriage of the *platzkart*, the third-class train on the Trans-Siberian railway network: the difficulties of making ends meet, the price of petrol and vodka, the results of the latest football match, rumours of political skulduggery. . . Sometimes they would mention the war in the east and their voices would grow quieter. Someone's son had joined the front, another's daughter was a volunteer nurse there. . . And then, after a silence, they would quickly change the subject.

After his breakfast, he drove to Poliske. Along the road, peaceful forests alternated with neglected fields, planted here and there with triangular signs warning of a highly contaminated zone – sad scarecrows that that had no effect on the large black crows hunting for rodents in the tall grass. He drove for more than two hours before Poliske appeared through a row of trees. Silent and deserted, the village seemed to be holding its breath. Hard to imagine that, prior to the accident, it had been the second biggest town in the region, with more than 12,000 inhabitants.

Since he had no idea where exactly this Kazimira lived, he drove slowly through the empty streets, searching for signs of life: a single lit-up window in an apartment block, smoke rising from a chimney, vegetables growing near an old izba, a tame-looking cat or dog.

On the wall of the old corner shop, graffiti proclaimed that the inhabitants of Poliske were Judases, that you should always remember your hometown, that the flowers were growing without them, and that their parents' graves would not forgive them for abandoning the town. A song from before the fall of the communist regime began looping inside Rybalko's head:

My address is not a house or a street
My address is the Soviet Union.

Like Pripyat, this place still seemed to belong to the U.S.S.R.: worn, crepuscular, decaying. Rows of collapsed houses lined the streets. Occasionally a sign in a garden would pronounce that the owner still lived there, but nobody answered the door when he knocked. These shaky izbas were all silent. Growing inside one of them he even saw a tree, its branches reaching out through the broken, ground-floor windows. A sort of inverted taxidermy, Rybalko thought: the inanimate becoming alive.

Near the church, he found an old woman sitting on a bench. She wasn't Kazimira, but she told him the way to Kazimira's house. He drove until he reached a wooden izba with blue shutters. In the garden behind the vegetable plot surrounded by a dilapidated fence, he saw a washing line hung with women's clothes.

"Hello, anyone here?"

He waited a moment, then walked around the vegetable garden. When he returned to the front door, he saw an old woman walking slowly up the road, pulling a small cart filled with firewood behind her.

"Hello, babushka," Rybalko called out.

The old woman's leathery face cracked into a toothless smile.

"American? Journalist?" she said, articulating exaggeratedly.

"Soviet. I was born near here. Are you Kazimira?"

"Yes, that's me."

"I have some questions to ask you about a man who might have come to see you. Does the name Leonid Sokolov mean anything to you?"

"Olga's son? He came here about a month ago."

"Olga? You knew his mother?"

"Of course. We were colleagues. We both worked at a school in Pripyat before the disaster."

She squinted at him.

"But I know you!" she exclaimed. "You're the poet's son. Little Pushkin!"

His throat swelled with emotion. He hadn't expected anyone here to remember him, let alone to know the nickname his mother had given him. Pushkin. . . She'd named him Alexander in homage to the most famous Russian novelist, Alexander Sergeyevich Pushkin, who had also been of mixed blood. Rybalko's mother had been the only woman of colour in Pripyat. A Cuban comrade who worked at the Palace of Culture and spoke Russian with a delicious accent.

"Come in, come in," the old woman said warmly. "Would you like some tea?"

He was in a hurry, but he did not have the heart to tell her no. He offered to help her with the firewood, but she refused and lurched slowly towards the house, dragging her burden after her. Inside, the izba looked like a village shop. The shelves were filled with round jars. Pickles, dried tomatoes, strawberries, mushrooms. There were tins of *tushonka* too – beef stew. Enough food to last for weeks. Most of the products appeared to come from her vegetable garden or the surrounding forest, like the aromatic herbs – mint and savoury – that were hung upside down from the ceiling to dry. In the small courtyard behind the house, he saw a high pile of firewood, interspersed with objects the old woman must have found in abandoned buildings: wooden chair legs, drawers, banisters sawn into bits. Nobody needed them now, after all, so she may as well use them to keep her house warm.

"Have you lived here long?" Rybalko said.

"A few years," she said vaguely. "I didn't like living in Slavutych. I had an apartment there and I found it hard to make ends meet. Here, I have my vegetable garden, and the forest is close by, so I have enough wood to keep me warm in winter, and enough herbs and roots to season my meals the rest of the year."

The water started to boil. Kazimira served the tea. Just before he took his first sip, Rybalko saw the well in the garden and realised that the water he was about to swallow had come from there. He thought about the rain soaking through the earth's polluted strata, then the contaminated liquid running down his throat and into his stomach before spreading radiation through his entire body.

He moved the cup away from his lips.

"Is there a problem?" Kazimira asked him.

She sipped her tea peacefully while he sat there motionless. Suddenly he saw the ludicrousness of the situation. What was he afraid of? He had less than six months to live. Refusing to drink this liquid when he was thirsty was as meaningless as worrying about the warnings on cigarette packets.

"No, no problem," he said, before taking a drink. It was very good.

For almost an hour they chatted about life in the zone. He learned that almost everyone in the abandoned villages was female now. Most of the men had died long before, killed by depression, alcohol and radiation.

The old woman's eyes misted over and she began to gaze nostalgically at a piece of cloth about thirty centimetres wide that hung on a wall in the kitchen. Perfectly white, the fabric was covered with delicate red and black embroidery. As he examined the patterns, Rybalko realised that this must be the *rushnyk* she had made for her own wedding. When he had married Marina, their hands had been tied together with a similar kind of cloth during the ceremony at the church.

At the bottom of the cloth, a pair of birds faced each other. Rybalko knew that every image on the *rushnyk* had a meaning.

"What do those birds represent?" he asked Kazimira.

"The doves? They symbolise harmony and love between the newlyweds."

"Did people ever embroider swallows on *rushnyki?*"

She thought for a moment.

"Hmm, I've seen peacocks and cockerels, but swallows? I don't think so."

"What about falcons?"

"Falcons. . . yes, sometimes. Actually, I remember now that the only bird you're supposed to avoid is a nightingale, because it represents a philanderer, luring young women with his beautiful words as the bird attracts its partners with its song. Oh, and the cuckoo too, because it symbolises widows."

A falcon, a swallow. . . was it possible the killer was using symbolism drawn from old Slavic rites? Rybalko put this idea in the back of his mind and decided it was time to question the babushka about Leonid Sokolov's visit.

"Why did Leonid come to see you?"

"He wanted to talk about his mother. She and I worked together for years."

"What exactly did he want to know?"

She turned her empty teacup in her wrinkled hands.

"Why are you interested in that, Alexander?"

"His father asked me to investigate what happened to him. You know he was murdered?"

She nodded sadly.

"I knew he was taking a risk by coming here," Kazimira said. "He told me he was trying to find out the truth about his mother's death. He had good reasons to believe that the killer was still alive and that he lived in the zone."

"How could he be so sure about that?"

"He had evidence. A locket that had belonged to Olga. Her photo-graph was inside."

"Did he show it to you?"

"Yes. He told me she'd been wearing it the day she was murdered.

He said he'd had it examined in a laboratory and they'd found two different D.N.A. traces: his mother's and that of a man who was not his father. That was why he'd come back to the region. He wanted to find the man whose D.N.A. it was."

"Like trying to find a needle in a haystack."

"Apparently he had someone in mind."

"Who?"

"I think he suspected Piotr Leonski."

"The husband of the woman who was killed on the same night?"

"That's right. Larissa. She worked at the school with Olga and me. And Leonid asked me. . ."

She hesitated. Rybalko nodded, encouraging her to continue.

"He asked me if I thought she'd been cheating on her husband."

"Had she?"

Kazimira looked embarrassed by this turn in the conversation.

"Larissa was a quite a. . . a liberated woman. But I don't know if that was just a façade or if she really had relationships with other men. There were rumours, of course, but Olga said they were all lies. It was normal that Olga should defend her. Their daughters played together, they regularly ate dinner at each other's houses, they belonged to the same clubs. . ."

"Wait a minute," Rybalko said. "Their daughters? Olga and Vektor Sokolov had a daughter?"

The only photographs he had seen at Sokolov's mansion had been of Leonid, so he had supposed he was an only child.

"Of course. She comes to see me sometimes when she's working in the area. You might know her. Her name's Ninel."

20

Half an hour later, he left Kazimira's house, his head buzzing with questions. He had been sickened when he found out that Ninel was Sokolov's daughter. Why hadn't she mentioned that when they first met? Why hide her connection with Leonid?

Outside, the pick-up truck was leaning oddly to one side. When he got closer, he saw that the two tyres on that side were flat. Thankfully there were two spare wheels under the tarp that covered the back of the vehicle. Punctures must be common around here, he thought, pulling up the sleeves of his jumper.

He was changing the first tyre when a black 4×4 appeared at the crossroads and drove slowly towards him. The passenger side window rolled down and a hard-faced man looked him over.

"You new around here?" the stranger said.

He had very short hair and there was something military about his bearing.

"I work for the 1986 charity," Rybalko said, nodding at the logo on the side of the truck.

"Oh yeah? So you work for those two bitches?"

The man leaned his elbow through the open window. There was a tattoo of a Third Reich-style eagle on his forearm. Rybalko tensed. He assumed that he was face to face with one of the men who had vandalised Ninel's office.

"You shouldn't wander around the zone like that," the man said, lighting a cigarette. "It's a dangerous place. Didn't your girlfriends tell you?"

Adrenaline was rushing through Rybalko's veins. He was unarmed, in the middle of nowhere, with no means of calling for help. His gaze flickered to the tyre iron he had left in the back of the truck. Would he have time to grab it if things turned bad?

"It's not just the radiation," the man said. "All sorts of stuff could happen to you here. Have you heard about the Russian they found dead in Pripyat? He was a guy like you, who had no business being here, didn't know anything about it. Didn't turn out too well for him, did it? So, if I were you, I'd get out of here quickly. This is no place for Russkies. Or for darkies..."

Rybalko was seething now, but he tried not to let it show.

"Round here, people who stick their noses into things don't live long. They get killed, and sometimes their bodies are never found. They get dumped in a cellar and then the house above it goes up in flames. And seeing how everything round here is contaminated, nobody ever comes to see what's underneath the ruins. So, a word of advice: fuck off home, *negro*."

The neo-Nazi tossed his cigarette stub at Rybalko's feet and the 4×4 sped off, leaving him alone with his flat tyres. And then as he looked at them, he saw that they had been slashed with a knife.

THE LIFE OF OTHERS

21

After his disappointment with the Russian green woodpecker, Melnyk decided to focus his investigation on the K.G.B. lead. He learned from Oksana that the Soviet secret service archives were kept in Kyiv, in a building belonging to the S.B.U., the intelligence agency that had replaced the K.G.B. when Ukraine became an independent country. Best of all, by dint of a law passed after the Maidan Revolution, the archives were accessible to all Ukrainian citizens, which meant he would not have to waste any precious time jumping through bureaucratic hoops.

Finding the reading room for the archives was less easy, however. Since the building was also home to the active departments of the S.B.U., access was strictly controlled. At the reception desk, he had to call an archivist from an old telephone with a round dial, then wait for him to come downstairs and accompany him to a metal detector where a guard checked all entries into the more sensitive areas of the building. After showing his I.D., he was finally allowed to enter the reading room, a small, austere room were historians carried out research and where curious citizens could find out what had happened to members of their family during the communist dictatorship. The room was big enough for six people, eight if they were squeezed close.

The archivist asked Melnyk to wait for a moment, then reappeared with a grey cardboard box and a pair of headphones that looked like the kind that airline pilots wore.

"There are cassettes as well as paper files," the S.B.U. employee explained.

"Do they still work after thirty years?"

"You can tell me that. I found an old tape recorder in the storeroom."

The archivist gestured to an ancient-looking black plastic machine. Melnyk smiled as he recognised the cassette recorder: it was a Legend-404, a genuine museum piece. Only the rich had been lucky enough to own one of these in the 1980s.

"I didn't think those old *sovok* things still existed," the archivist said, laughing. "I won't ask if you know how to use it. I bet you had one of these when you were young!"

Melnyk glared at him in silence. In Russian slang, the word *sovok* could be translated as "old-fashioned Soviet crap". It also meant dustpan. The archivist was in his twenties. He belonged to the Coca-Cola-iPhone-Internet generation, who regarded all remnants of the Soviet world with a mocking eye. Jolting old Ladas were *sovok*, and so were old men like Melnyk.

The archivist handed him the dossier and the headphones, then gestured to the reading room monitor. "If you need anything, ask my colleague over there. You can photocopy documents or photograph them with your mobile, but you're not allowed to take any archives out of this room. We also have a scanner, if necessary. For the cassettes, I doubt if we have anything that could record them, so I'd advise you to transcribe them manually."

"That could take a while."

"You have until closing."

Melnyk remembered 1980s cassettes containing an hour or two of recordings. It was highly unlikely that he would have time to transcribe the whole thing that day. And then there was the dossier itself, which he had to photocopy.

"I'm here for a criminal investigation, not to find out how Stalin killed my grandfather. Can't I take the cassettes with me?"

"Sorry, the rules are the rules. But if you haven't finished we could put the documents aside for a few days."

Melnyk did not insist. He sat at his little bit of table and opened the box. The first thing he found inside was a 300-page investigation report. Its pages smelled of old Soviet paper: a mix of mould and dried fish. He put it aside and concentrated on the audio cassette. He slid it into the tape recorder and put the headphones over his ears. As he pressed "play", he prayed that the tape would still be audible.

At first there was only static. That sound took him back many years, to when he would listen to music at the houses of friends whose parents were wealthy enough to have a cassette recorder. He had had to be content with his parents' old record player and some pirate vinyl made on Pyral engraving machines. Until the 1960s, when the Soviet regime stopped censuring all western music, they had had to make do with whatever they had to hand if they wanted to listen to the latest pop music from the other side of the Iron Curtain. Ever resourceful, the pirates stole X-rays from hospitals, made a hole in the middle with a lit cigarette, cut the X-ray into a circle, and engraved music onto it. That was how the teenage Melnyk had ended up with his father's strange record collection, twenty or so American standards recorded on images of sick people's chests.

What came through the headphones, however, was not American rock music, but the deep voice of a K.G.B. agent.

"Interrogation of Piotr Leonski, July 15, 1986. Comrade, identify yourself."

The voice was curt, authoritarian, a voice used to giving orders. Leonski's was frail and hesitant.

"My name is Piotr Mikhailovich Leonski. I'm twenty-six and I was born in Kyiv. My father worked in a metalworking factory and my mother was a bus conductor. But I already said all this, do I really need to—"

"I will decide what is necessary and what is not necessary. You will repeat it for as long and as often as I want you to, comrade Leonski. Understood?"

"Yes, comrade colonel."

"Now tell me about yourself."

"About myself? What do you want to know?"

"Everything."

"I don't understand."

"I want you to tell me the story of your life from birth until today, comrade."

"But why—"

"Do what I say."

There followed a long monologue punctuated by questions that were quite often private and embarrassing: did he love his mother or his father more? Did he report their anti-Soviet activities? His first girlfriend was secretly Orthodox – did he know that? How did it make him feel to learn that she had been deported to a gulag in Siberia?

"Did you tell your wife about what you did at the power plant?"

"Not much. I mean not at all."

"*Not at all* and *not much* are not the same thing, comrade Leonski."

"What I mean is. . . I didn't talk to her about the work itself, but the stuff around it. I'd say, 'We had a hard day today and I'm tired', or 'So-and-so told a joke in the cafeteria today and we all laughed'."

"Tell me that joke."

"Um. . . sorry?"

"You heard. Tell me that joke."

"A. . . a group of workers are walking past a school and there's a window open. . . the teacher is making one of the students recite his multiplication tables and, er. . ."

"Go on."

"The teacher asks: 'What is six times six?' and the student quickly answers: 'Thirty-seven'."

"Six times six is thirty-six," the investigator's cold voice says.

"I know, but that's why it's funny, because one of the workers turns to the rest of the group and says: 'Thirty-seven! Since Andrei Gromyko's been in power, everything's going up!'"

There was a staticky silence.

"Are you questioning our leaders' policies, comrade Leonski?"

"No, of course not!"

"Yet that's precisely what you just did."

"It was only a joke."

"Do you often make anti-patriotic jokes?"

"No, no. . . it was more my colleagues who did that."

"Give me their names."

"I. . . I don't remember."

"Comrade, I am sure you remember the name of the person who told that joke. Unless you would prefer to accept responsibility for the joke yourself?"

Leonski suddenly regained his memory: "Anton Winograd. He was the joker."

"Thank you, comrade. We're going to take a break now, while I transmit that information."

An awkward silence fell. Melnyk looked around him at the other researchers, absorbed in reading their files. With the headphones covering his ears, he felt like a Stasi policeman spying on a private conversation between two East German citizens. He leafed through the dossier, trying to spot the K.G.B. man's name, but found only a service number, which he wrote down in his notebook.

"Interrogation of comrade Leonski, starting again. Had your wife been asking you more questions about your work at the power station recently?"

"Will Anton be in trouble?"

"You're in a lot more danger than he is. Answer the question."

"No. She knew she wasn't supposed to ask questions about that."

"Are you sure?"

"Yes, why?"

"Because we need to categorically disprove a theory that is bringing my superiors out in a cold sweat, comrade Leonski. Your wife had access, through you, to strategic information on the functioning of the power station. . ."

"But I didn't tell her—"

"Do not interrupt me, comrade! As I was saying: your wife had access, through you, to precise technical data about the power station.

Comrade Sokolov's wife also had access to sensitive information via her husband. Do you see where I'm going with this?"

"You think my wife was involved in some sort of. . . plot?"

The K.G.B. man responded as if reciting something learned by heart:

"We are currently examining all theories that might explain how Reactor 4 of the Vladimir Ilyich Lenin Power Station could have exploded. One of them involves an outside intervention. And by 'outside', I mean the capitalist countries, and the United States of America in particular. If the Americans caused the explosion, they must have had precise information enabling them to carry out their sabotage operation. They would have needed contacts, people in a position to provide them with our nuclear secrets. Now, I know that your wife had family in Berlin. Some in the east, and some in the west."

"She hadn't been in contact with them for a long time. The ones in the west, I mean."

"Did you know that she had a brother under surveillance by the Stasi?"

"What? But why? What had he done wrong?"

Leonski seemed shocked at this news about his brother-in-law.

"That is not your concern. You need only know that our East German comrades have good reasons to believe that he is carrying out anti-Soviet activities. If we know this, then so do the Americans. They might have offered to exfiltrate him from Berlin in exchange for your wife supplying them with information."

"No, this is crazy! She would never have aided the enemies of our people!"

"Are you sure? You spent a lot of time at the power station. She could have done all this behind your back."

"I would have known. She'd never have been able to hide something that serious from me."

"So, there was nothing suspicious about her behaviour?"

There was a long silence. At last the K.G.B. officer said impatiently:

"Well?"

"She was a little more distant, but that's all. But I don't understand where you're going with this: if she'd given information to the Americans on how to sabotage the power station, why would they kill her?"

"Because that's how capitalists work. Once the crime has been committed, they get rid of their agent. The number of stab wounds would just be a way of throwing us off the scent by making it look like a crime of passion."

Melnyk thought about the discussion he had had with Arseni on his boat in Strakholissya. Was it really possible that the two women found dead in 1986 had been involved in the Chernobyl explosion?

"I never talked to Larissa about what I was doing at the power station."

"You told her about your friend Anton's jokes."

"But that's all! I swear."

"Very well. Let us hope that your brother-in-law backs up your claims. Our Stasi comrades are interrogating him at this very moment. If his sister had told him about a deal with the Americans, they will find out. You can trust them. They're very persuasive."

Melnyk could not help shivering at that.

"Let's change the subject. Comrade, how would you describe your relationship with your wife?"

"She was the love of my life, the apple of my eye, she—"

"Did you argue?"

"Of course. Just like all couples do."

"Did you beat your wife?"

Again, Leonski took some time to respond, as if he was weighing up how much to say.

"Well, comrade?"

"No."

"You took a long time to answer. Are you sure what you just told me is true?"

"I might have slapped her a couple of times, but nothing serious."

Melnyk thought how in the U.S.S.R. – and even in Ukraine now – the authorities were overly tolerant towards domestic violence. Leonski knew he would not get in trouble for this kind of confession. It was, unfortunately, part of the country's moral make-up.

"Who could have wanted your wife dead?"

"Nobody! Everyone liked her."

The officer asked him to repeat what he had been doing at the time when Larissa was killed. Leonski explained that he had been at the power station, working the night shift. He was working on a reactor – not the one that exploded. He said that after the accident, he had decided to get out of there so he could protect his family. His twins were spending the night at their neighbours' house for a birthday party sleepover, while his wife was at their dacha.

"Your wife had sexual intercourse before being killed."

"The killer raped her."

"We found alcohol and two glasses in the sink. Your wife was wearing expensive lingerie. She was with a lover."

"I. . . Larissa never slept with any other men."

"How can you be sure of that? You spent most of your time at the power station. Perhaps she wasn't alone in your dacha. Here's one possible scenario: she met her lover there, you went to find her, discovered him there, and you murdered her. Olga Sokolov heard something, she knocked at the door, then entered the dacha. She saw you with the knife, so you killed her too. You stabbed her in the heart."

"I would have been covered in blood!"

"You were in your dacha. All you had to do was get changed and bury your bloodstained clothes."

"This is crazy! So what happened to the lover?"

"Maybe you waited until he'd gone. Like a coward. Or maybe you didn't actually see him, you just sensed his presence. Maybe you smelled him on your wife's skin. A bottle of alcohol and two glasses. You wouldn't need to be a detective to work that one out."

"This is insane. . ."

The K.G.B. man continued impassively:

"If we eliminate the crime of passion and the American sabotage operation, only one possibility remains. And I'm not sure you'll like it. Have you heard about the lesopolosa killer, comrade?"

Lesopolosa. . . Melnyk wrote the word down and underlined it twice. As for the expression "the lesopolosa killer", Melnyk had heard it before. The lesopolosa were communal forests made available to the population by the Soviet government during the U.S.S.R. era. Anyone could go there to walk, hunt, collect firewood or pick berries. In reality, though, it was often used as a dumping ground. It wasn't unusual to find dead bodies in such zones.

"Four years ago, the corpse of a thirteen-year-old girl was found near Donskoy, a small town near the River Don, about one hundred kilometres from the Ukrainian border. Her body had been hidden in a strip of forest between a cornfield and the road leading to Zaplavskaya, a small village where a young girl had disappeared a few days earlier. Is this ringing any bells?"

This murder had occurred before Glasnost, the policy of freedom of expression implemented in the U.S.S.R. in 1986. Prior to that, newspapers rarely mentioned crimes and were heavily censored.

"The girl's corpse was badly damaged. It was the middle of the summer and the days were hot, so the body was in a state of advanced decomposition. She was naked, her legs spread. Her hands were raised, as if she'd been protecting herself. The coroner counted twenty-two knife wounds, some in the genital areas, others around the eyes, which had been gouged out."

Melnyk started to feel nauseous as he remembered Leonid Sokolov's sewn-up eyelids.

"How horrible! How could anyone do such awful things in our country?"

Leonski's naivety was almost laughable. By the mid-1980s, communist propaganda had made Soviet citizens believe that murder was extremely rare in the U.S.S.R., in contrast to what was happening in capitalist countries. As for rape and sexual deviance, they were regarded as nonexistent. In fact, hardly anybody talked about sexuality at all in those days.

"Other corpses were soon discovered in the region's forests," the K.G.B. officer went on. "Other women with stab wounds around their eyes and genitals. At this moment, we're talking about more than ten murders that have elements in common."

A serial killer, Melnyk thought. At the time, the police in western countries, particularly the United States, were beginning to understand the motivations of such murderers, but in the Soviet Union it was still an area of ignorance. For the militia, used to dealing with crimes motivated by money or jealousy, or crimes committed under the influence of alcohol, the idea of someone who killed for the pleasure, following a precise ritual, was scarcely imaginable.

What if the murderer of Olga Sokolov and Larissa Leonski had killed other people before? There were similarities between the bodies left behind by the lesopolosa killer and those two women in Pripyat. Larissa had been stabbed multiple times, including enough wounds around her face to heavily disfigure her. She and Olga had both had their eyes gouged out. Leonid Sokolov's eyelids had been sewn up. Maybe his eyeballs had been gouged out too?

"I believe you have family in east Ukraine, comrade Leonski. Do you visit them often?"

"Two or three times a year at most. Surely you don't think—"

"That you're twisted enough to have killed all those people in the Rostov region? I don't know. But I wouldn't hesitate to pin those crimes on you if you don't confess to killing your wife and Olga Sokolov. And the consequences would not be the same. A judge might be lenient towards a man who murdered his wife in a fit of anger and who killed a witness to save himself. Maybe you'd get away with a life sentence. But for ten murders you would undoubtedly be sentenced to death."

There was a cry of anguish, followed by sobbing. Leonski was about to crack. After a while, his trembling voice could be heard again.

"I'm innocent! None of this makes any sense. I didn't kill my wife. I didn't kill Olga Sokolov. I will never say I murdered them because it's not true."

"As you like. In that case, when your interrogation is over, we'll put you in a cell for as long as it takes for the truth to emerge."

"On what charge? You have nothing on me!"

"You deserted the power station during a major nuclear accident."

"I did it to save my family!"

"To save yourself, you mean. We're going to take a break now while you think about your situation. In the meantime, I'm going to call the militia in Rostov-on-Don to tell them that I might be holding the murderer they've been after for years." End of recording.

22

Melnyk removed his headphones and looked through the investigation dossier. He did not learn much. When he realised that he had only an hour left before the archives office closed, he began photocopying the pages in the dossier so he could go on reading it at home. That was when he noticed that some of the pages were missing. They had been neatly cut out, either with scissors or a sharpened blade.

He asked the reading room monitor to call the archivist who had given him the documents. A few minutes later, the young man appeared.

"I need a list of everyone who has consulted these archives," Melnyk whispered.

"Why?"

"There are some twenty pages missing. They've been cut out."

"Really?"

Incredulous, the archivist opened the grey box and began leafing through the dossier.

"That's unbelievable. . . the documents never leave here and there's always someone in the room watching over the readers."

Melnyk glanced at the monitor, who was calmly reading a newspaper.

"It's not exactly total surveillance, is it?"

"There's a camera too," the archivist said, as if trying to clear his colleague's name.

"Well, whatever, someone took those pages."

There was not much privacy in the room: it would have been difficult to cut out a page without the person beside you noticing. Melnyk suggested it might have been done with the complicity of an employee. The archivist took offence at this.

"This is the S.B.U. My colleagues and I don't sell archives!"

The archivist dismissed the idea with a contemptuous wave.

"That's not what I was suggesting."

"There'll be an internal investigation into this, you can be sure of that."

"What about the list of people who–"

"I don't have clearance to provide you with that information. But I can notify my superiors of your request. It shouldn't take more than two or three days before they respond."

Melnyk leaned forward and whispered in his ear: "In a murder case, two or three days is an eternity. It's just a few names. It'll only take you ten seconds."

"It's not procedure."

"Imagine I discover that the killer stole part of the archive. If your superiors learn that you made me wait three days before giving me the name of the people who consulted this dossier, you might get into trouble, don't you think?"

He saw the hesitation in the man's face. Was it better to follow the rules, or to bend them a little to cover himself in case it turned out he'd made a mistake? In the end, he took the safer option.

"I'm going to make an official request, which I hope will be successful," he said in a louder voice.

Melnyk sighed.

"Suit yourself. But if the delay messes up my investigation it'll be your fault."

The archivist carried the cardboard box out of the room, then returned to escort the captain from the building. In the corridor, just before the metal detector that led to the outside exit, he veered towards the men's room.

"We should wash our hands after touching those old papers," he said with a nod.

Inside the men's room, he checked that there was nobody else around, then took a scrap of paper from his pocket and unfolded it.

"Two other people have consulted those archives. Memorise their names. Don't write anything down."

Melnyk took the note from the archivist.

"Did you cut out those pages?"

"Of course not!" the archivist was outraged.

He seemed sincere.

"Don't you dare accuse me. And if you tell anyone that I gave you this information, I promise you, you will wish you hadn't."

"I have no reason to do that. One last thing: I noticed that the name of the K.G.B. agent who carried out the investigation did not appear in the dossier. There was just a service number."

"And you want the guy's name," the archivist sighed. "Alright. I'll send you a text when I find it."

Satisfied, Melnyk looked at the two names on the piece of paper. The first was not unexpected.

Leonid Sokolov.

The second, on the other hand, came as a complete surprise.

Officer Galina Novak.

23

Melnyk muttered a few insults as he left the archives office. How could Novak – a kid who had only been transferred to his police station a few weeks before – betray him by running a counter-investigation behind his back? He got into his car and decided to head straight to her apartment. He drove too fast, and eventually heard a siren wailing behind him. Blue lights flashed across the rear window of his car. He was being pulled over by the traffic police.

"*Blyad*," he hissed.

He parked on the roadside and the patrol car came to a halt behind him. A young male officer got out, wearing an American-style uniform like Novak's. He leaned down to the window and asked to see the vehicle papers.

Melnyk showed him his militia card: "We're colleagues."

"Militia, huh?" the young policeman said as he examined the old card with its well-thumbed corners. "I still need to see the car papers. And your insurance card."

Melnyk sighed and rummaged around in the glove compartment. He handed over the documents. After examining them, the officer took a few steps back and peered at the front wheel.

"Looks like you need new tyres," he said.

It was true. Melnyk should have changed his tyres a month or more ago.

"When the State gives me a raise, I'll buy new tyres," he said, forcing a smile.

"Sorry, captain, I'm going to have to give you a ticket."

"You've got to be kidding!" The words came out louder and angrier than he'd intended. He moderated his voice and said: "Listen, I've just come from the S.B.U. archives office. I'm in the middle of a homicide case."

"But this is a privately owned vehicle, not a patrol car," the young officer said in a prim voice. "That's the new policy. There's nothing I can do. No special favours."

Melnyk glanced at the rear-view mirror. The officer's patrol car was a brand-new Toyota Prius, a hybrid car. "Clean cars for clean police" was the official line. What bullshit, Melnyk thought. Were they going to use electric tanks in the Donbas too? He thought about his son again, stationed with his unit close to Donetsk, with their patched-up tanks and their lack of equipment. Meanwhile, in Kyiv, kids trained by Americans were driving round in state-of-the-art Japanese cars. And he was stuck in the zone, still driving a Lada so old that it was fit for the knacker's yard.

What hypocrisy!

His hands were gripping the steering wheel so tightly that the knuckles of his hands were white. He was angry. With his wife, with Novak, with the State, with the insurgents in the Donbas, with the politicians, with this stupid kid giving him a fine. As a general rule, he agreed with the principle of eradicating the rampant corruption in the police force and doing away with special favours, arbitrary arrests and banknotes slipped into driving licences to "thank" the officers. But if this same government had deigned to pay him a decent salary and to make the payments on time, if the army had been capable of providing his son with standard military equipment, if he had not been obliged to use his personal vehicle to investigate a murder because all the station's other cars were either in use or being repaired, he would not have been in a position where he had to drive around on bald tyres. That really pissed him off.

"Where do you work?" the young officer asked, thinking this would ease the tension.

"In the zone," Melnyk mumbled.

"The northern quarters? Which station?"

"I work in Chernobyl, not Kyiv."

"Ah."

The officer stepped away to write his ticket. On his face was the expression of someone who had narrowly avoided stepping into a steaming dog turd on a frozen pavement. It was one humiliation too many.

"Is that how you carry out a roadside check?"

"What?" the young officer asked, looking up.

Melnyk jumped out of his car.

"Return to your vehicle, captain..."

"You're not doing it properly. Didn't they teach you anything in that new school for super-police? You have to carry out a complete search. Check for illegal goods."

He walked to the back of the car and opened the boot.

"Look inside. Go on. You have my authorisation."

"It's all right, captain, you're in the militia and—"

"Oh, so that counts now?"

The young officer frowned, but he could think of nothing to say to this.

"What about the engine? Aren't you going to check that?"

Melnyk opened the bonnet.

"Go ahead. Put your hands inside, make sure it's all in order."

The young traffic policeman stood there paralysed.

"Well? What's stopping you? Don't worry, it's not radioactive."

"I don't think that's funny, captain."

"Nor do I, son. I'm not laughing, am I? I don't like people who don't do their job properly. So inspect this vehicle according to procedure or I'll call your chief and tell him you're lazy."

The young man hesitated.

"And get a move on. *My* job doesn't consist of just annoying my colleagues, I have a murder to solve."

The officer put the book of tickets back in his pocket. "It's alright, go ahead. But you should change those tyres. It's dangerous driving around like that."

The unintentional irony of this remark almost made Melnyk smile. Every day in the zone, he took far greater risks than that just by breathing.

"I'll change them when the State gives me a raise," he said again, getting back into his car.

He sped off. He knew he should probably have felt relieved, but in reality he was even more annoyed now. Maybe because that young officer reminded him of Novak, both of them in their stupid American uniforms.

He reached her apartment building ten minutes later. He knocked at her door. Novak opened it.

"Captain?" she said, surprised.

Her surprise turned to fear when Melnyk shoved her backwards and walked into her apartment.

"What the hell are you playing at, kid? Why did you go behind my back to investigate the 1986 double homicide?"

"The double homicide. . . What are you talking about?"

"Don't bullshit me. I went to the archives office. I know you consulted the K.G.B. dossier."

Novak was very pale.

"Darling? What was that noise?" a voice called from the other end of the apartment.

Melnyk took a step back. A second later, a young man appeared in the entrance hall. Brown hair, hazel eyes, grey suit, polished shoes.

"Is there a problem?" he said.

Novak composed herself and introduced the two men: "Vassili, this is Captain Melnyk. He's my boss at the police station. Captain, this is my husband, Vassili."

"Come on, then, Galina, don't leave the captain standing there. Come in, come in, we'll have coffee."

"I'm sure Captain Melnyk is very busy. . ."

"I'd love a coffee," Melnyk said.

Novak's face fell.

"Great!" said her husband, beaming. "I'll make us three coffees."

He went into the kitchen. Melnyk took off his jacket and handed it to Galina.

"You can't stay," she whispered.

"Just watch me!"

He heard the burble of a percolator and the aroma of hot coffee began to fill the apartment.

"Please don't mention Chernobyl," Novak begged him as they went back into the entrance hall.

Vassili and Galina Novak's living room suggested they were quite well-off. Computer, large flatscreen T.V., new furniture. . . Galina was certainly not paid enough to buy stuff like this, so presumably her husband's job was responsible for their upmarket lifestyle.

She stared pitifully at her shoes while Vassili placed a silver tray containing three cups of coffee on the table.

"So, captain, what's new at your station?" he asked. "Any exciting investigations? Galina never tells me anything."

"Yes, she's a secretive little thing, isn't she?" Melnyk said.

She blushed.

"Right now, we're working a homicide," he said in a neutral tone, so that Vassili would not guess at the irony behind his words. "A case from 1986."

"A cold case? And the murder took place the same year as the reactor explosion? That's fascinating. Why didn't you tell me about this?" he said, pinching his wife's shoulder.

"It's just an old case, not very interesting," she told him. "We're only investigating it because there's nothing else to do at the moment."

"Well, what did you expect? A town like Ivankiv is never going to have much for the police to deal with."

"Ivankiv?" Melnyk said, surprised.

Ivankiv was fifty kilometres from Chernobyl, in the safety zone. Melnyk turned to Novak, who stared at him wide-eyed as if imploring him not to say anything.

"It's true, I wasn't expecting it be so quiet when I was *transferred there*," she said, exaggeratedly. "Darling, could you bring us some milk?"

"Of course."

She watched her husband disappear into the kitchen. When she heard a cupboard door creak open, she leaned towards her boss and hurriedly whispered: "He doesn't know I work in Chernobyl."

"You lied to him?"

"I don't want him to know. Because of the radiation."

She sat back abruptly.

"What were you two whispering about?" Vassili said, putting the milk on the table. "Not me, I hope, captain?"

Galina gazed pleadingly at Melnyk.

"We were just discussing the investigation."

"Ah, professional secrets. . . I see. So, captain, how long have you worked in Ivankiv?"

"Call me Joseph. And. . . about seven years."

"Do you live there with your family?"

"No, my wife prefers to live in Kyiv."

Vassili placed his hand over his wife's.

"I don't know if she's told you: Lina drives there every day. But she'll have to stop soon." He turned to her. "Have you told him, darling?"

"I. . . no. I was going to talk to him about it soon. I wanted to be sure first. . ."

"But it is sure, darling. . ."

Melnyk instinctively grasped their meaning. "You're expecting a child?"

"I'm two months pregnant," Galina said, lowering her eyes to her coffee.

"We're very excited. It's our first child. Do you have children, captain?"

"Three," Melnyk said, somewhat thrown. "Two boys and a girl."

Why hadn't she told him that she was pregnant? The radiation around the police station was relatively light, but it was unwise for a woman in her condition to enter the zone.

"And what do they do?"

"Sorry?"

"Your children. What do they do?"

It took him a while to list his children's studies and professions; Galina avoided his eye while he was talking, until he mentioned Nikolai and the war in the Donbas.

"It's the government's fault if there's a war there," she said. "They shouldn't have denigrated the Russian language. That's what set things off in the east."

After the Maidan Revolution, one of the first measures implemented by the pro-Europeans in power had been to demote Russian from its status as an official language. In many regions of Ukraine, especially in the east, the population spoke almost nothing but Russian. There had been demonstrations against this measure in Donetsk and Kharkiv, and above all in Crimea.

"If Russia hadn't got involved, there wouldn't have been a war," Vassili retorted.

"Of course there would. The people there were never going to accept their history and culture being trampled."

"Nobody's stopping them speaking Russian," her husband said soothingly.

"That's not the point. The west has looked down on the east for years. No, decades! Imposing Ukrainian as their official language was the final straw."

Melnyk watched them bicker like this, until Novak's husband backed down.

"Her family is from the Donbas, captain," Vassili said. "This is a delicate subject. And now, if you'll excuse me, I should be getting back to work."

He stood up and shook Melnyk's hand.

"Pleased to meet you, Joseph. You and your wife should come and have dinner with us soon."

"That's very kind of you."

Vassili Novak kissed his wife on the forehead, picked up a leather satchel from the floor next to the table, and left the apartment.

"Have you been married long?"

"Two years. But we've been together for five."

"And you haven't told him that you're working in Chernobyl?"

"No. If I told him he'd be frightened. He'd want me to resign."

"What did you do wrong at the academy to be sent to Chernobyl?"

She smiled weakly.

"You know what place I finished in my class?"

"Well, given that you were sent to one of the shittiest places in the country, I'd have to guess that you didn't do brilliantly."

"I was top of the class."

"Really?"

"But my father is from the Donbas, remember?"

"That never harmed anyone's career."

"He was in one of the anti-riot squads deployed in the Maidan. The teachers at the academy found out and they lowered my marks."

Melnyk was not surprised. The Berkut, the riot squad that took its name from the Ukrainian name for the golden eagle, had been the government's main weapon against the protestors during the 2014 revolution. Hated by a large part of the population, the organisation had been dissolved after the opposition's rise to power.

"Since I don't want to stay in Chernobyl," she said, "my plan is to solve Leonid Sokolov's murder so I can get a transfer out of the zone."

She stood up and paced nervously around the living room.

"I don't want to quit and I also don't want to endanger my child by going into the zone. I paid a doctor to provide me with medical certificates so I wouldn't have to go to work on certain days. I used that time to investigate Sokolov's murder. I thought if I could solve the case, there'd be articles in the press and they'd have to transfer me to Kyiv."

She stopped pacing. She looked almost relieved to have confessed.

"Am I in trouble?"

Melnyk mechanically smoothed the end of his thick beard.

"You cost us time by going solo. I should report you, but. . ."

His anger had died away. Novak, like him, had only been trying to get out of Chernobyl. How could he blame her for that?

"I'm going to let you off the hook this time. Because I know what you're going through. My wife hates my job. Every week, she begs me to quit. She doesn't always come out and say it, but she makes me feel it. So I understand your situation. But you have to be honest with me from now on."

She sat down, relieved.

"How did you make the connection with the K.G.B.?" Melnyk said.

"I began by reading the militia dossier. What surprised me was that their investigations stopped after only a few days. That seemed illogical: one of the victims was married to a Communist Party dignitary. I researched and found some newspaper articles on the case. I noticed a journalist from Zhitomir had worked on the story for *Radianska Zhitomirchtchina*. I went to see him and he told me that the K.G.B. had taken over the investigation. You know the rest."

Clever, thought Melnyk.

"What about you? How did you find out?"

"I found the guy who was in charge of the militia investigation at the time, Arseni Agopian. He was not at all pleased that we were digging up his old case."

"Why?"

"I think he's afraid we'll blame him for the failure of the investigation. It's a familiar Soviet reflex: he knows we always accuse the subordinates here, while the real culprits get away with it. Like with Chernobyl."

One idea led to another. Abruptly he said: "What do you think of that story about the C.I.A. sabotaging the reactor? Agopian mentioned it, and the K.G.B. investigator questioned Leonski about it too."

"It's nonsense."

Novak got up and went to fetch a pile of documents from a drawer.

"There was a trial after the reactor explosion. The director of the power station, his assistant, the engineer in charge of Reactor 4, the head of the reactor workshop and the shift manager were all found guilty. But the whole thing was a farce."

She waved a bundle of stapled pages at him.

"I read everything I could find on the subject. This is an official report analysing the structural problems of R.B.M.K. reactors – the same model as the one that malfunctioned at Chernobyl. The heart of the R.B.M.K. is unstable when the reactor works at low power. It becomes difficult to control and the risk of an accident is increased. That's what happened on the night of the explosion. But the authorities had been warned about those problems long before the disaster. Add to that the human errors committed by a badly trained staff, and you have all the necessary conditions for a nuclear meltdown. The sabotage theory is a fantasy."

"Alright, so we can cross off sabotage. Olga and Larissa weren't killed by the Americans."

"Did you seriously think they might have been?"

Melnyk shrugged, slightly annoyed.

"Why not? It was the Cold War. The two camps would have done anything to destabilise each other."

"Blowing up a nuclear reactor is more complicated than derailing a train, though. The serial killer theory seems more interesting to me."

"That's a red herring," he said, with a certain satisfaction.

"How do you know? On the cassette, the K.G.B. officer said he gouged out his victims' eyes and–"

"The lesopolosa killer was the Butcher of Rostov."

Novak's face registered surprise then disappointment.

"The guy who killed women and ate their–"

"Yeah. That guy."

It had come to him not long after the traffic officer had stopped him. The Butcher of Rostov was a cannibal serial killer who had murdered twenty-one boys aged between eight and sixteen, plus fourteen girls and seventeen women in the region around Rostov-on-Don. After his trial, he'd been executed with a single gunshot to the back of the head. That was in 1994. So it was obviously impossible that he had murdered Leonid Sokolov.

"But he could still have killed Olga and Larissa in 1986," Novak objected.

"It wasn't that easy to travel around in those days. And it seems pretty hard to believe that the Butcher of Rostov would go to Chernobyl to kill two women on the very night when the reactor exploded."

"In that case, there are only two scenarios left," she said. "Either it was Larissa's husband who killed them or it was her lover."

"Which scenario seems more likely to you?"

"They both seem plausible. But I'm waiting to meet the K.G.B. officer who interrogated Leonski before I focus on one or the other."

"The guy on the cassette? His name wasn't in the dossier, just his service number."

"I know. But I managed to identify him by cross-checking with other documents in the archives."

She went to fetch her laptop. It was open on the VKontakte page of a deputy for Opposition Bloc, a pro-Russian political party. About forty years old, he had a predatory smile and a forehead smoothed by the magic of Photoshop.

"He's too young," Melnyk said, examining the man's face. "Our man is over fifty."

"I know. The K.G.B. officer is his head of security. Petro Lazarenko. You can see him there, in the background."

She pointed out a bald man, dressed in a dark suit. He blended into a crowd of people surrounding the deputy. You had to look closely to see that he was wearing an earpiece like the other bodyguards.

"Have you contacted him?" asked Melnyk.

"Not yet. I was planning to approach him during one of the deputy's public appearances. He'll be very busy this week. Here, for example. . ."

Novak pointed to the last message posted on the politician's VKontakte page.

"Tonight he's going to an art exhibition opening at the Arsenal. His head of security is bound to be there."

"And how do you plan to get into a private party like that? How do you plan to get to speak Lazarenko?"

"I'll use my police card. Why?"

Melnyk smiled at her naivety.

"If there's one thing politicians hate, it's a police officer crashing a party to ask them questions. Especially if those questions are about a murder case!"

"I don't see how he could stop me getting in, though. I mean, I'm a police officer and—"

"That doesn't matter. The guy you're trying to interrogate is ex-K.G.B. His men probably are too. You think they'll let you in just because you show them a bit of paper?"

"They're not above the law."

"Of course they are. Don't be so simple. This is what'll happen if you follow your plan: you'll turn up at the Arsenal, all dolled up, and they'll make you wait, telling you Lazarenko will be there soon, and instead they'll send you some guy with a mobile phone, and on the other end of the line there'll be a public prosecutor or someone in the ministry who will tell you in the most diplomatic way possible to shove your questions up your arse and leave Lazarenko alone. And even if you do manage to meet him, what do you think he'll tell you? Did you listen to that tape of him interrogating Leonski? You really think you're going to get anything out of a guy like that? He was K.G.B. The K.-G.-B. The bloke's a tyrannosaurus – he'd eat you alive."

Novak scowled. "You think you could do any better?"

"Him and me, we lived through an era that you never knew. I know how his mind works. That gives me a better chance of getting information out of him."

"So what am I supposed to do while you're interrogating him?"

She'd done a good job of investigating the case so far. He may as well use her talents.

"Find out everything you can about Piotr Leonski."

She nodded, glad to still be involved.

"One last thing," he said. "Did you notice something odd in the dossier?"

"The first thing that struck me was that there were some pages missing."

"How many?"

"About twenty. But you must have noticed that too. . ." Novak's expression changed as the penny dropped. "Wait, you think I did it?"

"Only two people consulted those archives. You and Leonid Sokolov."

"I didn't take them. Why would I do that?"

"To have a head start, in case anyone else decided to look through the dossiers in the hope of finding Sokolov's killer."

"You have a really low opinion of me."

"You kept information to yourself that could have saved me precious time. So, no, I don't completely trust you."

"I didn't take those pages," she said.

"If you lie to me again. . ."

Exasperated, she stood up and went to her office to fetch the photocopy she had made of the K.G.B. dossier.

"Go ahead and check," she said, handing it to him.

Melnyk glanced at it. It was missing the same pages as the dossier he had seen.

"Have you had time to read through the whole thing?"

"Yes."

"What were those missing pages about, in your opinion?"

Novak crossed her arms.

"No idea."

Melnyk gave her back the dossier.

"Alright, forget that for now. The fact that someone was so afraid of what was on those pages that he felt he had to steal them is a clue in itself. It means someone's trying to hide the truth about those murders from us."

24

Melnyk spent the rest of the afternoon in a public library. He had decided to corner Lazarenko at the opening of the art exhibition, so in the meantime he was methodically going through the photocopies of the K.G.B. dossier, hoping to find something that could help move his investigation forward.

Eight o'clock. After wolfing down a sandwich, he drove to the Arsenal. Surrounded by churches with green and gold domes, this nineteenth-century former military building had been turned into a museum of contemporary art in the early 2000s. Above the entrance, a red and gold banner displayed the name of the latest flagship exhibition, "Back in the U.S.S.R.", the title a reference to the Beatles song. At the doors, guards checked the guests' invitations. Melnyk went up to one of them and flashed his police card.

"Sorry, sir, this is a private party for charity."

"I have an appointment with Petro Lazarenko, the deputy's head of security. Tell him I've come on behalf of Olga Sokolov."

The guard disappeared for a moment. When he returned, he let Melnyk in and whispered: "Mr Lazarenko is waiting for you in the west wing. Have a good evening, sir."

"Thank you."

The exhibition began with a darkened room of metal shelves filled with televisions. Old and new, flatscreen and convex, they were all showing flashing images on a loop: speeches by Stalin; German soldiers in the Ukrainian countryside; Fidel Castro smoking a cigar; the Vostok-1 module piloted by Yuri Gagarin; the cacophony of a Soviet rock concert; a perfectly choreographed military parade in Red Square; nuclear warheads pointed at the sky; a Tarkovsky film; and many other fragments taken from the U.S.S.R. era.

After this, he walked along the Arsenal's quiet pathways, admiring the thick white columns that held up the high, vaulted ceiling. It looked like a monastery, except with paintings on the walls and sculptures perched on transparent plinths. The artist whose work was exhibited in that wing of the Arsenal did not seem particularly respectful of the country's history. He had chosen to exhibit the busts of Soviet dignitaries, some slathered with make-up like a 1970s rock star, others with false eyelashes and red lipstick, and others still wearing clown noses. A clear plastic table was covered with bits of a Lenin statue, laid out like slabs of meat on a butcher's stall. An arm, a leg, a head. Was there a message behind all of this? A metaphor for the U.S.S.R.'s disintegration? An encouragement to destroy all traces of the nation's communist past? There was no label to explain the work: the artist left it up to the spectator to decide.

Rounding a column, Melnyk spotted the deputy surrounded by a small circle of artists and flunkies pontificating about Russian realism. Lazarenko stood at a distance, watching his employer.

A man stood in his way as Melnyk approached the former K.G.B. agent.

"Having a nice evening, sir?"

"Captain Melnyk. I have to talk to–"

"The deputy is busy right now."

"It's your boss I need to talk to."

"For what reason, sir?"

"For police reasons."

"In that case, you will have to contact the deputy's lawyers."

The plural made it sound as if the deputy was protected by a platoon of legal experts.

"Tell your boss that I'm the guy who's here on behalf of Olga Sokolov."

"Olga who?"

"Sokolov. The wife of the former Russian energy minister. She was murdered in 1986. Your boss investigated her death thirty years ago. Please tell him that."

The bodyguard told Melnyk not to move and slipped away to discreetly contact his boss. A moment later, he was back.

"He'll join you in five minutes in front of the superhero mural."

"The what?"

"It's over there," the bodyguard said, pointing to an isolated room.

The mural turned out to be a life-sized photograph of a sculpture in memory of the soldiers of the Red Army. A Bulgarian graffiti artist had subverted it by painting the characters as American superheroes. There was a pistol-wielding Superman, a Captain America, a Joker, a Santa Claus, even a Ronald McDonald. A spray-painted message below explained that you had to move with the times.

"Thirty years ago, this 'artist' would have been sent to the gulag for less than that," someone grumbled bitterly.

He turned around. Lazarenko had just come into the small gallery. Despite his advanced years, he gave off an aura of menace. The gun bulging under his jacket was a part of this first impression.

"You mean *you* would have sent him to the gulag," Melnyk corrected.

"You're right," the former secret agent said. "I would have considered it my duty to send him to Siberia."

"Surely your protégé isn't a fan of this kind of art. Why come to the opening?"

"To show that if he's elected, he won't imperil freedom of creativity and all the other crap that goes with it: democracy, freedom of expression, the rights of queers and immigrants."

What a charming man, thought Melnyk.

"I hear you've reopened the investigation into the 1986 double homicide, Mr. . ."

"Melnyk. Captain Melnyk."

"Melnyk," repeated the old officer. "You've been sticking your nose into the K.G.B. papers, I suppose. That law about the free consultation of the archives is a real pain in the arse. Some things should stay in the shadows. I left the K.G.B. twenty years ago and since then I've worked for the good of this country. I would never have thought that my past actions would circle round to hit me in the face, like a boomerang."

"You have guilty secrets?"

Lazarenko shot him a look of contempt. "Who doesn't?"

"In that case, why didn't you get rid of the dossiers that mention you? You must still have friends in the secret services, right?"

Lazarenko stepped closer.

"Did you come here to blackmail me, Captain Melnyk?"

"What makes you think I could do that?"

"Don't play dumb. I know Olga Sokolov's son was found dead not long ago. I'll get blamed for not having arrested her killer."

"So what? That was more than thirty years ago. It won't affect your career now."

"Mine? No. But it could definitely affect his."

Lazarenko nodded almost imperceptibly at the deputy.

"We're in the middle of an election campaign. If my name appears as part of an investigation into a serial killer who I supposedly let get away, it could be disastrous for him. The pro-Europeans will do anything to defeat us. And besides, I don't really want my past in the K.G.B. to be spread all over the papers, given the anti-Russian climate in Kyiv at the moment. So I repeat: are you here to blackmail me? Because if you are, I'm warning you: if this information gets leaked to the press, you will wish it hadn't."

Melnyk was not thin-skinned, but even so he felt the hairs on the back of his neck stand up when Lazarenko stared into his eyes. This was not the kind of man to make empty threats.

"So? What do you want from me, Captain Melnyk?"

"I'm looking for answers."

"Just answers? Nothing else?"

"Nothing else."

"If I speak to you, will my name appear in the investigation report?"

"I'll make sure it doesn't."

Lazarenko gazed vacantly at the mural for a moment or two.

Finally he said: "Ask your questions."

"I listened to the cassette in the case file. Why did you focus your investigation on Piotr Leonski?"

"The fact that he deserted the power station made him the ideal suspect in the eyes of my superiors. Besides, I knew it was him. I had come across plenty of criminals and murderers in my career back then. I could sense this guy had it in him. Evil. Murder. When I questioned friends of the couple and their family, it became clear that Piotr Leonski was obsessively jealous. When he was younger, he beat a kid almost to death for hanging round his girlfriend. And then there were the footprints we found at the crime scene, in a pool of blood. Size 14. You don't see feet that big very often."

"The double homicide took place inside his dacha. Anyone could have taken one of his boots and stamped it in the blood to frame him."

"That was his line of defence. He said that a pair of his boots had disappeared."

"And he didn't alter his version of events even after you tortured him."

Lazarenko did not appreciate this remark.

"Don't get smart with me, Melnyk. We both know how things worked back then. I bet things haven't changed that much, have they?"

"I don't hit suspects."

"Maybe that's why there are so many criminals on the streets. They know the police have gone soft."

"So you did torture him?"

"We began by depriving him of sleep, water and food. When that wasn't enough, we applied some physical pressure."

Nice euphemism. The K.G.B., like all Soviet law-enforcement agencies, had a certain degree of expertise in how to inflict maximum pain while leaving minimal traces. For example, they would place a stack of files on the suspect's head, then hit them with heavy dumbbells. Or they would fill valenki boots with stones and smash them against the suspect's lower back. In some police stations, unfortunately, such methods were still in use.

"He never confessed," Lazarenko went on. "Not even when we locked him up in Lukyanivska with other criminals. We didn't have any evidence against him on the murder charge, but we still had him for deserting the power station."

Melnyk knew the old-school Soviet techniques. He had learned the same procedures when he was at the militia academy in Kyiv. After taking the suspect into custody, the prosecutor in charge of the case had a choice: either to free the suspect or to charge him. Without overwhelming evidence or a confession, he would be obliged to release the prisoner. But letting someone go after ten days of interrogation meant effectively admitting that you had made a mistake. And since mistakes were intolerable in the Soviet Union, they always found some pretext to keep the suspect in prison. Generally, he would be put in a cell with a *stukach*, an informer paid by the militia, whose job it was to become friends with the suspect and make him talk.

"You had ears in the cell?"

"Of course. It didn't give us anything."

"What happened after that?"

"We banned visitors, banned outings. Still he wouldn't confess."

Confessions. . . the Soviet police was obsessed with confessions. All criminals had to admit what they had done, like Raskolnikov in *Crime and Punishment*, like the defendants in all the great Stalin-era trials. It was the pinnacle of any investigation. Evidence was almost superfluous in comparison. You could always fabricate that afterwards.

"Leonski continued to plead his innocence, even after prison became a private hell for him. There was a rumour that he was involved in the reactor explosion. Back then, information didn't spread as rapidly or as easily as it does now. The press was censored and there was no Internet, there were no mobile telephones; quite often, there were no telephones at all. Even so, some of the prisoners knew about the disaster. Many of them had family in the affected areas. So when they got their hands on an engineer from the power station. . . you can imagine what they did to him. He was treated worse than an animal."

"So what did you do with Leonski, in the absence of any evidence or a confession?"

"Once he had served his sentence for desertion, we released him."

"Even though he was your prime suspect? Why so lenient?"

The old spy looked weary.

"You have to put yourself in our shoes. After the official investigation into the disaster, the Party wanted to bring the whole chapter to a close. An engineer accused of murder: that would have just dragged it all back up again. The culprit had to be someone with no connection to the power station. And since we couldn't find anyone, we pinned it on some lunatic who'd already killed three women in the Kyiv region."

"And you lied to the victims' families?"

"No. The investigation was secret. Nothing was made public."

"Except that the K.G.B. archives are now accessible. That's why some of the pages were cut out of the dossier. You did it, didn't you? Because those pages contained the name of the guy you framed for a crime he didn't commit."

"He committed plenty of other crimes."

"O.K. But meanwhile the real killer was on the loose. How did you sleep at night?"

"Things were different then."

The catch-all excuse! Melnyk thought.

"I want the pages you removed."

"Impossible. I destroyed them more than a month ago."

"After Leonid Sokolov's death?"

"Just before."

"Why?"

"He'd consulted the archives, just like you. He found my name and came to see me. That was when I decided to get rid of the more embarrassing parts of the dossier. I didn't think anyone would notice. I thought they would just assume it had been censored at the time."

"What did you talk about with Leonid Sokolov?"

"The investigation. And Leonski in particular. He had it in mind that Leonski might have killed his mother."

"And what did you tell him?"

"That he was wrong, and that the culprit had been executed."

"Did he believe you?"

"Not at all. When the interview was over, he told me he was going to find Leonski and prove that I had got it wrong in 1986."

Melnyk thought that Sokolov must have come to these conclusions after spotting something in the dossier. But what had he seen?

"What happened to Leonski after he got out of prison?"

"I think he went back to work at the power station for a while."

"They took him back despite his desertion?"

"There weren't crowds of people fighting to work there, as you can imagine."

"You think Leonid Sokolov found Leonski, and Leonski killed him?"

"It's possible."

"Leonid wouldn't be dead now if you'd made the right decisions thirty years ago. You know that?"

"You don't understand. The orders came from on high: the culprit must have no connection to the power station. God knows what would have happened to us if we hadn't obeyed."

"I grew up in this country, thanks, so I do understand. Except I was on the side of those who were tortured, imprisoned. Humiliated. My father was killed by a guy like you, who was just following orders. There have always been people like you and there always will be – bastards who shirk their responsibilities and make excuses about how they were just doing what they were told."

"If you think I'm going to let you–"

"What was your reward for denying justice to Olga Sokolov and Larissa Leonski? A promotion? A medal? A tin of caviar? A pat on the shoulder?"

"You'd better watch what you say," Lazarenko hissed at him. "Everything I did, I did in the best interests of my country."

"Of course you did, colonel. Of course."

He turned his back on Lazarenko and walked away without a word.

25

Rybalko was in a dark mood. He could not find Ninel anywhere in Chernobyl and she was not answering her mobile. He went to the 1986 office, where Sveta told him that Ninel had gone home to Kyiv. He immediately drove to the capital in search of an answer to the question that had been tormenting him since his meeting with Kazimira.

Why had she not told him that Leonid Sokolov was her brother?

Ninel's apartment was in a building that blended Art Deco with Soviet stylings: muscular male labourers and voluptuous peasant women were entwined around the front door. In the lobby, a mural filled with sheafs of wheat, hammers, sickles and machine guns led him towards a lift that appeared to date from the Stalin era. Over the years the floor numbers on the metal buttons had been worn to invisibility.

When he reached the third floor, he gave four hard knocks at Ninel's door. She opened within seconds.

"Alexander? What are you doing here?"

She frowned as she held the door half-closed.

"We have to talk. Can I come in?"

She hesitated. Like everyone else in the world, she knew that a discussion that began with the words "We have to talk" was not going to be particularly pleasant. Even so, she stood back to let him in then followed him into the living room. An old 1980s hit, "Elektrichka", was playing on a stereo system. Yet more Kino, he thought. Ninel must be a big fan.

I went to bed too late last night, I barely slept a wink
Maybe I should have gone to the doctor this morning
But now the suburban train is taking me where I don't want to go
Oh, the suburban train is taking me where I don't want to go

Boxes of burned C.D.s stood in neat lines on shelves made from Karelian birch. On their thin transparent plastic spines, he could read the names of bands from the 1980s underground scene: D.D.T., Auktyon, Nautilus Pompilius, Zoopark, all the Soviet rock classics. The living room was sparsely furnished: a desk with a computer, a sofa, a coffee table. There was an eerie sort of emptiness about the room, as if there were objects missing. On the walls, practically the only decorations were framed photographs of animals: birds perched on pine branches, horses running through snow, a wolf staring into the camera lens. The only exception was a snapshot of Ninel posing with Sveta in the middle of a square full of protesters: they were holding up a banner proclaiming: "Astravets – nuclear crime!" Behind them, a priest was carrying an icon of the Virgin Mary of Chernobyl.

Ninel noticed him studying the photograph.

"That was taken at a protest march in Minsk. Every April 26, there's a ceremony there in memory of the Chernobyl disaster."

"What's Astravets?"

"A city in Belarus, where the government decided to build the country's first nuclear power station. As if nuclear power hadn't done enough harm there already! Almost a quarter of Belarusian land was contaminated by the fallout from Chernobyl."

She gave the same exasperated sigh that followed all of her ecological speeches.

"You want a drink?" she asked.

He nodded. She took two glasses from the dishwasher and reached up for a bottle from a high kitchen shelf. As she stood, barefoot, on tiptoe, stretching to reach the chilli-flavoured vodka, he found himself staring at the curve of her hips. He lowered his eyes just before she turned around.

"Have you made any progress in your investigation?" she asked, filling the glasses.

"Well, I know that Leonid Sokolov was your brother."

A tense silence. She put the cap back on the bottle, gazing down at the kitchen countertop.

"How did you find out?"

"Who cares how! What I want to know is why you didn't tell me yourself."

"What difference does it make?"

She picked up one of the glasses and drank half the vodka.

"What difference? I'm investigating a murder! I'm looking for clues, witnesses. Why didn't you tell me?"

"I told Vektor everything I knew about Leonid."

Leonid and Ninel. Rybalko suddenly grasped the connection between the siblings' names. Leonid was named after Brezhnev, leader of the U.S.S.R. when Vektor's son was born. As for Ninel. . .

"Lenin backwards," he muttered.

She gave a mocking smile.

"My father thought his children's names were important. They had to be in line with his political ambitions. And flatter the people in power. If he had a son now, I bet you anything he'd call him Vladimir."

"Why didn't you tell me you were Vektor's daughter when we first met?"

"It's part of the deal I made with him. I help him investigate Leo's death, I get him permits to enter the zone for the men he sends, but they don't need to know that I'm his daughter."

"The *men*?"

"You're the third. The first one was got scared of the radiation and tore up his contract. The second one was beaten up by men in balaclavas. He's still in a Kyiv hospital, in a coma."

So that's why Sokolov was willing to pay so much, he thought.

"Why don't you want people to know that Vektor's your father?"

"Because he's a piece of shit."

Her lips were pursed and her voice shook slightly.

"Vektor is an arrogant, brutal monster. And a corrupt, selfish bastard. I left home at eighteen because I couldn't stand him. We've hardly talked since."

"And yet he funds your N.G.O."

"Yeah. In exchange for me staying away from his life as a respectable Muscovite businessman. And staying far away from his wife, who's young enough to be my sister. Far away from all those people who grovel at his feet. He's terrified that I'll turn up at one of his charity galas one of these days and vent my feelings. Everyone's under his spell over there – they don't want to see that he's a total scumbag."

Hate flamed in her blue eyes, like fire on ice.

"We've reached a sort of truce. He funds my N.G.O. and I leave him in peace."

"So you're a rich kid with a private income, basically."

"I don't keep any of it for myself. All the money goes to 1986."

"What about Leonid? Did you keep seeing him after you left home?"

Her blue eyes turned sorrowful.

"Leo was a great little boy when we were in Pripyat. Unfortunately, once our mother died, Vektor became his only role model, and he ended up resembling him. So I cut my ties with him too. I hadn't seen him for ten years before Vektor asked me to. . ."

A tear welled from her eye and rolled down her cheek. She wiped it away with the back of her hand.

"I was the one who had to identify the body," she said in a hollow voice.

She opened a drawer and took out a paper napkin to blow her nose.

"Did your brother ever try to get hold of you while he was in the region?"

"No. He must have known that I would send him packing."

"Your father thinks he was investigating his. . . I mean, your mother's death. You could have been a big help to him, with your knowledge of the zone."

"I told you: he didn't contact me. If I'd known he was investigating our mother's death, maybe I would have. . ."

Her gaze misted over. She took the other glass of vodka and downed it.

"Maybe I would have been able to help him. But there's no point thinking about that now. He's dead. All we can do is find his murderer."

"If Leonid's killer was involved in your mother's death, you're putting yourself in danger by staying in the zone. You could become a target."

"Nobody but you knows Vektor is my father. As long as you keep quiet, nothing can happen to me, can it?"

"I still think it'd be a good idea for you to get away from Chernobyl for a while. Until I've found the killer."

"I'm not afraid of him."

"You should be. You saw your brother's corpse. You know what this guy is capable of."

She turned pale. He regretted being so blunt.

"Sorry. I shouldn't have said that."

Her Ukrainian pride rose quickly to the surface.

"It's alright. I'm a big girl. I've been close to death before," she said fiercely. "I was in the Maidan when the special forces charged. I heard bullets whistling past. I was beaten. I saw people die around me. That guy doesn't scare me."

Despite her angelic looks, Ninel was tougher than most men he knew.

"You could go to Russia," he said.

"No way. This is my home. I'm not going into hiding because of some psychopath."

"I realise you're not on good terms with your father, but he has an army of bodyguards and his villa is like a fortress. Maybe this could be a chance for the two of you to bury the hatchet."

"Go to Vektor's house? Are you kidding? I will never set foot there again."

The way Ninel always used her father's name made him sound like some vague acquaintance.

"What exactly did your father do to make you hate him so much?"

"That's none of your business."

"It is if it has a bearing on my investigation."

"You've violated my private life enough for tonight. And if you don't mind, I'd like you to leave now."

She crossed her arms over her chest and stared into his eyes. She was even more beautiful when she was angry.

An animal urge tore through his body. He wanted to pin her to the countertop, rip off her clothes and take her right there in the kitchen. He wanted to suck the juice out of life while he still could. Desire pumped through his veins like fuel. He had to bite the inside of his lip to stop himself surrendering to this impulse. With a massive effort, he turned around and walked to the door. Just as he put his hand on the door handle, she called out: "I found you an expert on stuffed birds. He can see you tomorrow."

"Where does he live?"

"In the centre of Kyiv, near the Andriyivskyy Descent. I told him to meet us there at ten."

"I'll come by and pick you up in the morning."

"I'd rather meet you there."

"Suit yourself."

He hesitated for a moment, then turned back.

"My condolences for your brother."

"Keep them," she said coldly.

He opened the door and walked downstairs. Five minutes later he was in his car. Ten more and he was driving towards the red-light district. At a street corner, he spotted a girl. Tall, blonde, Lake Baikal-coloured eyes. She told him the price: a few hundred rubles. He promised to pay her more if she stayed with him all night.

26

Another day.

The next morning, he put another X on the small calendar he kept with him. He had followed this ritual since the day the doctor had told him about the cancer. He thought it would force him to use his time more efficiently, to remind him that every day was a race against time.

The girl he had brought back the previous night was still asleep. He left the money on the bedside table and went to the bathroom, hoping she would be gone by the time he returned to the bedroom. He felt no desire to talk to her. Or look her in the eye.

He took a long shower. The water poured over him as he stood there, eyes closed, vividly aware of the sensations on his skin. The liquid flow, the heat. After a while, he lowered the temperature until his muscles shivered and shook, fighting to maintain his body heat under the jet of icy water. Trembling in the shower cubicle, he felt more alive than ever, like those pilgrims who celebrate the Epiphany by cutting large crosses into the frozen surface of a Siberian lake and throwing themselves into the water to prove their faith.

He went to the bedroom. The girl was gone, and so was the money. She had also taken the small bag of weed he had bought from a dealer the previous night. On the whole, he felt relieved: at least this way he would not be tempted to start smoking the stuff again. He needed to keep a clear head.

Halfway through breakfast, he took the pills that the Moscow doctor had given him. A handful of different medicines designed to give him a physical boost. For now, the signs of the cancer were fairly low-key. A slight headache, the occasional bout of nausea, sudden feelings of exhaustion. But that might just as easily have been caused by an ordinary infection as by radiation poisoning. Then again, the fact that he had been exposed to radiation as a child meant that he got ill more easily and took longer to recover from even the mildest cold than the average person would have done.

And then there was the insomnia. He had slept only three hours the previous night, even less than the night before that. The anxiety he felt at letting another day slip through his fingers was enough to keep his eyes wide open. He still found it hard to accept that he would be dead in only a few months. He was not in pain, was not vomiting or suffering from nosebleeds. But he knew that would not last. The old doctor had warned him: his body would continue to function normally for some time, then his condition would rapidly deteriorate and he would find himself bedridden in hospital. In the meantime, he would have few symptoms: the disease would consume him silently, bit by bit, like a cigarette left smouldering on the edge of an ashtray.

After a hearty breakfast, he set out for the centre of Kyiv. He drove fast, ignoring the speed limits. On a boulevard, he passed a strange convoy: an articulated lorry carrying a huge statue of Lenin. Since it was too tall to be transported standing up, it had been lain on its side and strapped to the truck bed, making it look as if the bronze giant had been captured by Lilliputians. In all the villages Rybalko had been through since leaving the Donbas, the Lenins had been cut down like diseased oaks. Only their marble plinths survived in the middle of empty squares. The contrast between east and west was striking: the west was the land of old rusted idols lying like corpses, while in the east the vertical statues still gazed at the communist horizon, as if the U.S.S.R. had never collapsed.

His thoughts drifted back to Ninel. It could hardly be easy having a name like that in Ukraine when the country was in such a rush to rid itself of the old communist symbols. Hardly surprising that she and her association should have been targeted by neo-Nazis. Then he thought about her mouth, her breasts, her eyes. The night with the prostitute had not quenched his desire. And yet he knew it was idiotic. He would be dead soon. It wasn't the ideal time to start up a new romance. Besides, Ninel was a pain.

He had to wait half an hour at the meeting point on the Andriyivskyy Descent before she turned up. Late and bad-tempered.

"I had to take the bus. Someone slashed my tyres."

"The Right Sector again?"

"Probably. The taxidermist lives over there," she said, pointing at an elegant building with a yellow and cream façade. "His name is Lukas Romanenko. Tell him you were sent by Ernest. That's the name of my friend at the Natural History Museum in Kyiv."

"You're not coming?"

"I told you: I'm not a big fan of stuffed birds. While you talk to him, I'll take the pick-up truck and buy some tyres."

She held out her hand. Reluctantly, he gave her back the car keys she had lent him. He would have liked her to go with him, so she could give him her opinion as an ornithologist.

"Don't forget that thing," she said, pointing at a cardboard box on the back seat of the vehicle.

He picked it up carefully. Inside was the swallow he had brought back from Pripyat.

Ninel sped off with a roar, like someone slamming a door as they leave a room. He walked to the apartment building and rang the intercom. Romanenko calmly told him that he lived on the third floor, second apartment on the right as you came out of the lift. The taxidermist turned out to be a refined-looking man with a mane of long white hair.

The narrow two-bedroom flat smelled of polish and leather. He had made tea and the two men drank it while discussing his passion for stuffed animals. There were a few of them in his apartment: a pheasant on a chest of drawers, a ferret frozen mid-stride.

"I've worked for several museums, in Russia and in Ukraine. I used to restore damaged collections. Back when they were still exhibited, I mean. These days, naturalised animals tend to be kept in storerooms."

He spoke Russian with a Kyiv accent, his voice full of open vowels and softer Gs, throwing in the occasional word in Ukrainian. Now retired, he divided his time between taxidermy, his hobby, and the History of Art classes that he taught at the university. He did not know Ninel, but Ernest, her friend who was a curator at the Natural History Museum, had asked him to help out – and he was happy to do so.

"He said you wanted to show me a particular piece. A swallow, I believe?"

Rybalko took the stuffed bird from its cardboard box.

"A beautiful specimen," the taxidermist said. "Where did you find it?"

"In an old apartment."

He did not want to tell Romanenko that the bird was from Pripyat, for fear he would refuse to examine it.

"What exactly are you expecting from me, Alexander?"

He took out the photographs he had taken of the animals in the apartment where Leonid Sokolov's body had been found.

"I thought if you examined this bird and these pictures, you might be able to give me the name of the person who did all this. There can't be that many taxidermists in the region."

The old man delicately placed his porcelain cup on the table and put on a pair of glasses.

"The pieces in these photographs are badly damaged," he said as he looked through them. "Very different to the swallow. Its plumage is perfect, the stitching very fine, the posture extremely realistic. . . It's good work. I don't know many people in the region capable of work of this quality. Perhaps four or five. But, at the risk of disappointing you, I'm afraid I can't tell you who precisely was responsible for this naturalisation. To be sure, there is an element of individual style in taxidermy, just as there is in any artistic endeavour, but it's a long way from that to being able to identify a single individual's 'fingerprint' just by looking at one of his works. . ."

"Please think. I'm trying to track down a dangerous killer and this is the only clue I have."

The taxidermist frowned. "Ernest didn't mention that."

Rybalko explained that the murderer had left this bird at the scene of a crime and that he supposed it must be some sort of message. The taxidermist was silent for a while. At last he muttered: "It would be barbaric, but since it's a question of life and death. . . perhaps I. . . I hate to do it, but if this is truly important. . ."

He carefully picked up the swallow and got to his feet.

"Follow me. I have a way to find out more about this bird."

They walked through the living room to a small room that looked like a hermit's cave. The air there was dry and the windows were shuttered. Only a faint light came through between the half-closed curtains. The acrid scent of ambergris filled the room, as if they were entering the lair of some wild animal.

"This is my workshop," Romanenko explained. "I keep my hides here, away from the sun."

He turned on the ceiling lamp. Rybalko felt the hairs stand up on his arms as the light illuminated a zoo of unbreathing animals. They were everywhere he looked. Owls and dozens of other birds perched on shelves. Mummified snakes under glass covers. Squirrels that looked as if they were about to run away. Deer heads ready to be transformed into hunting trophies. Cracked hides in need of a facelift. Butterflies in bottles, killed with cyanide to avoid damaging their precious wings. Dead birds with multicoloured feathers, beautiful in a way that was both fascinating and cruel.

The taxidermist sat on a stool facing a large wooden work surface. The light from the ceiling lamp shone dazzlingly on the tools placed there: scalpels, pliers, files, saws, needles, hooks. In the middle of the work surface was a bright red parrot lying on a piece of newspaper. Its skin had been turned inside out like a sock, exposing the intimacy of its innards.

The old man moved the tropical bird aside and put the stuffed swallow in the centre of the desk.

"It's an art in itself, animating the inanimate," he began in a learned tone. "By naturalising an animal, you make its skin speak. The hide of an animal is a sort of musical score, and every taxidermist will interpret it differently. Just as no two pianists play Mozart in the same way, so each taxidermist has his own methods for giving the illusion of life."

Rybalko shivered again. This was all so macabre.

"There's great dynamism in this swallow. We have the impression that the author was seeking to capture the moment preceding movement, if you see what I mean? The crucial moment when everything is at play: the body has not yet been propelled forward, but the energy is spreading through its muscles."

There was a powerful halogen lamp above the work surface. He switched it on and turned its movable head towards the bird.

"The style of this work is familiar to me. Perhaps if I take a look inside this swallow, I will be better able to understand the artist's methods. But it breaks my heart to vandalise a colleague's work. It deserves to be in a private collection. Or in a museum."

Better not, thought Rybalko. He had measured the bird's radioactivity. It wasn't dangerous to handle, but it was sufficiently contaminated that regular and prolonged exposure would have an adverse effect. When the investigation was over, he planned to bury it somewhere in the zone.

The taxidermist put on a pair of gloves and picked up a small scalpel, which he used to make an incision in the bird's abdomen. The swallow looked so alive that Rybalko was surprised to see straw pour from the cut instead of blood.

"It's an old-fashioned method," the taxidermist remarked. "No polystyrene soul for this animal, of course. . . straw stuffing with horsehair inside."

"A soul?" Rybalko queried, frowning.

"It's a shape that we cut out to use as a support for the skin. For the past thirty years or so, it's been customary to use very light materials like polyurethane foam or polystyrene. They're easy to sculpt, so one can make a precise reproduction of the contours of the creature's muscles."

He pointed at the insides of the swallow.

"But for this bird, the artist has used traditional techniques. He's built a metal framework to keep the bird in the desired posture."

He held one of the wings and stripped away its feathers.

"Here he slid the metal wire along the wings to keep them open. There's wire in the feet too, to make them rigid. It's highly professional work. The skin filling has been done meticulously, proving that the author has a strong knowledge of anatomy, and the cuts are immaculate."

The old man caressed the feathers with the back of his scalpel.

"Another thing that strikes me is the care shown to the plumage. The naturalisation of a bird requires fewer steps than that of other animals, but it's difficult to obtain a good finish. I would tend to argue that it all comes down to the wings. The head is important too, of course, but the wings are essential."

He bent over the bird again.

"The eyes are perfect. Wherever we position ourselves, we have the impression that the swallow is looking at us. The work on the eyes is crucial to the effect of realism. The viewer should not be able to escape the animal's gaze."

He used a small pair of pliers to pluck out an eye, which turned out to be a sort of little glass bead mounted on a pin.

"Surprising. The sticking point between the glass and the metal pin suggests once again the work of a craftsman. He has cut the glass, then polished it to achieve the desired effect."

The taxidermist squinted.

"Wait a minute. . . this isn't glass. . . it's something else. . ."

He used a large magnifying glass to examine the eye.

"Fascinating. What attention to detail! The eyes were carved from amber. It demands great precision to carry out work like this."

"Is amber often used for the eyes?"

"Absolutely not. In fact, I've seen this only once before in my life."

The taxidermist took a heavy photograph album from a shelf. It contained pictures of stuffed animals and of Romanenko himself receiving medals at various taxidermy contests. He leafed through the pages in silence. Rybalko felt uneasy, spied upon by the dead animals observing him from every angle with their black, yellow or orange eyes.

"Here it is," the taxidermist said, tapping his finger against a photograph of a long, immaculately white bird. "It was during a contest organised by a hunters' association. One of the contestants won hands down with this egret. Its eyes were so realistic! I asked the artist how he had achieved the effect, but he wouldn't tell me of course. That's not the sort of thing that one discusses, one expert to another. It's like. . . like a magic trick. It has to remain secret or the charm is lost."

"But you knew it was amber."

The old taxidermist smiled.

"I knew the man who'd organised the contest. He let me examine the bird before he returned it to its owner. Using a magnifying glass, I could tell that there were typical inclusions proving that the eyes had been made from amber."

"Do you remember the guy's name?"

"Unfortunately, I am afraid I forgot that many years ago."

"Was he in Kyiv?"

"I have no idea. But I certainly noted the date of the photograph."

He took the photograph from its plastic pouch. On the back was written "1984".

"Before the explosion," Rybalko muttered.

"Sorry?"

"I was just thinking aloud."

Now he had confirmation that the man who stuffed the swallow had been active in the Kyiv region during the 1980s. Perhaps with a little luck he would find the man's name in the archives of the local newspaper, given that he had won the contest.

"Could you tell me about the work of naturalisation on the birds? It might help me understand how the killer works."

The old man put the photograph back in its place and closed the album with a muffled thud.

"Of course. What would you like to know?"

Remembering that the taxidermist had worn gloves to handle the swallow, Rybalko asked him why.

"To avoid damaging the feathers with my perspiration, but also to limit the risks of contamination. Toxic products are sometimes used in the naturalisation process."

"What sort of products?"

"Mercury, asbestos. . . For birds, it's common to use a kind of soap that contains arsenic."

"But that's a poison!"

"The doses used are not sufficient to kill a human being; there's just enough to prevent parasites eating the hide of the naturalised animal. Arsenic or borax are often used with birds, because it's impossible to tan their hides. There has never been a better method than that for conserving birds. But don't worry, I was handling it very carefully. I don't want to end up poisoned like Madame Bovary."

"Was she a taxidermist?"

Romanenko threw back his head and laughed.

"Madame Bovary was the heroine of a novel. Gustave Flaubert? The French author? You've never heard of him?"

Embarrassed, Rybalko changed the subject.

"Could you describe the process of naturalisation from beginning to end?"

"Certainly. But it will take a while."

The taxidermist turned on the halogen lamp again and lit up the red parrot on which he had been working. In a professorial voice, he explained that the word "taxidermy" came from the Greek *taxis*, "order", and *derma*, "skin". The science of the taxidermist consisted in best arranging the body of a dead animal to replicate the effect of reality.

While he started to explain the technique for skinning an animal, Rybalko imagined the murderer in a taxidermist's workshop. The acrid smells of treated hides and chemical products. The animals frozen for eternity. The thawed carcasses. The man sunk in a dark world of silent meticulousness. Striving every day to prolong life in a quasi-mineral form, trying to read the animal's secret life in its skin so he could recreate the way it moved. Did he poach his prey himself? Did he take pleasure in those tiny murders? Serial killers often begin by torturing and killing small animals. Is that where his first emotions as a murderer came from? Plunging his hands into the cold entrails, withdrawing them and cleaning off the dark blood. . . Frequent contact with skinned creatures would habituate him to lifeless flesh, would render death banal, desensitize the taxidermist. Pulling out the viscera. Removing the bones. Rubbing the skin to cleanse it of all fat and tissue. Did he cook the meat of those animals sacrificed in his kitchen? Can he smell it from his workshop, surrounded by his animal objects?

His gestures are methodical. His stitching precise and fine, as on Leonid Sokolov's eyelids. He shows great delicacy as he works with the feathers. He is not someone with a stormy temper, but rather a cool, calm character. He lays traps in the forest to catch animals. He also trapped Sokolov, in a way.

Patience is one of his qualities. He works slowly and meticulously. He took his time to hang Leonid's body outside the apartment block, having selected that as the best place to exhibit his work: a building overlooking the central square, seen by all the tourists who entered the zone.

There could be no further doubt: the man who had killed Leonid Sokolov had also naturalised this swallow. But why exhibit the body of his victim as if it were one of his stuffed animals?

Suddenly, an idea crossed his mind.

"Is it possible to apply the techniques of taxidermy to a human being?"

An expression of disgust twisted the old man's serene face.

"That would be despicable! It has been done though. We are animals, after all: our skin can be tanned into leather. Human skin has been used for book covers, mostly medical treatises. And then, of course, there were the horrors of the Holocaust. Apparently they found a lampshade made of human skin at the camp in Buchenwald. Among other things."

"What about stuffed humans? Has that been done?"

"Unless one considers mummies to be a form of taxidermy, I have never heard of it on the Old Continent. But the Shuar people in Peru and Ecuador, whom the Spanish called Jivaros, shrank human heads, and their technique was close to that used in taxidermy."

Rybalko swallowed painfully while Romanenko explained in detail how the indigenous Americans naturalised the heads of their enemies after decapitating them. Feeling nauseous, he decided to encourage the taxidermist towards a less morbid subject.

"Is it difficult to get hold of a bird? A falcon, for example?"

"Not really. You would simply need some contacts among the hunters or the forest rangers. Or you could hunt it yourself. It's quite a common species in this region."

"How do you get your animals? Are you a hunter?"

"Me? No. I have the bodies brought here. Or sometimes I'll travel to the place where the animal has died, the zoo in Kyiv for example. Anyway. . . I couldn't shoot an animal ever again."

He paused.

"I used to be a hunter. Quite a good one, in fact. But after Chernobyl. . ."

His voice sounded hesitant.

"After the disaster, I was summoned by the president of the association of hunters and fishermen in my region. He had been given orders to slaughter all pets in the forbidden zone and he was looking for men to carry out this dirty work. The authorities were afraid that the animals would spread diseases, or that they would carry radioactive particles embedded in their fur. I didn't want to participate in that. I loved animals. But I also loved my country and it needed me. And there was a thirty-ruble bonus. That was a lot of money at the time. So I agreed. We worked in brigades. Twenty men, plus an employee from the epidemiology centre or a veterinary doctor. We went to the abandoned villages with a tractor and a skip, and then we began the slaughter."

The taxidermist's lips were trembling. He avoided Rybalko's eyes.

"The first ones to die were the dogs. After days without their masters, they were happy to see human beings. We killed them all. A bullet in the head. Then we took the bodies to our skip and we dumped them in a pit. When the pit was full, we covered it with earth. As that was happening, there would sometimes be a few wounded animals trying to struggle out from under the pile of bodies. When we still had enough bullets, we would finish them off. But once we had exhausted our ammunition, we had to bury them alive. After we left, the earth would continue to move for days, as the wounded beasts tried to dig their way up to the surface."

The taxidermist stopped speaking. Rybalko said nothing. He sensed that the old man's confession was not over.

"The first dog I shot. . . I will remember that for the rest of my life. It was a German shepherd that was still guarding its owners' dacha. The door had been smashed down by burglars who had stolen almost everything in the house. The animal must have tried to defend its masters' belongings, because it had a nasty wound on one of its hind paws. When it came towards me, it was limping. It licked my hand. It was weak, and starving. I. . . I put the lunch my wife had made for me in its food bowl. A big beef sandwich. With the bonus, we could afford decent food. I watched the German shepherd as it ate. I was holding my rifle, the barrel aimed at it, but I couldn't pull the trigger. I knew I would have to do it eventually, though, and if I didn't, someone else would. The first time is always the hardest. Afterwards, we did it like automatons. The bonus meant we had plenty of money to buy vodka. That made everything easier. A bitch and its suckling pups: six bullets. A poodle hiding in a child's bedroom: one bullet. A cat. . . you needed a good aim to kill a cat. They hid under furniture. They slipped away like shadows. And if your aim wasn't perfect, you had to finish them off. With your boot heel or the butt of your rifle. So you didn't waste ammunition. But the German shepherd, that was my first. I didn't know all that stuff yet. I wanted to do it properly. First I waited until it had finished eating. And then I thought, if I was going to do it, I had to look it in its eyes before I killed it. I took a step back, I shouldered my rifle, and I put a bullet in the back of its head. Its skull exploded. The silence after the detonation. . . horrible. There were bits of bone and brain mixed up with the food in its bowl. And blood. So much blood. I haven't been able to eat meat since that day."

27

After leaving the taxidermist's apartment, Rybalko felt relieved to be on the busy streets. Birds chirped on wires. Dogs strained at their leashes, eager to sniff the city's odours. Their souls were flesh, not polystyrene. He felt as if he were again in the land of the living, after having journeyed through the realm of the dead.

As he waited for Ninel to return, he called Sokolov to give him an update.

"How's the investigation going?"

"I'm making progress. Has the autopsy been done?"

"The coroner just finished examining the body. He'll email us the results soon."

"Good. Did he manage to determine the cause of death?"

"Yes. He said it was poison."

Poison. . . This came as a surprise, given the extent of the damage to Leonid's body.

"What kind of poison?"

"Arsenic."

"Like for the birds," Rybalko said.

"Birds?"

"I just talked to a taxidermist. I showed him a stuffed bird that I found at the crime scene. He told me that people of his profession sometimes used arsenic to treat the hides of feathered animals, to stop them being attacked by parasites."

"You think the man who killed my son is some kind of taxidermist?"

"It seems to me highly likely."

Sokolov fell into a horrified silence. Innards removed, eyes gouged out, abdomen stuffed with horsehair. . . he realised that his son's corpse had been treated like an animal that was about to be naturalised.

"Do you have a list of suspects?" he demanded.

"Not yet. The taxidermist recognised it as the work of one of his colleagues, but he couldn't remember the guy's name. I just know that he used amber for his animals' eyes and that he took part in a taxidermy contest in 1984."

"Piotr Leonski," spat Sokolov. In a voice filled with hate, he went on: "The militia suspected him for a while, but those idiots let him go. He had a workshop next to his dacha. That degenerate used to prepare his disgusting stuffed birds there. He killed Leonid – I'd bet my life on it! That piece of shit! After all these years, he killed my son. My son. . . Why?"

"Leonid went to Poliske to speak with Kazimira, one of Olga's former colleagues. According to her, your son suspected Leonski of murdering his mother. It's possible Leonid found him and things got out of hand."

He thought about Kazimira, then about Ninel.

"Why didn't you tell me about your daughter?" he said.

The former minister played dumb: "What are you talking about?"

"Ninel. She's your daughter."

"It was her idea. She prefers me to remain discreet where that is concerned."

"I have the impression she doesn't like you much."

"Our relationship has been complicated since her mother's death. She took it very badly. And then the thyroid operation didn't help. She's prone to mood swings. Apparently it stems from that. As a teen-ager, she was always angry with the whole world. Especially with me. I think she's bitter that I got on with my life after Olga was killed. I had other women. Leonid accepted it, but not Ninel. She was so unpleasant to all my girlfriends."

"And how did she take Leonid's death?"

"They were brother and sister, but they were never very close. At least, not after we moved to Moscow. She was angry with him for 'taking my side'. But this kind of information isn't going to help your investiga-tion, is it?"

"No, that's true. Do you have any idea where I might find Leonski?"

"None at all. He was in prison when I left Ukraine. They put him behind bars because he deserted the power station."

"He never tried to get hold of you? No phone calls or threatening letters?"

"Nothing. I haven't seen him since Pripyat."

Rybalko saw the 1986 pick-up truck appear at the end of the street.

"I'm going to have to hang up now. I'll be back in touch when I have more to tell you."

"Find Leonski," Sokolov ordered. "And when you've found him, kill him. As we agreed."

"I should make sure that he's–"

"Kill him. It has to be him."

"But–"

Sokolov began to yell then, abandoning his veneer of civilisation.

"Are you stupid or what? What don't you understand, Rybalko? I want him dead. It's not complicated. So either you kill that piece of shit or you can kiss your money goodbye. Do you really want to miss out on fifty million rubles?"

Rybalko was gripping his mobile so hard that he feared he might break it. He was furious. No matter how much cash the former minister was paying him, it wasn't enough to let the bastard talk to him like that.

"So? Can I count on you or not?"

"You can," he said coldly.

"Good. Find Leonski. Kill him. I don't want that guy to get away with it a second time."

Sokolov hung up on him.

Ninel was double-parked. Rybalko got into the front passenger seat and slammed the door shut.

"Did you find out anything interesting?" she said.

"Apart from the fact that your father is a jerk?"

"That hardly counts as a scoop," she said, almost smiling.

"Your father is convinced that Larissa Leonski's husband is the killer."

"And you? What do you think?"

"That there are too many coincidences for it not to be him. According to your father, Leonski was suspected of the double homicide by the militia at the time, before being released. He also told me that Leonski was an amateur taxidermist and had a workshop in his dacha."

This connected to the macabre treatment of Leonid's corpse, obviously, but out of respect to Ninel, he did not mention it.

"I have to find him. I'll need someone who can help me track him down. Someone who works with the police or – better still – with the tax office. The tax office can always track people down. Which reminds me: my friend Kachin was supposed to send you a parcel. Did you receive it?"

Ninel seemed not to hear this question. She was staring straight ahead, as if lost in thought.

"Ninel?"

She parked the truck by the roadside.

"Is there a problem?"

"I opened the parcel. There was a pistol inside. Did my father ask you to kill Piotr Leonski?"

He feigned surprise. "Why would he do that?"

"Because he solves his problems using violence, intimidation or blackmail. So answer my question. Did he tell you to kill this guy?"

Her Baikal eyes stared deep into his. Lying became impossible. How could anyone lie to eyes like those?

"Yes. He wants Leonski dead."

She nodded.

"And you're going to do it?"

"Would that bother you, if I killed your brother's murderer?"

"Again, you haven't answered my question."

"You haven't answered mine either."

"I'd rather he went to prison. That whole eye-for-an-eye bullshit is what's destroying our country. So answer me: are you planning to kill him?"

"I'll do what needs to be done."

"So that's what you are: a murderer."

She shot him a look of disgust that set his teeth on edge.

"If what I'm asking you to do poses you a moral problem, you're not obliged to help me," he said angrily. "Call your father and tell him to find me another guide. He might stop sending you those generous payments though. Have you ever wondered where that money comes from, by the way? What's to say it's not stained with blood too?"

"It's not for me, it's for–"

"Your association? That's sheer hypocrisy! Your father's money pays for your rent too, doesn't it? Your clothes? Your food?"

"At least I'm not getting rich on others' misery."

"Don't judge me. You don't know anything about me. It's easy for you to play the heroine. If anything goes wrong for you, you'll always have your daddy to bail you out."

"I'm not a murderer. I don't kill people."

"Because you've never had to. You were born with a silver spoon in your mouth. Did you pay to go to university? Did you have to work while you were taking your ornithology degrees? Does your father send you a big fat cheque for your birthday every year?"

They stared each other out. Ninel looked away first. She lowered her eyes to the gear stick and started the car, each of her gestures stiff with anger.

"My hotel isn't this way," Rybalko said as she made a U-turn.

"I know."

"Where are we going?"

"You'll see."

"Are you kidnapping me?"

"Oh shut your mouth, for God's sake!"

She put the Kino CD into the player and the voice of Viktor Tsoi interrupted their conversation. They drove about twenty kilometres, heading north-west In the Pushcha-Vodytsya neighbourhood, Ninel kept going until they reached a sort of hospital in the middle of a forest.

There was a sign near the entrance.

"Ukrainian clinic for the protection of the population from radio-activity," Rybalko read. "What are we doing here?"

"You'll see."

Ninel parked and jumped out of the truck, her heels hammering belligerently against the tarmac as she walked to the front door. In the reception area, a nurse greeted her.

"Is Maria there?" Ninel said.

"The doctor is in her office."

Ninel headed towards the stairs.

"Who's Maria?" Rybalko asked.

"She knows a lot of people in the government. She'll be able to find someone who can tell you Leonski's address."

They went upstairs and she left him in front of a large door decorated with children's drawings.

"Wait for me inside. I'll be back in five minutes," she told him before disappearing.

Rybalko was still annoyed, so he went downstairs and lit a cigarette outside the building. Who the hell did this woman think she was? She was so full of moral certainties and ecological speeches, but what did she know about real life? She had never had to fight to survive, as he had. She had never been beaten up outside school because little white Russian kids didn't like the fact that a "darkie" could speak "the language of Pushkin" better than they could. She had never had to sell her integrity to make ends meet. She had never had to bow to a bunch of racist, incompetent, corrupt superiors.

A hospital employee was sweeping leaves outside the entrance. A strange-looking man, who smiled as he looked at Rybalko. He had no facial hair at all – even his eyebrows were bald.

"Bad day?" the hairless man asked him as he brushed the cigarette stub Rybalko had dropped on the ground into his dustpan.

"It is," Rybalko said, looking away.

A sweet melody came from one of the building's windows.

"That's the children," the man said. "The choir of little angels from Chernobyl. How can God cause them so much pain when they sing so beautifully?"

The man had a crazy look in his eyes that sent a chill down Rybalko's spine. He went back inside, up the stairs, and into the room where Ninel had told him to wait. It was a sort of games room, with fifteen or twenty kids playing in it. The room was divided in two by a long green curtain, so Rybalko couldn't see the other side. To start with, he did not notice anything unusual. Then a feeling of unease began to grip him as he spotted odd details. One of the children had a nosebleed. The others paid no attention to this, however. Rybalko watched the boy raise his head and pinch his nostrils. Soon another boy started bleeding from the nose and he went over to join the first boy on a bench.

He realised that none of the children could run for very long. The ones who were playing football kept stopping, taking deep breaths like old people who have just climbed two flights of stairs. Intrigued, he went further into the room, passing through the green curtain. Behind, he found some kids in wheelchairs, half-paralysed, with twisted arms and legs. He saw a child without legs and another whose only limb was a single atrophied arm. At the back of the room, some of the children were eating off the floor because they could not walk, while others were twitching, their eyes bulging, as if the only emotion they could feel was fear.

He took a step back. He wanted to get out of there. This place was unbearable. He did not mind seeing corpses or risking his life, but the idea of staying there, among all these mutilated kids. . . it was too much. He tried to turn, to escape this nightmare, but Ninel was standing there, blocking his path, staring at him with her fierce eyes, refusing to let him leave.

"You see? This is where some of my father's money goes. Does it seem useless to you? Is this just some spoilt rich kid's whim?"

"Let me go."

"Look at them," she said. "Don't you think it's worth taking dirty money to help them? Look at Oleg, with his legs like tree stumps. He has practically no lymphatic system, so his body produces toxins that he can't eliminate. Look at Viktor, the little boy without arms. After the Chernobyl disaster, the number of deformities among children sky-rocketed. So did cancer and leukaemia. We have diabetic newborns here. Kids whose limbs we have to amputate. You see? That's Chernobyl. That's the nuclear legacy. There aren't any mutant monsters or phospho-rescent creatures, just animals and people that are sick and suffering. Look at them!"

He pushed her out of the way and left the room. On the stairs, he took out a cigarette and lit it, ignoring the "No Smoking" signs all over the walls. Ninel came after him.

"What about you? What are you planning to do with my father's money?"

In a fury, he threw his cigarette away, ran up the stairs, and stood with his face only a couple of centimetres from hers.

"What are you going to do, hit me?" Ninel hissed.

Her eyes were cold enough to crack stones.

"I have a daughter," he began. "She's deaf. She needs hearing aids to hear. I accepted your father's offer so I could pay for an operation that will allow her to hear normally."

"Does she know her father's going to kill someone so she can have that operation?"

He really felt like slapping her then.

"No, she doesn't know that. She doesn't know her father will be dead in less than six months either."

He spun around and walked quickly downstairs. Outside, he lit another cigarette and paced the paths of the gardens to calm down. When he came back to the clinic, Ninel was waiting for him on the front steps.

"I'm sorry. I shouldn't have said all that stuff."

"It's O.K.," he said, his jaws still clenched.

"What's. . . what do you have?"

"Cancer. Thanks to Chernobyl, presumably."

"I shouldn't have used the children to make you feel guilty. I don't know why I did that. It's not me, it's. . ."

Her eyes grew misty.

"Forget it," he said.

A woman in a doctor's coat came out of the clinic and walked towards them. Ninel quickly dried her eyes.

"This is Maria. She's an honorary member of 1986."

Maria was a tall, slim woman with tired eyes and a vaguely anaemic complexion. She wasn't wearing make-up and her blonde hair was tied in a slapdash bun.

"Did Ninel show you around?" she asked Rybalko after shaking his hand.

Her voice was soft and composed; a reassuring voice for her young patients, he imagined.

"Briefly," he said. "I saw the games room and I heard the choir practicing. I. . . I never realised there were still so many problems caused by radiation."

Maria nodded sadly.

"And this is just a tiny fraction of the children affected by the disaster," she said. "People want to believe that the Chernobyl explosion is in the past. But not all the victims have yet been born."

She explained that the State had been trying to convince people otherwise for the past few years, by spreading propaganda that blamed the rise in serious diseases in the region on "radiation phobia". According to certain experts, people were falling ill because of the stress caused by all the information they read and heard about radiation.

They claimed this brought on premature ageing, cancer, even leukaemia.

"I don't know whether to laugh or cry," Maria admitted. "But you didn't come here to talk about that, did you? As I understand it, you're looking for someone's address."

"That's right. A man who was working at the Chernobyl power plant on the night of the explosion."

"That should make things easier. If he's still alive, I mean. Some of the plant's employees received a State pension or were paid medical expenses after the accident. I know quite a few people working at the Ministry of Health. I could find out where he lives, if he was given any kind of government aid."

"And if so, how long would it take to get his address?"

"I could have it by this afternoon or this evening."

"Perfect," said Rybalko.

This meant that, by tomorrow at the latest, Piotr Leonski would be dead and his mission would be over.

28

The next morning, Rybalko woke up in a cold bed. He had taken a handful of sleeping pills the previous night and had sunk deep into a chemical slumber disturbed by visions of eyeless bodies and mutilated birds. At one point during these nightmares, he had been back in Pripyat, in 1986. An orange sun was burning on the horizon. The air was warm. It was springtime. Blood-red flags flapped in the wind. Children ate ice creams, which melted over their chins. Shirtless men worked on building sites. Instead of the usual speeches, the loudspeakers were playing David Bowie's "Space Oddity", and a cosmonaut was walking beside Rybalko. Behind his midnight-blue visor, his face was invisible. Strangely, the people around paid the cosmonaut no attention; they were too busy enjoying this beautiful April day. He followed the cosmonaut to the river. The spaceman pointed to the horizon with his gloved hand. In the distance, he could see the red and white chimney of the Chernobyl power station. Suddenly a tongue of atomic fire shot from the reactor towards the sky. He tried to run, but the cosmonaut was holding him in place. Behind his visor, there was no face. Only a grinning skull with empty eye sockets.

Ugh, stupid sleeping pills. . .

After taking a shower and fixing his hair, Rybalko adjusted the tripod of the small camera he had bought the previous day and sat down on the bed. He took a deep breath, then pressed a remote control that began recording.

"Hello, Tassia, this is your father, Alexander. I asked your mother to give you this recording when you are eighteen, because I want you to know. . . to know. . ."

He pressed "stop". He could not speak. He had tried doing this the night before, but he had not been able to find the right words. He did not just want to leave his daughter an explanation, but a memory, something of his that she could keep after his death. He had not been able to keep any such memory of his father's. All his belongings had been thrown away when he arrived at the hospital in Moscow to be treated for radiation sickness. His clothes, his watch, his wedding ring. All the rest, or almost all the rest, had been left at their apartment in Pripyat. Rybalko did not even have a photograph of his father. It was as if he had never existed. And he did not want that to happen to Tassia.

He pressed "Record" again.

"Sweetie, it's Dad. I asked your mother to give you this video on your eighteenth birthday."

He was silent for a moment. He felt his throat tighten as he imagined his daughter watching this video.

"I've done lots of things I regret in my life. I have knowingly made bad decisions. More often I chose to do bad than to do good. I put my own desires before everything else. I've been selfish."

He was satisfied with this. It felt right to begin with a confession.

"I always thought I would die young. So I did not want to miss out on anything. I enjoyed everything I was allowed to, and abused everything forbidden. I thought that would be enough to make me happy.

I thought I would have no regrets when the time came to die, because I would have tasted everything that life had to offer."

He paused. Deliberately. He had rehearsed that part the previous evening, and he hoped it did not sound too artificial.

"But now the time has come when I have to look death in the face, it's what I have not done that really bothers me. And it's not the booze I didn't drink, the women I didn't kiss, the drugs I didn't try. All of that is just a waste of time, in the end. What I regret is not having spent more time with you and your mother. And I regret hurting you both. I know I wasn't a good father and that it's too late for me to change that. But I want you to know that I have dedicated the final days of my existence to you."

His eyes were stinging. A wave of emotion was rolling over him. He could feel it crushing his chest. He tried to slow his breathing, to control himself. He had to be strong, keep going until the end.

"I hope I'll be able to return from Ukraine before I'm too sick to enjoy my last moments with you. But if I die here. . ."

He thought about himself as a child, how he had stupidly blamed himself for being alive when his father was dead. As if he could have done anything about it.

"Whatever you do, don't feel guilty. I took on this final investigation because I wanted to give you a good future. I want you to be able to lead a normal life. . . no, a beautiful life. And I also want to do something good, at least once in my life. My father – your grandfather – sacrificed himself so that all Ukrainians, all Russians, all Europeans could continue to live normally. Without his sacrifice, I wouldn't be here and nor would you. He was a real hero."

His throat was so tight now that he was finding it hard to breathe. He had to bring the recording to an end.

"I love you, Tassia. You're the best thing I've done with my life."

He pressed "Stop" and stood up. In the bathroom, he buried his head under the jet of cold tap water. The shock electrified his whole body. The tension in his throat and his stomach melted away. He rubbed his head dry with a towel, then went to the hotel-room safe and took out the pistol that Sokolov had sent him through Kachin. The three magazines that came with it were filled with hollow-point bullets. As soon as they penetrated Leonski's body, they would open up like flowers, causing as much damage as possible to the surrounding tissue. Sokolov wanted to be sure that his son's killer was killed.

Thanks to Maria's government contact, he now had Leonski's address. He lived on the outskirts of Kyiv, in one of those neighbourhoods that housed the families evacuated from the zone. Rybalko himself had lived there with his mother in the late 1980s. Almost all his memories of the place were bad: his mother weakening from day to day, the hearses driven past every week, the other children who could not play football anymore because they did not have the energy, who were dying because their parents could not afford the hospital treatment. . . They always looked so tiny on their death beds, in the clothes that now hung off them. They had lost so much weight that when they died it was as quick and silent as a candle blown out in the night.

There were so many sick people in the neighbourhood that the cluster of tower blocks where they lived had been nicknamed the Cancer Estate by the people who lived in the next suburb, who were careful not to mix with them. The suicide rate was through the roof. The men killed themselves slowly by drowning in alcohol, or sometimes they would decide to end it all suddenly by jumping out of a window. Only the women remained. Apparently they were tougher and more adaptable in a crisis.

When he got there, Rybalko noticed that the neighbourhood had not changed much. It was still as grey and tired-looking. The suburb featured the same uniform Soviet apartment buildings that you could find in Moscow, St Petersburg or Vladivostok, crumbling tower blocks that made old U.S.S.R. hands like Rybalko feel as if they had come full circle into the past.

A parked van attracted a small gathering of scrawny drug addicts, staring vacantly into the white fog of intoxication. Inside the van, volunteers from the Snijenie Vreda ("Risk Reduction") programme handed out condoms and new syringes to limit the spread of Aids. In the dilapidated lobby of Leonski's apartment building, one of the pamphlets stuck to the wall promised to exchange used needles and syringes for new ones. Just above it, someone had pinned the list of inhabitants who had not yet paid their water or electricity bills. A little further on, another poster announced with cruel banality: "We buy natural hair, no dye, 40 cm minimum", with the address of the local hair salon printed beneath. These posters were everywhere in the suburbs of Kyiv, on walls and electric poles. Rybalko wondered if the guy who was buying the hair knew that radiation victims lived here. Would the American or French women who used those hair extensions end up with health problems as a result of Ukraine's cheap-rate locks?

Unsurprisingly, the lift did not work. It was an old Belarusian Mogilev, the same type that was fitted in almost all the Soviet-era tower blocks. By the time he had walked up to the sixth floor, Rybalko was soaked with sweat. He was amazed to discover a queue of men and women standing there, scratching their forearms and sniffing loudly. They were the same human shadows he had seen standing around the van on the street below. As he approached, he realised that the reinforced metal door outside which they were all waiting belonged to Leonski. Intrigued, he joined the line to see what would happen. Soon after that, a man opened the door. With his muscled torso in a too-tight T-shirt and his unfriendly expression, he looked like a nightclub bouncer. He shoved a middle-aged, white-blonde woman out of the door and she shuffled up the corridor, obviously high. The bouncer glanced at the next addict in line who, without a word, handed him a handful of wet, filthy, crumpled banknotes which looked as though they had been taken from the pockets of an old pair of trousers after an hour in a washing machine. The man took the money and nodded at the addict to go inside. Then he closed the door.

This was disturbing. Rybalko was looking for a one-time nuclear engineer, not a drug dealer. Could he have the wrong address? He walked past the queue and one of the junkies called out: "Hey, dickhead, wait your turn!" Rybalko glared at him and the junkie lowered his eyes.

Rybalko knocked on the door. The bouncer opened and crossed his arms.

"We're full. You have to wait."

"I need to speak to Piotr."

The bouncer frowned and a deep furrow appeared in his massive, cliff-like forehead.

"Piotr who?"

"Piotr Leonski. The owner."

"There's no Leonski here. Who are you anyway?"

Rybalko took a wad of rubles from his pocket. "I'm buying in bulk. I was told to see Piotr Leonski. Am I in the wrong place?"

"I've never seen you round here before. I don't trust people I don't know."

"I'm from the Cancer Estate."

The bouncer was caught off guard by this.

"Which village?"

"Pripyat."

The guy nodded. "All the same, I've never seen you before. And I think I'd remember a face like yours."

"My parents died in the Nineties. I had to move to Ivankiv," he improvised. "I do business in the zone down there."

"What kind of business?"

"Import-export. With Belarus. So anyway, does this Leonski guy live here or do I need to find someone else to supply what I need?"

The bouncer glanced at the line of junkies while he thought this over.

"Give me five thousand rubles," he said at last.

"Why?"

A sachet containing some white powder appeared in the bouncer's hand. Behind Rybalko, the junkies' faces lit up. It was cocaine – they all knew it without the word being spoken aloud. A rich man's drug, not the cheap shit that they had to inject into their own veins.

"I didn't come here to get high, I came to do serious business."

"You're not coming in if you don't snort that. Cops don't take drugs. I want to be sure you're not one of them."

Rybalko laughed out loud. "You obviously haven't met many cops! Go on, then, give me your shit."

He handed the bouncer the money, and the bouncer handed him the sachet.

"Have you got something I can use to make a line?"

The bouncer slipped away for a moment, then came back with a mirror and a plastic playing card. Rybalko poured the powder onto the mirror and used the card to form a little line. The jack of spades, he noted. The cocaine was as fine as flour. It left a smell of paraffin in his nostrils and a bitter taste in the back of his throat.

"That stuff is crap. I hope Piotr has something better to sell me. So, where is he?"

"Wait here. I'll go and see."

The bouncer closed the door and was gone for a few minutes, leaving Rybalko alone with the junkies. The drug started to take effect. He felt more lucid and focused. He could see clearly what would happen next. The bouncer would invite him in, then search him. He would hand him his gun, would talk to Leonski, negotiate a fake deal, then get his pistol back. Just then, he would shoot the bouncer, then kill Leonski. Thanks to the coke, he felt fully up to the task.

The bouncer reappeared at the door.

"O.K., come in."

He entered the apartment. To his surprise the bouncer did not search him. He led him through a living room transformed into a drug den: on the synthetic carpet were a dozen filthy mattresses occupied by junkies, their forearms decorated with blue, yellow or red scars. Empty syringes littered the floor.

These zombies would give him no trouble, Rybalko thought. After he'd shot the killer and the bouncer, the fittest of them would run for it while the others would be too high to move. And by the time the police got them to say anything, he would be on a plane back to Moscow.

He felt confident.

The dealer led him into another room and closed the door behind him. Rybalko found himself in a small bedroom, the air thick with the stench of rotting meat, nicotine and sweat. It seemed to be coming from the dealer, who was lying on a narrow bed. The man was in his fifties and he had a waxy, yellowish complexion. Liver disease, Rybalko thought. His face was gaunt from drugs, his cheekbones like knife blades. He was wearing a black T-shirt, a contrast with his pale skin. The lower part of his body was hidden by a thick sheet.

The dealer was smoking a Marlboro, which he put on the edge of an ashtray on the bedside table. The top of the table was covered with cigarette burns, like bullet holes on a target at a shooting range.

"My mate tells me you're from the Cancer Estate and you do business in the zone," the dealer said in a weary voice.

"Piotr Leonski?" was all Rybalko said.

"Himself. In the flesh."

That was the signal. Rybalko moved his hand behind his back to take his pistol and aimed it at Leonski. Despite all the adrenaline rushing through him, he hesitated just as he was about to pull the trigger. Leonski had recoiled not even slightly. He did not seem frightened. His lizard eyes stared coolly at the gun barrel. Taken aback, Rybalko examined the old man more carefully, then realised that something wasn't right. The sweat-soaked sheets were moulded to his body, but in the place where his left leg should have been, there was a hollow. Next to the bed, a pair of crutches was leaning against the wall.

"What are you waiting for?" the dealer said in a disinterested tone.

Rybalko swallowed his saliva. His throat felt numb. The cocaine must have been cut with lidocaine or something.

"Are you really Leonski?"

"Yes, that's me."

He palms were slick with sweat. None of this made any sense. This damaged guy couldn't possibly be Sokolov's killer. How could he have hoisted the body to the top of the apartment building?

He licked his lips and asked: "Does the name Sokolov mean anything to you?"

"I don't know that bird. Was it him who paid you to kill me? Thank him from me, won't you? Go ahead, shoot!"

"What was your wife's name?"

"Since when do hired killers ask questions?" the dealer said angrily. "Just do your fucking job!"

"Tell me your wife's name!"

"Nadejda, but why do you care?"

"I mean your first wife. The one who was murdered near Pripyat."

He saw blank incomprehension in the dealer's eyes and knew that he had the wrong man.

"You're not Piotr Leonski," he said, lowering his weapon slightly.

The old man suddenly threw himself to one side and tried to open the drawer of his bedside table. Rybalko instantly aimed at his head. The dealer took a metal object from the drawer and pointed it at him. Rybalko's index finger almost squeezed the trigger, before he realised that it was just a glasses case.

He lowered his gun again.

"Fucking hell," the man swore. "You're such a loser. If it had been a gun, you'd be dead now."

With a look of bitterness, he threw the case against the wall. It knocked a porcelain figurine from a shelf, and the ornament shattered when it hit the floor. The noise alerted the bouncer, who hammered at the door.

"You O.K., boss?"

"I'm O.K.," the man replied. "Leave us in peace."

He lit another cigarette, since the first one had fallen to the floor while he was opening the bedside table.

"Why didn't you tell him I was threatening you with a gun?" Rybalko said.

"Why bother? You're obviously not going to kill me." The man blew out a cloud of smoke and went on: "I mean, what kind of shitty hired killer refuses to bump someone off even when they're begging to be shot?"

"You're not my target. Why do you want to die?"

The man lifted up the sheet, revealing the stump of his left leg. It had been amputated at the thigh. He tore off the bandage that was covering the wound. It was recent: a seeping, suppurating mess. Rybalko looked away.

"What's the matter, you queer? Too scared to look death in the face?"

Rybalko felt a stirring of anger within, but he wasn't fooled. The man was clearly trying to provoke him into firing.

"It's a sort of gangrene. I'm rotting slowly from the inside. All I want is to snuff it, and quickly. But Pavel, my bodyguard, refuses to shoot me. He's afraid my wife will have him killed if she ever finds out he helped me to die. She wants to believe I can still be cured. She wants me to let them chop off the other leg. She thinks I'll be fine after that. The stupid bitch believes in miracles. But I know what's happening in my body. I'm going to die. No two ways about it. Anyway, why are you after Leonski?"

"Because he murdered someone."

"And you're being paid to kill him. By that Sokolov, I suppose?"

Rybalko ignored this. "This apartment is in Leonski's name. Did you steal his identity?"

The sick man smiled, exposing tobacco-wasted brown teeth.

"Answer me. How long have you been pretending to be him?"

"And what will you do if I don't answer, you moron? Kill me?"

"It won't cost you anything to give me that information."

"It won't get me anything either. If you want me to speak, you need to give me something in return."

The old man put his cigarette in the ashtray and sat up in bed.

"I'll tell you everything I know, on one condition: you have to kill me when I'm done talking."

It was a disgusting deal. And yet Rybalko heard himself reply in a hollow voice: "O.K."

The man smiled.

"Good. I never thought I would have been happy that some guy had been sent to kill me. Alright, what do you want to know, Snow White?"

"Your name, for a start."

"Call me Fyodor."

"How did you get Leonski's apartment, Fyodor?"

The man grimaced.

"It was twenty years ago. Things weren't going well for me. I mean, they were better than they are now, but still, I was deep in the shit. Where to start?"

Fyodor spoke for a long time, as if trying to make the most of his final moments. He kept losing himself in digressions. His athletic career, his days of drinking until he passed out, prohibition under Gorbachev, the thirst that had led him to take drugs. . . He explained the sordid greatness of his business. Junkies came to his place to get high because the syringes were clean and the drugs relatively pure. Here, his customers knew there was plenty of the right gear, like those 10ml syringes highly prized by junkies used to massive doses who didn't want to have to inject themselves more than once, or those fine needles used by diabetics which allowed the addicts without any visible working veins to go deeper into their flesh in search of tiny blood vessels. That was true for many of the poor bastards who came to Fyodor's place. And the cherry on the cake was that Pavel would inject them if necessary, without getting air into the syringe, without touching the needle with his fingers, without missing the vein because his hands were trembling.

"But how did you end up in this apartment?" Rybalko demanded, wearying of these details.

"At the time when I found this place, I was a *fartsovchtchik* – I worked as an intermediary between the people who wanted to pay for western clothes and the 'suppliers'. Sometimes I'd buy the stuff directly. I'd hang around in hotel bars run by Intourist, the State organisation that looked after foreign tourists. I'd buy jeans from westerners for thirty or forty rubles, then sell them for two or three times as much. I'd also buy designer clothes and luxury shoes from diplomats' wives: they were even more profitable. But it was a dangerous world. My troubles began when a B.Kh.S.S. officer started taking an interest in my little business."

Rybalko knew all about the B.Kh.S.S., the department that fought against the theft of socialist property. Some of the officers he had worked with in Moscow had been in that branch of the militia before it was dissolved in the 1990s. They were by far the most corrupt police officers he had met in his career.

"This officer turned up at my apartment. Thankfully I wasn't there.

After that, I stayed with friends for a while, so he wouldn't find me. But it couldn't go on like that. One day, one of my friends told me about some unoccupied apartments in Little Chernobyl, as people round here called this neighbourhood. My friend had heard that some old people were abandoning their apartments and going back to live in their rotten izbas in the countryside. I bribed the concierge and he told me this place had been empty for six months."

"But it's still in Leonski's name. So you must have stolen his identity too."

"There were cheques in the letter box. His compensation as a liquidator. It wasn't a lot of money, but it was better than nothing. It meant I could afford more than just the basics. Before I started selling drugs, I used to take them. At first, it was easy to get hold of them. There weren't many addicts in the U.S.S.R. and the authorities weren't vigilant about drugs. Doctors used to anaesthetise their patients with cocaine, if you can believe it! Fuck, those were the good old days. . ."

Dealer, liar, pension thief: Fyodor had quite the CV. Nobody would miss him, thought Rybalko, except his wife.

"Leonski didn't come back?"

"Just once. And that's the crazy thing: he turned up here and said he wanted to pick up his things. I took out a knife and yelled at him to fuck off. That bastard hit me with a right that I didn't see coming. I was out for the count! I thought he was going to kick me out, but he said he just wanted to take a few things and that he wouldn't be coming back so I could carry on living in his apartment. Fuck, I couldn't believe it. The State had given him an apartment after Chernobyl and he just abandoned it!"

"Did he say why?"

"He said he was going back home."

"Nothing more specific than that?"

"Nope. He just picked up his stuff and he went. I never saw him again."

"What did he take?"

"Photos, clothes. . . nothing special."

"Any stuffed birds?"

Fyodor blinked rapidly.

"No, but there were loads in the apartment when I got here. I got rid of all that crap straight away. Those things depressed the hell out of me. I could feel them watching me everywhere I went."

Junkie guilt, Rybalko thought. The dead animals' eyes brought out his feelings of shame at being an addict.

"The most ironic thing," Fyodor said, "was that I thought this apartment was like a gift from God. It was perfect for me because the police never came round, since the neighbourhood was full of radiation victims. They were scared of catching something. And the junkies couldn't care less about that, as long as there were cheap drugs available. But it was a poisoned chalice."

He scratched the end of his amputated leg.

"It was all those radioactive bastards who made me sick. They ooze fucking radioactivity. They breathe it out. It's because of them that I got this damn infection that's eating me alive. Bound to be. It's like the Chernobyl Aids."

Fyodor had stolen the identity of a Chernobyl victim, and now he was just like them: sick and dying. Poetic justice, thought Rybalko.

"Are you done? No more questions?" the dealer said. "Can we end it now?"

He tensed up. It was true: he had no more questions. He frowned, trying to think of something else to ask, anything to put off for a little longer the miserable chore he had agreed to perform.

"Are you sure this is what you want?"

"Totally."

"You could take pills – it'd be gentler. Or overdose on drugs."

"Pavel would never let me. He'd resuscitate me and call for an ambulance. I don't want to wake up in hospital in an even worse state. I want to die quickly and cleanly."

Rybalko thought about his own situation. In six months, he would be like this man, rotting slowly in bed. And he would be alone. Except he had a gun to end it himself. But did he have the courage to pull the trigger?

It was the moment to find out. He picked up a pillow and walked over to the dealer. Without a word, he pressed the pillow against the man's face. Fyodor did not resist. His rasping breaths grew shorter and faster. Rybalko held the barrel of the gun against the part of the pillow covering the dealer's forehead. The safety squeaked as he pulled it back. Seconds passed, as long as minutes. Fyodor was suffocating, but he didn't push the pillow away. He was determined to die. But Rybalko could not kill him. He let go of the pillow.

"Fuck, what are you... why did you stop?" Fyodor protested wheezily.

Without a word, Rybalko left the bedroom and walked through the living room full of junkies.

The dealer yelled: "You fucking black bastard! Fucking queer!"

Pavel came running. Rybalko aimed his pistol at the bodyguard.

"Hands on the wall," he ordered.

The bodyguard obeyed. Rybalko smashed him over the head with the butt of his gun and Pavel collapsed to the floor.

The dealer's voice was growing louder, closer. Rybalko turned around and saw Fyodor staggering towards him on crutches. He was drooling as he continued hurling insults. Suddenly afraid, Rybalko ran through the corridor as the dealer's curses echoed through the apartment.

"I hope you die in agony, you fucking bastard!"

29

Out on the street, he got into his car and sped away from the apartment building. He was a swarm of contradictory emotions. He could still feel the cocaine sharpening his senses, but his self-confidence had taken a severe blow. To give himself a pick-me-up, he parked by the roadside and snorted the rest of the powder in the sachet. A brief rush of euphoria, but it soon fell like a soufflé. Not only was Fyodor a bastard, his drugs were shit.

Even so, Rybalko still felt the shameful joy of being alive, even if he knew he was on borrowed time. He got out his wallet and found an old photograph of his ex-wife and their daughter. He had hoped this would make him feel better, but it had the opposite effect. He thought about all the time he had wasted on work, on futile pleasures that had kept him away from where he needed to be. At first, he'd refused to have a child. He was afraid that Marina would give birth to a monster. He had heard so many stories of stillborn babies and kids born with deformities when he was living in the Cancer Estate. Most of all, though, he was afraid of leaving his child an orphan. He did not want his son or daughter to grow up without a father, as he had done.

But then Tassia had been born. A wonderful parenthesis in his life. He made resolutions: no more drugs, no more girls, no more wheeling and dealing. For three years, he kept to these resolutions. But then his old demons returned. Violence. Fast money. Easy pleasures. His marriage began to collapse. To take his mind off it, he threw himself into work. His ambition was to make a purer world for Tassia to live in. To cleanse the streets of the most dangerous criminals. This pathetic crusade was his only objective in life. As he looked in the rear-view mirror now, though, what had he actually achieved?

His marriage had failed. His career was over. His dreams were all dead, if indeed they had ever existed. What would he leave behind him? Nothing of any worth.

Except Tassia. He had to keep going, for her.

He tried to think through what he had discovered. Leonski had told the dealer he was "going home". That could mean any number of things, but the most probable was that he had gone back to the zone. Rybalko had to check out that lead. He drove towards Chernobyl and reached the first checkpoint in less than two hours. He found an abnormally long line of cars waiting there. The drivers and guides around the guard's hut were all exasperated.

"What's going on?" he asked one of the men.

"No idea. The guard won't let us through. We've been hanging around here at least half an hour."

Rybalko waited for another ten minutes, until the guard delivered the bad news: "The zone is closed now. You should all go home."

"For how long?" one driver wanted to know.

"Until further notice."

"Why?"

"Police investigation. The police in Chernobyl just called: there's been another murder in Pripyat."

30

Pripyat was silent, as if in mourning. The light of a police car revolved in the darkness of Sportivnaya Street, throwing splashes of blue onto the bare concrete walls of the Lazurny swimming pool. The voice of Captain Melnyk was the only sound to be heard as he called the prosecutor in charge of the swallow killer case.

"What do you mean, a new murder?" the prosecutor demanded.

Melnyk stuck to the facts: "We found a dead body in the Lazurny pool."

"Is the victim Ukrainian?"

"I don't know yet."

"Good God, Melnyk. . . this is too much. I'm going to call Kyiv and ask them to send reinforcements."

"You're not taking me off the case?"

"Listen, I let you work on the murder of the Russian because nobody cares about a guy like that. The prosecutor general of Ukraine fought in the Donbas, you know. He's not a big fan of Russians. But this is something else. If the new victim is Ukrainian, this will be a big story."

"You can't do this to me. I've almost cracked the case. I have a suspect."

"Who?"

"His name is Piotr Leonski. His wife was murdered in 1986, at the same time as Olga Sokolov, the mother of our first victim. I think he killed them both."

"How sure are you that this guy is the killer?"

"Pretty sure. My men are looking for him right now."

The prosecutor did not seem enthusiastic, but he agreed to keep Melnyk on the case.

"Alright, you're in charge for now. But I'm still going to send reinforcements from Kyiv. We need more manpower. I have an idea this is going to blow up."

The prosecutor was right. Pripyat was world-famous thanks to its connection with the Chernobyl disaster. The first murder had gone under the radar, but with the second – and confirmation that a serial killer was on the loose in the zone – there was a chance that the region would soon be inundated with television crews from all over the world. That was one of the reasons why Melnyk had closed all the checkpoints: to keep out the voyeurs and at the same time try to confine the murderer within the zone.

"Don't disappoint me," the prosecutor warned. "We both have a lot to lose here."

"Don't worry, I have no intention of failing."

"Alright. And try not to kill the guy when you arrest him. I want a trial. You understand? I know you're angling for a transfer to Kyiv. If you bring me this killer alive, I'll support your request. But we have no time to lose. I'm under a great deal of pressure. My superiors want results fast. This could be good for both of us, captain: solve this case quickly, and I promise I'll find you a job in Kyiv, near your family."

"I understand."

He hung up. The entrance to the municipal swimming pool was guarded by a police officer. Melnyk saluted him and ducked under the red and white crime scene tape. Obviously, no bystander was likely to attempt to get inside, but Melnyk had anticipated that the prosecutor might call for reinforcements. These pointless security measures were designed to show the Kyiv police, who would be there in less than an hour, that the Chernobyl police followed procedure to the letter.

The Lazurny pool had once been magnificent. Large and modern, it had hosted regional championships besides being where the town's schoolchildren all had their swimming lessons. In those days, the basin was always full of chlorinated water. Now it was dry, its floor scattered with rubble, and the huge picture windows that surrounded it had long since been broken.

Novak was waiting at the end of the pool. She was wearing a mask that covered her mouth and nose. In her left hand she held a small gas lantern that cast a halo of light around it which reflected weakly off the white tiles of the empty pool. She had been on duty since a tourist guide had called her to report the discovery of a corpse in the pool. Even though Melnyk had exempted her from patrols in irradiated areas, she had joined the team sent to the crime scene and had kept it secure while she waited for her superior to arrive.

"Where's the body?"

"That end," she said, gesturing vaguely at the two large diving boards that overhung the deepest part of the pool, a dark chasm beyond the reach of her lantern's glow.

Melnyk noticed a rope at Novak's feet.

"We'll need this to get down to the corpse," she explained. "The ladders don't go all the way and it slopes down quite steeply in the middle of the pool."

"So you haven't been down to examine the body yet?"

"No, I just looked at it from the edge. I wanted to wait until you got here," she said, kicking the rope into the pool.

Novak bent down and put her lantern on the floor. At this end, the pool was only about one metre deep. She jumped down, raising a small cloud of dust as she landed. Melnyk joined her. He switched on his torch and swept the beam over the surface of the basin. It was littered with debris that had fallen from the roof and pieces of broken earthenware. On the dusty tiles, footprints were clearly visible. Some of them went down towards the other end of the pool, while others came back. Melnyk shone the torch at one of his own footprints. The mark left by his shoes looked tiny next to the others.

"Yeah, those are Leonski's footprints," he said.

Keeping clear of the killer's prints, they walked along the old swimming lanes bordered by lines of black tiles. Melnyk wondered if the water had been siphoned out in 1986, during the evacuation, or if it had simply evaporated over time.

"Who found the body?" he said.

"A guide."

"The same one as last time?"

"No, a different one. I sent him to the station with his tourist group so they can make their statements."

Novak was doing a good job. It made a change from his other subordinates: they were more battle-hardened but also more prone to sloppiness and laziness. They were also often drunk: more than once, Melnyk had had to drag one of his officers out of bed and stick his head under a cold water tap to sober him up before he could go to work.

"And the victim?" he asked. "Is it a man?"

"No, a young woman."

Midway along the swimming lanes, the bottom of the pool sloped downward. Novak tied the rope she had brought to the bars of one of the metal ladders and they slowly made her way to the lowest part. There, on the tiled floor, lay a young woman. Her azure eyes were staring sightlessly at the ceiling. She was wearing a white dress and her feet were bare. Her blonde hair was decorated with a crown of wildflowers. Melnyk crouched above the body and picked a petal. He crushed it between his fingers and a faint smell reached his nostrils.

"They're fresh."

Novak nodded gravely.

"We'll have to go through the list of women missing in the region," she said.

The young woman's torso was covered in deep cuts. Melnyk put on a pair of gloves and ran his finger along one of them.

"They look like knife wounds. Same as for the murders of Olga and Larissa."

He noticed that there wasn't much blood on the dress, despite these lacerations. Suggesting that the victim had been dead before she was cut.

"What do you think motivated the choice of this victim?" Novak said.

There was no way of being sure, Melnyk thought. But he tried out a theory anyway. "Larissa was twenty-six when Leonski killed her. This girl must be about the same age. Maybe he chose her because of that."

"But why kill a woman now, after so many years of inactivity?"

"Maybe murdering Leonid Sokolov gave him back his taste for killing."

Novak did not appear convinced by this story. Melnyk himself was not really convinced either. A killer remains a killer. A man who murders for pleasure is not going to wait years before he does it again.

"The real question is why he exhibits the bodies like that," he said.

"He didn't hide the two women's bodies thirty years ago," Novak responded.

"True, but that was different. He had to act quickly then. The power station was exploding and he wanted to get away from the zone as fast as he could."

"Maybe, in his sick mind, they're like trophies that he wants to show off?"

Melnyk noticed that Novak was staring at the woman's legs with a troubled expression on her face.

"Something wrong?"

"Do you think he. . . well, you know what I mean."

Yes, he knew what she meant. A man who enjoys giving life to dead animals. . . who takes pleasure in handling them. . . what emotion would he get from a dead woman? Did it excite him? Had he used his victim's body to satisfy his monstrous sexual desires? Or had he killed her after raping her?'

"We'll find out at the autopsy," Melnyk said.

He swept his torch beam across the bottom of the pool.

"There's something missing. Where's the swallow?"

Novak looked around.

"Perhaps he changed his routine? The victim's eyes haven't been gouged out either, like Olga and Larissa."

Suddenly Melnyk noticed a detail. As he leaned over the young woman, he had the feeling he could smell almonds. He asked Novak if she could smell it too. She took off her mask and sniffed.

"Bitter almonds, yes. . . that's the smell of cyanide."

She stepped back, hands over her nose.

"How do you know that?" Melnyk said.

"We had American trainers at the academy. Scientists. One of them taught a toxicology class."

Back in his day, Melnyk thought, they hadn't learnt that sort of stuff at the militia school.

"If Leonski naturalises animals," Novak went on, "he might have cyanide in his workshop. If I remember correctly, it's also used to kill butterflies without damaging their wings."

"Did the American teach you that too?"

"No. I read a few taxidermy books after you told me about the stuffed swallow. I thought it might be useful."

Melnyk could see why she had finished top of her class in the academy.

"Well, anyway, supposing there had been any doubt, I think we can be pretty sure now that Leonski is the killer," Melnyk concluded. "We have the enormous footprints, all the taxidermy stuff, and the knife wounds."

"There are some new elements compared to the 1986 murders though. The crown of flowers, for example."

"As I said, Leonski was in a very great hurry in 1986. Maybe he didn't have time to carry out all his fantasies."

As he examined the crown, Melnyk noticed something strange about the victim's left ear. When he folded it down, he saw a number of very old scars there.

"You think her ear was sewn back on?" Novak said.

Melnyk looked doubtful. The ear's texture was unusual.

"My bet would be reconstructive surgery. I've seen children born without ears, because of Chernobyl."

"So you think she's from the region?"

"It's possible."

Novak pointed at the victim's eyes.

"Why didn't he take them out this time?"

"No idea."

He peered into the dead girl's doll-like eyes, her azure irises and the white around it like porcelain. . . white like porcelain. . . azure and porcelain. . . porcelain. . .

Suddenly nauseated, he put his hand in front of his mouth and stood up shakily.

"Are you alright?" Novak said anxiously.

Melnyk leaned against the wall. Bent forwards, he tried not to throw up as his stomach heaved.

"Captain?"

"Just a minute. . ."

He took a few deep breaths until he started to feel better. Then he crouched next to the body again.

"What's wrong?"

"The eyes. . . I don't think they're hers."

Novak turned pale. Melnyk took a pencil from his pocket and moved it close to one of the eyes. A few millimetres from the surface of the eyeball, he hesitated. Then, gathering his courage, he tapped the cornea. A small dry sound, like a fingernail on a window.

"It's a glass eye," he breathed.

Chilled by that inhuman stare, Melnyk tried to close the woman's eyelids. But his finger slipped and grazed one of the glass eyes enough to make it spin horribly, creating an impossible, disturbing gaze, as if the dead woman wanted to look inside her own skull. Disgusted, he pulled the eyelids down.

"He's sick," Novak muttered. "He'll do it again. If we don't stop him, he'll keep killing people. Like the Butcher of Rostov."

Her voice was shaky now.

"It's my fault. If I hadn't gone solo, maybe we could have prevented this. Maybe he–"

"It wouldn't have changed anything," Melnyk interrupted. "There's no point going over all that again. It's what you do now that matters.

So focus on the crime scene. In half an hour, the Kyiv police and the prosecutor will be here. If we want to keep this case, we have to show we're capable of arresting this guy, O.K.?"

Novak swallowed.

"Yes, you're right. I. . . I'll be all right."

"Good. Now bring the lamp over here, I want to check something. Shine it on the abdomen."

Novak held the gas lamp above the corpse. The light danced gently as her hand trembled.

"What are you doing?" she asked as he ran his hands over the white dress, as if trying to smooth out the folds.

"There!"

Melnyk's hand stopped at the young woman's navel. He'd felt a rough patch through the fabric. Pressing the dress against the victim's skin, he was able to make out a scar sewn shut with black thread.

"Leonid Sokolov had the same scar on his belly. Since there was no autopsy, we have no way of knowing what that meant. But this time, radiation or not, they're going to have to do their job at the morgue in Kyiv."

He stood up and his knees made an unpleasant cracking sound.

"Now all we have to do is find the swallow," he said, taking out his torch.

He moved the yellow halo around the floor. No sign of a stuffed bird. Why wasn't there a swallow this time?

"The diving boards!" he said suddenly.

The highest one, several metres above them, was lost in darkness. Melnyk raised his torch and noticed something poking above the concrete edge.

"Is that. . . a bird's wing?" Novak whispered.

"Let's take a look."

They climbed up the slope to the shallow end. The tiles were slippery, but luckily quite a few were cracked or missing and the concrete beneath provided more grip.

At the deep end were the two diving boards. The lower one was about two metres above the water, the higher one closer to five metres. It was the higher board from which they had seen the bird's wing poking out.

Melnyk noticed a practical detail that he had not spotted when first entering the pool. There was a metal staircase between the two diving board platforms, but there was nothing between the lower board and the floor. It must have been removed years earlier as a precaution, to prevent nutcases going up there to take photographs.

"We could ask the fire brigade at the power station for a ladder," Novak suggested.

"We don't have time," Melnyk said.

Time was indeed short: he wanted to find the bird before the Kyiv unit arrived, just in case the prosecutor changed his mind and gave the investigation to the outsiders instead. For both him and Novak, this case was their ticket out of the zone. Their best chance of escape.

The platforms rested on reinforced concrete arms that joined at ground level to form a sort of V. Melnyk hoisted himself onto the lower part of this V; from there, he was able to climb up to the lower board by pulling on the metal guardrail that encircled it.

Novak raised the gas lantern above her head, looking worried.

"Be careful," she called. "That thing's more than thirty years old. It might give way under your weight."

As if to prove her right, the metal staircase that led to the second diving board shook when the captain set foot upon it to test its solidity. He hesitated. In the dust that covered the steps, he could see footprints: someone had already climbed this staircase, so what was he afraid of?

He climbed the first step, then the second.

"Just keep going, it's fine," he muttered to himself.

Another step, another creak.

"Just turn back," Novak shouted.

His legs started to tremble. The vibrations were transmitted instantly to the stairs, which began to make quiet clanking noises in the eerie silence of the abandoned pool. Melnyk closed his eyes and tried to reason with himself. You're already halfway there, just keep going.

"Are you O.K.?" Novak asked, a few metres below.

He did not reply, as if uttering a single word might break his fragile grip. He was only a few steps from the second platform. He raised his foot, put it down on the next step. The metal protested noisily.

"Turn back! We can send the firemen later."

Ignoring Novak's advice, he climbed another step. Was this determination? Misplaced pride? Masochism? Whatever it was, he refused to follow his subordinate's advice. One more step and he could see the bird perched in the middle of the diving board. A swallow.

A loud crack.

The screech of twisting metal.

One of the joints attaching the staircase to the top of the platform was about to give way. Melnyk felt himself veering sideways. The void beneath his feet grew slowly closer, as in a dream.

Then it stabilised.

Below, Novak stood wordless and paralysed. Without part of its anchorage, however, the staircase was coiling to the right. Melnyk gently shifted his weight to the left-hand side. No sudden movements, he told himself, or the second joint might come loose. He assessed the situation. He was almost at the top of the stairs. Either he kept going up or he turned back.

Going back made more sense. The base of the staircase was still firmly in place. A few steps and he would be safe.

His torch, which he was still holding in one hand, lit up the void. Some of the dust on the steps had been knocked off when the staircase had toppled sideways, and the air was filled with dancing motes. Melnyk slowly transferred his weight to his left leg and stretched his right leg backwards. The staircase wobbled dangerously. His foot groped at thin air, then came into contact with the step below. He supported himself on it. His whole body was stretched back.

Crack!

The staircase collapsed. Instinctively he pushed upward on his legs, hoping to throw himself back far enough that he would land on the lower platform and not on the ground three metres below.

His fall seemed to last an eternity.

His back hit the concrete with a thud.

Pins and needles all over his body. He couldn't move his lips. His arms and legs were like lead. His eyelids fluttered.

And then everything turned black.

31

Light.

Was this it, the famous tunnel that you saw as you passed through to the other side? At least there was a bulb in heaven's ceiling lamp. . .

Melnyk woke up in a hospital bed. He had a ferocious migraine. He felt the back of his head and discovered it was bandaged. He remembered his fall, the sound of a siren, faces leaning over him. Strangely, he also remembered floating in the air. They must have used some sort of cradle to bring him down.

"You gave us quite a scare, captain."

The voice was coming from a corner of the room. He turned in its direction.

"Novak?"

The young officer was sitting in a chair. There were dark rings under her eyes.

"Did you sleep well?" she asked.

Melnyk struggled to sit up. His back and backside ached. There was an unpleasant tickling sensation in his arm. He realised he was hooked up to an IV drip. He lifted his hand to his hair but when he passed it above the bandages he discovered he was bald.

"*Blyad*. . ."

"They had to shave your head and your beard."

"*Blyad!*" he said again, patting his chin.

"It was because of the radioactive particles. They sometimes stick to hair. You were covered with dust after your fall, so they shaved it off when you arrived here. You fell off the staircase onto the lower diving board – do you remember?"

Melnyk looked through the window. The sky was cloudy. Impossible to tell if it was morning or afternoon. He instinctively raised his left wrist to see what time it was, but his watch had been removed.

"Where are my things?"

"They threw them all away after your shower. You don't remember?"

She explained to him that the firemen from the power station had set up a makeshift decontamination shower near the pool, before cutting him out of his clothes and washing him.

"What time is it?"

"Nine in the morning."

He realised he had been unconscious for about ten hours.

"The body! Have they autopsied it yet?"

"They're doing it now. They prepared a special operating theatre for it."

Melnyk grabbed the needle stuck in his arm and pulled it out. Novak's mouth dropped open.

"What are you doing?"

"I'm not going to just lie here twiddling my thumbs while the others solve my case."

When he stood up, a sharp pain shot through his back and the back of his head, making him groan.

"The doctor said you had to spend a whole week in bed before you–"

"I'm fine."

"But they want to keep you under observation for at least forty-eight–"

"I said I'm fine," Melnyk interrupted.

In the wardrobe he found some clothes.

"Did you bring these?"

"Yes, I went to your apartment to get some of your clothes."

"In Chernobyl or in Kyiv?"

"In Chernobyl."

"Have you called my wife?"

"Yes, I reassured her. I told her that your life was not in danger and that the radioactivity tests had been positive. I mean negative. Well, I mean they were fine."

Melnyk cursed. Tatiana was not going to let him sleep at home after something like this. Maybe she would even leave him for good this time.

He took off his gown, untroubled by Novak's presence, and put on some clean clothes.

"You really ought to stay in bed," she said. "You almost fractured your skull."

"We don't have any time to lose, Novak. Do you want to get out of the zone or not? If the Kyiv unit arrest the culprit before we do, we'll both be stuck here for the next ten years."

He rummaged through the cupboard in search of some shoes.

"You didn't bring me any boots?"

"No, I couldn't find them."

"How am I supposed to go out? Barefoot, like a stupid hippie?"

At last the young officer let her exasperation show: "You weren't supposed to leave your bed for a week. And you could be a bit nicer. I spent the whole night at the crime scene and the hospital. I haven't slept since the night before last. And if you don't give a damn about your health, you may as well go out barefoot. Why not?"

"We don't have much choice."

Melnyk left the room, followed by Novak.

"My phone. . . did they throw that away too?"

"I assume so."

"*Blyad*. . . I have to call my wife."

"I can lend you mine," she said coldly.

"No, it's O.K. I'll do it later."

They went out to the car park. Given his lack of shoes, he let Novak drive.

"Have they identified the victim?"

"No."

"What about the swallow? Did they find out anything from that?"

"Not yet. The lab is examining it now."

"And Leonski? Have you found out where he lives?"

"Yes. In Kyiv. We called our colleagues in the capital and they're going to pay him a visit."

"Finally some good news. Although I doubt they'll find him there."

"Why?"

"He signs his crimes. He must be expecting us to turn up at his home eventually. I'd bet you anything that he's left by now."

They drove to the apartment building in Chernobyl where the police stayed while they were on duty. She accompanied him to the door of his apartment.

"Go back to the station and concentrate on trying to identify the victim."

"What are you going to do?"

"I'm going to Kyiv. I need to talk to the coroner."

And to my wife, he thought.

"We already have someone there."

"I'd prefer to take a look myself."

Novak did not argue. She drove to the police station while Melnyk took a shower. He rubbed his skin for a long time, trying to get rid of the smells left by the chemical products in the decontamination shower. He discovered his spare boots hidden under his bed (why the hell had he put them there?), put them on, and went out to find his Lada Riva in the car park.

A black 4×4 was parked next to it. The driver had opened the smoked-glass window and his forearm was leaning on the top of the door, exposing an eagle tattoo.

32

With his high cheekbones and gaunt cheeks, his dark eyes and salt-and-pepper stubble, there could be no doubt about it: the driver's face was all too familiar.

"Serguei Kamenev," Melnyk said, placing his hands on his hips, within reach of his handcuffs and his gun.

Kamenev was the right-hand man for an elusive criminal involved in all the zone's smuggling. It was said that his boss was a "thief in law", one of those tattooed criminals who secretly ruled prisons back in the U.S.S.R. days. But nobody had ever seen him in the area: he probably preferred to stay in Kyiv, far from his radioactive fiefdom.

"I almost didn't recognise you, captain. What happened to your hair and your beard?"

"Maybe he sold 'em," joked the man sitting next to him.

Dressed in a khaki bomber jacket with an orange lining, Kamenev's passenger had a long lock of hair combed forward in the style of the old Cossacks.

"I see you've brought one of your little Right Sector friends with you," Melnyk remarked. "Is he one of the morons who vandalised the 1986 office?"

"Never heard of it," Kamenev said.

He turned to his passenger: "Did you do something illegal in Chernobyl?"

The man laughed and swore he had not. Melnyk glared at them.

"I don't want any Right Sector thugs in my zone, Kamenev. If your little Nazis keep bothering the people at 1986, I'll have to lock them up. You won't get any more warnings."

"Who the fuck d'you think you are, you old fart?" the Cossack shouted at him.

Kamenev silenced him with a movement of his hand.

"Take it easy, Melnyk. These lads are just good patriots. They're fighting against the Moscow troops. Just like your son."

It was true that there were quite a few Right Sector members among the volunteers on the Eastern front. The knowledge that Nikolai was rubbing shoulders with people like that on a regular basis made Melnyk feel sick.

"I heard he was in the Donbas, near Donetsk," Kamenev said.

Melnyk twitched. "How do you know that?"

"It's a small world, the zone," the gangster said with a nasty smile. "How many people live in Chernobyl, a few hundred? News spreads fast."

He took out his mobile and showed Melnyk a picture of a group of men in uniform posing in front of a Cold War-era tank. Not one of them had the same equipment.

"My son's there too. He sent me some photos of his unit. It's a fucking mess, isn't it? An army of farm boys. The State gives them hardly anything – a bit of food, some ammunition, and that's your lot. Good thing he's got me to help him out."

Kamenev bent forward to open the glove compartment. Melnyk caught a glimpse of a revolver. He thought briefly about arresting him for possession of a prohibited firearm, but what was the point? Kamenev had supporters within the police force and he would undoubtedly be released before the case reached the courts. He was already free to move around the zone as he wished, despite the fact that it was supposedly sealed shut. Most of the guards got a nice *vziatka* – a backhander – from him, to let him go about his business.

The smuggler took a dog-eared magazine from the glove compartment.

"I bought him this gun," he said, showing Melnyk a wildly expensive sniper rifle. "And a telescopic sight. That way, I can be sure they won't put him in the frontline," he added with a wink. "How 'bout your kid, is he well-equipped?"

Melnyk thought about the ring his wife had sold to raise money for Nikolai.

"What's that go to do with you, Kamenev?"

"I heard he didn't have a bulletproof vest. Maybe I could get you some decent equipment for him."

Here we go. The attempt at corruption had begun.

"In return for what?"

The smuggler smiled.

"All this shit going on in the zone is bad for business... The cops from Kyiv, the journalists. . . ornithologists. . . There have been too many people around lately. But the worst thing is the closed checkpoints. That needs to end soon. It's not good for business, you understand?"

"What business, Kamenev?"

"Business that requires serenity. There have been too many outsiders hanging around recently."

"Like Leonid Sokolov?"

"I didn't kill the Russian, if that's what you're implying."

"I wasn't implying anything. I prefer direct questions. Were you involved in the death of Leonid Sokolov?"

"You think I'd tell you if I was?"

"No, I think you'd lie to me while looking me straight in the eye."

"I didn't murder that guy."

"Did you get one of your men to kill him?"

"Why would I need some poor rich kid dead?"

"Because he was sticking his nose in places you wanted kept secret."

"I didn't kill him and I'm not involved in any way in his death."

"Will you come to the station and put that in writing?"

"What would you do to us there, old man?" the Cossack said. "Give us a thrashing with your belt?"

"It wouldn't do you any harm, you little twat," Melnyk said.

"Oh yeah? You dirty fucking cop…" Furious, the man started opening his door to get out. Kamenev grabbed his arm.

"Stay where you are, idiot. As for you, Melnyk, you know perfectly well I'm not going anywhere near the fucking police station."

"I could arrest you."

"On what charge?"

"I'd find something."

"Let it go," the smuggler sighed. "Even if you did manage to make something stick, another guy would take my place within the week. You and me, we're the same, you know: just interchangeable pawns in someone else's army. So let's not waste time arguing. Anyway, I didn't kill the kid. I'm not a monster, I'm just a businessman. If I kill someone, I don't sew up their eyes and lips afterwards."

"How do you know that?"

Kamenev handed him an advertising pamphlet from the firearms magazine.

"The deal's on the table, Melnyk. Open the zone. And clean out the scum. There are too many outsiders sticking their noses where they don't belong. Especially that black who turned up recently."

"The ornithologist?"

"Yeah, that's the one. Make him go away, him and all the other rubberneckers. And open the checkpoints. And then your kid'll get all the equipment he needs at the front."

Kamenev twisted the ignition key and the 4×4's engine roared. He was about to put it into gear when Melnyk placed his hand on the door.

"How did you know about the sewn-up eyelids?"

Kamenev revved the engine.

"Better get out the way, Melnyk. Wouldn't want an accident, would we?"

"How did you know?"

Kamenev shifted into first and the vehicle lurched forward, forcing Melnyk to step back. The 4×4 drove to the road, then disappeared into the distance.

The advertising pamphlet lay on the ground, still open at the page of bulletproof vests.

33

On his way into Kyiv, Melnyk got stuck in an enormous traffic jam that ended his hopes of getting there before the end of the autopsy. He called the morgue and asked to speak to the coroner.

"We just finished," the coroner told him. "You won't have the report until tomorrow."

"I just want your first impressions. Were you able to determine the cause of death?"

"Probably poison. The body smelled of bitter almonds and I detected alkaline burns on the gastro-intestinal tract consistent with ingestion of cyanide salts. Of course, we'll have to wait for the laboratory to confirm that."

Just as Novak predicted, Melnyk thought.

"What else can you tell me?"

"Well, the young woman had undergone plastic surgery. There was a major aplasia that required reconstruction of her left outer ear, probably using cartilage from her ribs."

"Is that a common operation?"

"No, it's rare. Although less so since Chernobyl."

He took a mental note: this would help with identification.

"I noticed some stitches on her abdomen," Melnyk said.

"Ah, that. . ." the coroner said, sounding revolted. "In thirty years as a coroner, I've never seen anything that vile. The killer removed her intestines. And stuffed a dead bird in there. This guy is really sick."

"What species of bird did he use, a swallow?"

"No, it was a bird of prey. I'd say probably a falcon, but I'm no expert."

"*Sokol*," muttered Melnyk.

"Sorry?"

"My first victim was called Sokolov."

"A *sokol* in a Sokolov. . . Sounds like your killer has a pretty dark sense of humour."

"What else did you notice?"

"I found some post-mortem fractures, caused by a very violent blow. As if the body had been dropped from a great height. I'm guessing the killer thew her off the edge of the pool so he wouldn't have to drag her all the way there."

Melnyk wondered if Leonski had acted that way out of convenience or if there was another explanation for this *modus operandi*. The fall had damaged the body, and he was convinced that in the murderer's mind the corpses that he left behind were like works of art. This girl could not have weighed more than fifty kilos, so dragging her body into a swimming pool hardly seemed an insurmountable feat for a man in his fifties. Did that mean he was ill or injured?

"What about the eyes?" Melnyk said.

"Prosthetic. With kopeks behind them."

"Coins?"

"You heard me. One dated 1960 and the other 1986."

1986. . . the year that Larissa and Olga had died, the year; the power station had exploded; and Leonski had been sent to prison. . . there were so many events that might correspond to that date. For 1960, however, he could not think of anything. He wondered if there had been coins behind Leonid Sokolov's eyes too. A shame they could not do the autopsy. . .

Melnyk ended the call and kept driving through the slow-motion hell of afternoon traffic. He thought about his wife. How would she react if he turned up like this, head shaved and beardless? He rehearsed what he was planning to tell her. They checked me out, I'm fine. They only shaved me as a precautionary measure. Would she demand that he started shaving every day now? God, what a pain. . .

When he got home, the door was closed and he could not open it because someone had left the key in the lock on the other side.

"Honey, it's me," he said, knocking on the wooden panel.

"Joseph?" Tatiana said, sounding shocked. "You're not in hospital?"

"They discharged me. I'm fine."

His spine and the back of his head disagreed with this diagnosis, particularly after the three hours he'd spent in the car, but the pain was not debilitating.

"Can you let me in?"

Silence.

"Honey?"

"Get undressed first."

"Come on, I'm not going to strip off on the landing. . ."

He was whispering: the walls in their building were so thin that they could hear the neighbours snoring at night. He imagined them now, staring out of their spyholes, laughing their arses off at the policeman on the fourth floor who had to get naked before he could enter his own home. This was too humiliating to bear.

"Open the door. My clothes are clean. They decontaminated me."

"I'm not letting you in wearing those clothes. And what happened to your hair?"

"They shaved me as a security measure."

"Why?"

"It's protocol. Listen, it's stupid talking about this through the door. Just let me in and I'll explain everything. . ."

"I was told you fell into a pile of radioactive dust. Is that why they shaved you?"

He silently cursed Novak. Why had she told his wife that?

"Yes, that's right. But that means I don't have any radioactive particles left on me, you see?"

"I. . . I don't know, Joseph. Maybe you shouldn't come home."

He was speechless. Had he misunderstood?

"You don't want me in the apartment?"

"I just think you should stay away until they're sure."

"Sure of what, for Christ's sake?" he said, losing his temper.

"Don't speak like that in front of me, Joseph!"

"I'm not in front of you, there's a door between us. And that's what pisses me off. Come on, I told you I'm not radioactive anymore!"

Screw the neighbours. He needed to get this off his chest.

"Do you realise what you've put me through since I started working in Chernobyl? Making me get changed in the hallway, making me wash myself for half an hour, not letting me touch you because you're scared I'll contaminate you. . . Do you realise what I'm going through?"

"What, you think it's easy for me? I'm making sacrifices too. I spend all week without you. We never see our friends anymore. When I invite them to dinner, they ask me if you're going to be there. They're afraid of you. Afraid that you'll contaminate them."

"And you? Are you afraid of me?"

No answer.

"I'm not a fucking nuclear waste dump!"

He thought he could hear her sobbing behind the door.

"Let me in, Tatiana."

Still no answer. He waited another two minutes.

"Alright. I just came by to reassure you and to give you a hug. Well, at least you know I'm alive now. Since you won't let me in, I'm going back to Chernobyl."

He turned around. Tatiana's voice came to him through the door.

"You know I love you, Joseph, but we can't carry on like this. *I can't carry on like this.*"

He sighed.

"I know. We need to talk about it, when I've cracked this case. In the meantime, you're right – it's better if I don't come home for a while."

Another silence. He waved. He knew she was watching him through the spyhole, but even so it felt weird waving goodbye to a door.

"I love you," he called out before leaving.

"Be careful," the door said.

34

The next day began with a headache that felt like an axe splitting his skull open. Melnyk swallowed a few painkillers and skipped breakfast. He felt nauseous. He had had a few drinks the night before, to help him sleep and to help him forget the row with his wife, while working until very late, looking through the register of missing persons in the region. The alcohol and the painkillers were a bad mix, and he had woken feeling groggy in the room at the police station where he'd set up his camp bed.

Just before ten, while he was going through a mass of messages sent to him by the police in Belarus, Novak entered his office holding a sheet of paper.

"I found it! The victim's name!"

The young officer gave him the paper then crossed her arms, looking pleased with herself. It was a colour photocopy of an I.D. card. Melnyk put on his glasses and recognised the face of the girl in the pool. He felt queasy as he noticed that her eyes were brown, not blue like the glass eyes the killer had placed in her sockets.

"Natalia Winograd, born in Kyiv, 1987," he read. "So she's a post-Chernobyl kid. That explains the reconstructed ear. Does she have any family?"

"A sister in Kyiv. Her mother died in the 1990s. Her father is still alive. . . but guess where he was living thirty years ago?"

"Pripyat?"

"Exactly. He lives in Slavutych now."

"Have you called him?"

"No. I wanted to talk to you first."

"How did you find the girl's identity?"

Novak told him that she called all the police stations in the region, one by one, asking if they had had any suspicious reports of missing persons. She had struck lucky with the station in Slavutych: Natalia Winograd's father had reported her missing the day before.

Melnyk stood up and took his coat. Outside, the sky was turning grey. When he had gone out a little earlier for a smoke, the cold had taken his breath away.

"Let's go and see the father to break the bad news," he said. "Find us a car. I need to make a call first."

He dialled the prosecutor's number while Novak left his office. Barely had he opened his mouth when the prosecutor yelled that his chief suspect was a dead end.

'A dead end? What do you mean?

"I mean it quite literally. Leonski was found dead the day before yesterday."

"But. . . how. . ."

"Suicide. He slit his wrists with a razor blade, in his apartment which was being used as a sort of drug den. And guess what? Your Leonski was disabled. He had one leg missing and he'd been bedridden for weeks."

"Impossible," Melnyk muttered.

He could not believe his ears. Everything had pointed to Leonski. He had been suspected of the murders of Olga and Larissa. . . There'd been a stuffed swallow in his dacha. . .

"The coroner is a hundred percent sure. There's no way Leonski could have hoisted a corpse up the side of a building."

"There must be some mistake. . ."

"My mistake was entrusting you with this case. I should never have listened to you!"

"I've got things in hand. . ."

"Oh really? I keep getting calls from people in high places telling me to open up the zone that *you* shut down."

"We need to keep it closed for now. If the killer's inside, he can't get out."

"The zone is full of holes – you know that as well as I do! The only ones you're blocking are the tourists, and they're the region's chief source of revenue. You have to open the checkpoints."

"I refuse. We're making progress. If we lift the blockade now, it'll give the killer a chance to leave the zone without risk."

"May I remind you, captain, that you are in a precarious position, as an ex-militia man? You are still a 'temporary member of the police force' as far as I'm aware. Have you carried out the process of requalification? Has your passage to the new Ukrainian police been validated?"

He balled his fists. The prosecutor knew the answers to all these questions as well as he did.

"They're just political formalities," Melnyk said coolly.

"I know. But I'm taking a huge risk by leaving you in charge of this investigation. If there's another murder, Kyiv will hold me responsible. And if that happens, you're out on your ear. I hope I make myself clear?"

"What's the worst that can happen? They're not going to transfer me somewhere worse than Chernobyl, are they?"

The prosecutor said nothing: he had not been expecting this comeback.

"I just need a bit more time," Melnyk said. "I'm almost there, I can sense it."

"Alright," the prosecutor sighed. "I'll give you until the end of the week. If the zone isn't open by then and the case isn't close to being solved, I'm handing it over to the Kyiv crime squad. And if you fail, I will wash my hands of you. You alone will bear the responsibility for another murder. Understood?"

"Perfectly."

"Good. Now tell me about the victim."

Melnyk repeated everything he'd just learned about her.

"Have you contacted the father?" the prosecutor asked.

"Not yet. I'm going to see him myself. I think it's better that he hears about the death of his daughter from me."

He would certainly prefer that someone came to talk to him if Nikolai was killed on the front.

"As you like. Call me as soon as you have any news. Day or night."

"Of course," Melnyk said, then hung up, smiling bitterly.

The prosecutor no doubt wanted to give the impression that he was a competent official, always available to his subordinates, but Melnyk was not fooled: if he wanted to be kept informed of the investigation's progress in real time, it was so that he could drop the captain like a hot potato if anything went wrong.

As he walked towards the garage, he saw Novak coming towards him.

"There's only one car left and it's not in working order."

Melnyk glanced at his Lada. It was one of those models with a trapdoor on the floor of the passenger side, used to go fishing on frozen lakes in winter without having to leave the vehicle. In other words, it was almost as old as the Berlin wall.

"*Blyad*," he cursed. "What's wrong with it this time?"

"The gearbox is broken."

"In that case, we'll take the train at the power station," he decided.

They got in his car. At the crossroads, he did not turn onto Kirova Street, which led to Chernobyl and Pripyat. Novak looked surprised.

"I'm going to ask for some help first," Melnyk told her.

"From whom?"

"The one in charge of the entire zone."

The streets of Chernobyl were even quieter than usual, with tourists still banned. Few of the power station employees were based there: the city was too contaminated for anyone to live there year-round. They passed the empty offices of a travel agency, then the commemorative park with its signs indicating the names of vanished villages.

"I've been wondering: what is that statue?" Novak said as they drove past a giant sculpture made from long metal bars.

It was a winged creature blowing into a trumpet.

"The third angel of the apocalypse," Melnyk said. "The one that announces the arrival of the Absinthe star."

Novak raised her eyebrows. In Ukrainian, Chernobyl was the name of a brand of absinthe.

"And a great star fell from heaven, burning like a torch, and it fell on a third of the rivers and on the springs of water," Melnyk recited. "The power station was just next to the river. Hell of a coincidence, don't you think?"

They arrived at a small blue church painted blue, white and gold. Melnyk parked outside the gate and got out.

"The one in charge of everything in the zone?" Novak repeated. "Are you a believer?"

"No, I just want to buy some cigarettes. Are you coming?"

"No thanks. If God really exists, how could he accept all this?" Novak demanded, waving her arms at everything surrounding them.

Melnyk walked to the St Elias church. Inside, he muttered a quick prayer for his son, for his wife, and for God to help him catch this devil. After that, they drove to the power station. They were welcomed by a pack of stray dogs running towards the workers' cafeteria. It was lunchtime and the animals had come to beg for scraps. Most of these dogs were sick. Their life expectancy was rarely longer than five or six years.

Novak's anxiety went up a notch when they walked across the tarmac outside Reactor 4. Beside it was a half-constructed giant dome. When it was finished it would cover the old concrete shell, built in a hurry in 1986 to trap the radioactive elements still inside the reactor. The dome was supposed to give the Ukrainian authorities another hundred years to get rid of the radioactive waste. This was easier said than done, of course, since that lava-coloured mass of corium and other materials – nicknamed the Elephant's Foot, after its shape – was so irradiated that, according to the specialists, two minutes in its presence would be enough to make your cells start to decompose. Not only that, but since the Elephant's Foot was still active, there was no guarantee that it would not create another nuclear disaster. As for what would happen if it came into contact with the groundwater. . . well, that Bible passage about the star probably said it all.

Melnyk resolved not to tell Novak any of this.

At the station, they had to pass by a row of blue cabins equipped with Geiger counters before they could board the train. White as a ghost, Novak placed her feet and hands on the metal plates containing the machine's sensors. A green light shone and she sighed with relief. Melnyk followed, and he too was given the green light. In the line behind them, a worker took his place inside the machine. Another green light. Melnyk wondered if the machine actually had a red light to indicate too much radiation, or if the whole thing was just a charade to reassure people. Knowing governments' propensity for lying in such situations, he imagined that someone carrying a nuclear bomb in his backpack could probably get through without raising the alarm.

They had no difficulty finding two seats face to face in the carriage. The other seats were occupied only by engineers from the night shift. Inside the carriage there was the usual morose atmosphere to be found on sleepy suburban trains. Some of the passengers were nodding off, chins on chests, arms crossed. Others spoke in low voices. Nobody looked out of the window: they knew the passing landscape by heart. The dark forests, the deserted farms, the empty villages. A view as depressing as the leaden grey sky.

The accumulated weight of weeks of fatigue, mixed with the rolling, swaying carriage, lulled Melnyk to sleep. He woke to the sound of squealing brakes. At the station in Slavutych, the platforms were deserted. Melnyk and Novak walked the short distance to Chernihivska Street, where Natalia Winograd's father lived. As soon as the man saw the two police officers on his landing, he understood the reason for their visit. Melnyk offered his condolences and asked if he felt capable of answering a few questions. The man agreed.

Natalia Winograd's father was named Anton. He had a heavy, deeply wrinkled face. His skin was grey and scattered with liver spots. He was a good twenty kilos overweight and he wheezed as he breathed. His apartment smelled of neglect: the mingled odours of dirty laundry, greasy hobs, and blocked pipes.

Winograd sat in a faded flower-patterned cloth armchair. The ashtray on the coffee table was overflowing with cigarette stubs. A mobile telephone lay next to it, stuck to a brown alcohol stain. Natalia's father had probably stayed up all night, waiting for his daughter's return or a call from the Slavutych police station.

"How did she die?" he asked.

Melnyk sat on a creaky wooden chair. Novak preferred to remain standing.

"She was murdered," Melnyk said.

"A murder here in Slavutych?"

Violent crime was rare in this town: life was too short to waste it killing one another.

"Your daughter's body was found in Pripyat, not Slavutych."

"Pripyat," the man muttered.

A veil of sadness covered his eyes.

"Your daughter lived in Kyiv, is that correct?"

"Yes."

"Did she have a husband or a boyfriend?"

"My daughter was born without genital organs, because of the radiation. It's hard to have a love life when you're like that."

Novak decided to sit down after all. Her legs were trembling.

"Why did you contact the police station in Slavutych yesterday?"

"Natalia was supposed to come and see me in the evening. We were going to a restaurant, for my birthday."

"How did she come here usually?"

"She took the *marshrutka*. She didn't have a car."

Melnyk turned to Novak.

"We'll have to question everyone who drives a shuttle bus between Kyiv and Slavutych."

Novak took out her notebook and wrote: Question drivers of collective taxis.

"When was the last time you saw your daughter?" Melnyk said.

"Three months ago, in Kyiv. We didn't see each other very often, but we talked on the telephone regularly. The last time I heard from her was the day before yesterday."

"Did she seem anxious then? Stressed?"

Winograd's voice crackled when he spoke, as if his lungs were two old speakers. "No. She was the same as usual. Happy. She was a fighter, that girl. She shouldn't have been born at all. The doctor wanted my wife to get an abortion. Natalia was born prematurely. She was tiny. But she survived. She spent her whole life fighting to survive. Every day was a victory for her."

The old man balled his fists.

"You have to catch the bastard who did this. He deserves to rot in prison for what he did to my daughter."

"We'll put him behind bars," Novak swore.

Melnyk frowned. It was never a good idea to make that sort of promise to the victims' families. It was the kind of mistake young police officers were always making.

"Did your daughter ever enter the forbidden zone?" he said. "I know a lot of people go hiking there, despite the risks."

"She wasn't very healthy. She got tired quickly. I can't imagine her doing that. Where in Pripyat was her body found?"

"In the Lazurny swimming pool."

Winograd buried his face in his hands for a moment. Melnyk was expecting to see him weep, but when the old man looked up again, his eyes were dry, just lost in a fog of sadness.

"That's where her big sister learned to swim. She would have learned there too, if that damn explosion hadn't stolen our future from us."

The two police officers exchanged a look.

"Whereabouts in Pripyat did you live, Mr Winograd?"

"In the Voskhod apartment block."

Melnyk shivered. That was the building from where Leonid Sokolov's body had been hung.

"Did you ever know a man called Piotr Leonski?"

The old man looked distressed at this question. "Leonski... yes... I... he lived in the apartment next to ours."

Suddenly it all made sense. Winograd must be the employee who told jokes in the power station cafeteria, Melnyk thought; the one Leonski had denounced to the K.G.B.

"Did you have troubles with the K.G.B. in 1986–7?"

"Uh... what does that have to do with my daughter's death?"

"Please answer the question."

"Yes, it's true, I did have some problems with the K.G.B. First they threatened to arrest me for anti-Soviet propaganda or something like that. Because of some jokes I supposedly told. But Piotr was the joker there, not me!"

He sounded sincere. Had Leonski grassed up Winogard to save himself?

"And after that?"

"They asked me about Piotr. About his wife's murder. They thought he'd killed her. I told them the same thing I'd told the militia."

"Hang on... the militia interrogated you?"

That had not been in the investigation dossier that Melnyk had consulted at the archives office.

"Of course. My wife and I lived in the apartment next to the Leonskis and we were looking after their daughters on the night of the murder, so they were bound to question us. But anyway, I told the K.G.B. the same thing I'd told the militia that night: how Piotr had arrived at his apartment just after the explosion, his bloodstained clothes... I wasn't on duty that night. I tried to call the power station, but the lines were down. I was in the kitchen trying to find some news on the radio, when I heard a noise from Leonski's apartment. The walls between the apartments were very thin, you know. It was like the neighbours were living with us, and vice versa. We heard everything. I was worried, so I went to knock on his door. He opened it and... I don't remember exactly what we said to each other, but I do remember there was blood on the sleeve of his shirt. I went back to my apartment. We woke his daughters. He wanted to take them with him to Kyiv. Later, I learned that he had deserted the power station during his shift. He was a clever man, Piotr. The government never told us about the risks of nuclear power, but he realised that the zone was going to be seriously irradiated so he wanted to get out of there as quickly as he could."

"Was he angry with you for testifying against him?"

"I don't know... I don't even know if he was aware of my testimony."

"Is there any way he could have found out about it?"

"Maybe. You think he murdered my daughter?"

"That's what I thought, until I was told he was dead. He committed suicide."

"Leonski, kill himself? I don't think so!"

Winograd seemed confident on this point.

"He was very ill," Novak said.

"Like most of us," the old man said, showing them the scar on his neck from the operation to remove his thyroid. "But Piotr would never kill himself, I can promise you that."

"How can you be sure?"

Winograd pointed at a religious icon that stood on a dusty shelf.

"He was a devout Orthodox. There's no way he would have committed suicide. He took that kind of thing very seriously."

Melnyk made a mental note to check this out as soon as possible. He stood up suddenly, surprising his subordinate.

"We're going to leave you now, Mr Winograd, but we'll need you to come to the station to make your statement. You will also have to identify your daughter's body, to be certain that there's not been a mistake."

Winograd nodded, his face pale.

"We'll have to search her apartment in Kyiv. Do you have a spare set of keys?"

"No. But her sister lives there too. She must have some."

"You'll have to call her and tell her to come to Chernobyl to make her statement."

"Could she do it somewhere else? She's terrified of the radiation. She never comes to Slavutych because of that."

"Yes, that could be arranged," Melnyk said.

He left the old man his mobile number, then led Novak out of the apartment.

"What's going on?" she asked as they walked through the corridor to the stairs.

"Winograd said that Leonski would never have killed himself."

"So?"

"If he's right, then the Kyiv police have identified the wrong man. In that case we have to inform everyone involved in Leonski's arrest."

"Why?"

"Because this was an act of vengeance. Don't you see? First he kills Sokolov's son, then Winograd's daughter, whose testimony had strengthened the K.G.B.'s certainty that he murdered his wife. If I'm right, he must be getting ready to kill another son or daughter of someone who he believes wronged him."

"But why their children? It's not their fault what their parents did."

Novak's comment suddenly gave him an idea. He called the police station in Chernobyl.

"Ivan? Go to my office. . . Yes, right now. . . You see the blue folder? Open it and look for a piece of paper with Leonski's name underlined. . . Have you got it? Right, and it says that his daughter died in 1987, is that right? Ah, yes, that's right, there were two daughters. . . twins? O.K., can you tell me what she died of?. . . Perfect, thank you."

He hung up.

"Leonski had twins. One of them died in 1987. She had leukemia. She was nine."

"So you think Leonski's killing these people's children because of that? That's crazy!"

"To us, yeah. But maybe he sees it as a legitimate form of vengeance. I think I understand his reasoning. Remember, the night of the Chernobyl disaster, he had planned to leave Pripyat with his daughters. But he was stopped by a roadblock, and the militia arrested him when they discovered he had deserted his post. What do you think they did with his kids then?"

"Well, their mother was dead. So I imagine they were taken back to Pripyat."

"Exactly. At the very moment when the radiation levels there were at their highest. That's probably why Leonski is killing the descendants of the people he holds responsible for his arrest. The violence he suffered in prison, his daughter's death, his social fall from grace. . . he wants revenge against everyone who had him imprisoned. By taking their children."

"But why now? Why thirty years later?"

"I have no idea. But that doesn't matter now. What matters is stopping him before he kills again. We need to identify his next targets."

"Arseni!" Novak said. "The officer who led the militia investigation at the time – we have to warn him."

"He doesn't have a mobile. Call him at his shop."

They both took out their phones. Melnyk dialled Vektor Sokolov's number. It was the first name that came to his mind. He had already lost a child, but there was nothing to suggest Leonski wouldn't attack his family again.

The phone was answered by a secretary.

"This is Captain Melnyk. I need to talk to Vektor Sokolov."

"Mr Sokolov is in a meeting at the moment."

"Tell him I have news about his son's murderer. And tell him his family is in danger."

"I. . . Alright, I'll tell him. He'll call you back."

He hung up. Novak had finished her call too.

"What did you find out?" he asked.

"I talked to Arseni's son. I told him to warn his father and the rest of his family. What about you?"

"I left a message for Vektor Sokolov to–"

The mobile vibrated in his hand. He answered the call.

"Captain Melnyk?" said a commanding voice.

He had spoken only once with Vektor Sokolov during the course of the investigation, but the timbre of his voice was so unusual that Melnyk recognised him easily.

"My secretary told me that my family is in danger. What does that mean? What's going on?"

"Mr Sokolov, the recent advances in my investigation lead me to believe that your son's killer might be Piotr Leonski. I'm sure you're aware that he was suspected of murdering your wife, in 1986?"

"Of course. I always thought he did it, but he was released. The morons who carried out that investigation were even more useless than you."

Melnyk felt his blood boil, but forced himself to remain polite.

"In 1986, what was it that made you think Leonski might have killed your wife?"

"His dacha was only a stone's throw from mine and he deserted the power station on the night of the murder. What more proof do you want?"

"Did you try to interfere in the investigation at that time?"

"I don't like the tone of that question, captain."

"Allow me to rephrase it in a more explicit way: did you try to harm Piotr Leonski in any way in 1986?"

Sokolov was silent for a moment.

"I am *this* close to hanging up and calling your superiors to file a complaint against you, captain. Your insinuations are outrageous."

Melnyk was not intimidated.

"I've just spoken to Anton Winograd," he said. "Does that name mean anything to you?"

"Absolutely not. Was he an accomplice of Leonski?"

"No. His daughter was found dead yesterday. Mutilated in the same way as Leonid."

"Ah, now I understand. So a Ukrainian citizen had to die before you take this case seriously!"

Melnyk chose to ignore this venomous remark.

"Thirty years ago, Anton Winograd testified against Leonski," he said. "I think that's why he killed his daughter. So I'm going to repeat my question: did you try to harm Piotr Leonski in any way whatsoever?"

Sokolov hesitated.

"Anything you might have done would be well beyond the statute of limitations by now," Melnyk said, to encourage him. "And even if that wasn't true, nobody's going to risk extraditing you from Russia, are they?"

At last the former minister answered grudgingly: "Yes."

"Yes what?"

"Yes, I tried to take care of Leonski thirty years ago. I'm not the kind of man who can just stand there doing nothing when my family is attacked, captain. I paid some criminals in prison with Leonski to make his life difficult. I wanted him to suffer. Most of all, I wanted him to confess."

This confirmed his theory: Leonski was avenging those he thought had wronged him.

"Could he have found out?"

"I don't know. . . Probably. Maybe the men I paid told him why they were attacking him."

"That was a stupid thing for you to do. You could have hurt an innocent man."

"But that's not the case, is it? Leonski killed my wife, my son, and this girl. . . right?"

There wasn't a trace of remorse in his voice.

"Do you have any other children, Mr Sokolov?"

"I had only one son. And I'm still waiting for you to arrest his killer."

"I'm working on it."

"I hope so. Call me as soon as you've caught him."

"So you can have him beaten up in prison?"

Sokolov choked on a profanity.

"Lucky for you you're a policeman in Ukraine and not in Russia," he hissed.

THE DOMAIN OF WOLVES

35

A cigarette. Then another. And yet another.

Rybalko was pacing around the room he had rented in the centre of Kyiv. He could have gone back to his hotel in Slavutych, but to what end? Ninel had informers in Chernobyl, and they all said the zone was still closed and that the blockade might last several more days. An eternity when the time remaining to you could be counted in months, if not in weeks.

His investigation had ground to a standstill. He had read and reread all the documents and all his notes. They pointed to one suspect: Leonski. He had used his contacts – or, rather, Ninel and Sokolov's contacts – to try to track Leonski down. But it was no good: he was nowhere to be found. At this point, Rybalko could not even say with any certainty whether his prime suspect was in Ukraine or had left the country. Leonski was known to have spoken perfect Russian. He could have gone to Russia when the communist regime fell, when the borders became porous, controlled by corruptible officers. He could even have changed his identity. Bureaucrats in the 1990s were equally open to bribery. The only hope he could cling to was that Leonski had gone back to live in the zone. At least, with the blockade, he would be trapped there until further notice.

He lay on his bed and looked through the brochure he had taken from a travel agency in Kyiv the day before. He had ventured inside to take his mind off things, after going over the evidence in the case for the umpteenth time, like someone vainly trying to solve a puzzle with a missing piece. He had asked the woman who worked there to show him various all-inclusive trips to Cuba. He imagined starting in Havana, lounging on beaches, dancing the merengue and the salsa all night long. He had been promising himself for almost twenty years now that he would one day visit his dark-skinned ancestors' land. He could find the house where his great-grandfather used to live. Meet his distant cousins, who would be surprised to see someone who looked like them coming from Moscow, speaking Spanish with a Russian accent. They would drink rum and dance. Drink and dance. Dance and drink. To forget. And then he would die, in the amber warmth of a strange land.

He closed the brochure. This was stupid. He wasn't from Cuba. He was as Russian as a bottle of vodka, as a Kalashnikov rifle. And he would die in the middle of winter, in his blue-eyed homeland. Going to Cuba was a fantasy that would never become real.

Or maybe it would. But he would not go alone. With Ninel?

Despite their arguments, he could not get her out of his head. He was supposed to meet her at ten o'clock on Andrivskyy Descent so they could discuss the progress of the investigation.

He met her at a heated café terrace. She was smoking a light cigarette, staring dreamily at a bird with flecked white, brown and yellow feathers. The bird was pecking at breadcrumbs trapped between the paving stones of the street.

"It's a serin," she told him. "*Serinus serinus*, to be precise. It ought to be on its way to Africa by now."

"Maybe it doesn't realise summer is over."

"More likely it's sick. Birds of that kind can live on their own, but in autumn they rediscover their social instinct and they gather to migrate south, towards Mediterranean Europe or North Africa."

"And if it doesn't leave, it'll die?"

"Possibly. But it'll leave in the end. It's in the bird's genes."

She stubbed her cigarette out in the ashtray.

"Have you made any progress with Leonski?"

"No. I'm sure I need to go to his old dacha, where he killed his wife, to have any chance of finding him."

"But the zone is closed and nobody knows when it will reopen."

"That's why I needed to see you. I have to find another way to get inside."

"You want to enter the zone illegally?"

He nodded. He had thought about it long and hard: this was the best solution.

"It's madness," she told him.

"It's what Leonid did."

"And look what happened to him. It's a bad idea to go in there alone. Some of the places are highly radioactive, and most aren't indicated. When you don't know your way around, it can be dangerous. Fatal, even."

"That's why I need a guide."

"No official guide would risk their licence taking someone in illegally."

"Yeah, that's not what I had in mind."

He took out his mobile and showed her an article from an online magazine about a stalker.

"There are guys who regularly enter the zone. This one's done it more than fifteen times, always illegally. I need someone like that to help me."

"It's dangerous. If you get caught–"

"I can't waste a week waiting for the zone to reopen," Rybalko interrupted. "Can you find me a stalker?"

Ninel thought for a minute before replying: "I don't know any. But Maria could help you, I'm sure. She knows lots of people around here. I'll call her clinic."

She stood up and walked away from the terrace to make her call. He watched her for a moment, then noticed that she'd left her handbag open. Inside, he glimpsed a blue feather. Out of curiosity, while her back was turned, he took it out to have a look. The end of the feather had been turned into a pencil tip.

"What are you doing?" Ninel demanded, coming back to the terrace.

Caught red-handed.

"I noticed you had a pen," he improvised. "I wanted to write something down."

"I don't like people going through my things."

"I wasn't going through anything, I just needed a pencil."

She obviously didn't believe him, but she dropped the subject.

"I talked to Maria. She does know a stalker. He goes by the name Tomik. At the moment he's working in a restaurant near the Maidan. He agreed to meet us."

"When?"

"When his shift ends later today. The simplest thing would be for us to eat lunch there and wait for him to get off work."

"Good idea."

They drove back to the city centre. The restaurant where Tomik worked was called Veterano Pizza. As they entered, they were met by the delicious aromas of baking dough, melting cheese and simmering tomato sauce. The warm air was abuzz with conversation. Apparently the Veterano was a popular destination. Most of the tables were occupied.

Rybalko was surprised to see a fake machine gun hung on the wall, surrounded by the military badges of various Ukrainian units.

"The owners are veterans of the Donbas war," Ninel said.

She pointed to a section of the wall at the end of the room, behind the till. It was covered with military badges and children's drawings. There were also some knick-knacks on a shelf just below: blue and yellow bracelets, rag dolls, playdough Father Christmases, origami, Orthodox crucifixes, and a disarmed grenade. Lucky charms, thought Rybalko. He had known many soldiers on the front who had carried such objects around with them.

In a discreet corner, a poster in the colours of the national flag announced a workshop on pizza-making for children of soldiers who had died in combat. A waiter sat them at a table close to the corner. The centre of the wooden table had been hollowed out and covered with a thick glass lid. Inside was a circle of spent machine-gun cartridges.

268

"Have you been here before?" Rybalko said.

Ninel nodded and began reading the menu, cutting short his attempts at small talk. It really annoyed him, the way she kept rebuffing his attentions.

"Why don't you ever talk about yourself?"

She looked at him in astonishment.

"What do you want to know?"

"About your friends, your hobbies. . ."

"Would that help your investigation?"

He shrugged. "Probably not."

"Then why discuss it?"

"Isn't that what normal people do?"

"We could always talk about your life, if you like. You told me you were divorced. Who left who?"

"She left me."

"Why?"

He thought about this.

"Because I spent too much time at work, messed around too much, and I was carrying a lot of baggage."

"What kind of baggage?"

"I was in Chechnya. And my parents were killed by the Chernobyl disaster. That sort of thing changes you. Not in a good way."

"I understand," Ninel said. "I know what it's like, losing someone you love."

A shadow passed over her big blue eyes. She hid them behind the menu. She advised him to choose the same pizza as her, a Provence. It was the most popular item on the Veterano menu. Cream, mozzarella, gorgonzola, chicken, and a Neapolitan-style thin crust. And they sprayed it with mustard just before serving it. Rybalko doubted that a pizza like that would ever be eaten in France or Italy, but he took her advice anyway. Ninel hailed a waiter and ordered for both of them.

"And two suspended pizzas. And two sparkling waters."

The waiter thanked them and walked towards the counter.

"Four pizzas?" Rybalko laughed. "Wow, you're hungry!"

"The other two aren't for us. When you order a suspended pizza, it's sent to a wounded soldier at a hospital in Kyiv. Sometimes they send them to the train station too, for soldiers who are waiting to go back to the front. The restaurant owners are committed to helping our soldiers. Everyone who works here used to serve in the army. It helps them reintegrate into civilian life."

In the restaurant's kitchen, Ninel went on, there were ex-marines, members of the National Guard, special forces veterans. This must be the worst place in Kyiv to start a fight, Rybalko thought.

"They just stay here for a few months, long enough to develop a reintegration plan and start therapy with a psychiatrist."

"A shrink? They all see a shrink?" Rybalko said, surprised.

In Ukraine, as in Russia, talking to a psychiatrist was generally stigmatised as being only "for queers and loonies", as a Russian army bureaucrat had told him after he had complained about the lack of support for veterans returning from Chechnya.

"A lot of the men sent to the front have trouble finding their place in society when their war is over. They don't enjoy anything anymore. They've seen so many things that stop them sleeping at night. Horrible things. Most of the young people go to war full of pride and hope and come back broken."

"I've seen that myself," Rybalko said.

The waiter reappeared with their food and slipped the bill under one of the water bottles. Rybalko watched the man attentively. He was in his twenties, but he had an old man's eyes. How many times had he seen eyes like that? Many of his comrades had never managed to readapt to normal life after surviving the terrible war in Chechnya. They had been thrown back into a world where there was no-one to watch their back. For most of them, returning from the front meant living in a seedy apartment building and being unable to find a job because employers were afraid of former combatants. It also meant alcohol or drugs, sometimes both. Lost and alienated, many of them ended up becoming drug addicts or committing suicide. How many of their bodies had been found at the bottom of the Moskva River or inside a snowdrift, when the springtime sun finally melted the snow?

And then he thought: And me? Where will they find *my* body? Once again, the prospect of his fast-approaching death left him sick with fear.

"*Bon appetit,*" Ninel said, attacking her pizza.

He ate slowly, like a prisoner on death row consuming his last meal, his head full of dark thoughts. What if he had found out about his condition a month earlier. What if there'd still been a chance that he might recover. The same doubts endlessly circled his mind. He had read somewhere that there were six or seven stages of grief. First, what you experienced was pure shock. That had lasted a few hours after his visit to the doctor. Then came denial: he had wanted to get a second opinion, to make sure there had not been a mistake. Then came anger, accompanied by fear, depression, sadness. Now he was in the acceptance phase. He was no longer fighting against the inevitable. He was going to die and he knew it, he had accepted it. He had even contrived to find some meaning in his last days, carrying out one last investigation to help give his daughter a better future.

According to psychologists, the final stage of grief was serenity. That seemed a long way off. For now, he was still mired in dissatisfaction; in truth, he still felt angry. Maybe he would finally be at peace when he had killed Leonid Sokolov's murderer? Maybe he would feel, then, that he had at last put his affairs in order.

The waiter cleared away their plates. Ninel's was empty, his own half-full. They ordered coffees. As they were drinking them, a man came over to their table. He had a grey beard and on his head he wore a black forage cap covered with skulls. His apron was the colour of army camouflage.

"Tomik," he said by way of introduction. "Are you Maria's friend?"

Ninel stood up and shook his hand.

"I'm Ninel. This is Alexander."

"The one who wants to go into the zone," the veteran muttered.

Tomik sat facing him and stared into his eyes. Rybalko did not like the way the man looked at him. There was something scary about those blue-grey eyes. Like gazing into a bottomless pit.

"Tomik knows the zone like the back of his hand," Ninel said. "Maria says that he has been there dozens of times."

She turned to the stalker and waited for him to speak, but he remained silent, staring challengingly at Rybalko. The veteran was sizing him up.

"*Afghanets?*" Rybalko said.

This was the nickname given to Red Army veterans who had fought in Afghanistan. Tomik slowly nodded, then slipped his hand beneath the top of his T-shirt and pulled out a small gold medal. He turned it in his fingers while pronouncing an incomprehensible phrase in a foreign accent.

"With the gratitude of the Afghan people," he translated, his jaw tensed.

Rybalko had seen medals like that before. The message was written in Russian on one side and in Afghan on the other. Back then, the official propaganda hammered home the idea that troops were being sent to Afghanistan to help their communist brothers fight counter-revolutionaries. At the war's end, the medals had been given to former Red Army soldiers as a "gift of thanks".

"Were you in the army?" Tomik said.

"I was in Chechnya."

"I heard that was ugly."

"No worse than Afghanistan, I imagine."

"Why do you want to go to the Zapovednik?"

This Russian word meant "forbidden". Ninel had explained to Rybalko that this was the term that inhabitants of the border towns generally used to designate the Polesie State Radioecological Reserve, located in Belarus, and the Chernobyl exclusion zone in Ukraine.

"I need to go to Zalissya," Rybalko said.

"I know it. Radioactivity levels tolerable. But near a bridge. That's not good. Why there?"

Tomik spoke in short phrases, as though he were having a conversation by walkie-talkie.

"I'm looking for a dacha where someone lived before the explosion."

Tomik examined him shrewdly. His eyes had the hard, dark shine of the lazurite stone extracted from the Panjshir Valley.

"Why that house in particular? What are you looking for?"

Rybalko kept his answer vague. "I'm carrying out an investigation."

"Detective?"

"Sort of. I'm working on a double homicide case from 1986. Two women who were killed the night of the explosion."

Tomik nodded.

"It's dangerous, going into the zone. You know the risks?"

"I know about the radiation, yes. That's not a problem."

"Radiation?" Tomik snorted. "That's nothing. We've got vodka for that!"

His laughter was loud and staccato. Then his eyes grew hard and serious again.

"It's not like it was twenty years ago. The zone used to be like a sieve. The militia didn't pay much attention to it. Now, visiting is a business. There are more checkpoints. And there are hostile elements. Some of the villages are empty. Others are full of squatters. Tramps, criminals. Inside the houses, the floorboards are rotting. You can fall in a cellar and die. Break your leg. Nobody will ever hear you scream. And then there are the animals. Wolves, wild boar. Snakes."

"I'm ready for all that. What about you?"

"Depends on the price."

Rybalko took out his notebook, scrawled a figure, and handed it to the veteran. It was a tidy sum. Tomik raised his eyebrows.

"Departure date?"

"As soon as possible. Tomorrow?"

"You're in a hurry."

"Exactly."

Tomik scratched the back of his neck.

"It's feasible. Meet me in the Maidan at ten. A friend will take us close to the barbed wire. Far from a checkpoint. Away from prying eyes. We'll have to walk twenty kilometres or so in difficult terrain. Zalissya's on the other side of Chernobyl. And near a bridge that's usually guarded. We'll have to go there at night to minimise the risks. O.K.?"

Rybalko nodded. The veteran then listed the equipment they would need to take. He advised Rybalko to pack light and wear good shoes.

"There are all kinds of predators in the zone," he said as they were parting. "And the most dangerous ones are not four-legged."

He laughed fiercely, then added: "But you'll be safe with old Tomik, comrade. Don't worry about that. You'll be safe."

36

Outside the restaurant, Ninel asked him what he thought of Tomik.

"He seems to know his stuff."

"He seems pretty miserable to me."

"A lot of old soldiers are like that."

He wanted to reassure her, but there was undeniably something broken in Tomik. Still, he thought, beggars can't be choosers.

"What are you planning to do now?" Ninel asked.

"Buy some equipment. A backpack, some good walking boots. And tonight, I want to go out."

"You should get some rest instead. Tomorrow will probably be an exhausting day."

"It could also be my last, if Leonski finds me before I find him."

She shot him a strange look.

"How. . . how do you deal with the fact that you'll soon be. . ."

"Dead? I don't deal with it. I just focus on the present. And my mission. But I do want to give myself a break and relax before I go into the zone."

Rybalko sensed that she was troubled by this.

"What do you usually do to take your mind off things?" Ninel asked.

"Loads of things. I smoke. I fuck. I drink. I dance."

"In that order?"

He laughed.

"Not really."

"What sort of dancing?" she asked.

"If I said country, would you believe me?"

She almost cracked a smile.

"I find it hard to imagine you in a cowboy hat."

"Actually I look good in a cowboy hat. But I prefer Latin dances."

"Tango?"

"I'm more of a salsa man."

"I know a bar you might like. The Buena Vista Social Bar. I go there with friends sometimes. They play Latino music. The cocktails are good, and so's the music. There are often bands there."

"If you like, we could go together," he said.

She stared at him with her inscrutable blue eyes.

"That's not a good idea. You need to be on top form tomorrow."

She tapped her fingers on the steering wheel.

"I'll think about it," she said at last.

Well, that was something, Rybalko thought. He took out a cigarette.

"Not in the car," she reminded him.

He kept the cigarette between his lips, to save face, but he put the lighter back in his pocket.

"How long have you lived in Kyiv?" he said.

"Four years."

"That's all? What were you doing before?"

"I was working in Moscow, at a university. Then one day, I met Sveta at a protest march. She told me about Chernobyl and suggested we set up a charity together."

"So you gave up everything in Moscow for that?"

"Sveta is very persuasive."

"You didn't mind the idea of coming here to work?"

"If you respect the safety protocols, it's no more dangerous than being a police officer in Moscow. The radioactivity isn't as bad as it was thirty years ago."

"To be honest, I was thinking more about bad memories. Your mother's death and all that. . ."

Ninel opened up a little more than usual. "It was hard at first. But I got used to it. At least until Leonid was killed."

She was silent for a moment.

Rybalko asked: "You weren't ever tempted to do what he did? Investigate your mother's death, I mean?"

"I always reckoned there was no point. My father was head of the Gorkom in Pripyat. He must have used all his influence to find my mother's killer. So what could I do? And it was thirty years ago. I had had time to get used to the idea that the killer would never be caught. Or that he was dead. That's what I thought, until he struck again."

Her hand was trembling as she changed gear. The gearbox screeched in protest. Fifteen minutes later, she dropped him outside his hotel. In the distance a rainbow was visible in the fine rain falling on the west of the city.

"What time shall I pick you up?" he asked before she could drive away.

She looked uncomprehending.

"Salsa, remember? You said you'd think about it."

She hesitated for what felt like a long time.

"Meet me at the Buena Vista at nine," she said, as her window rose between them. "And be on time: I don't want to stay out late."

37

Alive.

That's how he felt as he shaved, brushed his dark hair, splashed cologne on his cheeks, and put on a shirt. He felt alive. For the first time since hearing that he had cancer, he felt a spark of excitement. And even if the promise of death glinted at him from every mirror, from the hands of every clock, in the sun's inexorable arc towards the horizon, he felt good: like an invincible conqueror.

His phone buzzed.

From: Ninel.

Going to be late. Can we make it 9:30?

He pulled a face. She'd already told him she didn't want to stay out late. Was she going to stand him up?

O.K., he replied, despite his misgivings.

He drove to the Buena Vista Social Bar. To kill time, he decided to have a drink outside. The air was cool, but that didn't stop the nicotine addicts from sitting on the terrace for a smoke. He ordered a Black Russian. Vodka and coffee liqueur: exactly what he needed to give him a pick-me-up. He was starting to feel the effects of his insomnia. For now, the price wasn't too high: trouble concentrating, absent-mindedness, slowed reflexes. If his symptoms got worse, he would have to take sleeping pills again. He needed to keep a clear head. The other solution was speed or coke. But it was too early for that kind of stuff. Better to save the drugs for the sprint finish. When he had so little time left to live that sleep would feel like a luxury he could not afford.

Thirty minutes passed. His phone rang in his pocket. He was expecting a call from Ninel, telling him she would have to cancel. But the name on his screen read: Marina.

"Alexander? How are you?"

He immediately noticed the quaver in her voice.

"I'm O.K. What's going on?"

"I. . . I received your letter. From the doctor. . ."

Shit. Those idiots must have sent it to my old address. . .

"Marina, listen, I. . ."

"Why didn't you tell me?"

He sensed concern beneath her reproach.

"I didn't want to scare you."

"Scare me? You're going to die! That's a good reason to be scared, isn't it? When were you planning to tell me?"

"When I got back from Ukraine."

"And what exactly are you doing there?"

"An investigation."

"Russian investigators don't work outside Russia."

"It's a private job."

"You're working as a private detective? What are you–" She changed her mind and started again: "No, I don't want to know what kind of skulduggery you're up to. I just want to know when you'll be back. You have to come home. So we can take care of you, Tassia and m–"

"Have you told her?" Rybalko interrupted.

"No. Not yet."

"Good. She doesn't need to know. . . not now."

"Then when, Alex? From what I read, they're only expecting you to live another six months. Well, less than that now. . ."

"This case won't take long."

"But–"

"Marina, listen: what I'm doing here, it's to give our daughter a better future. It's extremely well paid. If I succeed, we'll be able to pay for Tassia to get the operation she needs. . ."

"And if you die there without her having a chance to say goodbye? Have you thought about that? You can't do that to her!"

His heart contracted. He never had a chance to say goodbye to his father. He knew what Tassia would feel if things went badly for him in the zone.

"You'll have to explain it to her. Tell her what I did for her."

"Oh right! So I have to turn you into a hero? That's better than telling her about the drinking, the girls you picked up in bars, the drugs, the fights, the wounds I had to sew up by the ceiling light in the kitchen. . ."

"Marina. . ."

"Is that it, Alex? You're trying to buy yourself a place in heaven? Belatedly trying to make yourself look like a good father? For the past ten years you've neglected your daughter, you've neglected me, and now you're going to die a hero hundreds of kilometres away? So you get the lead role and I'm supposed to support you?"

"I'm not asking you to lie to Tassia. I haven't been a good father, I know that. And I was an even worse husband. I lived my life the way I wanted to. I was selfish. I wasn't faithful to you. I should never have treated you the way I did."

Marina fell silent, surprised at this sudden acceptance of his faults.

Surprised, perhaps, finally to be hearing these words which she had waited years for him to utter.

"I missed so many things with you and Tassia," he said. "And I can't change that. But for once in my life, I want to do something that can. . . not erase the past, I know I can't do that, but at least show you both that I loved you. That I love you."

God, this was so hard to say. He felt almost ashamed of himself. He heard Marina sobbing at the other end of the line and he felt wretched that he could not cry himself.

"You're a bastard, Alex."

"I know, Marina. I know."

He listened to her crying for a long time, and then abruptly she stopped.

"Do what you have to do," she said coldly. "But do it quickly. You are not allowed to die without saying goodbye to your daughter."

She hung up before he could answer. He walked back to the terrace. It was past 9:30 now. Perhaps Ninel had changed her mind. Oh well. . . he still had Black Russians and Latino music. He went into the bar and ordered another drink.

And that was when she appeared. Like a vision, a dream made flesh. Her blue eyes ringed with black eyeliner. Her sulky lips painted poppy-red. Her golden hair shining in the spotlights. She saw him and advanced towards him. She was wearing a party dress and high heels: he thought she looked like a model on a catwalk.

"I hope you haven't been waiting too long?"

What could he say? Nothing – just ask her what she wanted to drink. They didn't speak much. She wanted to dance too. The band was playing salsa. They joined the one-night standers on the dancefloor.

He held her hand delicately and began to lead. A few basic steps, and then he soon shifted into more complex moves. Ninel was graceful but not passive. He guided her, but she resisted, rebelled, bridled, stepped away, came closer. It was as close to fighting as to dancing. Long, exhausting, hypnotic. A mating dance. Their eyes were locked together. The world receded to a bubble around them, and they were safe inside the borders of their encircling arms, their rhythmic feet. Their bodies pressed together, their breaths merged.

"You didn't tell me you knew how to dance," he said.

"You didn't ask," she said, her lips brushing his ear.

The music grew calmer. Their heartbeats slowed a little. But the heat remained. They moved even closer together. A ballad, forcing their desire to be patient. A slow dance. Swaying together. Their skin, electrified at the faintest touch. Around them, the other couples no longer existed. The band was playing for them alone. Rybalko's hands ventured into zones that he thought forbidden. Ninel's big blue eyes gazed into his. He held her even more tightly. She did not seek to escape now. She was his willing captive.

They kissed, for a long time.

Then, for no apparent reason, she put her hands on his chest and pushed him away. She turned around, left the dancefloor, and walked towards their table. He followed her.

"Is something wrong?"

She took out a cigarette and lit it. A bouncer told her to put it out. No smoking inside. She grumbled as she stubbed it out.

"What's the matter?" Rybalko said.

"Nothing. I'm just tired. I'm going home."

She picked up her handbag. Disconcerted, he watched her walk away, then hurried to catch her up.

"Was it something I did?"

"No, it's me."

Outside, the cold was bitter. Her red dress had vanished under a raincoat. Her high heels clicked on the tarmac.

"Wait. . ."

He grabbed her wrist. She pulled away, her expression cold.

"It was a bad idea, O.K.? I'm going home now."

He stood there, alone on the pavement like an idiot. She disappeared around the corner of the street and he did not run after her. That bird had flown. He went back to his hotel, frustrated. On the street below, some prostitutes were hanging around. One of them was blonde and slim.

"Blue eyes and dark skin – you're just my type," she whispered as he passed her. "I'll give you a special price."

"Fuck off, bitch," he snarled, to her and to all the Ninels of the world.

Her pride hurt, the woman gave him the finger as he went into the hotel lobby. But Rybalko did not see her gesture, just as he didn't see the large black 4×4 parked a little further down the road. In his room, he opened the door to the balcony and leaned on the guardrail to smoke a cigarette, then another. After the third, he decided to go to bed. He started thinking about the investigation again.

He tried to imagine the killer working on one of his birds. The smell of glue, straw and horsehair that filled his lair. The dismembered bodies around him, skins pinned to little wooden boards, ripped-out guts macerating in a plastic bucket, whitened skulls and skeletons. Dead matter coming to life beneath his fingertips. Or being given the illusion of life, at least.

After a while, his thoughts began to drift. The sleeping pills were taking effect.

He was in a dacha. There was wine, two glasses. Latino music. He went upstairs to join her. His fingers on the banister came into contact with a sticky liquid. Blood. It was all over the bedroom too. The mattress was pierced with stab wounds. He called out her name: "Ninel?" No response. He went down to the cellar. There were cages, and in the cages were bird-women. He went up to one of them. She looked as if she wanted to cry out, but her eyes and lips were sewn shut. He touched her skin. It was cold. A tanned hide. These weren't women anymore, but museum pieces. The killer had done to them what he had done to the birds. He had killed these women to keep them close to him forever. Naturalised.

The sound of breaking glass, a high-pitched voice. . . He wasn't dreaming now, he was wide awake. The noise was close, urgent, threatening.

Instinctively he rolled off the bed and crouched on the floor, gun in hand. The bedroom window had been smashed, shards of glass were scattered across the beige carpet. Further inside the room, the projectile that had caused the explosion was lying next to the foot of a chair. It was a brick wrapped roughly in paper. It had shattered when it hit the floor and bits of red clay had flown in all directions.

He went to the window. At the crossroads, a black 4×4 spun into an alley with a squeal of rubber. Rybalko put away his gun and turned on the ceiling light. He picked up the projectile, unwrapping the paper around it. It had been partly ripped by the impact, but it was not hard to read the message written upon it: "Keep out of the zone, you black cunt."

38

He decided to rent a room in a different hotel, without telling the manager about the broken window. He didn't want to get bogged down in paperwork or end the night at the police station. He slept badly and woke up exhausted. After a large bowl of coffee that took the edge off his tiredness, he met Tomik in a car park near the Maidan. The veteran was wearing combat fatigues and biker boots so worn that the leather was starting to crack. He was with another man, a taciturn Belarusian who was going to drive them to a spot near the barbed-wire fence that surrounded the zone. This man was an old friend of Tomik's, so there was no risk of him informing the police about their activities, as sometimes happened with bus and taxi drivers.

All the way there, Rybalko thought about Ninel. Why had she rejected him the night before? Was it something he had done? Something he had said? Ninel was a mystery to him. A mystery who attracted and frustrated him in equal measure.

After a two-hour drive in almost total silence, the Belarusian dropped them close to a remote section of the fence. Rybalko greedily sucked in fresh air: the smell of pine resin was carried to his nostrils on the cool breeze. He felt a strange mix of euphoria and nausea, like a kid who's about to spend the night in a cemetery to impress his friends. Tomik crossed the road and walked towards the sinister snarl of metal spikes.

He threw his bag over the fence then began crawling along the ground.

"What are you waiting for?" he demanded, when he saw that Rybalko was not following him.

Rybalko crouched down. With one hand, he swept away the thin layer of snow that covered the earth, as if stroking the fur of an angry animal.

"There's nothing to worry about here," Tomik told him. "Get a move on."

He took the backpack off his back and threw it over the barbed-wire fence, then lay down and started to crawl beneath it. On the other side, he stood up, dusted the snow from his parka, and put his backpack on again, jumping up and down a little to settle the weight more evenly. Tomik immediately set off towards the forest, as if the trees were a lover he had not seen for a long time.

"Follow me. Don't speak. Don't smoke," he ordered.

By the time Rybalko had tightened the straps of his backpack, the veteran had disappeared into the white forest and he had to follow his footsteps through the thick snow. For a good hour they walked so fast that he felt like he was hunting Tomik. The old soldier was always about fifteen metres ahead of him and often he could see nothing of him but his khaki bag and the maroon military beret he'd put on after crawling under the fence. Sometimes Tomik would vanish into a dense copse of trees and Rybalko wound wonder if he was going to lose him, but invariably he would find his guide standing near a birch tree, sniffing the air as if navigating by smell, or staring at the blue line of the horizon to follow the sun's trajectory.

After two hours they took their first break.

"You see the building over there? We're going to stop there for a while," Tomik said.

He pointed at the ruins of an old State farm. The Soviet building, with its half-collapsed roof, did not seem welcoming, but Rybalko was glad for the chance to catch his breath. Tomik found an old stool that might once have been used by milkmaids, and sat on it. He took a plastic pouch from his bag. Inside was a lighter and some cigarettes.

"We can smoke here. The guards never come this way. And the wind won't carry it far."

He picked out one of the hand-rolled cigarettes and lit it. A strong scent of hashish filled the barn.

"Afghan. You want some?"

Rybalko stared cautiously at the joint.

"Not now. I need to keep a clear head."

"Suit yourself."

Tomik took a huge drag, then slowly exhaled the bluish smoke through his nose. He repeated this until the joint was nothing more than a glowing dog end that threatened to burn his fingers.

"If I hadn't had this in Afghanistan, I'd never have made it back," he said, tossing away the remains of the cigarette. "What about you? What kept you going in Chechnya?"

"My comrades. Vodka. Faith too. I believed in what we were doing there. At least to start with."

Tomik burst out laughing. Rybalko glanced anxiously at the broken windows. The guide's laughter was probably audible for a radius of a hundred metres. Who knew if the police were patrolling the area in search of Leonski? And then there were those men who'd smashed the window of his hotel room. He had no wish to encounter either police or criminals. Was the hash making Tomik reckless?

"The lies of the motherland," spat the veteran. "Call it what you want – the U.S.S.R., Russia, Ukraine – the lies are always the same. Be men. Defend your homeland. Be heroes. Kill the fascists. Kill the terrorists. Kill the fascists *again*. What a load of crap. . ."

This was the longest speech Tomik had made since Rybalko had met him. Even his diction had changed. There was a feverishness to the way he expressed himself.

"Why do you come to the zone?" Rybalko asked.

Tomik gave him a knowing smile.

"I was lost, after the war. Maybe you were the same? You find yourself back in civilian life and nothing makes any sense. They tell you to shave, to use pedestrian crossings, to wear a tie, where a few weeks before you were blowing up some Afghan family's home with a rocket. I travelled around quite a bit after Afghanistan. I didn't feel at home anywhere. I started taking drugs. I hung around with former comrades in Kyiv, out near Victory Park. I was just killing time. And then one day, I decided to come here. I don't know why. It was like the zone was calling to me. The first time I climbed to the top of one of those tower blocks in Pripyat, I knew it was the only place I'd ever be free."

The ex-soldier stared at him intensely.

"Coming to the zone is like getting a foretaste of the apocalypse. It's like what this world will be like without us, one day. And it's the only place that's any good for people like us. Here, we're free," he repeated. "Totally free."

The glint in his blue eyes faded for a moment, as if his soul had escaped his body to glide somewhere above Kabul. Rybalko did not dare question him on what he meant by "people like us", nor what this supposed "freedom" consisted of. For him, the zone was just a vast field of ruins, a desolate wasteland which he had entered for one reason only: to find Leonski. The less time he spent here, the better. For Tomik, it was something else altogether. A place of infinite freedom. But freedom to do what?

The veteran did not expand on those thoughts. He stood up and said it was time to go.

He was much chattier after smoking the hash. He seemed to know everything about the zone. The bird on that branch? A European crested tit. The hoof prints in some muddy earth near that pond? A wild boar. Some of them grew up to more than 300 kilos in weight, not because of the radiation but simply because men left them in peace now, apart from a few crazy poachers. The piles of sawn wood that they kept coming across? The work of illegal forest rangers. They had cut down trees a long way from the road to avoid being caught by the patrols. Once you were out of the zone, the Chernobyl timber could be sold without any indication of its provenance. After that, it was used to make tables or chairs that could end up on sale in Kyiv or in a Swedish furniture store in France. Tomik said there was no risk as long as the wood did not catch fire. But in the summer, when temperatures in Chernobyl rose, there would sometimes be forest fires, and the trees, stuffed full of caesium, would release radionuclides that flew into the air and were carried by the wind across Russia and Europe.

Following his own chaotic train of thought, Tomik started talking about Ukrainian nuclear power stations. He explained that, because of the war in the Donbas, there was not enough coal to fuel the thermal power plants; consequently, the government had decided to push all the existing power stations to maximum capacity to avoid electricity shortages. But those stations had all been built during the U.S.S.R. years. Half of them were already past the expiry date for their use that had been decided when they began working.

"And everyone turns a blind eye to this. You know why? Because everyday problems are always more important. The rising prices of petrol or bread. The shortages. The war. And because we can't live without that energy. The U.S.S.R. gave us a taste of the atomic drug and we're still hooked. Two-thirds of our energy is nuclear. Not bad for a country whose surface area is badly contaminated with radioactive particles. And all this because of the politicians. . . the same ones who sacrificed us in Afghanistan. The Soviet leaders – Brezhnev, Andropov, Chernenko – they're murderers! I hope they're all burning in hell."

After this outburst, Tomik reverted to his habitual silence. Darkness was starting to invade the forest and the veteran became nothing more than a cracked branch, a patch of crushed grass, a flattened plant stem. Just when Rybalko thought that his guide had left him behind, he saw a reddish light up ahead. Tomik had turned on his headlamp. He had also rediscovered his old military concision.

"We're getting close to the bridge over the Uzh River. Behind it is Cherevach. The police often lie in ambush there. We'll have to go without lamps from here. There are no clouds. The moon is almost full. That will be enough to see by."

The ex-soldier rolled up his sleeve to check his watch. The hands glowed faintly greenish. He pointed to a row of birches.

"The road to Chernobyl is just up ahead, beyond those trees. We'll need to walk about seven kilometres along that road. Then we'll be in Zalissya. We should get there in less than two hours, as long as they aren't watching the bridge."

He turned off his lamp and stood motionless for a moment, time enough for his eyes to adjust to the dim moonlight. Then they set off again. As Tomik had predicted, a line of cracked tarmac ran alongside the birch trees. They followed the road to the bridge, which they crossed quickly. When they reached the deserted village of Cherevach, Tomik told Rybalko to stay a dozen metres behind him while he forged ahead. The veteran advanced haltingly, staring through the darkness like a wolf, on the lookout for the glow of a cigarette end, the glint of moonlight on a car's bodywork, the slightest sign of a police ambush.

As they were about to enter a forest on the outskirts of the village, Tomik suddenly froze. Almost instantly, a powerful beam of light picked him out like an actor on a stage. Rybalko, still in darkness, threw himself to the ground and crawled behind a tree. The veteran took a step backwards. There was a gunshot and the bullet raised a clod of earth a few metres from where he stood. He froze again, then raised his hands. A fat policeman appeared in the halo of headlights. He forced Tomik to his knees, then pushed him flat on the ground.

"Where were you off to, lad?" the officer demanded.

From where he lay hidden, Rybalko could see his guide's face. Just before the policeman handcuffed him, Tomik winked, a signal that he was not going to talk.

"I've got a date with your wife," the veteran said.

The officer punched him in the ribs and Tomik groaned.

"On your feet," the officer ordered before yanking on the handcuffs to pull his prisoner up from the ground. Then they walked towards the patrol.

They moved beyond Rybalko's field of vision. A second or two later, he heard the roar of an engine, heard tyres whispering on the tarmac, and the car's headlights swept over the place where he was hiding. His heart started to pound, but the vehicle was just turning, and soon it set off towards Chernobyl.

Rybalko stood up and watched the rear lights shrink into the distance. When they had vanished, he felt simultaneously relieved and very alone. Tomik had saved his skin, but he was no longer there to guide Rybalko to Zalissya. He walked along the road, constantly on the lookout for headlights in the distance. He feared that if the police beat Tomik, the veteran would end up telling them about the man he was leading into the zone. At each crossroads, he lost precious time examining his surroundings for clues that he was close to Zalissya. For a long time all he saw were warehouses and abandoned homes, until at last a road sign pointed to the village where Leonski had owned a dacha.

Zalissya was far enough off the beaten track for Rybalko to safely use his torch. A village overgrown with plants appeared in the shaky beam of light. Trees were crushing houses, their branches scratching the walls, while creepers strangled crumbling rooftops. He saw bits of rusted old barbed wire in the grass, like metal brambles. The remains of cars were rotting in driveways. They had been gutted for parts. The scrap-metal thieves had taken everything that could be carried off, leaving only the bodywork skeletons. Some had even had their roofs and wings removed.

He searched through several dachas, but they were all empty. Anything worth stealing had been stolen. All that remained were a few souvenirs, of sentimental value only. Family photographs. Letters. A newspaper dated the day before the disaster. Around four in the morning, increasingly frantic, Rybalko was in the garden of a house when his torch illuminated the shape of a glinting metal object. It was a brand-new padlock on the door of a shed. The shutters on its windows were closed. Intrigued, he was about to try forcing the shed's door when a light came on in the house nearby.

39

Instinctively he turned off his torch. Crouching behind the shed, he stared at the house while fumbling in his backpack for his weapon. He checked that it was loaded, then aimed it at the house, silently watching for the smallest movement.

A minute passed. Two.

He decided to move. Slowly, eyes riveted to the lit window, he crossed the garden and circled the dacha. The front door was open, revealing the entrance hall. A bin bag lay on the ground. Through the semi-transparent plastic he could see the remains of a large dead bird.

Rybalko's heart hammered in his chest. Leonski was here.

He crept into the hallway. A dusty carpet covered the floor, stifling the creaks of the old floorboards. In front of him he saw the staircase. A bright light shone down from ceiling lamps upstairs. When he put his foot on the first step, it moaned slightly under his weight. Enough to be heard on the landing above. He held his breath. Not a sound. He took another step and. . .

Searing pain in his head. Stars exploding before his eyes. He fell forward, smashing his forehead on the edge of a step. The pain spread through every nerve in his body. With a superhuman effort, he turned and glimpsed a figure bursting out of the dacha through the front door. He aimed his pistol and fired twice into the dark silence. He struggled to his feet and tried to run outside. But he was still in a daze and he got his feet tangled in the carpet, fell sideways and crashed into a wall. His shoulder knocked off an old photograph frame which shattered on the floor and he felt shards of glass sting his skin. Gritting his teeth, he went through the doorway and out into the night. Sweeping his torch beam across the garden, he spotted the strange figure that had escaped his bullets, thirty metres ahead of him. It was dressed all in green – some sort of anti-radiation hazard suit.

The gap between him and his prey closed rapidly. He was seized with a fierce joy: if Leonski had not killed him, it could only be because he was unarmed. Rybalko kept sprinting after him. Accepting that he couldn't outrun his pursuer, Leonski headed for a big stone building and dived inside. Rybalko slowed down and entered the building cautiously, on the lookout for another ambush.

He found himself in a large, empty room with moulding on the ceiling. At the far end of the room was a stage, the wall behind it covered with slogans in praise of the glory of communism. Rybalko supposed he must be in a Palace of Culture. Through a window, he saw Leonski moving into an adjoining room. Rybalko set off, took three steps, and...

The floorboards collapsed. His fall lasted only a fraction of a second. Between the floorboards and the concrete foundations, the gap was only about one metre. He was trapped waist-high between the wooden planks, coughing and spitting out every radioactive heavy metal in Mendeleev's periodic table, after breathing in the cloud of dust raised by his fall. His torch had rolled along the floor and was lighting up his face. With a surge of horror, he realised he had let go of his pistol. Still stuck halfway through the floor, he began groping around for it when suddenly the torchlight rose into the air: Leonski had picked it up. Squinting into the dazzle, Rybalko saw the pistol on the floorboards, then the killer's gloved hand picking it up. Leonski raised the gun and aimed it at him. He was breathing heavily. In the glare of the torch beam he could not see Leonski's face, but from his laboured wheezing, Rybalko guessed his enemy must be wearing some sort of gas mask.

It was over. He closed his eyes. In a way, he felt relieved. He would not have to shoot himself. Someone else was going to do it for him. Tassia would receive a quarter of the sum promised by Sokolov. It was better than nothing.

He seemed to wait an eternity. But nothing happened. He opened his eyes. The gun was still aimed at his face. As was the torch.

"What the fuck are you doing, you bastard?"

No response. Then Leonski raised his right leg and kicked Rybalko hard in the jaw. Stunned, Rybalko spat blood. A second kick, in the temple. He had no time to ask the killer what he was playing at before a third kick collided with his chin, knocking him unconscious.

40

The fluorescent tube on the ceiling crackled and a door slammed in the hospital at the Chernobyl power plant.

"Well, someone gave you a good working over, Professor Rybalko!" said a rough voice.

Rybalko sat up in his bed. The man who had just entered the room was familiar to him: it was Captain Melnyk, the officer who had turned up at the 1986 offices after the neo-Nazi attack. The Ukrainian was barely recognisable: his head and cheeks were shaved now, whereas at their first meeting he had had a lumberjack's beard and a mane of blond hair.

Melnyk took a chair and sat close to the bed – on the side where Rybalko was not handcuffed. They had explained to him that the cuffs were to make sure he did not escape before his interrogation.

"I spoke to my colleagues, the ones who found you in Zalissya. According to them, you found a guy pillaging the ruins and he attacked you?"

Rybalko nodded. The Ukrainian took a stack of folded sheets from the inside pocket of his jacket.

"Could this be the person who attacked you?"

Melnyk showed him a photocopy of Tomik's passport.

"I don't recognise him."

"You're sure? We arrested him just before we found you."

"The person who attacked me was wearing an anti-radiation suit. I didn't see his face."

The officer sighed. His breath smelled of coffee, stale tobacco and too many sleepless nights. Outside, the sun had not yet risen. Rybalko guessed that it must be about five or six in the morning.

"What explanation can you give me, professor, to justify your presence in Zalissya when the zone was closed?"

He rubbed the top of his head, as if trying to order his thoughts. Soon after being beaten up by Leonski, he had woken in the Palace of Culture. He had barely had time to hoist himself out of the floorboards before a police patrol had discovered him. He had claimed he had been hit and could not remember anything else. Now that a doctor had examined him and had not detected any serious head injuries, he knew that this line of defence would soon fall apart.

"I wanted to observe nocturnal animals," he said. "Because of the curfew, it's not easy to watch birds hunting at night."

"It's a really bad idea to go for a night-time stroll through the exclusion zone of the Chernobyl nuclear power station, Professor Rybalko. It's illegal and it's dangerous. There are all sorts of unscrupulous people around at night."

"You're right, it was a reckless thing to do. I hope this isn't going to cost me my accreditation?"

"That depends on you, *professor*."

The officer unfolded another sheet of paper and turned it towards Rybalko. It was a photocopy of a page of illustrations from an ornithology manual and it showed a sort of sparrow with a yellow stripe on its head.

"Can you tell me what kind of bird this is?"

"Why do you ask?"

"Answer the question: what species is this bird?"

His guts twisted. Did Melnyk have doubts about his identity or had he simply discovered a stuffed bird in Leonski's house that he wanted to identify? Either way, his cover would be blown if he did not come up with the correct answer. He concentrated on the animal and tried to remember if he'd seen it in Ninel's ornithology book.

"So?" Melnyk prompted him.

"It looks like a passerine."

"Well, yes, it does belong to the Passeriformes order, but passerines represent more than half of all bird species, from what I've been able to gather. Could you be a little more precise: what is the name of this bird?"

Rybalko bit the inside of his lip. His bluff had failed.

"I'm sorry, I can't remember."

"It's a yellow-browed bunting. You didn't study this kind of bird at university?"

"It must be the blows I took to my head. I'm finding it hard to concentrate."

"In that case, let's try something easier."

Melnyk showed him another bird.

"What is this?"

A grey bird with stripes on its abdomen and under its wings. Rybalko had no clue what species it was.

"Cat got your tongue? It's a common cuckoo. You know, those birds that take over other birds' nests. The female cuckoo lays one of her eggs there, and the other birds have to do the work of feeding her young. Apparently, the baby cuckoos push the other eggs out of the nest to get more food for themselves. Nasty piece of work, the cuckoo. But right now, it's not the most harmful species to be found in Chernobyl – far from it."

Melnyk showed him one last picture. It was a swallow. Rybalko remained silent.

"So? You don't need a degree to recognise this one, do you?"

"It's a swallow," Rybalko said reluctantly.

"That's right. A swallow."

Melnyk put the photocopies back in his pocket, then crossed his arms.

"You're no ornithologist. And you weren't wandering around the forbidden zone to observe owls. Who are you really and what are you doing in Chernobyl, Rybalko?"

He thought as quickly as his numbed brain would allow him. Melnyk had surely realised that he was investigating Leonid Sokolov's death, so there was no point in denying it. True, the Ukrainian did not have much to charge him with: at worst, he might send him to the court in Ivankiv, where he could be given a few weeks in prison. But in his condition, a few weeks was an eternity.

"Your friend Tomik has entered the zone illegally several times before. My men are interrogating him now and I'm pretty confident he'll end up telling us the whole truth. So stop lying to me right now."

"I was hired to find out who killed Leonid Sokolov," Rybalko said.

Melnyk seemed to relax.

"Who hired you?" he asked in a gentler voice.

"His father."

"Vektor Sokolov! What a surprise," the Ukrainian said with bitter sarcasm.

He took out his phone and gave a few quick taps on its screen.

"Look at this," he said, handing it to Rybalko.

The screen showed a photograph of the wooden shed in Leonski's garden.

"Go on, scroll through them," Melnyk said encouragingly.

Rybalko swiped left and saw a picture of wooden floorboards. Dozens of footprints were mixed up in the dust and sawdust that covered it. One of them was clearly visible in the centre of the picture: a huge sole, very possibly a size 14. He scrolled to the next image and saw a shelf filled with spools of thread, scissors, scalpels and translucent pots. Chemical products, wood shavings, glass eyeballs. . . all of it reminded him of what he had seen at the taxidermist's workshop in Kyiv. There was even a water vaporiser, used to maintain the skin's elasticity during dismemberment.

This was Leonski's workshop.

"Why are you showing me this?"

"Keep going," Melnyk told him.

The next photograph made him shudder. On a large plank resting on two trestles, two dead swallows lay on their backs, wings outstretched. A piece of cotton wool blocked the beaks of both birds, to prevent bodily fluids dripping onto their feathers.

The other photographs were less grisly. A pile of branches waiting to be transformed into perches. Shelves containing books on European and Asian birds. Disturbingly white skeletons. And then suddenly. . .

He felt the blood drain from his face.

The image of a pale, emaciated corpse burned itself onto his retinas. The body was lying on a stainless steel table covered with peeling dark bloodstains. The face. . . the face was frozen in a silent scream that deformed the blue lips, and the empty eye sockets stared horrifically at the camera.

Struggling to swallow his saliva, Rybalko handed the mobile back to Melnyk.

"That's Ruslan Agopian. The son of the officer who led the investigation into the murders of Olga Sokolov and Larissa Leonski in 1986."

"Christ. . ."

Melnyk took out a pack of cigarettes and lit one, ignoring the poster on the wall that made it clear smoking was prohibited inside the hospital.

"Now our cards are on the table," he said, exhaling a cloud of smoke, "I want you to tell me about your investigation."

Here we go. This was where his fate would be decided: freedom or prison. It was negotiation time.

"What do I get in return if I tell you what I know?"

"I can throw you in prison just like that," – Melnyk snapped his fingers – "if you don't cooperate. We found you about thirty metres from the murder scene."

"How would that help you arrest the killer, though?"

Melnyk frowned.

"If you hide information from me, you'd be a criminal accomplice. What if someone else is killed? You'd be responsible."

"I can live with that. What about you? Would St Joseph forgive you for blowing a chance to get closer to the killer?"

Annoyed, Melnyk zipped up his jacket to conceal the holy medallion that hung around his neck.

"What do you want in exchange?"

"First of all, I want to talk as a free man."

He pulled at his wrists, making the handcuffs rattle against the metal bed base. Reluctantly, Melnyk took a small key from his pocket and unlocked the cuffs.

"What else?"

"I want you to drop any charges against me for last night."

"Oh, that's all?" Melnyk said sarcastically.

"No. I also want access to what you've discovered in your investigation."

"I have no intention of giving you anything whatsoever."

"Then I'm not saying a word."

"Don't push your luck, Rybalko. I could decide to send you to the prison in Lukyanivska. They're not very keen on people like you there."

"People like me? What's that supposed to mean?"

"It means you need to use your brain. A black Russian has a very short life expectancy in a Ukrainian prison."

"You're not going to arrest Leonski by putting me behind bars. He is your prime suspect, right?"

Melnyk stared at him appraisingly.

"O.K.," he said at last. "We'll swap information. You start."

"What guarantee do I have that you're not going to throw me in prison once I've told you what I know?"

"You have my word."

Rybalko could not help but laugh.

"The word of a police officer? I'm going to need something better than that."

"Either you trust me or this conversation ends here."

Rybalko sized up the Ukrainian in silence. He had known more lying, cheating, thieving policemen than honest ones. Yet something made him believe that Melnyk was an honest man. Besides, he did not have any other solution.

"As I told you, Vektor Sokolov hired me to find his son's murderer. . ."

He recounted how the ex-minister had recruited him, then began to describe the autopsy he had carried out in Donetsk.

"Hang on! Leonid Sokolov's corpse was highly radioactive. I thought it had been buried in a cemetery in Kyiv, under a concrete and lead screed?"

"Vektor is a very rich man. He arranged to recuperate the body before it was buried."

Rybalko went over the information he had gleaned from the autopsy. Melnyk listened attentively and wrote everything in a small notebook. When Rybalko mentioned the falcon he had discovered in Leonid's abdomen, the old police officer gave him some information in return.

"Leonski's second victim was called Natalia Winograd. We found her body in an empty swimming pool in Pripyat. She too had a falcon in her belly. And there was another bird at the crime scene. . ."

"A swallow?"

Melnyk nodded. So that was the common thread linking these murders: every time Leonski killed, he left a swallow behind. Melnyk explained that the killer had even had one delivered to his office, as if to taunt him. Rybalko wondered if the bird was a talisman used by the murderer to intensify his sadistic pleasure. Did he think about his future victims whenever he cut up a swallow to naturalise it?

"Why would he systematically leave that bird near the body?" he asked.

"To know that, we'd have to get inside the sick bastard's head, and that doesn't tempt me at all. But I have a colleague who thinks it's connected to his first crime. There was a stuffed swallow in the Leonskis' bedroom."

Melnyk asked him if the coroner had been able to determine the causes of Leonid Sokolov's death.

"He was poisoned," Rybalko said.

"With cyanide?"

"No, arsenic. So I assume from your question that he used cyanide for Natalia?"

"Exactly. And the common thread between those two poisons. . ."

"They're both used in taxidermy. Which tends to confirm that Leonski is the killer. The ritual of the murders is based around his fascination with stuffed animals. That's how I worked out that he murdered Leonid Sokolov."

He told Melnyk the genesis of this realisation: the swallow he had found at the crime scene, the discussion with the taxidermist, then with Vektor Sokolov, who remembered that Leonski had been obsessed with naturalising animals.

"All of that made me want to take a look at his country house, in the zone. That's why your men found me there."

He recounted his misadventures in Leonski's dacha.

"Did you see his face?"

"No, I told you, he was wearing some sort of anti-radiation suit. And he was shining a torch in my eyes."

"Did he talk to you?"

"No. He just aimed the gun at me. But he didn't shoot. I don't know why. But how did you understand that he was Leonid Sokolov's murderer?"

Melnyk told him about the archives that he had consulted on the double homicide in 1986.

"I talked to the K.G.B. agent who led the investigation. He was still convinced, all these years later, that Leonski was the murderer."

"So why wasn't he arrested at the time?"

"Political reasons. The Soviet government didn't want any scandal relating to the power station or its employees. They told him to bury the case by pinning it on someone who had already been sentenced to death. So they had to let Leonski go."

"I see. And the three victims? Have you found a link between them?"

"I have a theory," the policeman said. "Agopian, the father of the third victim, ran the investigation on the 1986 murders. Anton Winograd, the father of the second victim, was Leonski's neighbour. His testimony strengthened the militia's suspicion of Leonski and led to his imprisonment. As for Vektor Sokolov, he paid some other prisoners to 'take care' of Leonski while he was behind bars. My feeling is that Leonski is avenging himself on those he considers responsible for the death of one of his daughters. Thirty years ago, he was arrested at a militia roadblock as he was fleeing the zone with his twins. The two girls were taken back to Pripyat. One of them was diagnosed with leukaemia soon after and died."

"So the swallow left near the bodies would be his way of signing his crimes?"

"I think he wants the fathers of his victims to understand that he's killing their children because of what they did in the past."

This explanation made sense. And yet there was something about it that bothered Rybalko. By signing his crimes, Leonski was giving the police the chance to arrest him. He was acting as if he did not care about being caught. A suicidal method that had almost cost him his life in Zalissya, when Rybalko had found him. A suicidal method… Rybalko thought about the drug dealer who had taken over Leonski's identity. With his gangrenous limbs, the guy had wanted to die. But not at his own hands. He had wanted someone to kill him. To finish him off.

"He's sick," Rybalko muttered.

"It is barely credible," Melnyk said with a twisted grin. "A man who stuffs his victims' corpses with dead birds…"

"I mean literally sick. Leonski was working at the power plant when Reactor 4 exploded. I discovered that he was receiving a pension as a victim of the disaster. Maybe he has a terminal illness…"

"So he doesn't have long to live? That would explain why he keeps leaving behind corpses without apparently worrying about the consequences."

Melnyk put his hand to his face, as if to stroke his beard. Finding no hair on his face, he scratched his chin instead.

"So we're dealing with a madman hellbent on vengeance who is running out of time. In a way that simplifies things. He won't strike randomly. He must have a list of targets."

"The children," Rybalko mumbled to himself. Then: "Ninel!"

He remembered the photographs that Melnyk had shown him. In his workshop in the zone, Leonski had prepared two swallows. That meant that Arseni Agopian's son was not the last of his targets. What if it were Ninel?…

"Give me your phone," he said to Melnyk.

"Why?"

"I need to check something. It's very important."

The policeman reluctantly handed him his mobile. Rybalko dialled Ninel's number, but the call went straight to voicemail.

"Come on, pick up!"

"Who are you calling?"

He hesitated. Ninel had made him swear not to reveal her secret and she had been very sure that nobody else knew about her connection with Vektor Sokolov. But if she was wrong... if Leonski had recognised her... she did look like her mother, after all... He suddenly realised how careless he had been: even thirty years after killing her, Leonski would not have forgotten Olga Sokolov's face.

"I think I've made a terrible mistake," he said in a shaky voice.

He called again. Voicemail again. He left a message.

"Ninel, it's Alexander. Call me as soon as you get this message. It's urgent."

He wondered if he had just left a message with a dead woman. Wavering between hope and fear, he decided to call Sveta. The telephone rang about ten times before she finally answered.

"Alexander? Do you know what time it is?" she whined sleepily.

"This is urgent. Do you know where Ninel is?"

"Given the sun's not up yet, I'd say she's probably at home in bed."

"She's not answering. It keeps going straight to voicemail."

"Maybe her battery's dead. But what's wrong, Alexander?"

"All I can tell you is that she's in danger."

"The Right Sector again?"

The neo-Nazis... he'd almost forgotten them.

"Maybe someone worse... When was the last time you saw her?"

"I haven't seen her since the zone closed. But she called me yesterday morning."

"What time?"

"Around ten."

"What did you talk about?"

"The zone being closed, basically. She was asking me about the requests I'd made to have our access reinstated. . . But you're scaring me, Alexander. What's going on?"

"I. . . I'll call you later."

"Wait! Tell me why–"

He hung up.

"You need to send a patrol to Ninel's apartment," he told Melnyk as he handed him back his mobile. "Now."

"What's the connection with Leonski?"

"Ninel is Sokolov's daughter."

"Sokolov told me he didn't have any other children!"

"She made him swear not to tell anyone who she was. She's been in conflict with him for years."

"*Blyad!*"

Melnyk called Novak. "Hey, are you in Kyiv? Perfect. You need to go to Ninel's apartment. . . Yeah, that's right, the ecologist girl. . . No, she's not a suspect. But she may be in danger. Her address. . ."

He looked at Rybalko, who gave him the street and apartment number. Melnyk relayed these details to Novak.

"I'll call the nearest station to send you reinforcements. Whatever you do, don't go in there alone: if the Kyiv police aren't there when you arrive, just watch the entrance. She may be one of Leonski's targets. Yes. . . No. . . I'll explain later."

He hung up.

"Ninel shouldn't have hidden that from me. Nor should you, for that matter," Melnyk said. "If you'd told us she was a Sokolov, we could have protected her."

"Like you protected Agopian's son?" Rybalko said sharply.

Melnyk lost his temper then. "You are the very last person to lecture me about that kind of thing! And for your information, Arseni Agopian refused to let us put his son under surveillance until we had arrested Leonski, despite our warnings. Anyway, we need to go to the station," he said, getting to his feet.

Since Rybalko's belongings had been confiscated on the grounds that they might be radioactive, Melnyk left the room to find him a change of clothes. Rybalko immediately got up and examined the window. It was sealed shut, but they were on the ground floor: he could smash the glass with his chair and escape. But what good would that do? Even if he was able to steal a car and drive to Kyiv, he would be stopped at a checkpoint and arrested. He had no choice but to wait and obey. Melnyk was leading this investigation now.

The Ukrainian reappeared in the exam room.

"Put these on," he said, handing him a pair of the blue-grey overalls with orange trim worn by workers at the Chernobyl building site.

He also had a pair of safety boots that were slightly too big for him. Rybalko dressed without protest, then followed Melnyk out of the hospital.

They had almost reached the police station when Melnyk's phone began to ring. It was Novak. She had ignored his orders and gone straight to Ninel's apartment. The captain reprimanded her, then listened to her report. His face did not lose any of its anxious tension.

"So?" Rybalko said, fearing the worst.

"She's not at home and there are traces of a struggle in the apartment."

The policeman added in a toneless voice: "That's not all. Leonski left a message."

41

Time flew. For two hours, they interrogated Rybalko about his investigation. The questions kept being repeated, to check that his story was consistent. It drove him crazy. He did not have any time to lose. Ninel did not have any time to lose.

"I'd be more useful out there than locked up in here!" he roared when they asked him yet again about his pursuit of Leonski in the ruins of Zalissya.

"It's procedure," replied the officer who was questioning him.

"Where's Captain Melnyk? I want to speak to him."

"He's busy."

"What did they find at Ninel's apartment? What was Leonski's message?"

"I'm not authorised to tell you. And I don't know anything anyway. Now answer my question: how do you know it was Leonski who beat you up in the Palace of Culture?"

He sighed. "Who else could it have been? That sick bastard moved back to his old dacha. He must have installed a generator to provide it with electricity. He uses his shed to prepare his victims' bodies. But, for fuck's sake, you know all this already!"

He rubbed his temples. The painkillers they had given him at the hospital were starting to wear off. His face felt like it was burning and he kept getting shooting pains inside his head.

"I'm not going to tell you anything else. I want to see Melnyk. Go and find him."

"He's in a meeting. I can't–"

"Find him!"

The officer tried to reason with him, but Rybalko refused to say another word. Not knowing what else to do, the policeman picked up his phone and asked one of his colleagues to tell Melnyk what his witness had said.

"Better not push your luck," the officer warned Rybalko after hanging up. "You could be in big trouble: obstruction of justice, resisting arrest, illegally entering the exclusion zone. . ."

"Fuck you," Rybalko said. "Add that to your list: insulting a police officer."

The officer turned bright red. Thankfully, Melnyk entered the office just in time.

"I'll take care of him, Sasha," he told his subordinate, whose face still betrayed the anger he felt. "Rybalko, follow me."

Melnyk took him into a small room with grimy walls. Inside, a semi-circle of folding chairs had been arranged around a metal trolley on top of which was a very old television set: one of those fat 1990s models. Next to it hummed a video recorder. Rybalko had not seen one of those in almost ten years.

"Leonski's message was recorded on a video cassette," Melnyk said. "We had to dig these dinosaurs out of the cellar to be able to watch it."

He pointed to the large black plastic rectangle lying on top of the video recorder. Rybalko carefully picked it up and examined the label stuck to it.

"For Captain Melnyk and Lieutenant Alexander Rybalko," he read.

"So we're colleagues?" Melnyk snorted.

"Yeah. Moscow police."

"You don't have a Russian accent."

"I was born here. In Pripyat."

"A Russian policeman who speaks Ukrainian and knows the area. . . I'm starting to understand why Vektor Sokolov hired you."

"Except I didn't arrest Leonski and I don't know where his daughter is. Did you call Sokolov to tell him what was happening, by the way?"

"Yes."

"How did he react when he found out Leonski had kidnapped his daughter?"

"Apparently he smashed his phone to pieces. We had to call him back on his landline."

Melnyk inserted the cassette into the video recorder. The screen filled with a blizzard of black and white dots, then the image stabilised and a stuffed swallow with bloodstained feathers appeared. This lasted for ten long seconds before abruptly disappearing. More static, followed by a black screen.

Rybalko thought the recording was over, but then he heard something. Clicking, breathing, the sound of a hand touching a microphone. The tension mounted a notch as the old videotape kept rolling. Abruptly the lens cap was removed from the video camera. Rybalko was expecting to see something horrific. Ninel dead, her eyes gouged out, a long scar running along her belly. Instead of which he saw a squalid cellar with mouldy concrete walls. In the middle, on a metal stool, a woman was tied up.

Ninel.

Her head was slumped forward and her hair hung down towards the concrete floor. Was she dead or merely asleep?

"Look up," Rybalko whispered.

As if she'd heard him, Ninel raised her head and looked at the camera. She squinted, then her pupils started darting from right to left.

He realised that she was reading something.

"This. . . this message is for Vektor Sokolov. . . my. . ."

For half a second, her lips twisted.

"My father."

In the silence that followed, Melnyk turned to Rybalko. His face was a mask of anguish. Then Ninel's ghostly, strangely deep voice rose once again.

"If he wants his daughter. . . if he wants me to live, he has to come here, to Chernobyl, and. . ."

She paused. Rybalko imagined Leonski behind the camera, showing her a series of signs containing the text she had to read.

"And be ready to pay to have her. . . to save my life. He must bring a hundred million rubles. . ."

Ninel's face reddened.

"So you think that's fair? A fucking ransom demand?"

She stared defiantly at the person behind the camera. The screen suddenly went black. There was a shout, then some slapping, cracking noises. The image returned. Ninel's hair was dishevelled and her nose was bleeding.

"Motherfucker," Rybalko hissed.

In a deadened voice, Ninel recited: "Vektor Sokolov has twenty-four hours to come to Ukraine with the money. He must be in Lenin Square, Pripyat, at noon. If he's not there at that time precisely, he. . ."

She swallowed painfully.

"He will kill me."

The image froze on the young woman's face. Melnyk pressed a button and stark white light blazed from the ceiling lamp.

"What do you think?" he asked.

"It's ridiculous. Why ask for a ransom now? He's already murdered three people without asking for money."

"My thoughts exactly. I don't believe that Leonski is prepared to exchange Ninel for money. I think he's just trying to make Sokolov suffer a bit more."

Melnyk ejected the video cassette and slipped it into a transparent plastic bag.

"What do we do now?" Rybalko said. "Are you going to waste hours questioning me again?"

"No. I need you to convince Sokolov to come here tomorrow at the agreed time. He told me he wanted to talk to you before deciding what to do."

"So I'm free to go?"

"You are, so long as you help us arrest Leonski."

Melnyk accompanied him to the exit. In the car park, Rybalko was surprised to see Sveta. She was nervously smoking a cigarette outside the pick-up truck belonging to the 1986 association.

"We summoned Ninel's colleague here to make a statement," Melnyk explained. "She agreed to wait for you and take you back to Kyiv. When you talk to Sokolov, tell him that coming to Leonski's meeting is a way of gaining time for his daughter. We're still analysing what we found in that sick bastard's dacha. Maybe he left something there that will enable us to find his new hiding place before he kills her."

Rybalko doubted it. The cellar where Ninel was being held looked exactly like a thousand others built in the communist era. The building where Leonski was holding her prisoner could be anywhere in Ukraine. Or even in Belarus.

Melnyk shook his hand and went back into the police station. Rybalko joined Sveta.

"This is a nightmare," she said. "Ninel, kidnapped by that monster. . . how is it possible?"

She tossed her cigarette on the ground and crushed it with her heel. They got into the truck together and she drove out of the car park.

"Can I borrow your phone? I have to call Ninel's father."

"Of course," she said, taking from her pocket a mobile with a plastic protector in the colours of the Ukrainian flag.

Vektor Sokolov immediately went on the attack. "You fucking idiot! How could Leonski kidnap my daughter when you were looking after her?"

"You never told me to look after her, you told me to investigate—"

"She's a Sokolov! Leonski killed my wife and my son! Didn't it cross your tiny mind that he might go after her?"

"Ninel told me nobody knew she was your daughter—"

"Nobody? What about Piotr Leonski? What about Kazimira? What about everyone Leonid might have told that Ninel was his sister? Is that what you mean by 'nobody'?"

"You're just as responsible as I am for what happened," Rybalko said. "I discussed it with Captain Melnyk. He asked you if you had any other children and you never mentioned Ninel. If you had, he would have put her under protection."

Sokolov took this in silence, then started speaking again in a calmer voice.

"Alright. . . Well, this isn't the ideal time to apportion blame. . . The important thing is Ninel. Leonski's made a ransom demand. You will hand him the money."

"He wants you to come in person to Pripyat."

"Out of the question."

"But—"

"That's not negotiable. I'll send you the money through your friend Kachin. I'll come to Ukraine. But I'm not going to carry Leonski's suitcase for him like a fucking porter."

"He said he'll kill Ninel if—"

"He'll kill her anyway."

Rybalko was shocked into silence. How could Ninel's father accept her death so coldly?

"He'll kill her no matter what I do," Sokolov went on. "Don't be naïve, Alexander. Leonski isn't after a financial compensation for what I did to him. He wants revenge. He wants to drive me mad. He wants me to have hope just so he can tear it away from me. I refuse to play his game."

"But if there's even a small chance of saving Ninel, you still have to take it!"

"That's what we're going to do. You give him the money. We'll see if that works."

"It won't work! You're the one he wants to make the exchange."

"You've just hit the nail on the head, Alexander. It's me he wants. And why, do you think?"

"You think he wants to kill you?"

"Of course. Isn't that logical?"

He wished he could argue otherwise, but Sokolov was right to be suspicious. The ransom demand made no sense. Presumably it was just a way of luring Sokolov to a place where Leonski could hurt him. The former minister's villa in Moscow was as well guarded as a military fortress.

"Even so," Rybalko said, "she is your daughter. If I were you, I'd try anything to save her. Even if it meant putting myself in danger."

"I'm not going to change my mind. You will give Leonski the money. Be at the café in Pripyat tomorrow at noon. Kachin will find you there with the money."

"Wait. . ."

Sokolov hung up.

"That fucker," Rybalko muttered as he handed Sveta's mobile back to her.

"I take it that didn't go well?"

"The kidnapper wants Ninel's father to hand him the ransom in person, but he refuses to do it."

"Which means that monster's going to kill her. . ."

He tried to reassure her. "Not necessarily. And we still have time to find her."

They drove through Chernobyl, the streets free of traffic except for a few army vehicles transporting troops. The police had requested back-up to help them go over as much terrain as possible in search of

Leonski and his hostage. Once they were out of the city, the roads were deserted. The zone was still in quarantine: other than police and army, very few drivers were authorised to travel.

"So Ninel's father is the PetroRus boss," Sveta muttered as they headed along a country road towards Dytyatky. "Now I know why she never wanted to talk about him. She was involved in fighting against the oil and nuclear lobbies. It would have stripped her of all credibility if people had known. And our charity."

"You never saw her full name on a document or anything?"

"I did, but they were in the name of Ninel Ivanovna Balakirev."

"Balakirev? You're sure?"

"Yes. Why?"

"That's her mother's maiden name. Olga Ivanovna Balakirev."

Not only had Ninel cut off all contact with her father, she had even rejected his name. Her hatred of him seemed limitless.

"Did she ever tell you anything about her father, without naming him?"

Sveta looked embarrassed.

"Yes. Sometimes. I. . . I knew she had problems with him." She struggled to find the right words, then went on: "She told me that he'd more or less abandoned her when she was ten or eleven. He no longer took care of her, barely spoke to her. And when he came home from work. . ."

She took a deep breath.

"He hit her. I replied that my father would sometimes smack me too when I'd been naughty as a kid. But what she described. . . was something completely different. Every time he had too much to drink, he would take it out on her."

A car appeared in the rear-view mirror, moving fast on the road behind them. A large black 4×4. Sveta steered to the edge of the road to let it past.

"And then, when she was twelve, he sent her to a boarding school and stopped seeing her altogether. Even when she came home for the holidays, he would send her on summer camps or foreign exchanges. She grew up alone in a way. I thought that was very sad. But—"

Her mouth remained frozen on that last word. The black 4×4 was overtaking them. The passenger-side window was open. A man in a balaclava was aiming a sawn-off shotgun at them.

Rybalko reacted instantly. It was all or nothing. He grabbed the steering wheel and turned it sharply to the left. Their vehicle veered violently across the road, smashing into the 4×4. The sound of a gunshot. The rear-view mirror exploded and shards of glass and plastic sprayed over them. Sveta, in shock, had let go of the wheel. Rybalko held it firmly to the left, pressuring the side of their attackers' vehicle to force it off the road. The hard shoulder was getting closer, then a line of trees. He jerked the steering wheel suddenly to the right and the two vehicles separated. They spun out of control and the world began to whirl. When the pick-up truck finally came to a halt, Rybalko saw that the 4×4 had crashed into a tree.

Sveta, groaning, tried to restart the truck. The engine coughed uselessly, like an old man. After three desperate attempts, Rybalko got out of the truck and ran towards the black 4×4. Adrenaline was flooding his veins. The air around the crashed vehicle smelled strongly of oil and petrol. The passenger door opened and the man in the balaclava struggled out. Before he had time to raise his gun, Rybalko punched him in the face. He followed this with a judo move, throwing his enemy to the ground then breaking his arm. The man screamed, waking the driver, who'd been knocked out by his inflated airbag. Rybalko saw a look of surprise on the other man's face, then his hand reached towards the holster inside his jacket. Rybalko dived to the ground. Bullets whistled through the air, putting holes in the car door and sending clods of earth flying. In the grass beside him, Rybalko spotted the sawn-off shotgun. He picked it up and aimed by guesswork at the inside of the 4×4. In the gunpowder-flavoured silence that followed, he listened closely. No sound of breathing from inside the vehicle. Just the rustle of feet in grass: the other man was running towards the forest, holding his broken arm protectively to his side. Rybalko stood up and looked inside the black car. The buckshot cartridge, fired at almost point-blank range, had blown away part of the man's jaw and neck. Blood had spurted over the windscreen and side window, painting them dark red.

Some rifle cartridges had spilled onto the ground. Rybalko picked up a handful of them, reloaded the weapon, then looked around. The second attacker had disappeared. He went back to Sveta's pick-up truck. She had managed to start it and was holding tight to the steering wheel.

He leaned towards her.

"Are you hurt?"

She shook her head.

"Wait here for me."

"But. . . we have to get out of here!"

"No. I need to deal with this. Permanently."

Inside the boot, he found a few clamps, which Sveta and Ninel used to seal the bags containing their samples. He took them and walked towards the spot where the man had entered the forest. It wasn't difficult to trace his progress: the tall grass was pushed down where he had passed. Rybalko followed this path until reaching a series of earth mounds planted with triangular signs announcing a highly radioactive zone.

The man in the balaclava was running between two of the mounds. Rybalko fired a warning shot and the man froze.

"Don't move," he shouted. "Take off your mask."

The man obeyed, using his unbroken arm, ruffling his Cossack-style hair.

"What's your name?'"

The man spat on the ground and insulted him. His teeth were red with blood and he had a slight lisp. He must have bitten his tongue when the car crashed.

Rybalko aimed the shotgun at the man's knee.

"Tell me who paid you to kill me, or you lose your kneecap."

The man glared at him.

"Go ahead. Fire. What are you waiting for? If I talk, my boss will kill me anyway. Compared to what he'd do to me, a bullet in the knee is nothing. So go ahead, nigger. Shoot!"

Rybalko suppressed his desire to blow the man's head off and walked closer to him. He smashed the rifle butt into the man's face and watched him collapse to the ground. Rybalko put him in an armlock, then lifted him to his feet and walked him towards one of the mounds.

"What the fuck are you doing?" the man protested.

Rybalko used the clamps to attach the man to one of the triangular signs.

"Who is your employer?"

"Go fuck yourself!"

The man cursed him quietly before shutting himself into a furious silence. A few minutes passed. The man started to hop nervously from foot to foot.

"So? Are you going to talk?"

"Nope."

"Suit yourself. If you'd rather die of radiation poisoning, that's your business."

"You're getting it too."

"I already have cancer. I'll be dead in a few months. So I'm going to stay here until you answer my questions or until your eyes start bleeding."

The man stared him out for a long time, then spat at him.

"Fucker. My mates will find you. And they'll kill you."

He withdrew into silence once more. Rybalko pointed at the other mounds around them.

"I remember there was a village here before the explosion. Because of the contamination, they decided to bury everything. Every one of these signs was planted over a pit. The liquidators dug near houses, then pushed the buildings into the holes with their mechanical shovels. Sometimes they threw in animal carcasses too, and machines that were too contaminated to be saved."

He paused for a moment. The man still had not looked away, but the hate in his eyes was fading, being replaced with fear.

"When I was a kid, we had a neighbour who did that job. He said that after a few days of burying houses, he lost his appetite. Nothing tasted good to him anymore. You know why? Because the radiation destroyed his senses. What he ate had no taste. Some people lost their sense of smell too. Can you smell the pines?"

Unthinkingly, the man sniffed the air, but he said nothing.

"You won't have any after-effects. Not yet. But if you stay here too long, you'll start to get real problems. I know about this stuff. My dad was killed by radiation. He was one of the firemen in Pripyat. He was exposed to so much radiation, trying to put out the fire, that his skin looked tanned. They sent him to a special hospital in Moscow. They tried to give him bone-marrow transplants to save him, but it did no good. His skin melted. It stuck to the sheets when he tried to move. In the end, he vomited up his internal organs. Is that how you want to die?"

For an instant, he sensed the man wavering. He watched his face for signs he was about to capitulate. But still the man said nothing. Rybalko turned his back on him and walked towards the road.

"Where are you going?" the man yelled.

He didn't answer. Sveta was still behind the wheel. The car's engine was idling.

"Did you kill him?" she asked.

"Not yet. Do you have a dosimeter?"

"In the glove compartment."

He took it and went back to the mound. Grimacing with pain from his broken arm, the Cossack was moving his wrists up and down in the hope that he could wear down the plastic clamps by rubbing them against the metal signpost.

"The problem with radiation is that you can't see it, you can't feel it, you can't hear it. Thankfully, we have little devices that can measure it."

He turned on the dosimeter and tossed it at the neo-Nazi's feet. The device began to sizzle furiously.

This time, the man cracked.

"Fuck it, I don't want to die like that. Untie me and I'll tell you whatever you want to know."

"Talk first."

"My boss is Arseni Agopian."

"The ex-policeman?"

"Yeah, he runs everything around here. Now fucking untie me!"

"I will, when you've answered my questions. Why did your boss pay you to attack the 1986 staff?"

"Because those bitches are bad for business."

Desperate to be released, the man explained frantically that Agopian was the head of a vast smuggling network of irradiated metal. Rybalko knew that for many people in the area, Chernobyl was a sort of giant junkyard that they could use to their own advantage. Engines, car parts, bricks, doors, windows... they stole anything that could be moved. But what the Cossack told him sent shivers down his spine: Agopian's teams were moving ten to fifteen tons of metal out of the zone every night, with the complicity of the checkpoint police. Chernobyl's "black gold" was then sent to the east of the country, where it was melted down in the Donbas forges before being exported to China or India to be transformed into car bonnets, stepladders or scooters which were then sold in Europe.

According to this guy, the metal dealers were paid a pittance for their work in the zone: nine euros for a hundred kilos of merchandise. And they carried the contaminated metal on their backs, after stripping it with their bare hands, totally unprotected. Yet there was no difficulty in finding people to do this dirty work; in the villages around the zone, the inhabitants had no work, no future, no hope. They pillaged the zone like poachers hunting the last rhinos in Africa, with no thought to the consequences. Had anyone ever done anything to help them? No. So it was just tough shit for any kids who caught leukaemia from a radioactive scooter.

"The two women in that charity were starting to get on our nerves. A month ago, they posted photographs of a truck passing a checkpoint at night despite the curfew. The police opened an investigation because of that. Suddenly three of our police partners were fired. So Arseni told us to make those bitches understand that if they continued screwing us around, they'd regret it. He also told us to threaten anyone else working with 1986."

"Where can I find Agopian?"

"In Strakholissya. He has a legal business there, a fishing shop. His house is just next door."

Rybalko turned and began walking towards the road. He knew enough now.

"Oi! What the fuck are you doing? Untie me!" the man yelled.

Without turning around, Rybalko gave him the finger. That guy had smuggled irradiated metal out of the zone, probably giving thousands of innocent people cancer. It was time for him to get a taste of his own medicine.

Sveta drove them to the Dytyatky checkpoint. The guards looked curiously at their beaten-up truck, but Melnyk had told the local station that the two of them would be passing through, so they were allowed to go without being questioned. In Strakholissya, Rybalko asked Sveta to park about forty-five metres from Agopian's house. He took the sawn-off shotgun from the boot of the truck, where he had hidden it under a tarp.

"If you hear gunfire and I'm not back in half an hour, call Captain Melnyk and tell him what happened."

Agopian's home was a large villa overlooking the Kyiv Sea. The smuggler had made a fortune from other people's misery. How many deaths could this man have on his conscience? Shotgun at the ready, Rybalko knocked on the door. No response: just the creak of shutters in the breeze coming off the artificial lake. He put his hand on the door handle and noticed that the door wasn't locked. Behind, a wide hallway led to a lavishly decorated living room. Gun in hand, he walked through a number of empty ground-floor rooms.

He found Agopian at the back of the garden, where the grass gave way to a small sandy beach at the water's edge. The former militiaman was sitting on a folding chair, watching the lake's glassy surface. A half-empty bottle of vodka stood within reach, its base buried in the sand. Beside it, an old revolver lay on top of an icebox.

"Don't move," Rybalko said, aiming his shotgun at the man.

Agopian turned towards him, his face showing neither surprise nor concern, just an infinite sadness tinged with fatigue.

"The ornithologist. . . what are you doing here?"

"I got one of your men to talk. He told me everything about your little business."

Agopian's gaze caressed the barrel of the rifle.

"I knew you weren't a scientist. You're the one working for Vektor, I bet?"

"How–"

Agopian reached for his bottle. Rybalko raised his gun.

"Calm down," the old officer said as he picked up the vodka. "I have no intention of harming you."

"Two of your men just tried to kill me."

"A misunderstanding. I simply asked them to scare you. You were never supposed to be killed. Murder is bad for business. So what happened to them, out of interest?"

"One is dead and the other's tied to a warning sign above a radioactive dump."

Arseni nodded slowly.

"I imagine they got what they deserved."

He swallowed a mouthful of vodka. By the looks of things, he was already drunk.

"I just talked to Vektor on the phone," Agopian said.

"He called you? Why?"

"His daughter was kidnapped by Leonski. He asked me to find some guns and some men to help him out, and I agreed. So we're on the same side now, you and me," he said with a bitter smile.

"You tried to get rid of Ninel. Why would you help Sokolov find his daughter?"

"I tried to scare her so she'd stop meddling in my affairs, but there's no way I'd ever have risked the wrath of Vektor. I know what he's capable of when someone attacks his family."

"How did you know she was his daughter? She doesn't use her father's family name."

"She might be thirty years older now, but I vividly remember the face of the girl I talked to on the day the reactor exploded, when I had to tell her that her mother was dead."

"Vektor didn't tell her?"

"No, he was in Pripyat supervising the evacuation of the city. And all the telephone lines were cut, so it was impossible to call anyone. Ninel was in her parents' dacha on the night of the murder. She was still asleep when we started searching the place for clues."

"Who else knows that Ninel is Sokolov's daughter?"

"No idea. There are still a few former inhabitants of Pripyat living around here, but most of them are either dead or living in Kyiv these days."

Agopian took another swig of vodka.

"Alcohol and guns are not a good mix," Rybalko said, nodding at the revolver on top of the icebox.

"I'm just waiting for that bastard to come after me."

His eyes flared briefly with hate, before turning dull again.

"I should have listened to Vektor in 1986," Agopian said after drinking some more vodka. "I should have killed that piece of shit Leonski."

"Vektor asked you to kill him back then?"

"I told you, Vektor's merciless when it comes to his family. Thirty years ago, when I told him Leonski was my prime suspect, he said he didn't want his wife's killer to get away with just a prison sentence. He wanted him dead. But I refused. I may not be the world's most honest man, but I have my limits. Sure, I bribe people, I threaten them, if necessary I send some boys to beat up people who are screwing with my business, but I don't kill people in cold blood. I'm not like Vektor or Leonski."

Rybalko thought about Ninel. He was wasting his time here. He had to concentrate on her.

"If I find out you've lied to me..."

"Yeah, yeah, the usual threats," Agopian said, raising his bottle. "Death, torture... I know the score."

He finished the vodka and closed his eyes. Rybalko turned away. As he walked back up to the villa, he heard the ex-policeman sobbing.

42

Tick tock. Tick tock. Tick tock.

Chernobyl, the next afternoon. The clock on the wall of the town's only café counted down the seconds with atomic precision. Rybalko wanted to take out his gun and shoot the damn thing. It reminded him too much of the imminence of death. His own, but especially Ninel's.

The bar he was in was more like somebody's shed than a chic night-club. The furniture was rustic, there wasn't much choice of alcohol, the walls were wood-panelled, and the decorations were limited to a string of flashing electric bulbs and a few art prints. One of them showed some Cossacks writing a letter to the Ottoman sultan. One fine day in 1676, the sultan had ordered them to submit to his authority. The Cossacks had told him to go fuck himself, calling him an "Armenian pig", a "brewer of Jerusalem beer", an "Alexandrian goat-whipper", and advising him to park his august backside on a hedgehog.

Rybalko thought admiringly about the Cossacks while he drank his beer.

The bar was almost empty, and most of the customers were workers from the power station wearing combat fatigues. A small crowd of them was watching the news on a T.V. set fixed to the wall. When the presenter mentioned a suspicious disappearance connected to the swallow killer, Rybalko slumped further down in his seat.

Outside, fluffy snowflakes were falling onto car roofs and the tarps covering military trucks, weighing them down to expose the metal arcs beneath like the ribs of a thin man with greenish skin. Rybalko was staring vacantly through the window when a huge German 4×4 arrived in the car park. Nikita Kachin got out. He was wearing a long coat that made him look like a campaigning general and a chapka hat lined with silver fox fur. Another man was with him. Rybalko recognised the sidekick immediately: it was the man who had slashed his tyres in Poliske, the one with an eagle tattooed on his forearm.

"What the hell are you doing with that neo-Nazi cunt, Kita?" he asked his friend when the two men sat on the bench opposite his.

Kachin raised his hands appeasingly.

"Stay calm, Alex. His name is Serguei Kamenev. He's one of Arseni Agopian's men. He's on our side."

"He's a neo-Nazi. I'm black. Is there something you're missing here?"

"Relax," Kamenev said. "We're all on the same side. Arseni wants Leonski dead, and so does your boss. And I don't really have anything against blacks, you know. Nor against Russkies. We just don't want them living in our country."

"The main thing is we all have the same objective," Kachin said, before reciting: "My enemy's enemy is my friend."

"Bullshit," Rybalko muttered. "Tell him to piss off."

"Impossible. Sokolov insisted he go with you."

Under the table, Rybalko balled his fists. He wanted to smash them into Kamenev's face. The Cossacks in that painting would have approved. But to save Ninel and get his money, he had to keep silent and put up with Sokolov's demands. Even if he did not for a second doubt that Kamenev would stab him in the back if he had the chance, particularly after what he himself had done to two of the neo-Nazi's comrades.

"And where is Sokolov?" he said.

"Safe. Far from here."

"So he hasn't changed his mind? He's not coming?"

"No. He's sure that Leonski wants to lure him to Pripyat to kill him. Have you got the copy of the recording?"

Rybalko took out a memory card, which he gave to Kachin.

"I have the impression that Ninel's in a cellar, but that's all I know for sure. If the ransom deal falls through, we'll have to work out where she is before he is able to kill her."

"Is the building in the zone?"

"It's possible. The walls are covered in mould and the paint is peeling. But that doesn't mean much. There are thousands of cellars like that in Ukraine and Belarus. They've mobilised the army to search the zone, but we are talking more than a hundred square kilometres. They could search it for a month and not find anything."

Kachin pocketed the memory card.

"I'm going to send this to some guys I know in Moscow. They might be able to find something interesting on it. Does Leonski appear in the video?"

"No. You only see Ninel. I think he doesn't want us to know what he looks like. The most recent photograph of him I could find dates back to the 1980s. He may have changed beyond recognition. In fact, he could be here in this bar now and we wouldn't know it."

"Well, that's a cheerful thought," Kachin grumbled. "How do the police plan to arrest him after the exchange?"

"There are teams hidden at strategic points around Pripyat," Rybalko said. "As soon as Leonski's got the money, they'll seal the perimeter and he'll be trapped like a rat."

"He could still hide in Pripyat," Kamenev objected. "An abandoned town of fifty thousand people. . . there's no shortage of hiding places there."

"True, it might take them a while to find him," Rybalko conceded. "But at least he couldn't escape."

Kamenev did not seem convinced.

"This city has supposedly been inaccessible for thirty years, and yet people come and go as they please. Besides, Leonski's had plenty of time to prepare. If he's arranged a meeting in Pripyat, it means he's got a plan to get out."

Rybalko had to admit that the neo-Nazi had a point.

"Is it a perfect plan? Probably not. Do we have a better one? No. So let's just play our part and see if it works."

Kamenev smiled mockingly at him. "Well, I wouldn't like to be in your place, *Pushkin*. Leonski didn't choose the meeting place by chance. There are buildings all around Lenin Square. With a decent rifle, even a kid could take you down."

"I'm not his target."

Rybalko tried to sound confident, but his voice lacked firmness. The ransom was clearly just a way for Leonski to lure Sokolov to his death. In the absence of his prey, there was always a possibility he might decide to take his frustrations out on his enemy's emissary. But, again, Rybalko had no choice. It was a risk he had to take.

They stood up. It was time to go to Pripyat. Outside, he whispered to Kachin: "Kita, if I don't get out of this alive, I'm counting on you to make sure Sokolov pays what he owes me. The money's for Tassia, you understand."

"Don't worry about that," his old comrade reassured him.

Relieved, Rybalko got into the 4×4. The backseat was leather and the air was pleasantly warm.

As hearses went, it was pretty nice.

43

The birds had vanished from the sky. The Przewalski horses were taking shelter under the pines. The snowflakes danced over the quiet forests of Polesie. In the distance, beneath this white shower, Pripyat looked like one of those miniature towns imprisoned in a snow globe.

Strangely, Rybalko found himself thinking about Lenin. Perhaps because of Ninel, maybe because of the street they were driving along, which was named after the communist leader, as was the square where the exchange was to take place. Almost every city in the U.S.S.R. had boasted a Lenin Street, and it had often been the most central, most important road. In Pripyat, however, Lenin Square would keep its name for eternity. There was no danger of it being renamed one day: Pripyat was home only to ghosts now.

The 4×4 pulled up close to the square. Before Rybalko got out, Kachin handed him a pistol.

"Don't forget: Sokolov wants Leonski dead."

The gangster looked tense. If the ransom handover went wrong, he could kiss goodbye to his business partnership with Sokolov in Crimea.

"The priority is Ninel, right?" Rybalko said, slipping the pistol into the inside pocket of his coat.

"Of course," Kachin said. "Of course."

A cold wind swept through Lenin Square. Rybalko opened the car's boot and picked up the suitcase containing the money, then the vehicle drove away, leaving him alone in the middle of the deserted city.

"*Poyekhali!*" he said aloud before taking a deep breath.

"Let's go!" This was what Yuri Gagarin had said just before his rocket blasted off, on his way to being the first man in space.

Concealed by its blanket of snow, Lenin Square looked vaguely lunar. Rybalko waited one, two, five, ten minutes, glancing nervously now and then at his watch. Nothing on the horizon, apart from the white and grey buildings, like massive fossils. Not a sound, beyond the faint creaking of the pods on the big wheel as they moved in the snow-filled wind. Never in all his life had he felt so alone. It was as if he were the last human for hundreds of kilometres in every direction.

Then he heard a ringtone. He looked around, but saw nothing. Approaching the source of the sound, he accidentally kicked a plastic box beneath the snow. Inside, he found a mobile phone. A distorted, robotic voice blared loudly as soon as he put the mobile to his ear.

"Where is Vektor?"

"He's not coming. But I have the ransom."

There wasn't a trace of Leonski anywhere in sight. Rybalko held up the suitcase, then opened it to show off its contents. He turned around – three hundred and sixty degrees – so that the kidnapper, wherever he was hiding, would be able to see the money.

"You see? It's all there."

"It's not all there. Sokolov isn't there. He doesn't love his daughter enough to risk his life for her?"

"Listen, it's the money that matters, not who's carrying–"

"Call him. Tell him I'll kill his daughter if he isn't here in five minutes."

'Wait!

Leonski hung up. Feverishly, Rybalko called Sokolov using the satellite phone.

"Alexander? What's happening? Have you got Ninel?"

"No. He says he'll execute her in five minutes if you're not here."

"He's bluffing."

"He's serious. He showed that by killing Leonid."

"It's obviously a trap. He's manipulating us. He wants me dead. Tell him I'm not coming."

Anger overwhelmed Rybalko. "For God's sake! If I were in your shoes, I'd do anything he asked me to save my daughter! Are you going to be able to live with the deaths of both of your children on your conscience?"

"Stop lecturing me and just do your job. Negotiate. Find a way to convince him to hand Ninel over."

Sokolov hung up. Rybalko wanted to crush the mobile in his hand. At that moment, he would have willingly exchanged the few months of life that remained to him for Ninel's life. But his life was worth nothing to Leonski. That much had been made clear when the killer had spared him in the Palace of Culture. Rybalko had been trapped, at Leonski's mercy; all he'd had to do was pull the trigger.

The mobile buzzed.

"Let me talk to Vektor," the voice demanded.

"He. . . he's not coming."

Machine-like laughter echoed from the speaker.

"That old coward. I'm not surprised. He always got others to do his dirty work for him. Call him. Tell him his last child is dead."

"Wait!" Rybalko yelled. "It's not Ninel's fault that your daughter is dead!"

Leonski did not reply, but he had not hung up.

"I know what happened to her," Rybalko said quickly. "The leukaemia. I know you want revenge on Sokolov, Agopian and all the others who caused that. But Ninel is not her father. She's totally the opposite. She hates him. She changed her name. She disowned him. Take Sokolov's money and free her."

He could still hear the killer's hoarse breathing on the other end of the line. Had he managed to make him hesitate? He clung to this tiny hope during the eternity that it took Leonski to reply.

"Go to Elementary School number three. You have five minutes."

"I'll never make it, with all this snow. . ."

"Five minutes. The countdown has begun."

Rybalko put the mobile in his coat pocket and started to run. School number three was behind the apartment buildings on Kurchatova Street, several hundred metres from where he was now. Holding the suitcase tight to his chest, he ran as fast as he could without twisting an ankle in a pothole hidden by the snow. After crossing Kurchatova Street, he went between the dilapidated tower blocks and across an abandoned stadium.

The mobile vibrated in his pocket. He answered while he ran.

"Are you there?"

"Nearly... I can... I can see it," he panted.

"In the lobby you will find another phone. Take it and throw this one away."

At last he arrived outside the school. The metal pillars that held up the roof of the covered playground were rusted. The fibreglass that had been used to insulate it had fallen to the ground, where it formed a brownish matting that concealed the dangerous holes in the concrete.

A chair sat alone in the middle of the lobby, an old mobile phone on top of it. It started to ring. He answered and Leonski gave him new instructions.

"Go up to the second floor. There's a blue and yellow mural with four figures. Find it."

He ran through the corridors, the paint on their walls peeling, until he reached the staircase. In the classrooms he passed, he saw desks still neatly lined up. Red folders were piled on top of them, open to pages covered in children's handwriting. The floor was littered with sheets of paper and textbooks, all covered with a thick layer of dust. On the teacher's desk, Rybalko spotted an assemblage of iron rods and coloured balls used for chemistry classes. Perhaps that one represented a uranium atom...

On the second floor there were red flags and banners bearing communist slogans. The painting that Leonski had told him to find was hanging in the corridor. Oddly, it showed few signs of damage, whereas the paint on the walls was peeling off in large green flakes.

He called Leonski.

"Call Sokolov," the killer said. "I want a conference call between the three of us."

Rybalko dialled the ex-minister's number, but there was no answer. He sent a text explaining that he'd had to change to a different phone. A second later, Sokolov called him back.

"What's going on, Alexander? Why are you using a different phone?"

"Hello, Vektor," said the robotic voice.

Sokolov sounded horrified. "Leonski. . . you?"

"Yeah, it's me. I should have known you wouldn't have had enough guts to give me the ransom yourself."

"I don't take orders from scumbags like you, Leonski!"

"Don't lose sight of the situation, Vektor. Don't forget what I can do."

Sokolov was silent.

Leonski went on: "I've been waiting for this moment for thirty years, Vektor. Waiting to be face to face with you. But I suspected you'd chicken out. You always were a coward."

Knowing Sokolov's temper, Rybalko feared the situation would get out of hand, so he intervened: "Where should I put the money?"

"Don't be in such a rush. Tell Vektor what you see."

Rybalko looked at the painting. It showed four figures: a cosmonaut, a girl holding an ear of wheat, a man drawing plans for a rocket, and a woman with her hands joined, palms upward, feeding a bird. As he described this last figure to Sokolov, the truth seemed suddenly obvious.

"The woman with the bird. . . is that Larissa?"

The metallic voice crackled coldly: "It's her. My wife worked here. Go into the next room."

Rybalko saw a door surrounded by a sort of wooden casing. Behind it was a classroom with large picture windows, the glass broken. On the walls were portraits of historical figures, rendered almost unrecognisable by the spreading mould. He had to step over an old map of the U.S.S.R. to reach the teacher's desk.

"This was where Larissa worked. It was her classroom. Describe it to Vektor. . ."

Sokolov grew impatient. "I know what the fucking classroom looks like, Leonski. What's your point?"

"What are you complaining about, Vektor? Every minute we spend talking is another minute that your daughter is alive. But, oh well, since you're in a rush, let's move on. I want your friend to go to Apartment Building number eight. It's next to the Lazurny swimming pool. There's a mobile in the letter box for apartment fifteen. You have ten minutes."

"Number fifteen?" Sokolov choked.

Rybalko had already thrown away the mobile and run out of the school. He went up Serzhanta Lazareva Street and arrived, breathing heavily, outside the lobby of Building number eight. In the letter box of apartment fifteen, a telephone was ringing.

"I'm here," he gasped.

His lungs felt as though they were about to explode. Leonski again told him to arrange a conference call with Sokolov.

"So, Vektor, why don't you tell our friend why we're here?"

"It's the building where we lived before the disaster," Sokolov replied in a voice shaky with anger. "When are you going to stop playing these stupid little games, you sick bastard?"

"Soon. Go up to apartment fifteen, Alexander."

Rybalko frowned. How did Leonski know his first name? No time to think about that now. He climbed the stairs to apartment fifteen. Like most of the living quarters in the city, it had been pillaged and vandalised. In the living room, all that remained was an old Elektron 714 television set with a smashed screen and a few heavy, angular pieces of furniture. An old pennant for F.C. Stroitel Pripyat lay on the floor. The club had been challenging for promotion to the Soviet second division just before the accident. An even bigger stadium had been built on the outskirts of the city, in anticipation of the club's future victories. Like the amusement park, it was supposed to be ready for May 1, 1986. The reactor explosion had left it too radioactive to use. And most of the players had worked as liquidators in the months that followed. Suffice to say that they were incapable of kicking a ball after that.

"What now?" Rybalko asked.

"Go into the first room on your right."

He went through the hallway and entered what turned out to be an old bedroom. Here, too, looters had taken everything worth taking: the mattress, the small furniture, the bulbs, the electric wires. There were some children's toys on the floor: Misha the bear, a mascot from the 1980 Olympics, with its faded multicoloured belt and the five golden rings; the little bear Cheburashka with his big ears, and his accomplice Gena the Crocodile. It was disturbing, seeing them lying there covered in dust, as if waiting for someone to come back and play with them. He spotted a child's pink jumper with two woollen mittens hanging from the ends of the sleeves. His heart ached. Ninel had to have worn it as a little girl. Her mother had probably knitted it for her. And, just as all Ukrainian mothers did, so that their children would not forget their mittens outside, she'd sewn an elastic band into the collar that connected to both.

"You see the mannequin?" Leonski asked.

Near the broken window was one of those old mannequins that used to be found in Soviet clothes shops. It was wearing an old dress. Leonski told Rybalko to describe it.

"It's white, with a row of flowers sewn along the bottom. . ."

Rybalko stopped, realising with horror that it was the same type of dress that Ninel's mother had been wearing the night she was killed. Sokolov realised this too.

"You're sick," he hissed.

"Alexander, go into the kitchen," Leonski said. "Look under the sink, there's something for you."

He walked across the apartment. Empty tin cans, broken bottles, dilapidated Soviet cookbooks. The kitchen was in the same desolate state as the other rooms. In the cupboard under the sink, he found a large white icebox covered with reddish-brown stains.

"What is it?" he said anxiously.

No answer.

"Leonski?"

"What's happening?" Sokolov wanted to know.

"Leonski hung up. There's an icebox under the sink."

"Open it," Sokolov ordered.

The icebox was damp and cold to the touch. The lid was held on with thick brown sticky tape. Rybalko used an old fork he found on the floor to cut it free. He carefully lifted the lid and a smell of putrefaction and hairspray attacked his throat. He held his breath.

"What's in the icebox?" Sokolov asked.

Rybalko slowly moved the lid out of the way, as if afraid that whatever was inside the box would leap at his face.

"What's inside, for God's sake?" Sokolov yelled.

Rybalko wanted to tell him to fuck off, but the words died in his throat. The lid fell to the floor. It had slipped from his fingers. Inside the icebox was a mass of tousled hair. Not a wig: real hair. . . on a real head. He could see the pink scalp under the blonde roots. He moved his hands closer. His stomach whined, then nausea overwhelmed him. He just had time to stand up before vomiting into the sink.

"Alexander?" Sokolov panted. "Tell me what's happening!"

Rybalko crouched down again, shoved his fingers into the fibrous mass of blonde hair, then lifted up the head. It was surprisingly light. Slowly he turned it around and saw a pair of Baikal-blue eyes, cold and lifeless.

THOSE ABOUT TO DIE

44

Outside, Rybalko knocked the snow off a bench and sat down, insensible to the concrete's biting cold. A little later, a police car arrived. Melnyk got out.

"I'm sorry," the Ukrainian muttered.

Rybalko looked up. Melnyk appeared sincere. He genuinely felt sorry for his half-Cuban comrade.

"No, it's me... I'm the one who's sorry. I..."

He tried to find the words. How to tell him?

"It's not Ninel. The head in the icebox, it's not hers. Leonski took out the victim's eyes, like he did with all the others. And he put in glass eyes the same colour as Ninel's. But it's not her."

Hairs pricked up on the back of his neck. What he had seen in the icebox... he would never forget it.

"So who was the victim?"

"It's... it's Novak... your colleague... It's her head in there..."

The police officer was motionless for a long time, as if petrified, incapable of doing anything but staring at the plastic box, as white as the snow that fell around them. At last he reached out towards it.

"Don't open it," Rybalko said as Melnyk's fingers touched the lid.

But the Ukrainian wasn't listening. He swept away the thin layer of snow with a reverent gesture, as if he were dusting a gravestone, then lifted the lid. A swear word died in his throat. Melnyk let go of the lid, which fell soundlessly onto the immaculate ground. Feeling dizzy, he sat down on the bench. His irregular breathing formed little clouds of vapour in front of his mouth. Despite the cold, he unzipped his coat and fiddled with his St Joseph medallion.

"She was pregnant," he said after a long, frozen moment.

Rybalko shivered with horror. Leonski's crime was even more vile than he had imagined. Melnyk picked up the lid and placed it back on top of the icebox. He put it on the ground by his Lada's boot, which he was struggling to unlock. He went into a silent rage then, kicking the car until the boot finally opened. Emptied of anger, Melnyk leaned against the 4×4's battered side and lit a cigarette. Other police cars appeared at the end of the street. Now it was clear that Leonski was not going to show up, the police units hidden around Pripyat were converging on the central square. Melnyk sent them to examine the buildings that Rybalko had visited during the killer's macabre treasure hunt.

"I'm going to Kyiv to take her. . . to take the. . . I'm going to the morgue," he said, trying to control his emotions. "I also have to tell her husband. She was supposed to stay out of the firing line. In her condition. . ."

He bit his lip.

"She was inexperienced, but she would have been a good police officer." He nodded. "A very good one."

Then he seemed struck by a revelation.

"She must have found something. She didn't have any connection with Pripyat. She had never set foot in the zone before being transferred here. Leonski only kills the children of the people he considers responsible for his misfortunes. That's it: she must have discovered something. She had to stay in Kyiv to avoid being exposed to radiation. But she was still working with us on the investigation. I sent her a copy of the video. The ransom demand. She must have found something in it."

"Then why didn't she call you?"

"For weeks she ran a parallel investigation into Leonski without telling me. She thought if she caught him, she'd get a transfer out of the zone. Maybe she discovered where he was hiding and tried to arrest him on her own."

330

Rybalko reached into his pocket and took out the mobile Leonski had left in the letter box of the Sokolovs' former apartment.

"Leonski sent me a text," he said, handing him the mobile. "He's given us a new ultimatum."

Melnyk read the message out loud: "'Vektor Sokolov has until noon tomorrow to kill himself. If he doesn't, his daughter will die. . .' That piece of shit! We're going to catch that bastard. He made a mistake by killing Galina. . . Thanks to her, we're going to catch him," Melnyk said, his voice growing louder – as if he were trying to convince himself.

45

Melnyk dropped him in Chernobyl and Rybalko climbed into the 1986 pick-up truck. He made a brief call to Sokolov, who flat-out refused Leonski's deal. Clearly, he felt no desire to sacrifice his life for his daughter's.

Next, Rybalko went to Ninel's apartment in Kyiv. After searching it, he turned on the laptop he had borrowed from Sveta and plugged it into the video projector in the living room. He played the film of the ransom demand and spent two hours studying it, smoking cigarette after cigarette, examining each image one after another, without finding anything that gave him a new line of thought. But while he was drinking a coffee and watching the video for the umpteenth time, an idea crossed his mind.

"This. . . this message is for Vektor Sokolov. . . my. . . my father."

He stopped the video. Ninel's face showed no fear, only a sort of disgust. "My father": she never used that word to describe Sokolov. It was always Vektor this, Vektor that. She truly hated the man she referred to as "father" only because her gaoler was threatening her. A silent threat: at no point was Leonski's voice audible. Presumably he wanted to hide his voice. Ninel seemed to be reading a written text from something to the left of the camera. Maybe a computer screen or a tablet.

What if the clue was to be found in the soundtrack, not the images?

Maybe Novak had concentrated on the background noises. He found a pair of headphones next to the stereo and plugged them into the computer. Eyes closed, he listened to the recording. He soon noticed something that had escaped him until then: a regular noise that sounded like a muffled song. He turned the volume up as high as it would go. The melody was familiar. Where had he heard it? He listened to it several times, but in vain. Deciding to take a break so he could think, he took off the headphones, leaving the video playing.

He went out onto the balcony and lit a cigarette. He had new clues to examine, but he could not work out how they fitted together. The melody; the fact that Leonski was neither seen nor heard; the expression of disgust on Ninel's face; her calm demeanour. Ninel wasn't the type to piss herself with fear, but even so she seemed a bit too serene. As if she knew that nothing was going to happen to her.

No.

Not that.

It wasn't possible. His exhaustion was playing tricks on him. He had barely slept. His body was still stiff from his hike through the zone and the beating he had taken. He had a headache and the painkillers were having little effect. Obviously he wasn't thinking straight.

And yet. . . Leonski never appeared. . . Nobody had ever seen him.

He tossed his glowing cigarette stub and went back into the living room to call Melnyk. The captain did not answer. Maybe he was offering his condolences to Novak's family. Rybalko sent him a text.

"Did you find size 14 footprints on the floorboards that I crashed through when I was chasing Leonski?"

A message arrived five minutes later.

"Not size 14. Why?"

He did not reply and he declined Melnyk's call when the Ukrainian tried to contact him a little later. He had to concentrate. He had to follow the crazy idea that was buzzing inside his head to its logical conclusion. To make it seem more real, he spoke it aloud, as if questioning the image of Ninel that kept flickering in a loop on the wall.

"Was it you who did all this? Was it you who killed all these people?"

He stared into Ninel's hard eyes. Why was this idea polluting his mind? It could only be exhaustion.

And yet. All these little details were starting to fit together, like the pieces of a puzzle. Ninel hated her father and adored her mother. She had a violent temper. She had not revealed the fact that Leonid was her brother. She had refused to go up to the apartment from where he had been hung. She had refused to see the taxidermist. She had kept her mother's name and disowned her father's. Vektor Sokolov used to beat her when she was young. The voice on the message was disguised. Leonski did not appear in the video. His footprints were not in the Palace of Culture. What if it had been her, in the anti-radiation suit? What if it had been Ninel who knocked him out, when she could have killed him?

But why would she have murdered all those people?

She killed her brother because he was like her father and she hated him. She murdered Agopian's son because he failed to arrest Leonski, her mother's killer. And Natalia Winograd? No idea. And Leonski? Had she killed him too?

And then there were the birds. She was an ornithologist. She could easily have caught falcons. As for the stuffed swallows. . . maybe she had taken them from Leonski's workshop?

No, no, no.

He turned the whole apartment upside down in search of clues. In a wardrobe, well hidden, he found a box containing souvenirs of her mother. Photographs, little notes. But nothing related to her father.

He no longer knew what to think. He looked at his watch: another two hours had passed. He had to concentrate on something else. The melody. The songs. It was something he had heard recently, he felt sure. But where? It was like a choir. . . yes, a children's choir. . . that was it! It was the song the children at the clinic had been singing when Ninel took him there, when he was trying to find a guide to get him into the zone.

He ran out of the apartment.

46

It was late and the clinic was about to close for visitors. At the reception desk, he asked to see Ninel's friend Maria. He was told that she had gone home. He insisted that he needed to speak to someone in charge and, after a fifteen-minute wait, a small, energetic-looking woman with strawberry-blonde hair introduced herself.

"Dr Radecki. I was told you needed to speak to me urgently?"

"Yes. It's about Ninel."

"Is she alright?"

"Have you heard about the swallow killer?"

"No."

"Well, it's this man. . ."

But what if it's a woman?

". . . who has been active in the Chernobyl region. He. . ."

Or she. Ninel.

". . . has already murdered several people. Now he has kidnapped Ninel."

Or so she wants us to believe.

"My God!" the doctor exclaimed. "But what can I do to help?"

He took out his mobile.

"I would like you to take a look at this video and tell me if the room seems familiar to you."

Sickened by the first image, Radecki put her hand to her mouth and kept it there during the entire video.

"Do you recognise that place?" he asked.

"I. . . um. . . it resembles a room we have in the basement, but. . . my God, do you think she was held here? That's insane. . ."

"I have to see that room. Can you take me there?"

She agreed and guided him nervously to the depths of the building.

"Who has access to this part of the clinic?" he said.

"The maintenance people. The nursing staff, if they wish."

"The patients?"

"No, it's for staff only."

"And what is this room used for?"

"It's a storeroom, but we haven't used it for years because it's so damp. Everything we stored there ended up going mouldy."

"Do you need a particular key to get in?"

"It's the same type of lock as the other doors in the basement."

"And who has that kind of key?"

"At least ten people. And we keep one in the staff room."

When they reached the door, she took out a bunch of keys. She put one of them into the lock, but it wouldn't turn.

"That's strange. I'm sure it's the right one."

She tried some of the other keys, but none of them opened the door.

"I don't understand. It's as if someone has changed the lock!"

"Move to the side," Rybalko said, pushing her gently by the shoulder.

He took out the pistol that Kachin had given him. The woman turned a little pale.

"Stand back. The killer might be inside."

She stepped out of the way. He kicked the door. The wood was rotted by damp and the lock gave way on the fourth kick. Gun in hand, he walked into the storeroom. In the middle of the room was a chair exactly like the one on which Ninel had sat during the video of the ransom demand. On the floor he saw three round marks that formed an equilateral triangle. Almost certainly marks made by the camera tripod.

He searched the room, but there was nothing there except for a few mildewed pieces of furniture.

"You can come in," he told the doctor.

She appeared in the doorway.

"The killer used a camera here. An old one, with a cassette inside. There was also a tripod. Have you seen any of your employees with that kind of equipment?"

"Absolutely not."

And yet Leonski had clearly come here with the equipment and Ninel. Someone must have seen something. Unless. . . unless she came here alone. She could easily have found a copy of the key, given that she sometimes worked at the clinic. All she would have had to do was to discreetly bring the camera and the tripod down here, sit on the chair, and play out her little masquerade.

No. Forget that.

He took from his pocket a print-out of an old black-and-white photograph of Leonski, dating from the time when he still worked at the power station.

"Do you recognise this man?"

For several long seconds, the doctor examined Leonski's round face, his bushy eyebrows, his dark hair.

"No, that face means nothing to me."

"He'd be thirty years older now. Concentrate on his eyes. Anything?"

"Maybe. It's really strange, but he looks a bit like Hanss."

"Hanss? Who's that?"

"Our handyman. He's been working here for about a year. You've probably seen him in the corridors, when you came the first time. He's hairless now. He doesn't even have any eyebrows."

He remembered the man in the blue overalls who had spoken to him when he was waiting for Ninel outside the door of the games room. Could that have been Leonski? He tried to remember the man's eyes. Yes, there had been something disturbing in the way that man had looked at him. And he had smiled strangely too, as if he knew him. Leonski must be ill; he could have lost his hair as a result of some medical treatment.

"I have to see this Hanss. Where can I find him?"

"He's not here tonight, but he usually sleeps in an attic room when he's on duty."

"Can you show it to me?"

They went upstairs. The room occupied by the handyman was quite small and contained no personal objects. Rybalko searched, but found nothing.

"Does Hanss like birdwatching?"

"Sorry?"

"The swallow killer naturalises birds. He's fascinated by them."

Her face screwed up in concentration.

"I've never noticed Hanss doing anything like that."

"Does he have big feet?"

"Yes. Very big."

He was relieved. He had been wrong. Ninel was a victim, not the murderer.

"Ninel and Sveta often give presentations on animals. Does he attend those?"

"He was there for Ninel's speech two days ago. He was sitting at the back."

"Where does he live when he's not sleeping here?"

"I have no idea."

"Did he work today?"

"No. He called in sick."

"And yesterday?"

"He left very early. He wasn't feeling well," he said.

"Did a woman come to see him?"

The horrifying sight inside the icebox haunted him for an instant.

"I don't know. I spent most of my day with the children. You'd have to ask one of the secretaries, but they've all gone home now."

He would deal with that later. Novak must somehow have discovered the connection between Leonski and the clinic. There were no visible blood stains in the basement room. Did that mean Leonski had cleaned it, or that he had killed the police officer somewhere else?

"How does he get to work? Does he have a car?"

"No. I think he gets here by bus, or maybe by carpool... oh my God!"

She covered her mouth with her hand again.

"Yesterday. . . I saw him leaving with Maria. She. . . she was going home and he asked her if she could drop him at his apartment. She didn't come to work today. Do you think he took her?"

A scenario suggested itself: Novak turns up at the clinic. She asks questions. Leonski kills her. He hides the body, maybe in the room where he is standing now. But he knows he has to get rid of it quickly. He doesn't have a vehicle. He asks Maria to take him home. He uses an excuse to lure her into his apartment. Maybe he plays on her professional sympathies: he's ill, she's a doctor. She can't refuse to help him.

But as soon as the door is closed, he kills her. Then he takes her car to pick up Novak's body. He knows that Maria's death will be discovered within a few days, but he doesn't care: his vengeance is almost complete. He only needs to gain a bit of time.

"Can you give me Maria's address, quickly?"

They went to the office, where the doctor consulted the database for clinic employees and gave him Maria's details. She lived ten minutes away. Rybalko told the doctor to call the police, then set off for Maria's apartment. After parking the pick-up truck outside her building, he called Melnyk. No answer. He left a message telling the captain to join him and went into the apartment block.

The doorbell to Maria's apartment was not working. He hammered on the door before realising that it wasn't locked. He went inside, pistol raised. The entrance stank of blood and dead flesh. When he moved closer to the bathroom, the smell intensified. The bathtub was behind a transparent shower curtain, through which he could make out a horizontal form. Breathing fast, he pulled back the plastic curtain and found a headless woman's body. The body of Novak. Retching, he turned around and – just before he blacked out – saw a baseball bat swinging towards his head.

47

When he opened his eyes, he was tied to a chair. His head was boiling with pain. He was in the living room. The shutters were closed. The air was thick with the smell of leather and chemicals.

He tried to loosen his binds, but it was useless: his ankles and wrists were firmly attached with ropes to the wooden chair. A few metres away, the electronic eye of a camera was pointed in his direction.

Leonski entered the room.

"Awake already?"

Rybalko tried to move his lips. He realised his mouth was taped shut.

"Just a precautionary measure," the killer said, taking out a pistol.

He scratched at the edge of the tape and lifted up part of it.

"I'll take it off, but if you yell I'll have to kill you. Understood?"

Rybalko nodded. Leonski tore the tape off and his prisoner suppressed a cry. He stretched his lips, which burned unpleasantly.

"What did you do to Maria?" he said.

"Same thing as the others."

The others? A torrent of ice rushed through his guts. Was Ninel already dead? Or was he talking about the other three victims?'

"Ninel. . . is she alive?"

"You should worry about yourself, not her."

Behind the camera, Leonski pressed a button and a red light lit up.

"What are you doing?"

"You were here to arrest me, weren't you? You want me to confess my crimes? Then let's do it."

He brought over a chair and sat next to Rybalko.

"My name is Piotr Mikhailovich Leonski," the swallow killer began in a steady voice, "and I was born in 1960 in Kyiv. I killed Leonid Sokolov. I also killed Anton Winograd's daughter and Arseni Agopian's son. Two days ago, I kidnapped Ninel Sokolov."

"Where is she?" Rybalko asked.

"In a safe place, waiting for her father to accept my offer."

"You know he never will."

"Then his daughter will die."

"Why are you—"

"You want to know my motive? That's simple. Vengeance. Hatred. Anger."

"Vengeance for what?"

"For what Sokolov did to me."

"I know he paid some men to beat you up in prison. That doesn't justify murdering his entire family."

"*Beat me up?* That expression hardly describes what he put me through in prison."

He lifted up the T-shirt he was wearing, revealing horrific lacerations across his skin.

"My torturers did this with the lid of a tin can. They stuck it between my ribs until I begged them to stop. And that wasn't the worst of it, believe me. The death of his bastard son was payment for that."

Leonski fell silent. Rybalko sensed that he was awaiting the next question.

"And Ninel? Why kill her?"

"To settle the score. I lost my daughter because of him. He will lose his too."

"She's innocent."

"As were my daughter and my wife."

"You killed your wife!"

The ghost of a smile appeared on Leonski's lips.

"Was it Arseni Agopian who told you that? Arseni. . . that corrupt piece of shit. He did what Sokolov told him. He didn't imagine even for an instant that Vektor could have been the murderer."

Shocked, Rybalko stammered: "But. . . wait, are you saying—"

"I didn't kill my wife. It was Vektor Sokolov who killed her. Along with Olga."

"But why—"

"You're slow on the uptake. Think about it. Why would Sokolov kill my wife and his own wife on the same night?"

Rybalko replayed the film of the night of the double homicide in his head, trying to add Vektor Sokolov to the cast. What was he doing at Leonski's dacha?

"Vektor was your wife's lover. Olga caught them. Things got out of hand and he killed them."

Leonski shook his head.

"Not all love triangles are the same. Think about it a different way. There are two dead women and a killer. Conclusion?"

Two dead women, a love triangle.

"Your wife wasn't cheating on you with Vektor Sokolov. She was cheating on you with Olga. They were lovers!"

Leonski's face grew serious.

"Maybe you're not that stupid after all. It took me weeks to accept the truth. When I was cleaning the bedroom in our old dacha, I found love letters addressed to my wife."

He moved out of frame for a moment to pick up a yellowed sheet of paper.

"This one dates from March 1986. It's one of the last letters that Olga sent. She talks about her relationship with her husband: his violence, his jealousy. She says he wouldn't hesitate to kill her if he discovered their relationship."

He placed the letter gently on a coffee table.

"Sadly, that's exactly what happened. They must have spent the night together, the day of the murder. Sokolov presumably went to pick up his wife so he could take her away from the radioactive fallout. When he didn't find her at his dacha, he went to mine. He knew my wife and his were close. He just didn't know *how* close. Back then, nobody used to lock their doors at night. There were no burglars in the Soviet Union, according to State propaganda. He must have gone in and heard noises coming from the bedroom. He must have recognised his wife's voice. He found a knife in a drawer and went upstairs. When he found them both in our bed, he went mad with rage. He must have stabbed his own wife first, then attacked Larissa. After that, I assume he dressed Olga and moved her body so the militia would not suspect that she had been Larissa's lover."

"Not long after the reactor exploded, I fled the power station. I went to our apartment in Pripyat and I took our things. I picked up my daughters, who were sleeping at the Winograds' apartment for their eldest daughter's birthday party, and I drove with them to Zalissya. When I reached our dacha, I found the two bodies. There was blood everywhere. My Larissa. . . he'd attacked her so violently that her whole body was red with blood. And there were splatters of blood everywhere, on the mattress, on the walls. . ."

"On the stuffed swallow."

Leonski's eyes blazed with fury.

"Yes. On the swallow. It was to remind people of Sokolov's crime that I left one near every person I killed. I knew he wouldn't be able to resist sticking his nose into the investigation. I wanted him to be frightened. I wanted him to fear that his secret would be revealed to the world."

"But why did you kill Arseni Agopian's son? And Anton Winograd's daughter?"

"Agopian never really searched for the truth. He sacrificed me. As for Anton, he told the militia that I had blood on my shirt, which was false. He said that to avoid getting into trouble. Agopian or Sokolov must have told him what to say. Vektor had no problems hiding his own guilt. I was the ideal suspect. All he had to do was to encourage the militia to go after me. And yet that wasn't enough for him. He wanted me to confess, to put him totally in the clear. But I never gave in. I loved my wife. I wasn't a murderer. Not back then."

A bitter smile deformed his face.

"I nurtured my vengeance for years. I studied every detail I could find about that bastard. I realised that he had murdered my wife because he couldn't accept his own wife was a *lesbiyanka*. He'd have been a laughing stock if that had come out. His career would have collapsed. That's why he killed them both. So they could never talk. So that nobody would ever know the truth."

These words shone a new light on everything Rybalko had seen and learned. Sokolov's mood swings, his repressed violence. He was exactly the kind of man who would kill in a fit of rage, then destroy his victim's corpse afterwards.

"To carry out my revenge, I gave up the apartment the State had given me and took the identity of someone with no family. That was easy: the U.S.S.R. was falling apart; with a bit of money, you could buy anything. I went to Russia. I had a series of crappy jobs and put enough money aside to start my own electronics shop. That did pretty well. I bought a gun. I thought about shooting Sokolov, but I soon realised that would be impossible. He was constantly surrounded by bodyguards and I am not a good shot. So I bided my time. I found out that Ninel had started a charity in Chernobyl. I decided I would kill my targets in the zone. It was poetic justice: it had all begun there, after all. The most complicated thing was luring Leonid there. I had to make him believe that his mother's true killer lived in the zone. I'd picked up some old things belonging to Olga from the Sokolovs' dacha. I gave Leonid a locket as evidence and he agreed to travel to Ukraine. And I had a suspect all ready and waiting: me! I sent him to consult the K.G.B. archives, where he discovered that I had been suspected of the killing at the time. I knew I wasn't putting myself in any real danger. Leonid knew me only by my false identity, and even if there were photographs of me in the dossier, there wasn't much chance he would recognise me. As you may have noticed, I don't bear much resemblance to the man I was in 1986. It took me a while to persuade him to follow me into the zone, to see the dacha where his mother had been killed. He thought there was no point. I told him there might be some clues there that the police had missed, and in the end he fell for it, the idiot. I took him to my workshop, where nobody would hear his screams. And I showed him what his father had taught me about suffering."

"And Ninel? Does she deserve to pay for her father's crimes too? She started an N.G.O. here. She's fighting to alleviate the consequences of a disaster caused by people of your generation. And she hates her father almost as much as you do. He used to beat her when she was a kid. Did you know that?"

Leonski looked almost sorry. "That's regrettable. Ninel is a good person. But she must die to atone for her father's sins."

"And Maria? What did she do? And Officer Novak?"

"Necessary sacrifices. I'm sorry about those. They saw things they shouldn't have seen. I killed the policewoman to send a warning to Sokolov and the police. Maria. . . I'll take care of her later."

"Your vengeance is out of control, Leonski. You're killing innocent people. You're no better than Sokolov."

"In a war, there are collateral casualties. You know that, don't you? You served in Chechnya."

How did Leonski know that? The only person Rybalko had told was Ninel. Had he tortured her to make her tell everything she knew about him?

"You spared my life in the Palace of Culture. You could easily have shot me. Why didn't you?"

"I had no reason to kill you. Your investigation wasn't a threat."

The murderer's eyelids started to twitch. He was nervous, Rybalko could sense it. Why now?

"I don't believe you. You killed an innocent young woman just because she was a witness. There must be a particular reason you didn't want to kill me. . ."

He looked down at Leonski's skinny legs and his enormous trainers tapping nervously on the carpet. He thought again about how he had chased him. He saw the killer running ahead of him through the ruins of Zalissya, his silhouette visible in the light from the torch he was carrying. He saw him picking up the dropped pistol and aiming at him. He remembered the kicks aimed at his face.

The kicks. The footprints. The doubts he had had about Ninel returned to him.

"It wasn't you that night, in the zone!" he shouted. "You had an accomplice."

His face twisted with rage, Leonski stood up.

"Who is it? Who helped you? Sveta. . . no. . . Maria!" Rybalko yelled.

"Shut your mouth!" Leonski ordered, smacking him in the face with the back of his hand.

Pain exploded through his head and he tasted blood on his tongue. Leonski walked over to the camera and ejected the video cassette.

"You ruined it. Now we're going to have to do it again," he grumbled.

"Why is Maria helping you?"

Suddenly Rybalko understood.

"Maria is your daughter. She's the twin who survived. *She's* the one I was chasing in Zalissya. And unlike you, she isn't a killer. She couldn't fire at me. But what was she doing in your old dacha that night?"

Leonski glared at him.

"She knew you were going there. She was the one who gave you the guide's name, remember? When the zone was closed, I was trapped outside it. Maria has contacts among the people in charge of the checkpoints.

She arranged to go back into the zone at night, to pick up a few compromising things I'd left with the corpse of Arseni Agopian's son."

"That was risky."

"She thought she'd taken care of everything. She'd called her friends in the police to warn them some stalkers would try to cross the bridge near the village of Cherevach that night. But you slipped through their net. Thankfully she managed to get away from you."

"She's with Ninel now? Is she the one holding her prisoner?"

Leonski ignored this question. He was busy lighting a fire in the hearth, with some wood and petrol. Once the flames were high enough, he tossed the video cassette he had just recorded onto the pyre.

"How could you do that to your own daughter?"

The foul stench of burning plastic filled the living room, while the cassette crackled and melted.

"She's doing it to avenge her mother. Since that bastard Sokolov killed her, Maria grew up without a mama. She watched her twin sister die. Can you imagine what she went through?"

"What is her role in all this?"

"She got a job at the clinic. She was a brilliant medical student, so that wasn't complicated. No-one is going to turn down an excellent doctor who agrees to work for almost nothing in a half-abandoned clinic. I knew that her work would give her better access to the zone. She just had to claim she was running experiments on the health of the permanent residents."

The killer loaded another cassette in the camera.

"We're going to do another take. And this time you'll cooperate or I will kill you and make the recording on my own."

"You want to protect your daughter by pretending that you did all this alone?"

"Exactly. After that, I'll set fire to the apartment. I'll call Maria and tell her to kill Ninel. Then she can call the police and tell them that I kidnapped her and was planning to kill her too. And everyone will believe it, particularly after I send this video to the police."

A chess player's strategy, Rybalko thought. Leonski confessed again, as if for the first time. Rybalko decided to play along, at least until Leonski got up to turn off the camera. At that point, he was planning to yell that Maria was his daughter, forcing him to make another recording.

But a few minutes after they started, there was loud knock at the door of the apartment.

"Captain Melnyk. Police. Open up!"

Before Leonski could move a muscle, Rybalko shouted: "Watch out! He's armed!"

Leonski pistol-whipped him and he fell, still tied to the chair; the wooden back smacked against the floor. The ceiling was spinning above him as he fought to remain conscious. He heard the crash of broken wood, then gunshots. The floorboards shook as a body fell to the ground, then there was silence. After a while, Rybalko heard someone breathing, a heavy, disturbing wheeze.

"Melnyk?"

The chair, which was old and wobbly, had been damaged when it hit the floor. He pulled hard on his ropes and one of the chair's arms gave way, then the second. He managed to untie the ropes around his ankles and climbed unsteadily to his feet. He saw Leonski lying on the floor. His mouth was open to suck in air. His chest was oozing blood.

A groan.

Rybalko turned towards the hallway and saw Melnyk leaning against a wall. He was holding his stomach in both hands. His face was pale and he was panting.

"Melnyk. . . shit!"

He crouched next to the wounded officer. Dark blood was flowing through the cracks between his fingers.

"It went through your bulletproof vest?" Rybalko said.

"Don't have. . . a vest."

The policeman grimaced with pain. Rybalko found his mobile and called the emergency services.

"There are two men here with serious bullet wounds. Send ambulances."

He gave the address, then hung up.

"Hold on," he told the policeman.

Melnyk was shivering. There were beads of sweat on his forehead. Rybalko went up the hallway to find a blanket to place over him.

"Just keep breathing. I'm going to see if Leonski's still alive."

The Ukrainian nodded. In the living room, Leonski's chest was still rising and falling in time with his breaths, but it was clear that the swallow killer had only minutes to live. Rybalko knelt next to him. An odour of blood and burned fabric rose from his shirt, where the bullets had pierced his torso.

"Your vengeance is over," he whispered. "You took the life of Sokolov's son, and everyone will know what he did. I'll make sure of that if you tell me where Ninel is."

"It's not enough. . . He has to suffer more. . . he has to lose. . . his daughter."

Leonski closed his eyes. Rybalko took hold of his head and shook it gently.

"Leonski! Look at me!"

The killer opened his eyes. There was a glassy look in them now.

"Ninel and Maria. . . tell me where they are! It's too late for you, but not for your daughter. She hasn't killed anyone. Ninel doesn't need to pay for your mistakes. And nor does Maria. Neither of them should have to pay for their father's sins."

Leonski tried to speak, but his voice was too quiet to hear. Rybalko put his ear next to the killer's lips to listen to his final words.

"They are. . . they are in the. . ."

He hiccupped. Bubbles of blood foamed at the corners of his mouth as he mumbled incomprehensibly.

"Where? Where are they?" Rybalko demanded.

"In the. . . in the hands of God."

Leonski tensed, then the life drained out of his eyes. He was as inert as his stuffed animals.

Rybalko went back to the hallway to care for Melnyk. A blood stain had soaked through the blanket.

"Christ, Melnyk. . . why didn't you wear your bulletproof vest?"

A weak voice answered in a wheeze: "I. . . I gave it. . . to my son."

A woman's deafening scream in the doorway. The neighbours had finally dared to come out and see what was happening.

"Go and get help instead of yelling!" Rybalko told her. "Is there a doctor in the building?"

"Yes. . . on the fifth floor," the neighbour told him.

"Go and get him then!"

He looked at Melnyk. The police officer was as white as a sheet, and it sounded as if there was a whistle trapped in his throat.

"Hang in there!" Rybalko told him.

The doctor arrived soon afterwards, carrying a large first aid bag.

Melnyk was in good hands. Rybalko estimated that he had at most five minutes to look for clues to where Ninel was being held. After that, the police would be here and he would be forced to waste precious hours explaining what he was doing in Maria's apartment.

He kicked the pistol away from Leonski's dead hand and searched the corpse's pockets. All he found was car keys and a flick-knife.

Four minutes.

He went into the hallway and checked the drawers, the shelves and anything else that might contain some kind of information: diaries, Post-Its, notebooks. . . He tried to unlock the computer, using various passwords – SOKOLOV, SWALLOW, MARIA – but it was a stupid act of desperation and he knew it.

Two minutes.

He had to think. Stop rushing around like a headless chicken and use your brain. Leonski had known from the beginning that he was going to keep Ninel a prisoner. So he must have long ago chosen the place where she would be held.

One minute.

Symbols, symbols. . . a Bible lying on a table in the living room.

"They are in the hands of God," Rybalko said to himself.

That was what Leonski had said just before dying. What if Maria was keeping Ninel in a church? He hurried out of the room. Still no police sirens, but the ambulance had already arrived. The medics were crowded around Melnyk's prone body.

Reluctantly, he left the Ukrainian in the hands of the experts and took advantage of their agitation to slip away. He had to find Maria before she learned about her father's death.

48

Once he had driven far enough away from Maria's apartment, Rybalko parked by the roadside and dialled Sokolov's number. The ex-minister quickly picked up.

"Do you have news?" he said at once.

"You've been fucking me around, you piece of shit."

"What the hell is wrong with you? Have you lost your mind?"

"I just talked to Leonski."

"He's alive?" Sokolov demanded, in a voice full of surprise and fear.

"Not anymore. The police. . ."

He thought about Melnyk, lying in the hallway, and felt his throat tense.

"The police shot him."

"Did he say where Ninel was?"

"No. But he talked about his crimes. And yours."

Sokolov understood instantly.

"Whatever Leonski told you, don't repeat it to a soul until you've seen me again," he ordered.

"Oh, so you don't want me to tell anyone that you killed Olga? And Larissa?"

"Don't talk about that, not on the phone!"

"Everything that happened – your son's death, all the other murders, your daughter's kidnapping – all of that is because of you, because of your crimes and your lies."

"Shut up! Have you forgotten who you're working for? Do you want your money or not?"

"Go fuck yourself, Sokolov. You'll give me the money, or I'll tell everyone that you're a murderer."

"Nobody will believe you!"

"We'll see about that. There must still be witnesses. The guys you paid to take care of Leonski in prison. And Agopian, who you tried to bribe to keep his mouth shut. . . you think he'll hesitate to tell the truth about you once he learns that you're the reason his son is dead?"

"Shut your fucking mouth!"

"No, you're the one who's going to shut it, you bastard. I think I know what kind of place Ninel is being held in. I still have a chance to save her, but I need to act quickly. If Leonski's daughter discovers that her father is dead, she might panic and kill Ninel."

"Leonski's daughter? She helped him commit those murders?"

"She didn't kill anyone herself, but she gave him logistical support. I think Leonski chose a religious building in the zone to hide Ninel, and that she's being guarded by his daughter. There can't be that many temples here. . ."

"There's Saint Elijah in Chernobyl, which is still active," Sokolov said.

"I was thinking of an abandoned church or monastery. Does anything come to mind?"

"Yes, yes. . . There was a beautiful church in one of the villages we evacuated. Krasno, I think."

Krasno was in the one of the most remote corners of the zone, where nobody ever went. It would be the perfect spot for keeping someone hostage.

"That might be it. I'm going to look."

"I'll send you reinforcements."

"No way. I'm going alone."

He was about to hang up, when Sokolov called out: "Wait! I'd like you to do something for me."

"What?"

"Kill the daughter."

"Sorry?"

"Kill her. I want her dead. Do that, and I'll double your money."

He considered this offer in silence. Was he willing to damn himself even more for more money?

350

"Come on, Alexander, say something!"

"I'll see," he said.

"You don't have a choice, my boy: either you kill that bitch or you don't get your money. Don't fuck me around. I could crush you, you and your family, like ants."

"You shouldn't threaten the man who holds your daughter's life in his hands. And your reputation."

Sokolov hissed an insult.

"Kill her. Kill Leonski's daughter!"

He hung up. That monster made him feel sick. Sokolov had murdered two people and ruined the lives of countless others, and he seemed to feel no remorse at all. For him, every problem could be solved with a few million rubles. And to think that he had sold the last days of his life to that bastard.

He stepped on the accelerator and sped along the empty road. All the way there, he thought about Maria. She had spared his life in the Palace of Culture. He sensed she was nothing more than a pawn in this game, manipulated by her father. He could save her.

Then he thought about Sokolov's offer. Fifty million rubles for taking a life. He would be dead soon, so he wouldn't have to live with his bad conscience very long. Come on, Rybalko. Since when did you have scruples? Think about the poor sods you killed in Chechnya. They told you to shoot, and you shot at unarmed men. They told you to burn, and you burned entire villages. They told you to throw, and you threw grenades into houses where civilians were living. You won't be going to heaven now, whatever you do. Besides, you never really believed in God. If you had, you wouldn't have committed all those atrocities.

He reached the Dytyatky checkpoint. He showed them his papers and they let him through, even though it was late. Melnyk had spread the word: "Let the ornithologist through, day or night, and don't ask questions." He drove for more than another hour before he reached Krasno. He parked away from the outskirts of the village and walked to the wooden church. Its silent presence amid the mist that glided over the forest was disturbing. He had the impression that the dead from the neighbouring cemetery were about to rise up, that a Carpathian demon was about to fall from a tree and suck his blood.

Outside the door, he hesitated. Should he knock, or call Maria's name? Instead, he just pushed open the wooden door, which creaked loudly on its hinges. At the back of the church, in front of the iconostasis with its images of saints, Ninel was standing, hands tied and mouth gagged. Next to her, Maria was aiming a hunting rifle at Ninel's head.

"Stay calm, Maria," he told her.

"How did you find me?"

"Your father told me. He wanted to protect you."

"My father? Impossible! He would never tell you where I was."

"And yet he did."

"Where is he? Is he in prison? Have you arrested him?"

"No. He's in hospital. He shot a police officer, who fired back."

"Which hospital?"

"I don't know. The main thing is, he wanted you to surrender. . ."

He took a step forward.

"Don't move!" she shouted, aiming the rifle at him.

Despite this warning, he kept walking. He felt strangely calm. His life had no importance. He was there to accomplish one last mission. Afterwards, there would be nothing for him but disease and death. So why be afraid?

"Calm down, Maria, you're not a murderer. You chose to spare me when I chased you in Zalissya. You had the chance to kill me then, but you didn't."

"I should have done. My father wouldn't be in hospital if I'd had the guts to shoot you the first time."

"If you kill me, you'll go to prison for the rest of your life. But if you put down your weapon, the judges will find mitigating circumstances. All you've done is help your father. You were under his influence."

"I don't care. Prison or death – it's the same to me."

"You're not like your father, Maria. That wasn't a killer I saw in the orphanage, with those children. It was a woman full of love and generosity. You don't have to carry out your father's vengeance."

"Vektor Sokolov has to pay!"

"He's already paid. He lost his son. And soon everyone will know what he did, but. . ."

He broke off and looked at Ninel. Did she know the truth about her mother?

"But only if you stay alive. If you testify at your trial."

"He'll get away with it. He always does."

"Not this time. He's in Ukraine. He has no political support here. The police will be thrilled to arrest him. A former Russian minister accused of murder: that's too good to miss. It doesn't matter how rich he is: he'll rot in prison for the rest of his life."

Maria hesitated. He kept walking forward.

"Give me the rifle. You're not a killer. Your father trained you to help him with his vengeance. You helped him set a trap, but you're not a bad person. . ."

"We had no choice. . . he was untouchable in Russia. . . we had to lure him here. . ."

"And the other victims?"

"They paid for their parents' sins. . . My sister died because of them. Her body started rotting from the inside. Every day she grew weaker. It was like watching myself die. . . can you imagine that? They deserved to suffer for what they did to us."

"And Novak? Did she deserve to die?"

"The policewoman? She's dead?"

"I found her body in the bathtub of your apartment. Your father killed her. He didn't tell you?"

"No. . . You're lying! You're saying all this to confuse me."

She turned to aim the rifle at Ninel's temple.

"No!"

He took another step forward.

"Stay where you are," Maria ordered.

Another step forward.

"Shoot me if you want to, but let her live."

"Stop!"

"You are not a killer, Maria," he repeated, as if trying to convince himself. "Put down the rifle and come with me. I'm not going to tell you that everything will be fine. I'm not going to lie to you. But I swear that if you put down the rifle, we will go to the police together and they will take your statement. Sokolov will be arrested."

Another step.

"Don't. . . don't move!"

"There will be a trial. You can testify. Tell them about your mother's death. They'll listen to you. Everyone will know the truth about Sokolov. I'm sure your father told you that nothing matters more to Sokolov than his reputation. It will be destroyed. Everyone will know what he really is. Isn't that what your father wanted, deep down?"

He stepped forward again. He was only two or three metres from her. Suddenly the sound of a gunshot echoed inside the church. He stopped dead. Maria's shotgun had fired. Ninel fell to her knees.

"Not another step! I'll kill you, I swear I will. One more step and I'll shoot!"

She took aim at him. At her feet, Ninel was pressing her bound hands to her face.

"Go ahead!" Rybalko thundered. "Shoot me. And kill Ninel too. Then what? What happens after that?"

"I'll kill Sokolov."

"How will you do that, if you don't have a hostage to lure him here?"

"I. . . I. . ."

"Did he come here in person to hand over the ransom as your father demanded?"

She muttered something incomprehensible.

"Was he there? Yes or no?"

"No," she breathed.

She was close to cracking, he could feel it. Too much pressure: she was about to collapse, to surrender. He felt sure of it.

"I've got two facts for you, Maria. Fact number one: if you kill Ninel, Vektor Sokolov will board a plane for Moscow tonight, and you will never be able to harm him. Fact number two: he'll never put his own life in danger to save his daughter. You know that, don't you? He'll never do that, because... because..."

He looked at Ninel. What he was going to say would break her heart, but he had no choice, if he wanted to save her life.

"Because he doesn't love her. He always distanced himself from her. Not because he hated her. But you know why, don't you? Because she constantly reminded him of his crime. By her simple presence... she reminded him that he had... that he had killed her mother."

Tears rolled down Ninel's cheeks. A long, muffled moan came from her gagged mouth, then she burst into tears and crumpled to the floor.

"She's the living double of her mother. As long as she's alive, Sokolov will never be able to forget his crimes."

Maria looked at Ninel. There was compassion in her eyes. Rybalko sensed he was winning her over.

"She suffered too, you know. She too was a victim. She lost her mother, just as you did. Both of you are Sokolov's victims. Don't make Ninel pay for her father's crimes."

She hesitated. The barrel of her rifle wavered, then slowly lowered. He advanced, but almost instantly Maria's eyes filled with hate and she raised the rifle again. Fire burst from the barrel. Two detonations filled the air and the hot breath of a bullet brushed past Rybalko's cheek. By the time he realised it had come from behind him, the bullet had hit Maria's face. Shocked, he watched her fall backwards onto the floorboards, which gave a sad creak as her frail body landed.

"Nicely done," said a voice behind him.

49

Ninel's face was buried in her palms. Her golden hair was flecked with a rain of blood. When Rybalko reconnected to reality, Kachin was already moving towards the two women. He kicked away the gun, which lay on the floor close to Maria, and bent over Ninel.

"It's over. We're taking you home."

He grabbed her arm and raised her to her feet. Ninel let him do it. She looked like she'd been drugged. Her eyes were vacant. Rybalko wanted to talk to her, but he felt a hand on his shoulder.

"Nicely done, Pushkin," said Kamenev, the neo-Nazi with the eagle tattoo on his forearm. "We couldn't do a thing while her gun was aimed at the girl. You suckered her brilliantly."

In his hands, a thin plume of smoke rose from the barrel of the precision rifle he'd used to kill Maria.

"She. . . she was about to surrender," muttered Rybalko.

"Sure she was! She was a nutcase. She might just as easily have killed you – and the girl too."

The neo-Nazi slung the strap of his rifle over his shoulder and walked towards the body.

"Pretty girl," he said, pushing Maria's head to the side with one of his boots. "What a waste."

Her mutilated face fell sideways, exposing the half-exploded back of her head.

"We need to get her out of here. Don't just stand there: help me put her in the boot," Kamenev said.

"In the. . . boot?" Rybalko asked, frowning.

"Yeah, yeah, in the boot. You don't think we're going to just leave her here, do you? We need to get rid of the body. Your boss wants us to leave as little evidence as possible behind."

Kamenev ordered him to take the dead woman's legs while he lifted up her arms. Rybalko obeyed unthinkingly. They carried the corpse through the church. Maria's long hair, dragging along the aisle, left a streak of red all the way to the door.

An enormous grey 4×4 was parked outside. The boot was open. They put the body inside.

Suddenly Rybalko realised that Ninel and Kachin had disappeared.

"Where is she? Where's Ninel?"

"With her father and your friend. They already left."

He'd been so stunned by what happened that he hadn't heard the vehicle drive away.

"I have to talk to Ninel. She's in shock. . ."

"First we need to get rid of the body. We'll meet them after that. Come on, get in."

Kamenev drove them out of the village. Rybalko imagined Ninel sitting next to her hated father who had killed her beloved mother. What could be going through her head now?

The neo-Nazi leaned towards him.

"So, Pushkin, what will you do now that you're finished here?"

"Go back to my family," he muttered.

"That's good. Family is important. In fact, Sokolov has decided to give us a bonus so we'll keep our mouths shut about everything we did here. Good news, huh?"

They drove to a solitary house by the side of the road.

"This looks like a good spot," said Kamenev.

He manoeuvred the car so that its rear end was facing the entrance of the house.

"We'll dump the body inside and siphon a bit of petrol from the tank so we can pour it on the floor there," he said. "Then we'll set fire to the place."

They took the corpse from the boot and went inside the house.

"There's a cellar. Let's take it down there."

Putting the body down for a moment, Kamenev opened the broken door that led to the basement and took a flare from his pocket. He lit it and threw it down the stairs.

"We don't want to fall and break our necks! Careful as you go. If you fall, so do I."

The tattooed man went first, cautiously walking backwards. The light from the flare gave his skin a reddish glow, making him look like a demon straight out of hell. The descent was slow and difficult. The wooden steps whined under their weight and seemed on the verge of collapse. Kamenev did not appear worried about this.

A feeling of unease overtook Rybalko. The neo-Nazi was too relaxed. Too happy. Suddenly he recalled the threats that Kamenev had made to him when they first met, in Poliske: "Round here, people who stick their noses into things don't live long. They get killed, and sometimes their bodies are never found. They get dumped in a cellar and then the house above it goes up in flames. And seeing how everything round here is contaminated, nobody ever comes to see what's underneath the ruins."

He stopped halfway down the stairs.

"What are you doing? This thing weighs a ton!" Kamenev complained.

"This is supposed to be a tomb for two, isn't it?"

Kamenev frowned.

"Don't be stupid. We're working together."

"How much is Sokolov paying you to kill me?"

Rybalko stared at him, watching his face for an expression, a tic, a nervous twitch that would betray him.

"Stop your bullshit, man. This bitch is really heavy. We can't just stand here like idiots in the middle of the stairs. . ."

"You said it yourself: Sokolov doesn't want any witnesses. He paid you to kill me, you bastard."

A homicidal gleam appeared in Kamenev's eyes. He had realised there was no point protesting his innocence any longer. He didn't make a move though. Both men were armed. Kamenev's gun was in a shoulder holster, while Rybalko's was jammed in the back of his belt. Both men knew that the shoot-out would begin the moment one of them let go of the corpse.

Except that Rybalko had one advantage over his adversary: he was already used to the idea of dying.

"O.K. You're a clever guy," Kamenev said. "You're right – your boss paid me to kill you."

"Why? He knows I need his money."

"He thinks you might talk to a prosecutor when you get back to Russia. About his wife. Or that you might try to blackmail him."

A large drop of sweat ran from his hairline down his left temple.

"You think you're quick enough to kill me before I shoot you?" Rybalko asked with a swagger.

"Yeah, I think so," Kamenev said.

The tension went up a notch. Their breathing grew louder. Kamenev's left eyelid started to twitch. At the foot of the stairs, the flare was smoking in silence, giving off an acrid stench and an increasingly feeble light. They both knew they would have to drop the corpse and shoot before it went out.

"This is what's going to happen," Rybalko said. "I'm going to put the body down and grab my gun. If you do the same, I'll shoot you."

His shoulders were starting to ache. Maria's body felt as if it was made of lead.

"And then?"

"I drag you back upstairs. I tie your body to a tree. I take the 4×4 and I find Sokolov."

Kamenev laughed nervously.

"And then what? You'll kill him? What's the point, eh? What will it all have been for? Will your daughter get a better life? Because if you kill Sokolov, you can kiss the money goodbye!"

"How do you know about my daughter?"

"Your mate, Kachin. He briefed us on the situation. He was the one who told us to kill you. He really played you for a fool, man. He told us about your cancer."

"How–"

"How does he know you only have a few months to live? You stupid prick, he paid your doctor to tell you you were going to die!"

Kamenev burst out laughing and Rybalko felt a shiver run through his whole body. It wasn't possible. . . it had to be a lie. Suddenly he felt Maria's body falling. Kamenev had let go of her wrists and was reaching for his holster. Rybalko grabbed for his own gun a fraction of a second too late. A detonation boomed. A violent pain in his left shoulder made him cry out. He fell backwards, onto the steps. Thankfully he was still gripping his pistol. His finger tensed around the trigger and he fired. The bullet hit Kamenev somewhere in the belly. His bulletproof vest absorbed the blow, but the impact knocked him off balance and he fell backwards, tumbling down the steps to the bottom, where he was soon joined by Maria's corpse. Before Kamenev could react, Rybalko shot him in the head.

Silence fell. His left arm was on fire and shoots of pain were spreading from his shoulder. He slowly climbed the steps. Outside, the door of the 4×4 was open. He sat in the passenger seat, turned on the ceiling lamp, then took off his coat. The cold air rushed against his skin. He tore his shirt and examined his shoulder. The bullet had not exited. It was lodged somewhere between his muscles, bones and tendons.

Kachin's 4×4 had left marks in the fresh snow. He followed them, driving as fast as he dared given the state of the road. He had the impression that his whole body was burning up. Maybe it was the shock of the bleeding. Or the radiation? He thought again about Leonid's autopsy, how he had plunged his hands into those radioactive guts, about the tea made from contaminated well water that he had drunk at Kazimira's house, about the dust he had inhaled when he fell through the floorboards of the Palace of Culture, about the radioactive mound where he'd tied up one of his attackers...

Every pothole sent stabbing pains through his shoulder, and changing gears was torture. Thankfully, adrenaline and anger were helping him through the agony. He was determined to find Sokolov and Kachin. To make them pay. He thought about Ninel, stuck with those two bastards. About the horror she must be feeling now that she knew her father had murdered her mother. Anxiously, he wondered if they would silence her too. Ninel was not the kind of person who would just give in. She would refuse to keep what she'd learned to herself. Sokolov was going to kill his own daughter, if Rybalko didn't find them quickly enough.

All of a sudden, he spotted a car by the roadside, at the end of a long furrow that zig-zagged through the snow. The vehicle had veered off the road and ended up scything through a copse of young birch trees. Rybalko stopped at a safe distance, took out his pistol, and advanced cautiously. There was nobody in the car. Footprints went off in the direction of the forest. Here and there, a bloodstain punctuated the snow. One of them had been injured in the accident.

He heard yelling. Ninel. Rybalko gritted his teeth and ran until the forest gave way to a barbed-wire fence, barring access to a vast junkyard.

Hundreds of vehicles were piled up there: cars, trucks, even helicopters. They were all relics of the U.S.S.R. era. Machines that had been used during the Chernobyl disaster. Radioactive wrecks.

It was too late to turn back now. He found a gap in the fence and strode through. As he walked between skeletons of military vehicles, he tried not to think about the numbers painted on their bonnets, indicating the crazy radiation levels of each one. He felt abruptly aware of his own fragility. The certainty of his imminent death had turned him into a fearless machine. Now he felt vulnerable. His hands were trembling.

He heard raised voices, very close. Ninel was screaming. His heart started to pound. His shoulder throbbed. Mind sharpened by adrenaline, he moved more quickly, less cautiously. In an aisle of dismembered helicopters, he finally caught sight of Ninel. She was about forty-five metres ahead of him, trying to pull away from her father, who had his hands around her throat. Rybalko was running towards her when he glimpsed a shadow to his left, only a few metres away. It was Kachin. He was observing the scene with indifference. His rifle hung harmlessly behind his back, from a shoulder strap. When the gangster in turn saw Rybalko, his face briefly registered surprise, then he dived headlong towards him. Rybalko just had time to fire a bullet at him before Kachin rugby-tackled him.

He crashed against the icy earth. The pain in his shoulder exploded. Kachin was pressing him down with his body weight, but he didn't take advantage of his position to land a punch. He grimaced. The bullet had hit him in the side. Rybalko pushed up with his legs and overturned his enemy. Perched on his torso, he repeatedly smashed Kachin's face with his right fist, until the gangster kicked him away. Rybalko fell on his injured shoulder and let out a cry of pain.

At the end of the aisle, he saw Sokolov turn in his direction. Ninel took advantage of his distraction to escape his grip and try to run away.

Kachin went on the attack again. He leapt at Rybalko. Handicapped by the wound he had received, he could not punch hard, but his blows were still enough to send Rybalko into agonies every time his shoulder was touched. But as Kachin raised his fist to punch him in the face,

Rybalko kicked him in the ribs, at the exact point where a bloodstain was starting to spread. The gangster howled. Rybalko slapped him hard in the throat. Kachin fell backwards and began to choke. Rybalko jumped on top of him, turned him onto his front, and buried his head into the muddy snow. High on rage, Rybalko wanted the liquid earth to fill up his former friend's throat, his lungs, he wanted the radioactive particles to infect every cell in his body, he wanted Kachin to die slowly, painfully. Then he realised that Kachin was no longer struggling. He lifted up his head. The eyes were bloodshot and bulging from their sockets. Rybalko stood up and looked at his hands. They were covered with the contaminated soil. His whole body was contaminated. Since that bastard had made him believe he only had a few months left to live, how many years had he shaved off his true life expectancy?

There was the sound of a gunshot, and a bullet ricocheted from the cabin of a helicopter centimetres from where he stood. He dived behind the helicopter.

"Come out or I'll kill her!"

Rybalko glanced through the helicopter's windscreen. Sokolov was holding his daughter against him, a gun barrel pointed to her temple. Ninel's eyes were filled with pure terror. She knew her father was not bluffing. That he would kill her to protect himself, just as he had killed her mother.

"I'm going to count to three!" Sokolov shouted.

Rybalko's pistol gleamed faintly in the snow. He picked it up. The former minister was perhaps ten metres away. At that distance, in normal conditions, a trained policeman could not miss. But these were not normal conditions: there was no way he could hold his gun in both hands to steady his grip.

"One..."

He checked there were still bullets in the magazine.

"Two..."

If he missed, Ninel would die. If he did nothing, Ninel would die. He had to try. To jump out from his hiding place and aim at Sokolov's head.

"Three!"

He rushed out, pistol raised. Surprised, Sokolov turned his own weapon away from his daughter's temple and towards Rybalko. A gunshot exploded. Rybalko felt a bullet hit his thigh and he fell to his knees. A second shot ricocheted off the helicopter beside him. Ninel had pushed her father's arm as he was about to shoot. She scratched Sokolov's face now and he shoved her to the ground. Rybalko did not give him time to raise his weapon again: he fired a bullet at his chest, killing him instantly.

Then the pistol slipped from his hands and he felt suddenly, extremely cold. The iciness was spreading from the inside of his thigh, pervading his body like mist. Blood was pouring from the wound, turning the snow dark red. His head was spinning. A vein or an artery, he thought as he lay down on the frozen ground. A shot to the leg could kill you. He had seen that in Chechnya.

Ninel knelt beside him.

"I'll call for an ambulance, it'll be O.K.," she told him. "Do you have your phone?"

"In my jacket. . ."

With one hand, she unzipped his jacket, found the mobile in the inside pocket, and dialled the number for the Chernobyl police station. As soon as a policeman answered, she yelled at him that a man was bleeding in front of her, that they had to come as quickly as possible.

Rybalko closed his eyes for a moment. His eyelids felt heavy. Just as he was about to lose consciousness, he was woken by a sharp pain in his cheek. Ninel had slapped him.

"Stay with me," she told him.

She tried to stem the flow of blood by pressing down on the wound.

"Don't close your eyes. They'll be here soon."

"It's too late. . . we are beyond reach. . ."

"Don't talk rubbish. They've got a helicopter. They'll be here soon. Just stay with me for twenty minutes. Talk to me. . . tell me what you'll do afterwards. . . tell me about your daughter. . . tell me what you'll do when you see her again."

"I don't know. . . I'd like to. . . to go to Cuba. . . with her. . ."

"Cuba, yes. It's a beautiful island."

"Will you come?"

She removed her hand from his wound and delicately caressed his feverish brow.

"I'll come."

He saw scratches on her neck, where her father had tried to strangle her. She noticed him looking.

"My mother. . . I should have known all along that it was him. It all seems so obvious now. When he beat me, he was hitting *her* through me. I should have guessed the truth. In the car, he tried to convince me not to say anything. How could he have imagined for a second? How could he believe I would ever agree to that?"

Ninel kept pressing down on the wound, but she could not stop the bleeding. His whole body was tense with cold now and his field of vision was nothing more than a narrow tunnel directly ahead of him.

He realised that this was the end.

"No. . . no. . . you're going to live!" Ninel protested. "You can't go like that. You can't. . ."

She started to sob. The helicopter wasn't going to get there in time. She had known it, but had not wanted to admit it.

"Promise me," he said. "My daughter. . . promise me you'll watch over her. . . her operation. . . her education. . ."

"I promise."

"Tell her that her father. . . that her father. . ."

He couldn't speak any more.

"I'll tell her. Don't worry."

She held him tight against her. The gentle warmth from her body did him good. In the sky, birds glided over the treetops ablaze from the setting sun. He closed his eyes and felt himself drift into darkness.

It wasn't the worst place to die, after all.

EPILOGUE

No Ukrainian wedding can ever be sad. Despite the war, despite the deaths, people sing, they dance, they wish the young newlyweds all the happiness in the world.

Nikolai and Oksana Melnyk made a handsome couple, even if Mrs Melnyk thought her son looked a little too thin. During the months he had spent at the front, he had lost his healthy, round-cheeked boyishness. But how elegant he was, in his wedding suit! And he would have plenty of time to put some weight back on. He had decided not to return to the Donbas after the wedding. Oksana was pregnant. He did not want to risk the possibility that his son would grow up fatherless. It was what happened to Joseph, his father, that had changed his mind. In fact, he had decided to become a policeman, like him.

That night, when Tatiana Melnyk found herself alone in the living room of her apartment, she leafed through some old family photograph albums. How her children had grown. . . On the coffee table lay a postcard sent from the United States by Ninel, the young woman that Joseph and the Russian policeman had rescued from Leonski's clutches. She was writing to say that Rybalko's daughter's operation had gone well. Tatiana put the postcard with some other important letters, like the one from Galina Novak's family, thanking them for the speech he had given at her funeral.

"*Blyad!*"

The swear word, followed by a groan, came from the bedroom. She ran in there.

"Is everything all right, Joseph?"

Major Melnyk grimaced with pain.

"I stubbed my toe against that damn coffee table," he said, massaging his foot.

He was shirtless and on his stomach was visible the scar from the bullet that had pierced his stomach a few months earlier. His hair and his beard had grown back since his accident in the Pripyat swimming pool, but he had had to agree to trim them regularly now that he worked at an office in Kyiv.

"Oh, you're such a wimp," Tatiana joked as she hugged him.

ACKNOWLEDGEMENTS

Thank you Sophie, for being with me since I took my first steps as a novelist.

Thank you Caroline, for your patience, your commitment and the quality of your work. Thank you Lina for having believed in my book. Thank you to everyone at Albin Michel who worked on this novel.

Thank you David Khara, for your advice and kindness.

Thank you to my family, my friends, my colleagues, thank you to the people of Cancale, thank you to everyone who took the time to read my first novel and to tell others about it. Without you, this second book might never have existed.